WHITE LIES

WHITE LIES

JAYNE ANN KRENTZ

LARGE PRINT PRESS
A part of Gale, Cengage Learning

Detroit • New York • San Francisco • New Haven, Conn • Waterville, Maine • London

LIBRARY OF CONGRESS CATALOGING-IN-PUBLICATION DATA

Krentz, Jayne Ann.
   White lies / by Jayne Ann Krentz.
     p. cm.
   ISBN-13: 978-0-7862-9115-1 (hardcover : alk. paper)
   ISBN-10: 0-7862-9115-X (hardcover : alk. paper)
   1. Arizona — Fiction. 2. Large type books. I. Title.
   PS3561.R44W52 2007b
   813'.54—dc22
                                           2006031480

ISBN 13: 978-1-59413-244-5 (pbk. : alk. paper)

ISBN 10: 1-59413-244-5 (pbk. : alk. paper)

Published in 2008 in arrangement with G. P. Putnam's Sons, a member of Penguin Group (USA) Inc.

Printed in the United States of America
1 2 3 4 5 6 7 12 11 10 09 08

For Suzanne Simmons,
with thanks for an extraordinary
and enduring friendship.
I've said it before and I'll say it again,
you are not only a fantastic writer,
you are one of the sisters I never had.

PROLOGUE

Eight months earlier . . .

Clare Lancaster sat in the café of a large bookstore in Phoenix, Arizona, waiting for the half sister she had never met. A chaotic mix of anticipation, anxiety, longing and uncertainty churned her insides to such an extent that she could not drink the green tea she had ordered.

Even if she had not seen photographs and read articles about Elizabeth Glazebrook and her wealthy, influential family in the Arizona newspapers and house-and-garden magazines, she would have recognized her the moment she walked through the door.

It certainly wasn't because there was much in the way of family resemblance, Clare thought. At five feet three and a half, she was accustomed to having to look up, not only to most men but to many women as well. She was aware that, like Napoleon, she sometimes tended to overcompensate.

Friends and those who were fond of her called her feisty. Those who were not friends tended to go for other descriptors: difficult, stubborn, assertive and bossy. On occasion the words "bitch" and "ballbuster" had been used, often by men who had discovered the hard way that she was not nearly as easy to get into bed as they had assumed.

Elizabeth was her polar opposite: tall and willowy with a cloud of honey-brown, shoulder-length hair brightened by the desert sun and the discreet touch of a very expensive salon. Her features had a lovely, patrician symmetry that gave her an elegant profile.

But what one noticed most of all about Elizabeth was her style. Her half sister did not have merely good taste in clothes, jewelry and accessories Clare thought, she had *exquisite* taste. She knew the precise colors to wear to enhance her natural good looks, and she had an unerring eye when it came to detail.

Until her recent marriage to Brad McAllister, Elizabeth had been one of the most successful interior designers in the Southwest. Things had changed dramatically in the past few months. The once thriving business had fallen apart.

Elizabeth hesitated briefly in the doorway of the café, searching the small crowd. Clare started to raise a hand to get her attention. There was no reason why Elizabeth should recognize her. After all, she had never had her work featured in glossy, high-end magazines and she'd certainly never had her wedding photographed for the society pages of a newspaper. She'd never had a wedding. But that was another issue.

To her amazement, Elizabeth stopped scanning the room the instant she noticed Clare sitting in the corner. She started through the maze of tables.

My sister, Clare thought. *She knows me, just as I would have known her, even if I had never seen a photograph.*

When Elizabeth drew closer Clare saw the barely veiled terror shimmering in her hazel eyes.

"Thank God you came," Elizabeth whispered. The beautifully crafted leather handbag she carried shook a little in her tightly clutched fingers.

Clare's anxiety and uncertainty vanished in a heartbeat. She was on her feet, hugging Elizabeth as if they had known each other all their lives.

"It's all right," she said. "It's going to be okay."

"No, it's not," Elizabeth whispered, tears drowning the words. "He's going to kill me. No one believes me. They think I'm crazy. They all say he's the perfect husband."

"I believe you," Clare said.

CHAPTER ONE

Jake Salter was standing in the shadows at the far end of the long veranda, all his senses — normal and paranormal — open to the desert night, when he felt the hair stir on the nape of his neck. It was the first warning he had that something was about to put his entire, carefully laid strategy in jeopardy.

The hunter in him knew better than to ignore the disturbing sensation.

The ominous indicator of disaster took the shape of a small, nondescript compact car turning into the crowded driveway of the big Glazebrook house.

Something wicked this way comes. Or something very, very interesting. In his experience, the two often went together.

"It looks like we have a late arrival," Myra Glazebrook said. "I can't imagine who it is. I'm sure that everyone who was invited tonight is already here or sent regrets."

Jake watched the little compact crawl

slowly forward. The driver was searching for a parking place amid the array of expensive sedans, heavy SUVs and limos that littered the drive. *Like a rabbit approaching a desert watering hole that had already attracted a lot of mountain lions.*

Good luck, Jake thought.

There was no space left in the wide, circular court that fronted the big house. The Glazebrooks were entertaining this evening. Archer and Myra Glazebrook called their annual July cocktail gala the Desert Rats Party. This evening, everyone who was anyone in the affluent community of Stone Canyon, Arizona, who had not fled the merciless summer heat for cooler climes was here.

"Must be someone from the caterer's staff," Myra said. She watched the compact with growing disapproval.

The little car finished one complete circle of the drive without finding a place to alight. Undaunted, it scurried around for a second attempt.

Myra's jaw firmed. "The caterer's people were told to park at the back of the house. They're not supposed to take up space in front. That's for the guests."

"Maybe this particular member of the staff didn't get the word," Jake said.

The compact was sweeping toward them again, headlights bouncing off the gleaming fenders of the larger vehicles. Jake was sure now that the driver was not going to give up.

"Sooner or later he's going to realize that there is no room left in the drive," Myra said. "He'll have to go around to the back."

Don't bet on it, Jake thought. There was something very determined about the manner in which the driver was searching for a parking space.

The compact abruptly came to a defiant halt directly behind a sleek silver-gray BMW.

Out of all the cars here tonight, you had to pick that one to block, Jake thought. *What are the odds?*

The part of him that he did not advertise to the world — the not-quite-normal part — was still running hot, which meant he was flooded with parasensory input in addition to the information collected by his normal senses. When he was hot, data came to him across a spectrum of energy and wavelengths that extended into the paranormal zones. He was *aware* of the wild, intoxicating scents and the soft sounds of the desert night in a way that he would not have been if he were to close down the parasensitive side of himself. And his hunter's intuition was operating at full capacity.

"He certainly can't park there," Myra said sharply. She looked down the veranda. "Where is the attendant who was hired to handle parking this evening?"

"Saw him go around to the back a few minutes ago," Jake said. "Probably had to take a quick break. I can handle this for you."

Oh, yeah. I want to handle this.

"No, that's all right, I'd better deal with it," Myra said. "There's always the possibility that it's someone who was accidentally left off the guest list. Once in a while that happens. Excuse me, Jake."

Myra went briskly toward the veranda entrance, fashionable high-heeled sandals clicking on the tiles.

Jake clamped down on his eager senses. *Try to act normal here.* He could do that fairly well most of the time. He had learned long ago that people, especially those who possessed a measure of psychic ability and who understood exactly what he was, got nervous when he didn't. Others, which included the majority of the population — most of whom would never admit to believing in the paranormal — simply became uneasy for reasons they could not explain. He wondered which group the new arrival fell into.

He leaned against the railing, absently

14

swirling the whiskey that he had not touched all evening. He wasn't here tonight to relax and enjoy the hospitality. He was here to gather information with all his senses. Later he would go hunting.

The door of the compact popped open. A figure emerged from behind the wheel. The newcomer was a woman. She was not dressed in the uniform that the other members of the catering staff wore. Instead, she had on a severe black-skirted suit. A pair of black, heeled pumps and an oversized shoulder bag finished off the outfit.

Definitely not from around here, Jake thought. This was Arizona and it was July. No one went beyond "resort casual" at this time of year.

He prowled quietly forward along the veranda. When he reached a deep pool of shadow at the side of one of the stone pillars that supported the overhanging roof, he stopped. He propped one shoulder against the pillar and waited for events to unfold.

The newcomer's neat black pumps echoed crisply on the paving stones of the drive. She walked boldly toward the main entrance where Myra waited. Jake could see that the somber black suit skimmed small, high breasts, a trim waist and hips that, if one wanted to get technical, were probably too generously proportioned to suit the scale of the rest of the petite frame. He, however, had no problem, technical or otherwise, with her curves. They looked just right to him.

This was the kind of woman you looked at twice, even though you knew she wasn't beautiful. At least she was the kind that *he* looked at twice. Make that three times, he decided. The big, knowing eyes, proud nose and determined chin were striking in a compelling, unconventional way. The veranda lights gleamed on lustrous dark hair that was secured in an elegant knot at the back of her head.

But it wasn't her looks that grabbed his full attention across the spectrum of his senses. She had something else going for her, something that didn't depend on physical attractiveness. It was in the way she carried herself, the angle of her shoulders and the tilt of her head. Attitude. Lots of it. It would be a mistake to underestimate this woman.

Automatically he cataloged and analyzed the data that his senses were collecting, the way he always did when he was hunting.

She wasn't prey. She was something a lot more intriguing. She was a challenge. You couldn't charm a woman like this into bed. She would make the decision based on whatever criteria she had established. There

would be some fencing involved, certain negotiations, probably a few showdowns.

He felt the blood heat in his veins.

Myra stepped into the woman's path. He
could see that she had dropped the gracious
hostess role. It didn't take any paranormal
sensitivity to detect the tension and wariness
vibrating through her. The first words out of
Myra's mouth told him just how much trouble he was looking at.

"What are you doing here, Clare?" Myra
asked.

Well, damn. Jake mentally sifted through
the files he had been given to read before he
was sent to Stone Canyon two weeks ago.
No mistake. Right age, right gender, right
amount of hostility from Myra.

This was Clare Lancaster, Archer's *other*
daughter, conceived in the course of a brief,
illicit affair. The probability analysts em-
ployed by Jones & Jones, the psychic investigation firm that had hired him for this job,
had estimated that the likelihood of her
showing up here while he was working undercover was less than ten percent. Which
only went to show that just because you were
a psychic with a special flair for probability
theory didn't mean diddly-squat when it
came to predicting the behavior of a woman.
Plain, old-fashioned guesswork would have

yielded better results.

He knew he should be worried. Clare's presence here was seriously bad news. If the rumors about her were true, she was the one person in the vicinity who could blow his cover to pieces.

According to the Jones & Jones files, Clare was a level ten on the Jones Scale. There was no level eleven, at least not officially.

The Jones Scale originated in the late 1800s. It was developed by the Arcane Society, an organization devoted to psychic and paranormal research. Back in the Victorian era a lot of serious people took the paranormal very seriously. The period was the heyday of séances, mediums and demonstrations of psychic abilities.

Of course the vast majority of practitioners in those days were charlatans and frauds. But the Arcane Society had already been in existence for two hundred years at that point, and its members knew the truth. Paranormal talents did exist in some people. The Society's goal was to identify and study such individuals. Over the years it had acquired a large membership of psychically talented people. Those who joined got tested, and they brought their offspring to be tested.

The Jones Scale was designed to measure the strength of a person's psychic energy. It was continually being updated and expanded as modern experts in the Society created new methods and techniques.

It wasn't just the knowledge that Clare was a strong sensitive that raised red flags. According to the files, her talent was extremely rare and highly unusual. The strength of a person's pure psychic energy was fairly easy to measure these days, within limits, at least. Identifying the exact nature of an individual's talent was often far more complicated.

In the vast majority of cases psychic abilities fell into the realm of intuition. Those endowed with a measurable amount of paranormal talent were often good card players. They got lucky when they gambled, and they were known for their very reliable hunches.

But there were some major exceptions. Among the members of the Society, such exceptions were usually termed "exotics." It was not a compliment.

Clare Lancaster was an exotic. She had a preternatural ability to sense the unique kind of psychic energy generated by someone who was attempting to prevaricate or deceive.

In other words, Clare was a human lie detector.

"Hello, Myra," Clare said. "I can see from your expression that you weren't expecting me. I was afraid of that. All I can say is that I've had a bad feeling about this right from the start. Sorry for the intrusion."

She didn't sound sorry, Jake thought. She sounded like a woman who expected to have to defend herself; a woman who had done just that frequently in the past and who was fully prepared to do so again. A scrappy little street fighter in conservative pumps and a badly wrinkled business suit. He was a little surprised that she didn't have "Don't Tread on Me" tattooed across her forehead.

"Did Elizabeth ask you to come here tonight?" Myra demanded.

"No. I got an e-mail from Archer. He said it was important."

Now, that was interesting, Jake thought. Archer had said nothing at all about his other daughter, let alone bothered to warn him that she might show up unexpectedly.

Clare turned her head quite suddenly and looked straight into the pool of shadow where he stood. A small shock electrified his senses. Something had alerted her to his presence. He hadn't intended for that to happen. He knew how to blend into the background. He had a predator's talent for concealment when he chose to use it and he had been using it instinctively for the past couple minutes.

Aside from the rare handful of other sensitives who possessed exotic psychic abilities similar to his own — other hunters — there were very few people who could have detected his presence in the shadows. Clare's intuitive awareness was especially impressive given the amount of highly charged emotional electricity that was vibrating in the air between her and Myra. If nothing else, the tension alone should have distracted her.

Yes, indeed, here comes trouble. Can't wait.

"I was not aware that we had gotten a call from the guards at the front gate," Myra said stiffly.

Clare turned back to her. "Don't worry, there was no major breach of security. The guard called the house before he waved me through the gates. Someone on this end vouched for me."

"I see." Myra sounded uncharacteristically nonplussed. "I don't understand why Archer didn't tell me that he invited you."

"You'll have to take that up with him," Clare said. "Look, it wasn't my idea to come all this way for a cocktail party. I'm here because Archer said that it was very important. That's all I know."

"I'll go and find him," Myra said. She turned and walked quickly across the veranda, disappearing through the open

French doors.

Clare made no move to follow. Instead she switched her attention back to Jake.

"Have we met?" she asked with a chilly politeness that made it very clear she knew they had not.

"No," Jake said. He moved slowly out of the shadows. "But I have a feeling that we're going to get to know each other very well. I'm Jake Salter."

CHAPTER TWO

He's lying, Clare thought. *Sort of.*

She should have been prepared. She was always prepared for a lie. But this wasn't a pure, full-on lie. It was a subtle, nuanced bit of misdirection wrapped in truth, the kind of lie that a magician might use: *Now you see the coin, now you don't. But there really is a coin. It's just that I can make it disappear.*

He was Jake Salter but he wasn't.

Whatever he was, he was definitely a powerful talent. The strong but confusing pulses of energy that accompanied the half-truth jangled her senses. She had developed her own private coding system for lies. The spectrum ran from the hot ultraviolet energy that accompanied the most dangerous lies, to a pale, cool, paranormal shade of silvery white for the benign sort.

But Jake Salter's lie generated energy from across the spectrum. Hot and cold. She knew intuitively that Jake could be extremely dangerous but he wasn't, at least not at the moment.

Adrenaline flooded through her, making her edgy and hyperalert. Her paranormal senses flared wildly, disorienting her on both the physical and the psychic planes. Her pulse kicked up suddenly and her breathing got very tight.

She was accustomed to the sensation. She had been living with her rare brand of sensitivity since it developed in her early teens. Heaven knew she had practiced long and hard to learn how to clamp down on her physical as well as her paranormal reactions. But unfortunately her unusual senses were hardwired to the primitive fight-or-flight response. The Arcane House parapsychologist who had helped her deal with her unique type of energy had explained to her that psychic talents that triggered such basic physical instincts were exceptionally hard to control.

When she did her own search through the genealogical records of the Arcane Society, looking for examples of others like herself, she had stumbled across two disturbing facts. The first was that, although human lie detectors popped up occasionally among the membership, the majority were fives or lower. Powerful level tens were extremely rare.

Disturbing Fact Number Two was that of the handful of level-ten lie detectors in the historical records, the majority had come to bad ends because they never learned to control their talent. They wound up in asylums or took to drugs to dull the effects of the steady barrage of lies that assailed them day after day, year in and year out. Some committed suicide.

The truth was, everybody lied. If you were a level-ten human lie detector you either got used to it or you went crazy.

If there was one thing she had taught herself, Clare thought, it was control.

She pulled her senses — all of them — together with an effort of will and adjusted her psychic defenses.

"I'm Clare Lancaster," she said. She was proud of the fact that the words came out evenly and politely, as if she wasn't on the downside of a mini–panic attack.

"Nice to meet you, Clare," Jake said.

Okay, he wasn't lying now. He really was pleased to meet her. More than pleased, in fact. She did not need her psychic sensitivity to detect the masculine anticipation in the words. Old-fashioned feminine intuition worked just fine. Another little thrill quivered through her.

He walked, no, he *prowled,* toward her, a

half-filled glass in one hand. She got the impression that he was factoring her presence into some private calculation. Fair enough. She was doing the same thing in reverse.

"Are you a friend of the family, Mr. Salter?" she asked.

"Call me Jake. I'm a business consultant. Archer hired me to consult on a new pension and benefit plan for Glazebrook."

Another lie wrapped in truth. Wow. This man was scary good. And scary interesting.

He had moved into the light cast by one of the wrought-iron veranda lamps, allowing her a good look at him for the first time. She had the feeling that had not been by accident. He wanted her to see him. She understood why. Even his choice of clothing was an act of misdirection.

She wondered if he actually believed that the black-framed glasses, the hand-tailored button-down shirt and the business-casual trousers that he wore were an effective disguise. The conservative cut of his very dark hair didn't work, either.

Nothing could conceal the watchful intelligence in those dark eyes or hide the subtle aura of controlled power that emanated from him. He was all fierce edges and mysterious shadows. She would have bet the tiny amount of money left in her bank account that, like any proper iceberg, the really dangerous part of Jake Salter was hidden beneath the surface.

You didn't have to be psychic to figure out that this was not a guy you wanted to encounter in a dark alley late at night. Not unless he was promising some very kinky sex.

The last realization made her catch her breath. Where had that come from? She was definitely not inclined toward kinky sex. Actually, she wasn't really into sex of any kind. Sex meant letting go, becoming vulnerable and taking risks with someone you trusted. When you were a human lie detector, you had a lot of trust issues. When she did go to bed with a man, she made certain she was in control.

One of the great things about Greg Washburn was the fact that he had been quite content to let her take charge of the physical side of their relationship, just as he allowed her to control every other aspect of it. In fact, theirs had been a near-perfect engagement. She and Greg never argued about anything right up until the day he dumped her.

"You're a little late," Jake observed.

"My flight out of San Francisco was delayed," she said.

"Clare."

Clare jerked her attention away from Jake

Salter and smiled at her half sister. "Hi, Liz."

"I just saw Mom." Elizabeth swept forward, her attractive face glowing with delight. "She told me you were here. I didn't know you were coming down to Arizona tonight." She threw her arms around Clare. "For heaven's sake, why didn't you tell me?"

"Sorry," Clare said, hugging her. "I assumed you were aware I had been invited."

"Dad probably wanted to surprise me. You know how he is."

Not really, Clare thought, but she didn't say it out loud. She had met the man who was her biological father for the first time a few months before. The circumstances had not been ideal. The truth was, she knew very little about Archer Glazebrook, aside from the fact that he was a legend in Arizona business circles.

"It's so good to see you," Elizabeth said.

Clare allowed herself to relax a little. With her sister, at least, she was on safe ground.

"You look terrific," she said, glancing down at Elizabeth's elegant white sheath. "Love the dress."

"Thanks." Elizabeth returned the survey. "You look —"

"Don't say it. You know I'll know you're lying."

Elizabeth laughed. "You look as if you've

been traveling for half a day."

"Now that's the honest truth," Clare said.

She smiled. It was so good to see her sister happy and cheerful. Eight months ago Elizabeth had been a woman in the middle of a nervous breakdown. The change was little short of miraculous. No doubt about it, widowhood had been good for her.

Elizabeth, like her mother, was a registered member of the Arcane Society. Myra was a level two on the Jones Scale, which meant that, generally speaking, she had slightly above-average intuition. If she had not descended from a long line of Arcane Society members and been tested, she would have gone through life oblivious to the psychic side of her nature, taking her flashes of insight for granted, the way so many people did.

Elizabeth, however, was a five with a strong sensitivity to color, visual balance, proportion and harmony. Her psychic abilities were one of the reasons she was so successful as an interior designer.

"There you are, Clare," Archer Glazebrook roared from the open doorway. "What the hell took you so long?"

"My flight got delayed," Clare said.

She kept her voice perfectly neutral, the way she always did when she was around the larger-than-life Archer Glazebrook. Since their initial meeting she had spent very little time with him. She was not yet sure what to make of him.

Archer could have been cast as the aging, hard-bitten gunslinger in an old-fashioned western film. He was sixty-one, with craggy, sun-weathered features and shrewd hazel eyes. Appearances were anything but deceiving in Archer's case. He was born and raised on an Arizona ranch located close to the border and had spent most of his life in the Southwest.

Archer no longer rode the land. He bought and sold it, instead. And he developed it. He did all of that so successfully that he could buy and sell just about anyone in the state.

Eventually he would turn over his empire to his son, Matt, to run. But for now he was still in charge. Clare knew that this summer Matt, who was in his late twenties, was managing a Glazebrook job site in San Diego.

Clare had once asked her mother what she had seen in Archer Glazebrook that made her want to have a one-night stand with him. *Power is an incredible aphrodisiac,* Gwen Lancaster had said simply.

There was no doubt that Archer wielded power, not only through his business empire but also on the paranormal plane. In fact, one was linked to the other. He descended from a long line of Arcane Society members. His particular psychic ability allowed him to map strategies in unique ways. Many sensitives with similar talents wound up in the military or in politics. Archer had applied his psi-senses to the world of high-stakes deal making. The results had been spectacular.

At the sight of him tonight, flanked by two members of his *legitimate* family, Clare felt the old, familiar wistfulness well up inside her. She suppressed it with the same ruthless will that she used to control the psychic side of her nature. Just as she had since she first discovered that she had a father and that he did not know that she existed, she chanted her private mantra. *Get over it. You're not the only person in the world who was raised by a single parent. Worse things could happen to a kid and Lord knows they do, all the time.*

She'd been lucky. She had a loving mother and a doting great-aunt. That was a heck of a lot more than many people got.

"Well, come on inside and get yourself something to eat," Archer ordered. He started to turn back toward the doors, intent on resuming his duties as host.

"I can't stay long," Clare said quickly.

Archer stopped and looked at her. So did everyone else, including Jake Salter. Okay, so it had been an odd thing to say, given that she had just flown all the way from San Francisco.

Elizabeth frowned in dismay. "You're not planning on going back to San Francisco tonight, for heaven's sake? You just got here."

"No, I'm not going back tonight. I plan to catch a flight home day after tomorrow."

"Forget it," Archer growled. "We've got business to talk about. You'll need to stick around longer than that."

"I have things to do back home," Clare began, speaking through clenched teeth.

Jake was suddenly beside her, taking her elbow, drawing her toward the French doors.

"You could probably use a little food after that flight and the long drive from the airport," he said.

It was a command, not a suggestion. Her first inclination, as always in such circumstances, was to dig in her heels. That intention got even stronger when she realized that everyone, including Archer, was clearly relieved to see Jake taking charge of her.

Jake must have felt her incipient resistance. He gave her a slightly amused smile and raised his brows, silently asking her if she really wanted to cause a scene over a trivial matter like hitting the hors d'oeuvre table.

What the heck. She hadn't eaten anything

since the small carton of yogurt she'd had for lunch.

"All right," she said.

"Where are you spending the night?" Elizabeth asked.

"At one of the chain hotels near the airport," Clare replied.

Elizabeth was appalled.

"It's an hour's drive back to the airport," she said.

"I know," Clare said.

"You'll stay here," Archer declared decisively. "Plenty of room."

Myra's mouth opened and then closed abruptly on the objection. Clare felt sorry for her. Having your husband's long-lost daughter, the product of his one-night stand with another woman, show up on your doorstep thirty-two years later had to be in the top ten of every wife's worst nightmares.

"Thanks, but I prefer the hotel. I've already checked in and left my suitcase in the room."

"If only I hadn't just moved out of my apartment," Elizabeth said, "you could have stayed with me. But like I told you on the phone last week, I'm here with Mom and Dad until the deal closes on my new condo."

"It's okay," Clare said. "I don't mind the hotel. Honest."

Archer's jaw flexed ominously but Jake had Clare almost to the doors.

"She has plenty of time to decide what she wants to do," he said, drawing her through the opening. "Let me get some food into her first."

Every head in the crowded room turned when Jake escorted her inside. A split second later, everyone looked away. The noise of hastily resumed conversations and false laughter rose rapidly, filling the large space.

Clare had been prepared for the uncomfortable reaction but it nevertheless hit her like a psychic shock wave. She had to remind herself to breathe. She felt Jake's hand tighten on her arm but he said nothing.

He steered her toward a leather padded bar at one end of the long, spacious room, evidently unfazed by the covert glances and curious stares.

"Let's start with the drink first," he said. "If you've been in the Valley of the Sun for more than five minutes at this time of year, you need water."

"I am a little thirsty," she admitted.

He brought her to a halt at the bar and looked at the attendant. "Sparkling water and a glass of Chardonnay for Miss Lancaster, please."

"Never mind the wine. I won't be staying

long and I've got the drive back to the airport."

Jake shrugged agreeably. "Just the water, in that case."

The man on the other side of the bar nodded, deftly filled a glass with bubbly water and handed it to Clare.

"Thank you," she said.

"Now we do a surgical strike on the buffet," Jake said.

He guided her to a rustic, wooden plank table that looked as if it dated from the early 1800s when Mexico controlled a large chunk of what was now Arizona. She knew the table was probably a genuine antique. Myra had excellent taste and could afford the best.

The buffet was decorated with colorful, hand-painted pottery dishes that incorporated a variety of Southwestern motifs. A large, tiered ice sculpture with hollowed-out bowls held an assortment of cold hors d'oeuvres. At the other end of the long table stood a line of silver chafing dishes. Steam wafted up from the contents of the trays.

It dawned on Clare that she was hungry.

"You were right," she said to Jake. "I do need something to eat."

"I recommend those miniature blue-corn tortilla things." He handed her a pepper-red plate. "The filling may be a little too hot for someone from San Francisco, though."

"Obviously you don't know much about San Franciscans." She piled several of the tiny tacos onto the plate and moved on to the cold shrimp and salsa.

Elizabeth materialized just as Clare collected a napkin and fork.

"Everything okay?" she asked. She looked intensely relieved when she saw the assortment of food on Clare's plate. "Oh, good. You're eating."

"As you know, that's one of the things I do well," Clare said. "Don't worry about me, Liz. I'm fine. Go back to your guests."

"I wish Dad had told us you were coming. We could have made some other arrangements." Elizabeth glanced around uneasily. "I realize this must be very uncomfortable for you."

"I'm fine. Go mingle. Don't worry, now that I'm here, I'm not going to skip town without spending some time with you."

Jake looked at Elizabeth. "I'll take care of her."

Elizabeth clearly drew strength and reassurance from that statement.

"Well, in that case, I'd better go talk to some people," Elizabeth said. "If I don't, Mom will be upset. Thanks, Jake." She gave

Clare a warm smile. "I'll catch up with you later."

"You bet," Clare said.

Elizabeth disappeared back into the crowd.

Jake did a quick study of the room. "I suggest we go outside. It's a little crowded in here."

"Fine by me."

She munched a mini-taco, feeling remarkably better, and let him pilot her out a door on the far side of the room and onto another long veranda. This one fronted an elegantly curved pool. The underwater lights made the water glow a strange shade of turquoise.

They left the veranda, walked across the patio and sat down at a round table that overlooked the pool.

"Nice night," Clare said around a mouthful of taco.

"Hit a hundred five today. Supposed to be hotter tomorrow."

"Yeah, well, it is Arizona and it is summer." She drank some of the sparkling water and lowered the glass. "Any idea what Archer wants to talk to me about?"

"No. I didn't even know you'd been invited to this party."

He was telling the truth, she realized. That made for an interesting change.

"I got the feeling that you were taken by surprise," she said. *And you don't like being taken by surprise,* she thought. "You're used to being three steps ahead of everyone else, aren't you?"

"Obviously I screwed up this time."

She smiled cheerfully. "Don't blame yourself. Everyone else seems to be equally startled to see me. Looks like Archer played his cards close to his chest on this one." She paused, thinking about that. "Which, I admit, makes me a little curious."

"Is that why you came down here? Curiosity?"

"Nope. I'm here because Mom insisted." She raised her brows. "You do know a little of my family history, I assume?"

"Some," he said. "I'm aware that you're all registered members of the Arcane Society."

"You, too?"

"Yes."

She nodded. That explained some of the aura of power that radiated from him. It also explained why Archer had hired him as a consultant. Society members often preferred to work with other sensitives. They tended to choose their closest friends and their spouses from the Arcane community, as well.

"Actually, I was referring to the somewhat complicated aspects of my parentage, not our Society affiliation," she said to Jake.

"I know something about that, too."

"The thing is, I never met Archer or Myra or Elizabeth or Matt until this past year. We're all still feeling our way. Elizabeth and I get along great and Matt is friendly. But my presence upsets Myra for obvious reasons so I try not to inflict myself on her very often."

"What about your relationship with Archer?"

"Still under construction."

"Why did your mother want you to come down here tonight?" Jake asked.

"It's kind of complicated. The background is that Mom and Aunt May asked me to wait until I was in college before deciding whether or not to introduce myself to Archer. I respected their wishes. By the time I actually did go off to college, I had decided I didn't want to establish contact after all."

"Why not?"

She hesitated, uncertain how to put it into words. "Every time I saw a photograph of the Glazebrooks in a magazine or a newspaper they looked like the perfect family. I knew that would change if I showed up at the front door. I guess part of me didn't want to destroy what they had."

"No such thing as a perfect family," Jake said.

"Maybe not. But the Glazebrooks sure looked like they had come mighty close. Earlier this year I finally did contact Elizabeth, though. Now that the damage has been done, Mom and Aunt May have decided that Archer and I should bond."

"Family," Jake said. "Gotta love 'em."

She smiled and drank some more water.

"The situation with your relatives isn't the only complication you've got in your life, is it?" Jake lounged back in the chair and stretched out his legs. "You're a level-ten parasensitive with a rather unique talent."

She stilled. "You know?"

"That you're a human lie detector? Yeah. I did some background research on the family before I took this job. I may not have all the facts but I think I know the basics. Must be tough at times. People lie a lot, don't they?"

"Yes," she said. "All the time, in fact."

She wondered if he had been testing her earlier when he gave her his name or if he thought he could beat her sensitivity. Maybe he just didn't give a damn if she knew that he was lying. The more she thought about it, the more she was convinced that was probably the right answer.

"What's your sensitivity?" she asked.

Jake didn't answer. He turned his head to

look back toward the house.

"Damn," he said softly.

She followed his gaze and saw a stick-thin woman silhouetted against the lights of the house.

The woman hesitated. Clare realized she was searching for someone. With luck she would not think to check the heavily shadowed sitting area on the far side of the pool.

But at that moment the woman started purposefully forward. It was obvious that she was making for the table. So much for luck, Clare thought. Hers was not in good form tonight.

"Valerie Shipley," Jake said.

"I know. Just what I need to make my evening complete." Resigned, Clare put down the uneaten portion of a small taco.

"You know her?" Jake asked

"I met her once. That was the night her son, Brad McAllister, was murdered."

"McAllister was your sister's husband, wasn't he?"

"Yes." She watched uneasily as Valerie came toward them with an unsteady gait. This was going to get ugly.

"Just so you know," Jake said quietly, "Valerie drinks. A lot. I'm told the problem started after her son's death."

"Elizabeth said something about it."

Valerie stopped near the edge of the pool. She had a glass in one hand. Clare could see that she was tottering on her high heels.

Valerie was in her late fifties with dyed blond hair cut in a sleek bob. Six months ago she had looked fit and healthy. Tonight she appeared almost emaciated in her tight cocktail dress. The bones of her face were knife edges; the hollows of her cheeks were very deep.

"I can't believe you had the gall to walk into this house tonight, you murderous bitch," Valerie said. The words were slurred but the rage embedded in them was unmistakable.

Clare got to her feet. Beside her, Jake did the same.

"Hello, Mrs. Shipley," Clare said.

"Who's that with you?" Valerie peered into the shadows beneath the ramada. "Is that you, Jake?"

"Yes," Jake said. "I think it would be a good idea for you to go back inside, Mrs. Shipley."

"Shut up. You work for Archer. You don't tell me what to do." Valerie turned back to Clare. "You don't give a damn about the pain you've caused me, do you? You think you can waltz back here to Stone Canyon as if nothing happened."

Clare started slowly toward her.

"No," Jake said in a low voice.

Clare ignored him and came to a halt at the edge of the pool, facing Valerie.

"I'm sorry for your loss, Mrs. Shipley," Clare said.

"You're sorry?" Valerie's voice rose, anguish and fury inextricably mingled. "How dare you say that after what you did. *You murdered my son and everyone inside that house knows it.*"

Without warning, she dashed the contents of her glass across Clare's face.

Clare gasped and closed her eyes. Instinctively she took a step back.

Valerie gave an inarticulate cry of rage. Clare opened her eyes in time to see the other woman coming straight at her, arms outstretched. In the eerie glow of the underwater lights, Valerie's face was a demonic mask.

Jake was closing in with astonishing speed. He caught Valerie's arm before she could strike but Clare had already taken another step back to evade the blow. The heel of her black pump found nothing but air to support her.

She toppled sideways into the pool with an ignominious splash.

At least the water was warm, she thought

43

as she went under. On the rare occasions when she was in Glazebrook Territory, she was grateful for whatever luck came her way.

CHAPTER THREE

Jake looked at Valerie Shipley's twisted features.

"That's enough," he ordered. "Go back inside. I'll take care of this."

She jerked her attention away from the sight of Clare surfacing in the pool.

"Stay out of this, Salter," she hissed. "It has nothing to do with you. That whore tried to seduce my son. When that failed, she murdered him."

"Valerie?" Owen Shipley hurried toward his wife. "What's going on?"

Valerie started to cry. "The bitch came back here. I can't believe it. She actually came back. After what she did, it's not right."

She covered her face with both hands, whirled unsteadily and rushed toward the veranda.

Owen came to a halt. He was an athletic man in his early sixties with strong features and a ring of neatly trimmed gray hair. Under most circumstances he appeared relaxed and confident. But at the moment he looked awkward and helpless.

Jake felt some sympathy for him. Years ago Shipley had helped Archer found Glazebrook, Inc. The two men had been partners for nearly three decades until Archer bought out Owen's share of the business. The pair were still close friends and golfing buddies.

A year ago Owen met and married Valerie. It was a second marriage for both of them. Archer had told Jake that Owen and Valerie had met through the auspices of arcanematch.com. Jake had a hunch that the matchmaking computers at Arcane House, designed to help single members of the Society find life partners from among the community of sensitives, had failed to allow for the possibility that Valerie would morph into a full-blown alcoholic. It wasn't the first time arcanematch had made a mistake.

"I'm sorry," Owen said heavily. He looked at Clare. "Are you all right?"

Clare stood shoulder-deep in the water. "Don't worry about it, Mr. Shipley."

"Are you certain?" Owen asked.

"Yes," she said, her voice gentling. "It was an accident. I lost my balance and fell into the pool."

46

Owen's features tightened. "Valerie hasn't been herself since Brad was murdered."

"I know," Clare said.

"I've been trying to get her to go into rehab. But she refuses."

"I understand," Clare said.

Owen nodded humbly. "Thank you." He looked back toward the house. Valerie had disappeared into the shadows of the veranda. "I'd better take her home."

He walked back toward the house, shoulders slumped.

Jake waited until he was gone. Then he went to stand at the edge of the pool.

Clare flung her wet hair out of her eyes and looked at him, hands moving rhythmically under the surface.

"Don't say it," she warned.

"Can't help myself." He crouched down on the coping. "I did warn you not to confront her."

She made a face. "I thought consultants were supposed to do something helpful and productive in a moment of crisis."

"Right. Almost forgot."

He rose, walked to the nearby cabana and opened the door. Inside he found a stack of oversized towels on a shelf. He picked up one and carried it back to the pool.

"How's this for helpful?" he asked, unfolding the towel.

"Much better."

She took a deep breath and dove back under the water to retrieve her shoes. When she surfaced again she trudged toward the wide steps where he waited.

"There's a robe inside the cabana," he said, draping the towel around her shoulders.

"Thanks."

Clutching the towel, she made her way toward the small cabana. The black suit clung to her body, outlining her lush, rounded hips.

She stripped off her jacket just before she reached the door. The thin, pale silk shell she wore underneath had been rendered transparent by the water. Jake could see the straps of a dainty bra.

She disappeared inside the cabana. He considered his options. There was no question now but that Clare Lancaster was a spanner that had just been thrown into the works of his carefully crafted scheme. He had to decide how to deal with her, but first he needed more information.

The cabana door opened. Clare walked out muffled from head to toe in a thick white terrycloth robe. Her hair was wrapped in a towel. She carried her sopping-wet clothes in one hand and her soaked shoes in the other.

"I think the party's over for me," she said. She paused at the table to pick up her shoulder bag.

"Looks that way," he agreed. "I'll take you home."

"Hotel," she corrected automatically. "I don't live around here, remember?"

A small shock of awareness slammed through him. Talk about a slip of the tongue. He had spoken without thinking, meaning *his* home, or rather the house he rented. What the hell was that about? Probably something to do with seeing her in a robe and knowing that she was naked underneath the pristine white terrycloth.

"I'll take you back to your hotel," he said.

"Thanks, anyway, but I've got a car."

"It's not a problem. It will give me an excuse to leave early. Cocktail party chatter bores me."

"Why come, in that case?"

He shrugged. "Archer invited me. He's the client."

She gave him an odd look. She knew he was lying to her, he thought. But he sensed that she wasn't going to call him on it.

She was trying to figure him out, he realized. Fair enough. He was doing the same thing to her. He smiled slightly.

"What is so amusing?" she demanded crossly.

"We're like a couple of fencers," he said. "Testing each other's defenses. Looking for openings. Makes for an interesting game, don't you think?"

She went very still. "I didn't come here to play games."

"I know. But sometimes the game finds you."

"I don't know what you think you're doing, Jake Salter, but whatever it is —"

He took her arm. "Let's get you back to your hotel."

"I told you, I'm fine. I can drive myself."

"Be reasonable." He steered her toward the veranda. "You're soaked to the skin. You've had a long day. You've been through some family drama and a major scene with a woman who seems to hate your guts. On top of everything else, you probably don't know your way around Phoenix very well. Let me take you back to your hotel."

"No, thank you." Polite but determined.

"You're as stubborn as Archer."

They reached the veranda. Clare halted abruptly and looked at the open doors.

"I'm not going to go back inside," she said, glancing down at her robe. "Not like this."

"No," he agreed. He tightened his grip on

her arm and drew her along the veranda. "We'll go this way."

He walked her around the side of the house. When they reached the crowded driveway Jake saw the parking attendant. The young man was hovering over Clare's rented compact.

"Looks like my car is blocking another vehicle," Clare said.

"That would be mine."

She gave a small start and then smiled ruefully. "What are the odds, huh?"

"I figure maybe it was psychic karma."

"You believe in psychic karma?"

"Didn't until tonight," he admitted. He didn't like the way the attendant was studying Clare's car. "I think we may have a problem."

"What?" She looked up, keys in hand.

They were close to the compact now. Jake could see the spiderweb of cracks in the windshield. Clare noticed them a couple seconds later.

"Oh, damn," she whispered. "The rental agency is not going to be happy about this."

The attendant saw Jake. "I was just about to go talk to my boss."

"What happened?" Clare asked.

"Mrs. Shipley came outside a little while ago," the attendant said unhappily. "She

51

wanted to know which car had arrived in the last half hour. I told her that it was this one."

"Good grief," Clare said. "What did she do to my windshield?"

"She, uh, smashed it with a rock," the attendant said.

"Where is Mrs. Shipley?" Jake asked.

"Her husband came after her. Said he was going to take her home. He apologized and said to tell you that he'll make things right with the rental company."

Jake released Clare. "That settles it. You won't be driving yourself back to the hotel tonight." He took the keys from her unresisting fingers. "I'll move your car so we can get mine out."

She sighed, resigned now. "Okay. Thanks."

"Psychic karma, remember?" He opened the door of the compact and got behind the wheel.

Clare waited, her hands stuffed into the pockets of the robe, while he switched the positions of the two vehicles. When he had reparked the compact, he settled Clare into the front seat of the BMW and went around to the driver's side.

He got behind the wheel and drove down the drive and out onto the road that looped through the gated golf course community. The security guard waved him through the massive wrought-iron gates.

Clare looked out the window, evidently absorbed by the night and the lights of Phoenix in the distance.

"I knew that Brad McAllister was murdered six months ago," he said after a while. "Archer mentioned that the cops believe he interrupted a burglary in progress at his home here in Stone Canyon."

"That's the official theory." Clare did not turn her head away from the inky-dark view. "But as you may have noticed, Brad's mother is convinced that I murdered her son. She's had several months to promote her theory. I understand she's been quite successful, although Elizabeth assures me that most people in Stone Canyon are very careful not to speculate too loudly in Archer's hearing."

"Archer sure as hell wouldn't want that kind of gossip going around."

She turned her head to look at him. "The police did question me, you know."

"Be surprising if they didn't. You were the one who found the body."

"Yes."

He glanced at her. She had gone back to studying the night.

"Must have been bad," he said quietly.

"It was."

He said nothing for a moment. "How did it happen that you were first on the scene?"

"I flew into Phoenix that evening to see Elizabeth. There was a mix-up with a message I had left for her. She thought I was due in the following morning. She was out attending a reception for the Stone Canyon Arts Academy when I arrived. I drove straight to her place. The front door was open. I walked in and found Brad's body."

He didn't need his parasenses to pick up the lingering traces of shock and horror under the simple, straightforward words.

"Archer told me that the safe had been opened," he said. "It certainly sounds like an interrupted burglary scenario."

"Yes. But that hasn't stopped Valerie from concluding that I was the killer. She thinks I was having an affair with Brad and that I murdered him because he refused to leave Elizabeth."

"Elizabeth and McAllister were separated at the time. Any idea what he was doing at her house that evening?"

"No," she said.

He did not want to ask but the hunter in him needed to know.

"Were you sleeping with McAllister?" he asked without inflection.

She shuddered. "Lord, no. There's no way

54

I could have been attracted to a man like that. Brad McAllister was a liar."

His stomach clenched. She probably hated liars.

"Everyone lies at one time or another," he said. *Including me.*

"Well, sure." She sounded startlingly casual about that simple fact. "I don't have a problem with most lies or the people who tell them, at least, not since I learned how to handle my talent. Heck, I tell lies myself sometimes. I'm pretty good at lying, actually. Maybe it goes with having a gift for detecting lies."

He was dumbfounded. That did not happen very often, he reflected wryly. It took him a couple seconds to regroup.

"Let me get this straight," he said. "You're a human lie detector and you don't mind that most people lie?"

She smiled slightly. "Let me put it this way. When you wake up one morning at the age of thirteen and discover that because of your newly developed parasenses you can tell that everyone around you, even the people you love, lie occasionally and that you are going to be driven crazy if you don't get some perspective, you learn to get some perspective."

He was reluctantly fascinated. "Just what

kind of perspective do you have on the subject?"

"I take the Darwinian view. Lying is a universal talent. Everyone I've ever known can do it rather well. Most little kids start practicing the skill as soon as they master language."

"So you figure there must be some evolutionary explanation, is that it?"

"I think so, yes," she said, calmly serious and certain. "When you look at it objectively it seems obvious that the ability to lie is part of everyone's kit of survival tools, a side effect of possessing language skills. There are a lot of situations in which the ability to lie is extremely useful. There are times when you might have to lie to protect yourself or someone else, for example."

"Okay, I get that kind of lying," he said.

"You might lie to an enemy in order to win a battle or a war. Or you might have to lie just to defend your personal privacy. People lie all the time to diffuse a tense social situation or to avoid hurting someone's feelings or to calm someone who is frightened."

"True."

"The way I see it, if people couldn't lie, they probably wouldn't be able to live together in groups, at least not for very long or with any degree of sociability. And there you have the bottom line."

"What bottom line?"

She spread her hands. "If humans could not lie, civilization as we know it would cease to exist."

He whistled softly. "That's an interesting perspective, all right. I admit I've never thought about the subject in those terms."

"Probably because you've never *had* to think about it. Most people take the ability to lie for granted, whether or not they approve of it."

"But not you."

"I was forced to develop a slightly different perspective." She paused. "What I've always found fascinating is that the vast majority of people, nonparasensitive and sensitive alike, *think* they know when someone else is lying. That's true around the world. But the reality is that the research shows that most folks can detect a lie only slightly better than fifty percent of the time. They might as well flip a coin."

"What about the experts? Cops and other law enforcement types?"

"According to the studies they aren't much better at picking out liars, at least not in a controlled lab situation. The problem is that the cues people assume correlate with lying, such as avoiding eye contact or sweating, generally don't work."

"You can't count on Pinocchio's nose growing, huh?"

"It's not a total myth," she said. "Physical cues do exist but they vary a lot from one individual to another. If you know a person well, you've got a much better shot at picking up on a lie, but otherwise it's a crapshoot. Like I said, lying is a natural human ability and we're all probably a lot better at it than we want to admit."

"You said that Brad McAllister's lies were different."

"Yes."

"What did you mean?"

"Brad was a different kind of liar," she said quietly. "He was ultraviolet."

"Ultraviolet?"

"My private code for evil."

"Heavy word."

"It was the right one for Brad, trust me. The ability to lie is a very powerful tool. In and of itself, I consider it to be value-neutral, sort of like fire."

"But like fire it can be turned into a weapon, is that it?"

"Exactly." She folded her arms. "You can cook a meal with fire or burn down a house. In the hands of a person with evil intent, lying can be used to cause enormous damage."

"What makes you think Brad McAllister was evil? From all accounts he was a devoted husband who stuck with Elizabeth through her nervous breakdown."

She whipped around in the seat, suddenly fierce and furious. "That image was the biggest Brad McAllister lie of all. And it really pisses me off that it still stands, even though the bastard is dead."

He absorbed that. "What did McAllister do to make you dislike him so much?"

"Brad didn't stick by Elizabeth while she went through her nervous breakdown. He *caused* her breakdown. But Elizabeth and I have given up trying to make anyone, including Archer and Myra, believe that. As far as the whole town of Stone Canyon is concerned, Brad was a heroic choirboy right to the end."

Jake gave that some thought. "Okay, what's your theory of the murder?"

She hesitated and then sank slowly back into the seat. "There doesn't seem to be any reason to doubt the cops' version of events. Brad probably did interrupt a burglary in progress."

"Now who's lying? You don't believe that for a minute, do you?"

She sighed. "No. But I don't have a better answer, either."

"Not even a tiny theory?"

"All I know is that Brad was evil. Evil people collect enemies. Maybe one of them tracked him down and killed him that night."

"But you have no motive, aside from the fact that Brad was not a nice person."

"Sometimes that's enough."

"Yeah," he said. "Sometimes it is."

There was a short silence.

"By the way," Clare said after a moment. "We need to watch for the Indian School Road exit."

"Why?"

"Because my motel is on a street off Indian School Road," she said patiently.

"Thought you said your hotel was out at the airport."

"I lied."

CHAPTER FOUR

The best that could be said about the Desert Dawn Motel was that it made no pretense of being anything other than what it was: a run-down, low-end, budget-class establishment from another era. The two-story structure was badly in need of a coat of paint. Rusted air conditioners thundered in the night.

Most of the landscaping had died back in the Jurassic. Only a few hardy barrel cacti and one wilted palm had survived. The letter s in the red and yellow neon sign snapped and crackled and blinked annoyingly.

Clare felt a distinct pang of embarrassment when Jake eased the BMW into a parking space near the entrance to the shabby lobby. She suppressed it immediately.

Jake turned off the engine and regarded the limp palm tree that graced the cracked concrete sidewalk.

"You know," he said, "if you had mentioned that you were coming into town this evening the Glazebrook travel department would have been happy to make reservations for you at a slightly more upscale hotel. I'll bet they could have found you something where the bathroom isn't down the hall."

"There's a bathroom in my room, thank you very much." She unclasped the seat belt and opened the door.

Jake got out and took her wet clothes out of the trunk. Together they walked toward the lobby.

"Mind telling me why you chose this place?" he asked politely.

"Maybe you didn't know that I was fired from my job six months ago. I haven't had much luck finding a new position. So I'm on a strict budget these days."

"Your father is one of the wealthiest men in the state," he pointed out mildly.

"I don't consider Archer Glazebrook to be my father in anything but the biological sense."

"In other words, you're too proud to take any money from him." He shook his head, amused. "The two of you sure have a lot in common."

He pushed open the grimy glass door. Clare went past him into the postage stamp–sized lobby.

The desk clerk stared at Clare, taking in the sight of the bathrobe and towel turban.

"You okay, Miss Lancaster?" he asked uneasily.

"Late night swim," Clare said.

"I'm going to see Miss Lancaster to her room," Jake said.

The clerk sized him up and then shrugged. "Sure. Whatever. Just keep it quiet, will you? There's a couple from the Midwest in the room next door."

Clare frowned. "What are you talking about? Why should I care if there are people next door?"

The clerk rolled his eyes.

Jake grabbed her arm and hauled her toward the stairs.

"What's going on here?" Clare asked, bewildered. "Am I missing something?"

Jake waited until they reached the next floor and started down the dingy hall before answering.

"The guy at the desk thinks you're a call girl who is using this motel to entertain clients."

"You being the client?"

"Yes."

"I suppose the bathrobe gives a poor impression."

She stopped in front of room 210. Jake

63

took the key from her and inserted it into the lock.

The door to room 208 opened. A middle-aged woman with a helmet of graying curls peered disapprovingly through the crack.

Jake nodded politely. "Evening, ma'am."

The woman slammed the door shut. Jake heard voices through the walls. The door opened again. This time a balding, over-weight man dressed in a pair of plaid Bermuda shorts and an aging white T-shirt looked out. He stared hard at Clare through the opening.

Clare inclined her head. "Nice night, isn't it?"

The man shut the door without speaking. Jake heard the loud snick of the dead bolt sliding into place.

"I don't think the night clerk is the only one around here who is wondering about your career path," he said.

"Little do they know that I don't even have a career at the moment."

Jake opened the door.

The interior of the small room was as un-prepossessing as the exterior. At the far end cheap sliding glass doors opened onto a tiny balcony that overlooked a small pool. Clare switched on the weak overhead light.

Jake glanced at the single, roll-aboard suitcase sitting on the stand.

"Doesn't look like you packed for an extended stay," he said.

"I'll give Archer one day to explain why he dragged me down here. As long as I'm in town, I'll spend some time with Elizabeth. But after that I have no reason to hang around."

"Going back home to San Francisco?"

"I'm job hunting. Six months of unemployment has put a major dent in my savings. I don't want to have to start borrowing from my mother and my aunt. I need to find work."

He nodded. "Probably for the best."

He was obviously looking forward to getting rid of her. Why was that depressing?

"Thanks for the ride," she said. "It has been an interesting evening, to say the least."

"My dates say that a lot."

She smiled. "In case you didn't notice, this wasn't a date. You were just doing your job. Taking care of problems for Archer Glazebrook."

She closed the door very gently but very firmly in his face.

CHAPTER FIVE

Jake drove back to Stone Canyon and parked in the garage of the house he rented. He opened the trunk of the BMW, took out the computer that was never far from his side and went indoors.

He had intended to spend the night prowling through a couple more homes belonging to members of the Glazebrooks' circle of acquaintances, searching for some indication of what he had been sent here to find. It was how he had spent most of the other nights in Stone Canyon. Thus far he had managed to rummage through the closets, drawers and wall safes of twelve residences.

But the arrival of Clare Lancaster had changed his plans for the evening. Ever since his first sight of her, his hunting senses had been on high alert. She was important. He could feel it. And not just because he wanted to take her to bed, although that was pretty damn important, too.

In the kitchen he flipped on a light and set the thin laptop on the table. He poured himself a glass of scotch, sat down and powered up the computer.

He did not want any more surprises.

The heavily encrypted files on the Glazebrook family that had been given to him contained only sketchy information on Clare Lancaster. He reviewed it quickly.

Clare came from long lines of registered Society members on both sides of her family. There was an asterisk next to her Jones Scale number. It meant that, although she had been assigned a ten, her particular type of sensitivity was so rare that the researchers did not have enough examples to guarantee that the rating was accurate.

There was a similar asterisk next to the number ten on his para profile, too.

Clare had been raised by her mother, Gwen Lancaster, an accountant, and her great-aunt, May Flood, in the San Francisco Bay area. She had a degree in history from the University of California at Santa Cruz. He knew enough about the reputation of that branch of the UC system to be aware that she had probably emerged with not only a respectable education but a slightly offbeat view of the world, as well.

He paid attention to that small fact because here in Arizona, Glazebrooks were not inclined to be offbeat. They were pillars of the community, active in civic, business and charitable affairs.

He dug a little deeper into the files and found the item he was looking for. There was a small note to the effect that following graduation Clare had applied to work for the West Coast branch of Jones & Jones. Her application was rejected.

In the intervening years she had applied several more times. And been rejected several more times.

Following her failure to obtain a position at J&J, Clare had gone to work for a small nonprofit foundation. She stayed there three years before accepting a managerial position in the larger, more prestigious Draper Trust.

The Draper Trust was a private foundation that specialized in making grants to organizations that worked with battered women and homeless families, and in the fields of early childhood health and education. She had evidently been very successful at the trust. At least, that had been true until six months ago. That was when she was questioned in connection with the murder of Brad McAllister.

When she had returned home to San Francisco she was fired from her position at the

Draper Trust. Her engagement to another executive at the trust, Greg Washburn, ended at the same time. She had spent the intervening months searching for a new position in the charitable foundation world without any luck. She had also sent another application to the West Coast branch of J&J.

Rejected again.

Jake did a quick search on Greg Washburn in the Arcane Society records. There were a few Washburns listed, but not the Gregory R. Washburn who had been Clare's fiancé. She tried to fake it with a nonsensitive, he thought, just as he tried to do with Sylvia.

That gave them something in common. They both knew that very few members of the Arcane Society were interested in marrying a level-ten exotic of any kind, let alone a hunter or a human lie detector. They had each gone outside the community to find mates. The results had been spectacular failures for both of them.

He sat back in his chair and sipped the scotch, thinking.

After a while he pulled up the data on Brad McAllister's murder.

There was a good deal of information available because McAllister's death had been big news among the country club set in Stone Canyon. Most of the material was unhelpful, however, and superficial at best. The investigation had gone nowhere.

Clare had given a statement to the police but was never an official suspect. It didn't take much imagination to figure out why she was cleared so quickly, he thought. She was, after all, Archer Glazebrook's daughter. No one affiliated with the Stone Canyon Police Department would have been eager to press an investigation without solid evidence. It would have been a career-breaking move.

He sipped more scotch and thought about what Clare had told him. She had called Brad evil and claimed he was responsible for Elizabeth's nervous breakdown. That was pretty heavy stuff. It was also the first hint of negative gossip he'd picked up concerning Elizabeth's sainted husband. As far as the rest of Stone Canyon was concerned, Brad had been a damn near perfect husband.

But what if Archer Glazebrook had suspected that Elizabeth had been abused? Jake didn't doubt for a moment that Archer was capable of gunning down a son-in-law if he thought said son-in-law had done something terrible to one of his children. Archer grew up on a ranch and spent time in the military. He knew guns.

The problem was that Archer, Myra and Elizabeth had all been seen at the Arts Academy reception that evening. There was no shortage of witnesses.

Then again, how hard would it be to slip away from a crowded reception long enough to kill someone who was only a couple miles away?

Jake pulled up the Bradley B. McAllister file. There wasn't much of interest in it.

McAllister and his mother, Valerie, were both members of the Society, but neither had tested high on the Jones Scale. Valerie was a two and Brad a four. Both had been rated as possessing "generalized parasensitivity" with no special aspects.

As a four Brad had probably been a very good card player. The talent also explained his success as an investor. McAllister had been a very wealthy man.

The Arcane Society members were statistically more inclined to possess varying degrees of paranormal talents because of the group's long history of encouraging marriage between psychically talented people. Like every other human trait, genetics played a role.

He went swiftly through the rest of the information Jones & Jones had on McAllister. Brad appeared for the first time in the local area a few months after his mother married Owen Shipley. Brad had no previous marriages, according to the file. He was well educated, had a flair for the financial world and had worked for a medium-sized brokerage house before going out on his own as a private investor. By the time he arrived in Stone Canyon, he had amassed a sizable fortune.

Didn't mean he hadn't married Elizabeth for her money, Jake reminded himself. Some people never had enough.

After a while he opened his cell phone and punched out a familiar number. Fallon Jones answered on the first ring.

"I hope this call is to tell me that you've finally made some progress in Stone Canyon," Fallon said.

The low, dark voice suited the man, Jake thought. Fallon was a brooding loner. He was probably at his desk. Fallon was nearly always at his desk, hunched over his computer. He resembled some mad scientist. The analogy was apt. Fallon Jones could trace his lineage straight back to the founder of the Arcane Society, Sylvester Jones the alchemist.

Like most of the men in the founder's long line, Fallon Jones was a strong sensitive. He was also uniquely qualified to head up a psychic investigation agency because his exotic paranormal abilities allowed him to discern patterns where others saw only randomness;

conspiracy where others saw coincidence. He was invariably right.

When Fallon sent his agents out to hunt, you could count on the fact that there was prey out there somewhere.

"There's been a new complication," Jake said. "Her name is Clare Lancaster."

"Glazebrook's other daughter?" Fallon paused. "Hell. The probability guys told me she wasn't likely to show up."

"Well, she's here. I think it's safe to say that she knows there's something not quite right about my story."

"Damn. You can't let her screw this thing up. There's too much riding on the project."

"She doesn't seem inclined to blow my cover," Jake said. "Says she's used to the fact that everyone lies. In any event, she's scheduled to fly back to San Francisco day after tomorrow."

"Think you can control her until then?"

"I don't think anyone can control Clare Lancaster," Jake said. "At least not for long. But with luck she won't wreck the project. I called because I've got a question about her."

"What?"

"I came across a file that says she has applied for a position at Jones & Jones on several occasions."

"Every six months, regular as clockwork. She's been persistent, I'll give her credit for that."

"Why does she get rejected?"

"Why the hell do you think?" Fallon said patiently. "Because she's a level-ten lie detector. Make that a level ten with an asterisk."

"Seems to me like someone with her talent might be very useful to a business like yours."

"Maybe. But not a ten. They're way too unstable. When her first application came in I had one of the analysts do some background research on other members with her kind of talent. Turns out there have only been a half-dozen or fewer in the entire history of the Society. Most of 'em were either extremely neurotic or downright crazy. Four committed suicide. It's a tough talent to handle."

"You rejected her because you thought she'd be unable to do the job?"

"This is an investigation agency, Jake," Fallon pointed out drily. "You know as well as I do that in our business everybody lies — the clients, the suspects and the J&J agents. No level-ten-with-an-asterisk lie detector could last long under that kind of pressure. She would have been a risk to herself and others in the field."

"You may have underestimated her."

"It's possible, but I have to go with the probabilities," Fallon said philosophically. "Whatever you do, don't let her mess up your assignment."

"I'll see what I can do."

CHAPTER SIX

Fallon Jones got up from behind the battered mahogany desk and went to stand at the window. He was always aware of the weight of Jones family history when he was in his office.

The desk, like the distinctive glass-fronted bookcases and the Egyptian motif wall sconces, was in the Art Deco style. They had been among the original furnishings in the West Coast branch of Jones & Jones when it opened for business in Los Angeles back in 1927.

Eventually Cedric Jones, one in a series of Joneses to head the branch, had made the decision to move the office to the secluded beachside town of Scargill Cove on the northern California coast in the late 1960s. Cedric had brought most of the L.A. furniture with him. When Fallon inherited the job, he kept everything, right down to the wall sconces.

Back in the 1960s, Scargill Cove had been a remote village populated by an eclectic group of hippies, New Age types, artists, craftspeople and others seeking refuge from the relentless forces of the modern world. A psychic detective agency fit right in with the rest of the neighborhood.

Not much had changed in Scargill Cove over the years. It sometimes seemed to Fallon that the town was trapped in a time warp. That was one of the things he liked about it. He worked here alone, supervising his far-flung team of part-time investigators, analysts and lab techs via the Internet and his cell phone. Once in a while he considered hiring an assistant but had yet to act on the notion.

He knew what Jake and the others thought about his decision to run his empire from this hidden place on the coast. But he needed his privacy in ways the others could never understand. Virtually all the members of the Jones family were strong sensitives of one kind or another, but his particular talent was unique in the Jones line. No one else understood it. He didn't understand it himself most of the time. All he knew was that to do his best work, he needed the solitude and tranquillity of Scargill Cove.

It was late. The fog-shrouded moon illuminated the looming outlines of the natural foods grocery, the craft galleries and a handful of other shops that composed the town's tiny commercial district.

This was July but the windswept cove, with its slice of rocky beach and looming cliffs, attracted few tourists. Those who found their way into town never stayed long, primarily because there was very little in the way of lodging. The Scargill Cove Inn had only six rooms. Visitors hung around just long enough to browse the arts and crafts galleries. They left before sunset in search of accommodations and restaurants farther down the coast.

Cedric Jones, with his level-ten intuition, had sensed that Scargill Cove would stay undiscovered for a long, long time. He had been right.

Jones & Jones was a family business with branches in the United States and the United Kingdom. It was founded in the aftermath of the First Cabal in the late 1800s. All the branches were headed by members of the Jones family who had descended from the alchemist founder, Sylvester Jones.

Most of the time the firm's various offices were kept busy handling a wide range of security and investigative work for members of the Society and others in the general population who chose to seek the assistance of psychic detectives. But those in the Society who were aware of J&J's history understood that its primary client was the governing Council of the Arcane Society.

As far as the Council was concerned, J&J's chief job was to protect the Society's most extraordinarily dangerous secret: the founder's formula.

The original formula was created by Sylvester Jones. In his private journals he claimed it could greatly enhance psychic abilities in those who possessed at least some traces of paranormal talent. Over the years the formula had become just one more Arcane Society legend as far as most members were concerned. But the Jones family and the Council knew the truth. The formula had existed and it had worked.

The para-enhancement elixir had also proved to be exceedingly dangerous, its effects wildly unpredictable. Those who had tried it had, indeed, developed frighteningly powerful psychic abilities. But they had also become obsessed with the drug. Inevitably the formula had transformed its users into ruthless, psychically enhanced, highly unstable sociopaths.

Despite the risks, however, it seemed that in every generation some power-hungry sensitive came along who would stop at nothing to re-create the founder's formula. Whenever that happened it was understood that it was J&J's job to deal with the problem.

In some instances, the person intent on obtaining the formula was merely an unbalanced eccentric or someone who had become fixated on the legend of Sylvester Jones. Generally speaking such individuals did not get far before J&J stepped in to deal with the problem.

But this latest situation was different. The information that had filtered in thus far suggested that they were dealing with a highly disciplined, carefully structured, utterly ruthless organization. In fact it had all the earmarks of a full-blown conspiracy along the lines of the First Cabal.

The cabal was another Arcane Society legend, and, like the story of the founder's formula, it was based on more than a nugget of truth. The original conspiracy formed in the late 1800s. Its goal was to take control of the Society and, using it as a base of power, to extend its tentacles into the highest levels of business and government in the UK.

The shadowy outlines of this new, modern conspiracy had been revealed over the past few months. At least two Arcane Society lab researchers had disappeared under suspicious circumstances. Their bodies had never been found. A month ago a technician who worked in an Arcane Society facility turned up dead. Just over two weeks later, a trusted informant was killed in a car crash.

In addition, Fallon was certain that some of the Society's carefully guarded computer files had been hacked into by someone who was very good when it came to not leaving tracks.

The new conspiracy appeared to be centered on the West Coast. That meant that he was in charge of stopping it. He had a dozen agents working on various leads but he desperately needed a break. His best hope at the moment was Jake.

The arrival of Clare Lancaster was not a good thing.

CHAPTER SEVEN

Clare closed the lid of her laptop, got up from the chair and went to the balcony door. The slider did not want to move in its metal track. Eventually she was able to force it open. It made a harsh grating, grinding sound as it retreated, fighting her every inch of the way. She had a hunch the noise carried to the room next door.

She went out onto the narrow balcony and stood looking down into the murky pool.

According to what she had just learned from her online search, Jake Salter was exactly what he claimed to be: a successful pension-and-benefits consultant. She had found a few pieces and a brief profile on him in the financial press.

There was also a small reference to a marriage that ended in divorce after less than a year.

She remembered the little frissons of energy that had whispered across the nape of her neck during the drive back to the Desert Dawn Motel.

Unlike most people, Jake didn't just tell lies. He was living a lie.

CHAPTER EIGHT

The cell phone rang just as Clare emerged from the shower. She tried to wrap one of the paper-thin towels around herself and discovered that it wasn't long enough. She used it to dry a hand and picked up the phone.

"It's me," Elizabeth said. "Are you up for breakfast?"

"Sounds like a very good idea," Clare said. "I'm a little hungry after my late-night swim."

"I heard about that. I'm pretty sure everyone at the party knows what happened. Saw what Valerie did to your car, too. Dad said that Jake took you back to the hotel last night."

"That's right."

"Look, since you don't have your car, why don't I drive out there to the airport and pick you up? We can have breakfast at one of the resorts on Camelback Road. Afterward I'll take you out to Stone Canyon so you can deal with the rental car situation."

Clare surveyed the seedy-looking motel room. She really did not want Elizabeth seeing the Desert Dawn Motel. Jake's reaction last night had been bad enough. Her sister would be downright horrified.

"I can get a cab," she said quickly.

"Forget it. Let's see, it's seven-thirty now. Rush hour. Going to take a while to get out to the airport. See you in about an hour."

Clare sighed. "I'm not at the airport."

There was a short, startled pause.

Elizabeth cleared her throat. "Uh, don't tell me you wound up at Jake Salter's house last night?"

"No." Clare felt the heat rise in her cheeks. "For Pete's sake, Liz, whatever made you think I went home with Jake? I just met him. You know that."

"Okay, okay, take it easy," Elizabeth said. "I was just asking. Didn't mean to upset you."

"I'm not upset."

"Right. So, if you're not at Jake's house and you're not at an airport hotel, just where the heck are you?"

"Things have been a little tight lately," Clare said. "Let's just say that I'm staying at a budget establishment."

"Dad asked you to come down here to Arizona. Didn't he pay your way?"

"He offered," Clare admitted.

Elizabeth groaned. "You, of course, turned him down. I swear, you're as stubborn as he is, you know that? All right, give me the address of this 'budget establishment.'"

"It's a dump," Elizabeth declared.

"It's not a dump," Clare said.

"It's a dump," Elizabeth repeated flatly.

She had known Elizabeth would be horrified by the Desert Dawn Motel, Clare reminded herself. The only hope was to try to change the subject.

They were eating breakfast on the outdoor dining terrace of one of the luxurious golf course resorts near Scottsdale. The tiered swimming pools and the unnaturally green expanse of the course beyond gave an illusion of balmy comfort. In reality, although it was only eight forty-five in the morning, the heat was building fast. It would have been uncomfortable sitting outside had it not been for the awning, the overhead fans and the misters that spewed forth a cloud of tiny water drops that evaporated almost immediately.

"Are you sure I can't convince you to stay at Mom and Dad's place?" Elizabeth asked one more time.

"No," Clare said.

"I'll be there, don't forget."

"It wouldn't be fair to Myra. I cause her enough stress as it is."

Elizabeth made a face, acknowledging the truth of that statement without words.

"Stop worrying," Clare said. "I'm fine where I am. I'll only be in town for one more night, anyway. No big deal."

The waiter appeared, bearing a cup and saucer.

"Your green tea," he said to Clare.

Clare looked at the bag perched on the saucer. The tea was a generic brand, and she was pretty sure the water was going to be lukewarm.

"Thank you," she said. She unwrapped the little bag and lowered it into the cup.

She had been right about the water.

Elizabeth chuckled. "You ought to know better than to order green tea in Arizona. This is coffee country."

"Unlike the Desert Dawn Motel, this is a high-end resort that caters to affluent travelers from around the world. You'd think they would be able to provide a decent cup of tea."

"You remind me of Jake. He's the only other person I know who drinks tea. I think he likes the green stuff, too."

Clare pondered that while she dunked the tea bag up and down in a desperate effort to extract some flavor and caffeine.

"What do you think of him?" she asked.

"Jake?" Elizabeth raised one shoulder in an elegant little shrug. "He seems nice enough. He must be competent or Dad wouldn't have hired him."

"Do consultants always get invited to Glazebrook cocktail parties?"

"It's not so unusual." Elizabeth forked up a bite of her eggs Benedict. "Dad has always made it a practice to invite his upper management team to social functions. He gives them memberships at the Stone Canyon Country Club, too."

"But Jake is an outside consultant, not a vice president."

"Dad wants him treated with respect at the office," Elizabeth said. "That means he has to get the perks of upper management."

"I suppose that makes sense."

Elizabeth smiled. "What's with the curiosity about Jake Salter?"

"I'm not sure, to be honest," Clare said. "He just struck me as a bit unusual, that's all."

Talk about a bald-faced lie. Jake wasn't just a *bit* unusual. He was off the charts, at least as far as she was concerned. No other man had stirred the hair on the nape of her neck or aroused her feminine instincts the way he had last night.

"That's funny," Elizabeth said. "Jake always strikes me as being just what he is. A pleasant, somewhat dull business consultant."

Were they talking about the same man? Clare wondered.

"He's registered with the Society, you know," she said.

"Yes." Elizabeth stirred her coffee. "But what's so odd about that? It's not surprising that Dad would look for a sensitive when he decided to employ a consultant."

"No," Clare agreed.

"My understanding is that Jake is a mid-range talent. Maybe a level five or six. No more."

Clare went still.

"What?" Elizabeth's brows rose. "Don't tell me he hit on you last night?"

"No."

She did a quick rerun of her conversation with Jake. It occurred to her that he had never actually mentioned his level of sensitivity. She had just assumed it was very high; no, she had *known* that it was high with every intuitive fiber of her being.

What was going on here? Were her instincts

that far off or had Jake lied to Archer and the rest of the Glazebrooks about the strength of his psychic abilities? If so, why?

Maybe he thought it would make things awkward for him, she reflected. Heaven knew her high Jones number had never served her well, socially or in her career. Members of the Society, who understood the significance of it, tended to put some distance between her and themselves. It wasn't uncommon for people to feel uncomfortable around level-ten sensitives of any kind. Then, too, there were always those at the opposite extreme who were attracted to power in a sick kind of way.

Upon reflection she had to admit that advertising a high-level talent could complicate Jake's professional life.

Give the man a break, she thought. Jake had a right to his privacy.

"You were correct about Valerie Shipley," she said to change the subject. "She's got a serious drinking problem."

"Yes, and it's getting worse. Valerie always liked her cocktails but after Brad was killed she really started to hit the bottle. Poor Owen. I think he's at his wit's end. Mom said he talked to her about putting Valerie in rehab."

"Did she encourage him to do that?"

"Of course. But it's easier said than done. Valerie won't even discuss her problems. If she doesn't quit the heavy drinking, I think Owen will probably divorce her."

"Who could blame him?" Clare said quietly. "But I'm not sure Valerie will find what she needs in a rehab clinic, even one run by the Society. She's a mother who lost a son to an act of violence, and as far as she's concerned, justice has not been done. I doubt if that kind of thing can be resolved with a twelve-step program."

"As far as I'm concerned, justice *was* done," Elizabeth said, abruptly fierce. "I just wish Valerie knew what a bastard Brad really was. I wish the whole world realized it, not just you and me."

"How do you tell a mother that her dead son was a sociopath? Your own parents wouldn't even believe it when you tried to explain to them that you had married a handsome monster. Archer and Myra thought you were having some sort of mental breakdown."

"Brad could be unbelievably convincing." The fork in Elizabeth's hand trembled a little. "He always had evidence of my craziness to show people. He was even able to convince Dr. Mowbray that I was a nutcase."

"The creep really did a number on you. All

that stuff about how you were suffering fugue states during which you tried to kill yourself. It was like something out of a horror film."

Elizabeth made a face. "He seemed so *perfect* at the beginning. It gives me chills every time I realize how wrong I was about him."

"Don't blame yourself," Clare said. "You weren't the only one who thought he was wonderful. Archer and Myra and Matt and all your friends bought into his phony persona, too."

"I honestly believe that I would have been dead by now if it hadn't been for you, Clare." Tears glittered in Elizabeth's eyes. "And the worst part is that everyone except you would have been convinced that I committed suicide."

Clare touched her arm. "It's all right. It's over. Brad is the one who is dead. That's all that matters."

"Yes." Elizabeth dabbed at her eyes with her napkin. "He's gone. That's the important thing. But no one realizes how evil he truly was. I just wish we could find a way to let everyone know the truth. After the funeral, the more I tried to talk about the situation, the more Mom and Dad tried to make me keep quiet."

"In their defense, I'm sure they think it's

best for all concerned if the whole thing just goes away. Murder in the family is never good for business, let alone your social life."

"It's more than that," Elizabeth replied. "I think Mom's afraid that everyone in Stone Canyon secretly believes I'm unstable. She's worried that I won't be able to find another husband."

Clare smiled. "Are you looking for one?"

"No." Elizabeth shuddered. "It's going to be a long time before I even think about marriage again, if ever."

"You'll get past what Brad did to you," Clare said. "You just need a little time."

Elizabeth put her fork down. "Actually I'm more concerned about you than I am about myself. You paid a very high price for rescuing me from Brad. First you got dumped by your fiancé and then you got fired. We both know it was because of the gossip that went around after the murder."

"What the heck." Clare reached for the small blue ceramic pot that contained salsa. "Screw 'em if they can't take a joke."

She concentrated on spooning salsa over her scrambled eggs. It took her a couple seconds to realize that Elizabeth was staring at her.

Clare looked up. "What?"

Elizabeth shook her head and then, unex-

93

pectedly, started to giggle. The giggles turned into laughter. She clapped a hand across her mouth in a vain attempt to stem the tide.

Clare ate her spiced-up eggs, waiting for Elizabeth to get herself back under control.

Eventually Elizabeth sobered and reached for her coffee cup. "Thanks, sis, I needed a good laugh."

"Happy to be of service."

Elizabeth tipped her head to the side. "Are you really that laid back about what happened to your career and engagement?"

"I wasn't at the time but in hindsight, it did not turn out to be the end of the world. As far as the engagement goes, I was having a few doubts anyway. I don't think Greg and I would have made it for the long haul."

"I agree. You didn't even feel that you could confide in him about the paranormal side of your nature."

"That was certainly part of the problem."

"You couldn't have kept that secret forever. Sooner or later it would have come out and Greg probably would have assumed that you were delusional. That's how most non-sensitives react when told that someone has psychic abilities."

"True." Clare hesitated, thinking. "But

there was another aspect of our relationship that was starting to worry me, too."

"What?"

"In the whole time we were together we never had a single fight."

"What's wrong with that?"

"I'm not sure," Clare admitted. "But it started to get irritating. We always did what I wanted to do. I made all the decisions. I picked the restaurants where we ate. I chose the shows. He always let me set the pace in bed. It got old."

"Whoa, whoa, whoa." Elizabeth waved her hand in Clare's face. "Back up to the part where he always let you set the pace in bed. I thought that was one of the things you liked about him. You told me you appreciated the fact that he let you control things in that department."

"Sometimes you just want someone else to take charge for a while."

"Really?" Elizabeth smiled knowingly. "And just when did you come to that little epiphany?"

"I don't know," Clare admitted. "The thing is, I could only allow someone else to take charge if I trusted him completely."

"You will recall that I did warn you that it was probably a mistake for someone with your level of talent to marry someone who

95

could never in a million years understand your true nature," Elizabeth said.

"It seemed like a good idea at the time," Clare said.

"Famous last words."

"In fairness to Greg, my paranormal issues aside, I'm just not the type who can hand over the reins to someone else."

"You can say that again." Elizabeth chuckled. "In your case I think someone will have to come along who is strong enough to take the reins away from you."

Clare winced. "Not sure I like the sound of that."

"See? You're resisting the very thing you say you want. That control streak in your personality probably goes with your level-ten trust issues."

"Probably. Catch twenty-two, I guess."

Elizabeth sobered. "Well, I for one will always be profoundly grateful for your particular talent. I don't want to think about what would have happened if you hadn't seen through Brad's wall of lies."

"Luckily we don't have to worry about Brad anymore."

"Thank heavens," Elizabeth said. "But I'm starting to get concerned about Valerie Shipley."

"I think it was seeing me last night that set

her off. Once I'm out of town, she'll calm down."

"I'm not so sure of that. In fact I wouldn't be surprised to find out that she's the one who picked up the phone and spread the gossip that got you fired and caused Greg to end your engagement."

"I wouldn't dream of arguing with your intuition," Clare said. "You may be right that Valerie got me fired from the Draper Trust. But I don't know for certain that it was the rumors about my connection to Brad's murder that caused Greg to dump me."

"Hah. You asked him why he was ending things, remember?"

"Yes," Clare admitted.

"And what did he do?"

"He told me there was someone else."

"Which was?"

"A lie," Clare said.

"I rest my case."

CHAPTER NINE

The voice mail message from Jake was waiting for Clare when she turned on her cell phone after leaving the resort restaurant. It was brief and to the point.

"This is Jake. When you're ready to pick up your car let me know. I'll come and get you and take you out to Stone Canyon."

Clare punched the key to erase the message. "Talk about a take-charge type," she said. "I think Jake Salter could give me lessons."

Elizabeth pulled dark glasses out of her purse. "What was that all about?"

"He just left me a message telling me, not asking, mind you, *telling* me that he will come and pick me up and take me back to Stone Canyon."

"I'm sure he was just trying to be helpful."

"Oh, yeah."

"I sense undercurrents," Elizabeth said.

"So do I," Clare said. She put on her own

dark glasses. "But darned if I have any idea what's going on."

They waited while the parking attendant brought Elizabeth's Mercedes around. When it arrived Elizabeth slipped behind the wheel. Clare got in beside her.

"For what it's worth," Elizabeth said, driving out of the resort and onto Camelback Road, "I really don't think you need to worry too much about Jake Salter. Dad trusts him and that says a lot."

"Can't argue with that," Clare said. "Are you sure you don't mind running me out to the house?"

"No problem. I don't have any appointments until this afternoon. Are you bound and determined to fly back to San Francisco tomorrow?"

"That's the current plan."

"Well, if you change your mind and stay over another day or two, I'm free tomorrow afternoon. We could go to the spa."

"Thanks, Liz, but I wasn't kidding when I told you that my budget is *very* tight at the moment."

"My treat."

"I really don't —"

"Oh, for pity's sake. This is me, your sister, remember? I'm not Dad. It's okay to let me treat you to an afternoon at the spa."

"We'll see," Clare said.

The compact was waiting precisely where Jake had left it in the otherwise empty driveway in front of the Glazebrook house. The fractured windshield glittered in the hot sun.

Clare got out of the car, hitching her bag over her shoulder. She leaned down to look back at Elizabeth.

"Thanks," she said.

"Call me when you find out whether or not you'll be staying for another day or two."

"I will."

Clare closed the door. Elizabeth drove back down the driveway.

The front door of the big house opened. Archer came out onto the veranda.

"Thought Jake was going to bring you back here this morning," he said without preamble.

"Elizabeth and I had breakfast. She offered me a lift. It was more convenient. I called the rental company on the way here. They're going to deliver a replacement car and send a tow truck for this one. They said the new car will be here in about an hour."

"Good. Too hot to sit out by the pool. Let's go inside."

"I thought you would be at the office by now."

"Been waiting for you."

Might as well find out what this is all about, Clare thought. She tightened her grip on her purse and walked toward the veranda.

"Sorry about Valerie last night," Archer said gruffly. "She's got a problem with the booze these days."

"I noticed."

She followed him warily into the house.

"Where's Myra?" she asked.

"There's a meeting of the board of directors of the Arts Academy this morning. She's the president."

"I see."

They sat opposite each other on two leather chairs facing the view of the pool and the mountains. The housekeeper brought iced tea.

"I'll get right to the point," Archer said. "I know you've had trouble finding a new job."

"Something will turn up sooner or later," she said, stirring her iced tea with the long swizzle stick.

"Like what?"

"Well, I hear there are a lot of opportunities selling time-shares in Las Vegas."

"I'm asking you a serious question, damn it."

She hesitated and then gave a mental

shrug. "I'm thinking of opening my own business."

Archer frowned. "What the devil do you know about running a business?"

"Not much." She smiled blandly. "But it sounds like fun so I thought, what the heck, why not give it a whirl?"

He narrowed his eyes. "Do you always have to be so damned sarcastic?"

"No. I only get that way when I'm feeling pressured."

Archer settled deeper into his chair. "Look, I know that the reason you lost your job and your fiancé was probably the gossip that went around after Brad got killed."

"It didn't help, that's for sure."

"Figured the rumors would die down fairly quickly, to tell you the truth."

"So did I," she admitted. "But it doesn't seem to be working out that way."

"That's why I want to offer you a job," Archer said.

She choked on her iced tea. It took a minute to catch her breath.

"No thanks," she said automatically.

"Hell, I knew you were going to say that. So damned stubborn."

She set her half-finished iced tea on the coffee table. "Maybe I should go now."

"Hear me out first. It's the least you can do."

She smiled a little at that. "The *least* I can do?"

"You're my daughter, damn it. Not my fault I didn't know you existed until a few months ago. Your mother had no right to keep that secret from me."

"She thought she was doing what was best for everyone concerned."

"Yeah, well, she was wrong."

Clare exhaled slowly. "I didn't come here to argue about a decision that was made more than three decades ago and over which I had no control."

Anger and frustration flashed across Archer's face. "Why did you come, in that case?"

"Mom insisted."

Archer grimaced. "Should have guessed."

"Maybe we should change the subject."

"Fine by me," Archer said grimly. "Here's the deal. I'm thinking of setting up a charitable foundation and I want you to take charge of it."

She was too flabbergasted to respond. She just sat there, staring at him.

"Well?" Archer said, scowling. "What do you have to say about my offer?"

"I think," she said, spacing each word with

exacting precision, "that setting up a charitable foundation is a terrific idea. You've got more money than any one human being needs. You could do a lot of good with it."

Archer seemed satisfied. "Right."

"I'm sure you're aware that foundations require large endowments."

"I'm not stupid, Clare."

"Really, really *big* endowments," she emphasized. "The kind that can have a serious impact on what is left over for your heirs."

For the first time he seemed amused. "Starting to worry about your inheritance, after all? I thought you told me you weren't interested in my money."

"Now who's being sarcastic?"

He made an obvious bid for patience. "Yes, Clare, I'm aware that setting up a well-endowed foundation will cut into the inheritance I plan to leave for my heirs. Don't worry about it. There will be plenty left over for them and for any children they might have. Matt will take the company into the future and make even more money for the next several generations. Trust me, I can afford to fire up a foundation."

"Have you discussed this with Myra?"

"No. I talked it over with Owen but I asked him to keep quiet about it until I had a chance to discuss it with you."

"Why the secrecy?" Clare asked, opening her parasenses cautiously.

"Because I wanted to get you on board first."

The pulse of truth reverberated in the words.

"You're not planning to set up this foundation of yours just so you can give me a job, are you?" she asked.

"It's something I've been thinking about for a while."

Not an outright lie, she decided. But Archer was not telling the whole truth, either.

"Since when?" she asked.

His mouth twitched a little. "You're the skeptical type, aren't you?"

"I have trust issues."

"The idea came to me a few months back."

"Right after you found out that I got fired from my job at the Draper Trust and it became obvious I was having trouble finding a new position?"

Archer moved one hand negligently. "I'm not saying that there was no connection. I'm telling you that it all came together in my head a few months ago."

"Far be it from me to discourage you from giving away some of your money but I honestly don't think it would be a good idea to

105

put me at the head of your new foundation."

"Why the hell not?"

"Well, for starters, you'd want to be in charge," she said. "My ultimate goal has always been to be my own boss."

"I'd give you your head. It's not like you haven't had plenty of experience in the field. You'll know what you're doing."

"Let's not kid each other, Archer. We both know that you've dedicated your life to building your empire. You'll certainly want the final word when it comes to deciding who gets your money and what they spend it on."

He snorted. "Well, it would be *my* foundation, after all. I ought to have some say in where the money goes."

She picked up her tea. "I agree."

"Doesn't mean you wouldn't be in charge."

"Yes," she said. "It means exactly that."

Annoyance hardened Archer's sun-weathered face. "Doesn't look to me like you're going to get a better offer anywhere else."

Clare's stomach knotted. "Please don't tell me you're the one who's been calling every potential employer I've contacted in the past six months and warning them not to hire me."

"Hell, no." Archer slammed his hand flat on the table. "You really think I'd do something low-down and nasty like that just to get my way?"

"If it was sufficiently important to you, yes."

For a few seconds she thought he was going to explode. Then he heaved a heavy sigh. "Your mother told you a little about me, huh?" he said.

"She said you could be ruthless. At least you were in the old days."

"You don't build the kind of company Owen and I built unless you're willing to play hardball."

"I don't doubt that for a minute."

"I did what I had to do," Archer said. "But I had my own rules and I stuck by them. As God is my witness, I never took advantage of anyone who was weaker than me or anyone who didn't know how to play the game."

He was telling the truth, Clare decided.

"That sounds fair enough to me," she said quietly. "But you have to admit those rules do leave some wiggle room."

"Won't argue with that. But I didn't use that wiggle room to call up people in San Francisco to tell them not to hire you."

"Okay. I believe you."

He looked at her. "Be reasonable, Clare. It

doesn't look like you're going to get a better offer anywhere else."

"I know. That's why I'm thinking about setting up my own business."

"Why did you get into the charitable foundation field?"

"It wasn't my first choice, but I have to admit that it turned out to be a reasonably satisfying alternative." She paused. "At least until recently."

"What was your first choice?"

She hesitated and then decided there was no harm in telling him the truth. "For the past several years, I've dreamed of going to work for Jones & Jones."

Archer was clearly taken aback. "Your goal was to become a psychic investigator for J&J?"

"I thought it would be exciting and a perfect way to use my talents. I've sent in applications to the West Coast office every six months for the past few years."

"No luck, I take it."

"The dumbass who heads up the regional office, Fallon Jones, always rejects my applications."

Archer blinked. "Dumbass?"

"I assume that is an appropriate description because he is obviously too dumb to realize how much I could contribute to J&J."

"I see."

"Every time I apply, I get a letter informing me that there is no position available. Doesn't take a human lie detector to know that's a bunch of bull. Fallon Jones has decided my sensitive nature is too delicate for the work."

"How do you use your talent in the philanthropy field?"

"Lots of frauds and scammers out there who will go to any lengths to get their hands on a foundation's money. It just so happens that I am uniquely qualified to detect frauds and scammers. Until six months ago that's what I did for my employers."

Archer turned thoughtful. "Must have been tough all these years, living with that lie detector talent of yours, though."

"Mom and Aunt May saw to it that I got some help from a really insightful parapsychologist. Dr. Oxlade helped me figure out how to control my sensitivities."

"That fiancé of yours. Was he a member of the Society or a sensitive?"

"No."

"He ever figure out that there was something a little different about you?"

"I don't think so," Clare said. "At least not in the way you mean."

"You're better off without him, then. Anyone as strong as you would have been miserable with a nonsensitive."

She said nothing. Given that it was unlikely she would ever find a sensitive who was willing to risk marriage with her, there didn't seem to be much to say.

"What makes you so damn sure we couldn't work together on my foundation?" Archer asked after a while.

"Intuition." She paused a beat. "Archer, if you're making the offer because you feel guilty about the past, forget it. It's not your fault you didn't know I existed."

"Yes," he said. "It is."

Startled, she looked at him. "Why do you say that? Mom told me that she quit her job and left Arizona forty-eight hours after the two of you had your one-night stand. She said she never contacted you again."

"I should have checked up on her," Archer said. "Made sure she was all right. But the truth was, her quitting like that made my life a whole hell of a lot simpler. I had enough problems on my plate at the time. I concentrated on dealing with them."

"What kind of problems?"

"The company was going through a bad patch. Myra and I were having trouble. By the time I had my head above water again a year or so had gone by."

"So you concentrated on the future, not the past."

"I don't look back too often," Archer said. "Not my way. I told myself that it was highly unlikely your mother got pregnant that one time and that if she did, I sure as hell would have heard from her. Most women in her situation would have come looking for the kid's inheritance. And she'd have had every right to do just that."

"Mom's a very proud and independent woman."

"I remember." Archer smiled wryly. "Probably why I was attracted to her. That and the fact that she was a hell of an accountant. At any rate, she never got in touch after she left so I figured that was the end of it."

"What's done is done. I understand and accept that you feel some responsibility to take care of me financially. I respect that. I appreciate it. But it's not necessary. I can take care of myself."

"I never said you couldn't. But what the hell is wrong with taking a job from me?"

She heard a car in the drive. "That will be the guy from the rental car company."

"You didn't answer my question."

She collected her purse and stood. "It wouldn't work."

He got up and faced her. "Before you run

111

off, give me your word that you'll at least think about taking the position I'm offering."

"It's not a good idea. Trust me."

"I hit you with it cold today. You haven't had a chance to give it serious consideration."

"I don't think —"

"Forty-eight hours," he said, cutting in swiftly. "And stay here in Phoenix while you're thinking about it. Is that too much to ask?"

"Why do I have to stay here while I'm mulling over your offer?"

"Because if you go back to San Francisco you'll find it easier to say no," he said. "Besides, like it or not, I'm your father. You owe me some consideration."

She smiled in spite of herself. "Never let the client walk away on a no, right? Congratulations. You get an A in Business Psychology one-oh-one."

For the first time Archer's eyes gleamed with amusement. He grinned. "Honey, I've been doing deals since before you were born."

She realized she had just caught a glimpse of the Archer Glazebrook her mother had known. Three decades ago he would have been hard for any young woman to resist.

She hesitated. It was a mistake.

"Forty-eight hours," Archer urged softly. "That's all I'm asking. As long as you've come all the way down here, you'll want to spend some time with Elizabeth, anyway. Just give me a couple of days to show you some of my ideas for the foundation."

"You're serious about establishing one, aren't you?"

"Yes."

"All right," Clare said. "I'll stay a couple of days. You can show me some of your plans. But I am making no commitments. Is that understood?"

"Understood."

"Good-bye, Archer."

A few minutes later she was behind the wheel of the replacement compact. On the way down the drive she glanced in the rearview mirror a couple times, contemplating the sight of the big house where her sister and brother had grown up.

Archer watched the little compact turn onto the main road. All his life he'd known exactly where he was going, he thought. His goals had been clear: money, success, power, the woman he loved and heirs to whom he could leave what he had built. He had acquired everything he set out to get, never questioning any of the decisions he had made along the way.

He was not proud of some of the things he had done in the past but what the hell. He wasn't a saint. Saints didn't put together financial empires. Saints usually came to bad ends.

He went back inside and stood looking out at the pool. As he had told Clare, it was not his habit to contemplate the past. He got through life by staying focused on the future. But he could no longer pretend that what he had come to think of as his Lost Year had never taken place.

He had been married to Myra for two years when the company he and Owen had worked so hard to get off the ground started to implode. The economy went south. Business was almost nonexistent. Bankruptcy loomed. Myra's father, the senator, who had been dubious about the marriage from the start, was dropping heavy hints to his daughter about the wisdom of divorce.

To make matters worse, Myra had been upset when he told her he wanted to wait until the company was on its feet before they started a family. She became cold and withdrawn in bed. He was pretty sure she had begun to turn to Owen for sympathy and understanding.

Myra had dated Owen before he succeeded in sweeping her off her feet. When things turned bad, he wondered if she regretted her decision.

Somewhere in the midst of that jumble of impending disasters, he had found himself on a business trip with his young, attractive head of accounting, Gwen Lancaster. Gwen was a strong parasensitive with a talent for finding the patterns in financial data that eluded most people. She was the reason he was on the business trip. Gwen had located a possible contract opportunity. If they moved fast and if Archer could convince the client to go with Glazebrook, Inc., it might be possible to avoid going off a financial cliff.

Archer had closed the deal, dazzling a reluctant client with a strategy for developing a high-end shopping mall.

That evening, alone together in the restaurant of the cheap hotel where they were staying, he and Gwen had toasted the future of Glazebrook, Inc. One toast led to another and before he realized it, he ended up telling Gwen that he was pretty sure his marriage was falling apart. Gwen commiserated with him. They wound up in bed together.

In the morning Gwen realized the enormity of the mistake even before he did.

"You called out her name," Gwen said, looking at him in the cracked mirror over the dressing table as she put on an earring. She smiled wistfully. "You love her. You will always love her. Go back to her."

"What about you?" he said, feeling helpless.

"I'm handing in my resignation, effective immediately." She put on the other earring. "I can't stay with Glazebrook now. We both know that."

She rented a car and drove back to Phoenix rather than fly back on the same plane with him. He never saw her again, although he knew she had returned to her office long enough to clean out her desk. He heard through the rumor mill that she went to San Francisco to stay with an aunt while she hunted for a new job. He'd had no concerns about her finding a good position. Her talent for accounting was, after all, preternatural.

Myra had known the moment he returned what had happened, of course. She was a member of the Arcane Society, too, although she preferred to ignore that fact as much as possible. Her father, the senator, had been strict on that subject. He had taught his family that their connection to a group of people who actually believed in the paranormal had to be kept a deep, dark secret. Voters tended to be wary of politicians who claimed to possess psychic powers.

Myra had immediately made his worst nightmare come true. She filed for divorce. He spent the next several months crawling on his knees while simultaneously trying to kill the pain with work on the shopping mall project.

In the end Myra relented and came back to him. *After* the divorce was final, of course. She wanted to make her point.

They remarried, and nine months later Elizabeth was born. At about the same time the shopping mall project was completed on time and on budget. Glazebrook, Inc., was off and running, a fierce competitor in the high-stakes world of Southwest commercial real estate development.

He never looked back.

Until eight months ago that policy had served him well. But sometimes the past returns to slap you upside the head with a two-by-four.

CHAPTER TEN

Clare heard the unmistakable warble of her personal phone just as she went through the Stone Canyon security gate. She pulled over to the side, reached into her purse and retrieved her phone.

"Where are you?" Jake asked.

"Just leaving Stone Canyon in my shiny new rental car. Why?"

"Thought we agreed that I'd take you out there to make the swap."

She smiled. "That's funny, I don't recall agreeing to anything of the kind. What I recall is getting a message *telling* me that you would pick me up and take me out to Stone Canyon. As it happens, I had breakfast with Elizabeth. She very kindly drove me out here."

Silence hummed while he processed that. She couldn't tell if he was irritated, amused or merely surprised to discover that she had paid no attention to his instructions.

"You don't take direction well, do you?" he said eventually, sounding thoughtful.

"I'm usually okay with directions. It's orders that I don't take well."

"How about invitations? Do you accept those?"

A light, fluttery sensation sparkled through her. She stomped on it immediately. She must not forget that Jake worked for Archer. She was dealing with not one but two strong-willed men, each with his own agenda. This was cowboy country and she was the tenderfoot from San Francisco.

"Depends on the invitation," she said carefully.

"Will you have dinner with me tonight?"

Her mouth went dry.

"Still there?" he asked after a while.

"Yes."

"Do I get an answer?"

"Yes."

"Thank you," Jake said. "I'll have a car service pick you up at that flophouse where you're staying at five-thirty. It will take you close to an hour to get back out here."

"Wait," she said quickly. "I meant, yes, you get an answer. I didn't say yes was the answer."

"What is the answer?"

"Before I give it to you, will you swear on

your honor as a consultant that this invitation is coming from you and you only and that you are not doing this because Archer asked you to do it?"

"My honor as a consultant?" He sounded amused. "I give you my word that I am inviting you to dinner because I want to have dinner with you. Not because your father asked me to entertain you."

He sounded sincere, she thought. But when it came to her type of paranormal sensitivity, nature had not allowed for the complications of modern technology. She had learned the hard way over the years that phones, e-mail and the other varieties of electronic communication rendered her talent unreliable.

Nevertheless, anticipation welled up deep inside. Some risks were definitely worth taking.

"All right," she said. "Yes. Thank you. I'll look forward to it."

"So will I."

She cut the connection. When she glanced in the rearview mirror before pulling back onto the road she was startled to see that she was smiling.

Then the horrifying truth struck her full force. She had not come to Arizona prepared for a date with a fascinating man. The only clothes she had with her were the severe black business suit that had been ruined by the dunk in the pool, two pairs of black trousers and two T-shirts.

She needed to go shopping.

Her phone rang again two hours later, just as she emerged from the stairwell into the deep gloom of the mall parking garage. It took some major scrambling to locate the device in her purse because she was clutching two shopping bags.

She finally got the phone open.

"Hello?" she said.

"It's me, Elizabeth. Where are you?"

"At a mall."

"You went shopping without me? How *could* you?"

"It was an emergency," Clare said. "I got invited out to dinner tonight."

"Who do you know down here except for me?" Elizabeth demanded.

"Turns out I know Jake Salter."

"Oh. My. God."

"Yeah, that was my first reaction, too," Clare said. "I was sure that Archer put him up to it for devious reasons but Jake swears that's not the situation."

"Do you believe him?"

"He made the invitation by phone. You

121

know I can't trust my senses unless I am face-to-face with the person. Guess I'll find out the truth tonight."

"You know, this is all very interesting."

"I certainly thought so."

"I wouldn't have thought that Jake Salter was your type."

"Who knows what my type is?"

"Okay, there is that," Elizabeth admitted. "Take notes tonight. I'll want a full report in the morning."

"Of course."

"Did you find out what Dad wanted?"

"He plans to establish a charitable foundation. He wants me to run it."

"You're kidding. He hasn't said a word about a foundation. Wonder if Mom knows."

"He told me that the only person he's discussed it with is Owen."

"Well, that's not surprising," Elizabeth said. "After all their years together in business, he trusts Owen's opinion on anything involving money."

Clare started down the long aisle between rows of parked cars, trying to recall the precise color of her new rental. It was some silvery gray shade that was both exquisitely neutral and completely forgettable. Why didn't they paint rental cars shocking pink or emerald green so you would remember them and locate them in alien parking garages?

"I'm not sure what the driving force is behind Archer's decision to establish a foundation," she said into the phone. "Like a lot of wealthy people, he probably thinks it's a great way to be able to control his fortune even after he's gone."

"Sounds like Dad."

"If that's the case, I've got some bad news for him. A charitable trust or foundation has a way of taking on a life and an agenda of its own after the founder has passed."

"Maybe he thinks he can control the future if he puts you in charge."

"Maybe," Clare said. She spotted a familiar-looking compact and started toward it.

"What are you going to do?" Elizabeth asked.

"My first inclination was to say not only no, but hell no."

"Naturally," Elizabeth said drily.

"Appointing me the director of his foundation is his way of making up for what happened in the past. That bothers me on some deep level."

"That's your pride talking."

"I realize that. And after spending the past two hours doing some serious retail therapy and running myself deeper into the black hole of credit card debt, I've had some second thoughts."

"Clare, that's wonderful. I love the idea of you running the Glazebrook Foundation."

"Not about taking the director's job," Clare said hastily. "I know that wouldn't work. Archer and I would be at loggerheads every minute. But I'm thinking of setting up my own security consulting agency."

"Really?"

"I'll tell you about it later. But if I do go out on my own, the Glazebrook Foundation could be my first client."

"Okay, that works," Elizabeth said. Enthusiasm vibrated in her words. "Either way, you'll be spending a lot more time down here in Arizona. We'll be able to see more of each other."

"I like that part, too," Clare agreed.

She stopped in front of the silvery gray compact she had been closing in on. The upholstery was blue. She was pretty sure it should have been beige.

"Damn," she said.

"What's wrong?" Elizabeth asked.

"I've lost my car. There are a zillion silver cars in this place."

"Light colors are popular for cars in Arizona," Elizabeth said. "They reflect the heat. You know, if you're having dinner with Jake tonight it means you'll be here tomorrow."

"I told Archer I'd stick around for forty-eight hours."

"Fantastic. Let's do the spa thing tomorrow afternoon. It's short notice but I'm sure I can get us into the Stone Canyon Spa."

Clare did not doubt that for a moment. Very few people in Stone Canyon said no to a Glazebrook.

"Sounds great," she said.

"Call me in the morning with that report on your big date," Elizabeth reminded her, and ended the call.

Clare dropped the phone back into her purse and started down another aisle of almost identical vehicles.

She wondered if she was on the wrong floor. Belatedly it dawned on her that there was an unlocking device attached to the key chain the rental agency had given her.

She fished around inside her purse again and came up with the keys. She punched the unlock button.

Two-thirds of the way down the aisle in which she was standing, taillights flashed in response.

"About time," she muttered.

Clutching the shopping bags and her purse, she hurried forward.

A car engine revved violently in the shadows behind her. Unease trickled through her. She had not noticed anyone in this section of the garage. It was unnerving to realize that there was someone in the vicinity and she had not been aware of it. This was how innocent people got mugged in parking garages, she thought. They failed to pay attention to their surroundings.

Calm down. Whoever he is, he's in a car. He's not trying to sneak up on you. He's just heading for the exit.

The vehicle's engine roared.

She glanced back over her shoulder.

A massive, late-model SUV was bearing down on her. Behind the heavily tinted windows, the driver's face was only a dark silhouette.

Shock flashed through her. The SUV was not slowing down. The driver evidently didn't see her. Probably had his sunglasses on in preparation for heading out into the intense midday light. Or maybe the idiot was talking on the phone.

The possibilities flashed through her mind in an oddly serene, orderly manner, as if nothing out of the ordinary were happening; as if she were not standing directly in the path of an oncoming vehicle.

"Oh, shit."

Adrenaline kicked in. Instinctively, she

tightened her grip on the shopping bags and purse and rushed toward the side of the aisle.

The SUV abruptly swerved toward her, as though in pursuit.

Teens gone bad, she thought.

She dropped the bags and flung herself into the narrow crevasse between two parked cars, fetching up hard against a fender. The vehicle's alarm went off, blasting her eardrums.

Beep, beep, beep. Whoop, whoop, whoop.

The SUV thundered past, missing by inches the front bumpers of the two cars that shielded her. It turned the corner at the far end of the aisle, tires squealing.

Clare waited, feeling like a cornered rabbit. What would she do if the SUV came back? Could she make it to the stairwell?

Mercifully, the hungry growl of the big engine faded. The SUV was heading for the exit.

Hands trembling, heart pounding, she looked for the fallen shopping bags and her purse.

The good news was that, although the dress had spilled out onto the concrete floor, it was still safely encased in its plastic sheath. The strapless bra she had bought to go with it was also safe. The shoes had tumbled out of the box but there was only a small mark on the left sandal.

She found her purse lying next to the front wheel of one of the cars that had given her shelter.

Collecting her belongings, she took a steadying breath and trudged toward the rental car. When she was safely behind the wheel she made certain the doors were securely locked. Then she sat quietly, waiting for her nerves to settle down.

It took a while before she felt calm enough to drive. She hadn't experienced this kind of edgy shock and raw fear since that night six months ago when she went to Elizabeth's house and found Brad's body; the night she wondered if she had been the intended victim.

CHAPTER ELEVEN

The chauffeur eased the big car to a smooth stop in front of the house. Clare studied the expensive-looking residence through the window of the vehicle. The house had been done in the Spanish colonial villa style, complete with red tile roof, that was so popular in this part of the country.

An exquisite little thrill, part warning, part excitement, flashed through her.

"I assumed you were taking me to a restaurant to meet Mr. Salter," she said to the driver. "This is a private residence."

"It's the address I was given," the chauffeur said.

He climbed out and opened Clare's door. She collected her purse and extricated herself from the dark interior of the vehicle.

She did a quick survey of her surroundings on her way to the front door. The house was one of a number of elegant, low-profile homes scattered about Stone Canyon. Unlike the Glazebrook house, which was situated on a golf course, this residence was surrounded by a lot of open, rolling desert.

The door opened before she could knock. Jake stood in the tiled entranceway. He was dressed in a pair of black trousers and a midnight blue shirt. The collar was open and the sleeves were rolled up on his forearms. He was not wearing his glasses, she noticed.

He examined her from head to toe, taking in the sleek, off-the-shoulder black dress and the high-heeled black patent sandals. Masculine approval and something she was pretty sure was sensual heat darkened his eyes. The excitement that had been stirring inside her intensified, stirring the hair on the nape of her neck.

"Great dress," Jake said.

"Thanks. You're lucky to see it in one piece." She stepped into the hallway. "It nearly got run over in the parking garage at the mall where I bought it this afternoon."

"Yeah?" He closed the door and turned to face her. "What happened?"

"Some fool driving a monster SUV either didn't see me walking toward my car or else decided to play a game of chicken. I had to scramble to get out of his way. Dropped the shopping bags in the process. Fortunately nothing got damaged."

His expression sharpened. "You're all right?"

"Oh, yes. I'm fine. I was just a little shaken up, that's all."

"It was that close?"

"Certainly seemed like it at the time, although I may have exaggerated the incident in retrospect. I've got a creative imagination."

"Get a look at the car?" he asked.

"Not really. It was big. Late model. Like every other vehicle in the garage it was sort of silvery gray." She smiled. "Don't worry about it, Jake. It was probably a teenager playing games or someone talking on the phone. Either way, no major harm was done." The incident in the garage was the last thing she wanted to talk about tonight, she thought. She searched for another topic. "This is a nice place for a rental."

He followed her gaze, taking in the tile floors, Mediterranean yellow walls and dark wooden beams as though he had not previously noticed them.

"It serves my purpose and it's convenient to the Glazebrook offices," he said. "Would you care for a glass of wine?"

"That sounds like a really terrific idea."

"This way."

He ushered her along the wide hallway that

divided the living room and a library, through an arched opening and into a large kitchen that gleamed with a lot of modern, high-tech appliances.

Clare stopped short. "Wow. You could film a cooking show in here."

He opened the door of a wine cooler and removed a bottle. "The kitchen was one of the reasons I chose the place."

"You like to cook?"

He set the bottle on the large island in the center of the kitchen and went to work on the cork with an opener. "If I didn't, I'd have to eat out or order in every night."

"You could afford a housekeeper," she pointed out.

"I like my privacy when I'm home. Besides, cooking is a form of relaxation for me."

She walked forward slowly and came to a halt on the opposite side of the island. "I enjoy cooking, too. But when you live alone —"

"I know." He set the cork down on the island. "Part of the pleasure of food is sharing it."

He filled two glasses and handed one to her.

"To shared pleasures," he said, tapping his glass lightly against hers.

She smiled. "To shared pleasures."

She took a sip, savoring the crisp, elegant white. When she looked up she saw that Jake was watching her very intently. She was suddenly conscious of the intimacy of the situation. She was here, on his territory, drinking wine that he had poured for her. Why did that make her shiver ever so slightly?

He handed her his glass, breaking the small spell. "If you'll take this outside for me, I'll get the bruschetta."

She carried his glass and hers through the open sliding glass doors. The wings of the house framed the pool and patio on three sides. On the fourth side a decorative wrought-iron fence and gate were all that stood between the house and the wildness of the desert landscape.

Jake followed her, carrying a wooden tray.

They settled into a pair of cushioned patio loungers. The heat of the day had faded to a comfortable temperature. Beyond the wrought-iron fence the desert was cloaked in the long shadows of twilight.

Clare helped herself to some bruschetta, wondering why something as simple as a slice of grilled bread topped with excellent olive oil, a little salt and delicately chopped tomato and basil leaves could taste so good.

"Wonderful," she said, munching happily.

"Absolutely fantastic."

"Glad you like it." Jake leaned back in the chair and cocked one ankle over a knee. "How did the talk with Archer go?"

"I'm not sure. Archer wants to establish a foundation. He wants me to run it. I told him no but I agreed to hang around here in Arizona for another forty-eight hours. I'm very sure I don't want to run his foundation, but I might consider consulting for him."

"What kind of consulting?"

"Well, since you ask, getting fired from the Draper Trust has pushed me into making a decision that I have been considering for quite a while now."

"You want to set up an independent consulting firm?"

"Not exactly. I'm going to establish my own psychic investigation agency. Detecting scam artists and frauds for private foundations and charitable institutions will be one of the services I'll offer."

Jake just looked at her. "Huh."

"Thanks for the enthusiastic encouragement."

"Huh," Jake said again. "You want to be a private investigator?"

"It's been my dream for a while now. I've applied several times to the West Coast office of Jones & Jones but the dumbass who runs the firm won't hire me."

"Dumbass?" Jake repeated neutrally.

"Fallon Jones." She made a face. "I know those Jones men are legends in the Society, at least the Joneses who trace their descent back to Sylvester Jones are. But if you ask me, Fallon Jones is a narrow-minded, hidebound, dumbass jerk who can't see past the myths about my kind of talent long enough to realize that all human lie detectors are not the same."

"Huh."

"Honestly, you'd think that of all people in the Society, a Jones would be especially open-minded. I mean, it's not like a lot of the Jones men haven't been pretty extreme talents, now, is it?"

"No," Jake admitted, sounding very cautious. "No, it's not as if there haven't been some exotics in that family."

"Exactly. A Jones should be able to look beyond the myths and stories and rumors about certain kinds of unusual talents. But Dumbass Fallon Jones obviously can't do that."

"Huh," he said again.

She smiled, satisfaction bubbling up inside her. "So, I'm going to start up my own psychic investigation agency and give J&J a little competition."

"Should be interesting."

"I expect it will be. Getting fired unexpectedly from the trust kind of put a crimp in my business plan. I had intended to work for another year in order to put together enough capital to open my agency. I was also hoping to persuade the trust to become my first big client after I left. But that all went up in smoke when the rumors about my connection to the McAllister murder reached management. So, to make ends meet, I tried to find another position right away."

"But that didn't work out."

"No," she admitted. "And now I think it was for the best. As I said, it has given me the impetus to take the big leap out on my own." She polished off the rest of a piece of bruschetta. "Speaking of your professional activities, Mr. Salter, I went online and did a little research on you."

"Learn anything interesting?"

She cleared her throat. "Came across your website and some personal stuff. That's all."

"Personal stuff." He crunched bruschetta. "That would be an oblique reference to my divorce?"

"As you can see, I have a natural talent for inducing people to give up information."

"Probably be useful in the investigation business," he said. "What do you want to know about my divorce?"

"It's not really any of my business."

"True. But that doesn't alter the fact that you're curious, does it?"

"Okay, I wondered if your ex was a sensitive," she said.

"No." He turned the wineglass in his hand, studying the contents. "That was a deliberate choice on my part. I thought maybe she wouldn't notice my little eccentricities."

She watched him closely. "They're not so little, are they?"

He did not respond immediately. For a few seconds she wondered if he was going to lie.

He met her eyes. "I'm a level-ten parasensitive."

The truth at last. She whistled softly. "Well, that explains a lot."

"Such as?"

"Such as why you let everyone think you're a mid-range strategy talent. Level tens of any kind tend to make a lot of people nervous."

He watched her with an unwavering gaze. "It doesn't bother you?"

"I'm a ten, too, remember? What happened to your marriage?"

"Let's see." He stretched out his legs and assumed a reflective air. "As I recall, about three months into the marriage, she started to complain that I was being overprotective and that I was trying to run her life."

"Let me guess. Before the marriage your protective streak seemed very romantic to her."

"Don't know about that. All I can tell you is that she didn't mention the problem until three months into the marriage."

"Any other complaints?"

"I believe she may have mentioned that I was overly demanding."

"Overly demanding?"

He looked at her. "In bed."

"Oh." She gulped some wine and swallowed hard. "I see."

"Four months into the marriage she started talking about needing more space. Six months in, she went to see a divorce lawyer."

"Your marriage only lasted six months?"

"It was a disaster from the start." He drank some more of his wine. "I should have known better. The experts always tell you that strong parasensitives don't do well with people who are not also sensitive. Hate to admit it, but I think they're right."

"Maybe." She settled back in her lounger. The wine was starting to have an effect. She was feeling much more relaxed than a few minutes before. A lot more insightful, too. "But in your case I'm not so sure that your marriage went on the rocks just because you married an outsider."

He raised one brow. "Got a better theory?"

She contemplated the glowing pool. "You're the take-charge type. Not your fault. It's part of who you are."

Jake made no comment. Inspired by his lack of argument, she warmed to her theme.

"The way I see it, your ex-wife was probably telling you the truth when she said that you were trying to run her life. Running things is what you do." Clare raised a finger. "But your instincts weren't the problem. Neither were your intentions. The real issue was that she didn't know how to hold her own with you."

"Think that was it?" Jake asked in an odd tone of voice.

"She probably couldn't set boundaries and, when necessary, put you in your place. So, in the end, she panicked and fled the scene, leaving you confused and bewildered and wondering what the hell you did wrong."

"You sound very certain of your analysis."

"Yep." She nodded, feeling very sage now. "You are what they sometimes call an alpha male. Leader of the pack. Trouble is, in the modern world, there aren't a lot of packs to lead so your natural talents get applied to whatever comes into your orbit. Family, spouse, business, whatever."

Silence greeted that statement.

Clare turned her head to see how he was taking her brilliant insights. A cold shock went through her when she realized that he was watching her with an unnervingly enigmatic air.

"How did you know?" he asked evenly.

She cleared her throat. "Sorry. Just a wild hunch, honest."

"How did you know?" This time the question sounded distinctly dangerous.

"That you are a much stronger talent than you lead others to believe?" A trickle of unease penetrated the pleasant wine haze. "Uh, well, it really isn't all that hard to tell. I mean, it's sort of obvious."

"No, it is not obvious." He put his half-finished wine down on the table. "And it isn't in the Arcane Society's genealogy files, either, at least not the ones that are open to the public. So how did you figure it out?"

"I'm getting a little confused here, Jake. What, exactly, is so secret about you being a take-charge type?"

"I'm talking about your alpha male comment. Don't try to slide out of this. You know, don't you?"

Understanding finally dawned on her.

"Oh. I see. You're a hunter."

He watched her with the steady, unblinking gaze of a top-of-the-line predator.

"Yes," he said.

"Actually, I hadn't guessed that part. Just that you're a high-end talent."

The corners of his eyes tightened ever so slightly.

She cleared her throat. "Well, you have to admit that it does sort of explain your little problem with your marriage. Everyone knows that hunters are very difficult to match."

"Some people think that's because our type of sensitivity is so damned *primitive,*" he said. There was a gleaming edge on every word. "They used to call us throwbacks. Some people still do."

"Get over it. We're all primitive beneath the surface. That's why they invented civilization, remember?"

"Civilization doesn't always work."

"Maybe not, but it's definitely way ahead of whatever is in second place." She frowned at the nearly empty plate. "Are you going to eat that last piece of bruschetta?"

There was no response to what seemed to her to be a perfectly polite question. When she looked up from the plate she saw that Jake was still studying her with a disturbing gaze.

"What now?" she asked.

"It doesn't bother you."

"Knowing that you're a hunter? Nah. It's kind of reassuring."

"Why?"

"It explains why you have to lie a lot. I respect secrets, Jake. And I know how to keep them. Trust me. Now, about that last piece of bruschetta."

"Help yourself," he said.

"Thanks." She scooped up the bruschetta and took a crunchy bite. "What with having to shop for this dress and nearly getting run down in the garage, I didn't have time for lunch. I'm starving."

"Dinner will be ready soon."

"Lovely." She drank a little more wine, ate the last of the bruschetta and settled back to enjoy the descent of the desert night.

"Level-ten hunters often make other sensitives nervous," Jake said after a while.

"Hey, you want to narrow your social life down to a humiliatingly small vanishing point? Try telling everyone you know that you're a human lie detector."

"I can see where that might do the trick," he said.

"I blame the whole negative attitude toward hunters on the Jones men," she said. "The Joneses who are the direct descendents of the founder, that is."

"Why do you hold them responsible for the bad image?"

"They haven't all been what we call hunters by any means, but some of them were and over the years that bunch managed to make themselves legends in the Society, right?"

"I've heard that," he agreed.

"That's all well and good. Every community needs its legends. But the problem with a powerful legend is that it usually consists of a little dollop of truth surrounded by several layers of fluffy lies. After a while the lies conceal the truth at the core and everyone starts to believe the lies. In the case of hunters, there has been a decidedly dangerous image associated with that type of talent because so many of the stories connected to the Jones men who were hunters involve violence."

"So?"

She took another sip of wine. "The way I see it, hunters, in general, get a bad rap simply because of those darn Jones men. If they had pursued normal, ordinary careers the way you have instead of chasing after bad guys, no one would think twice about a sensitive who happened to be a hunter today."

"You don't think that answer might be a

143

little too simplistic?"

"Makes sense to me."

He let that ride for a while.

"Did your engagement end because of your sensitivity?" he asked eventually.

"Nope. I did a pretty good job of covering that up. It ended because of what happened here in Stone Canyon."

"The McAllister murder?" he asked.

"Uh-huh. Between you and me, I think someone right here in Stone Canyon phoned Greg and warned him that he was engaged to an ax murderer."

"McAllister wasn't murdered with an ax."

"Details." She waved that off. "The bottom line is my fiancé had good reason to get cold feet."

"Did he?"

She frowned. "Well, yes. What would you have done in his shoes?"

"If I had questions, I would have gone hunting."

She stilled in the act of taking another sip of wine. Slowly she lowered the glass. "I beg your pardon?"

He stretched out his legs and contemplated the jeweled pool. "You heard me."

"You would have gone hunting for what, exactly?"

"Answers." He picked up his wine and

drank what was left in the glass.

"Answers aren't always available. This isn't exactly a pension and benefits issue. The police think a burglar killed Brad. That kind of crime is notoriously hard to solve. It's quite possible the murderer is in jail now for some other offense."

"Do you believe that?"

It was getting a little hard to breathe. She tried another sip of wine in hopes of calming her jittery nerves.

"It's comforting to think that the killer is probably off the streets," she said.

"You don't look particularly comforted. I assume that is because you believe that whoever murdered McAllister is probably not sitting in jail."

How had the conversation strayed into such dangerous territory? Not an accident, that was certain. It was time to take the offensive.

"Why are you so interested in Brad's death?" she asked coolly.

"Because you interest me, Clare Lancaster. What happened to your sister's husband had a major impact on your life. It cost you a fiancé and it's the reason you're currently unemployed. Therefore it follows that I'm curious."

She dared not move. "Why are you interested in me? Is it because Archer is your client?"

"No, Clare." He smiled slowly, letting her see the hunter beneath the surface. "This is personal."

CHAPTER TWELVE

The incident in the parking garage had been a reckless, idiotic, potentially disastrous act, Valerie thought. She was still shaking.

She had made the mistake of giving in to impulse and an irresistible moment of opportunity. That must not happen again.

Luckily she had failed. What if she had succeeded? Yes, Clare would have been dead or grievously injured and that would have been enormously satisfying. But there would have been so many problems. How would she have concealed the damage to the car, for instance? Owen would most certainly have demanded an explanation. There would have been blood or some other type of forensic evidence left behind.

She might have been arrested, Valerie thought, horrified.

Shuddering, she gulped down half the martini and topped off the glass.

She had not followed Clare from the

Glazebrook house with the intention of running her down. The plan had been to find out where she was staying in Phoenix. No one seemed to know anything other than that she was at a hotel near the airport.

Valerie clenched one hand into a fist. This morning she had opened a city map of Phoenix and drawn a circle around Phoenix Sky Harbor. She methodically called every hotel and motel within a two-mile radius of the airport. There was no Clare Lancaster registered at any of them.

Clever bitch. You know you've got a reason to be careful, don't you?

The idea of watching the entrance to the gated community where she and Owen and the Glazebrooks lived had come to her that morning. Owen had said Clare had returned to Arizona because she was summoned by Archer Glazebrook. It made sense that sooner or later she would show up at the house again, if only to deal with the damaged rental car and pick up a new one.

The detour into the mall parking garage had come as a surprise. Valerie remembered how she had sat there, waiting, for nearly two hours in the damned heat before Clare returned. At the sight of her carrying shopping bags and acting so *normal,* just as if she hadn't murdered Brad in cold blood, rage boiled up and spilled over.

Stupid, Valerie thought. *So stupid.*

Cradling the full martini glass in both hands, she walked gingerly across the white-on-white great room and sat down on the white leather sofa. She had to be careful. Owen had been furious two days before when she accidentally spilled a whole pitcher of martinis on the rug.

But she needed this drink badly. Her nerves were shot. She took another long swallow and set the glass on the table.

She held up her hand and stared at her shaking fingers. Maybe she ought to take one of the pills the doctor had given her. He warned her not to mix the meds with booze but she knew for a fact that people did it all the time. She had done it herself, more than once, recently. A good night's sleep had been impossible to come by since the night of Brad's murder, but she had discovered that a judicious mix of pills and alcohol made it possible to escape into oblivion for a few hours at a time.

No pills this evening, she decided. She did not want to sleep. She needed to think. She had to concentrate on what to do about Clare Lancaster.

Rage flashed through her. How dare Clare come back here after what she did?

Valerie took another fortifying gulp of martini and looked out the wall of windows toward the mountains.

She hated this place. She detested everything about the desert with its harsh, ugly plant life, its stinging insects and snakes, the relentless summer heat and the intense light. But most of all she hated knowing that Brad's killer was walking around Stone Canyon as free as a bird.

Seeing Clare enter the Glazebrook house just as though she deserved to be treated like a member of the family was too much. No mother who had lost a son could be expected to tolerate that kind of affront.

She used both hands to raise the martini glass to her lips again. This time she hesitated. Then, very carefully, she set the glass back down on the white stone coffee table without taking a sip.

She really did need to think.

For a while the vengeance she had pursued these past six months had been enough to satisfy her. The first phone call, the one to Clare's fiancé, had been extremely gratifying. Poor Greg Washburn was horrified to discover that Clare had been having an affair with her half sister's husband. He was even more stunned to discover that, although she had not been arrested, many of those closest to the victim were convinced that Clare killed him. That kind of gossip was too much for any decent man. He'd had no choice but to end the engagement.

The phone call to the head of the Draper Trust where Clare worked had been just as satisfactory. Valerie placed the call in her capacity as president of the board of the Stone Canyon Arts Academy. *Due diligence and all that. Just a word to the wise.* Everyone in the charitable foundation business understood that the employees had to be purer than Caesar's wife. If word got out that a member of the staff had been involved in an illicit love triangle that ended in murder the impact on future fund-raising efforts could be devastating. Reputation was everything in the world of high-end philanthropy.

She had refined her story as the months went by, perfecting it with additional phone calls to each of Clare's prospective employers. It wasn't that hard to learn the names of the charitable organizations that were considering her application. The world of charitable gift giving in the San Francisco Bay Area, after all, was relatively small.

No, she assured each scandalized board director in turn, there was no hard evidence implicating Clare Lancaster but it was *common knowledge* in certain circles in Stone

Canyon that she had been intimately involved with the victim. It was also well known that Archer Glazebrook had pulled a lot of strings to keep his illegitimate daughter out of jail. He had only done what he'd had to do, of course. After all, he had the reputation of his family to protect. But *everyone* knew the truth.

The phone calls that had destroyed Clare's engagement and her career provided some justice. But now, Valerie thought, she had to face the possibility that those calls were the reason Clare had come back to Stone Canyon. Last night Owen told her that Archer was setting up a charitable foundation just to make sure Clare had a job.

It was too much, Valerie thought. Her plan of revenge had backfired on her. Clare was going to come out of this smelling like a rose. She would have the Glazebrook money and the Glazebrook power behind her.

That wasn't right. Clare should be made to suffer for what she did to Brad. She had to pay.

Valerie focused on the mountains, trying to concentrate. It was so hard to keep her thoughts clear these days. She desperately needed to talk to someone.

There was only one person who understood the pain she was going through; only one person on the face of the earth who had suffered as she had suffered when Brad was killed.

She reached for the cell phone.

CHAPTER THIRTEEN

This is personal.

That was nothing short of the truth, the whole truth and nothing but, Jake thought. Way too much truth, probably. He had a strict policy when it came to dealing with the truth. He never used more of it than absolutely necessary when he was working. The truth often made people nervous. That was the last thing he wanted to do in Stone Canyon. It would only complicate an already extremely complicated project.

The smart thing would be to put some distance between Clare and himself until he had finished what he came here to do. But he was pretty sure that wasn't going to be possible. Not now.

In spite of all the invisible flashing red warning lights going off around her, he felt compelled to get closer. Something inside him resonated with her gutsy attitude; made him want her on a visceral level. He had an overwhelming urge to find out how a woman who was clearly accustomed to fighting for everything she wanted responded when she went to bed with a man who applied the same technique to life. A man like him.

Dinner alone with her at the house had been a bad decision in what he suspected would be a long line of similarly bad moves. But somehow he could not bring himself to regret any of them. So much for the virtues of twenty-twenty foresight.

"It's late." Clare put down the empty teacup and checked her watch. "I should be getting back to the motel. Is the driver still around?"

"No." He got to his feet, fighting a deep reluctance to let her go. "I'm going to drive you back to your motel."

He backed the BMW out of the garage. When he bundled Clare into the front seat he experienced a proprietary satisfaction from the small act. His woman in his car. And they were going to drive off into the night together.

When he got behind the wheel the dark, intimate confines of the front passenger compartment closed around him, sealing his doom.

So why wasn't he a lot more worried?

So he had a rule against sleeping with anyone involved in a case. So what? Rules were made to be broken.

Of course, things usually went south when that kind of thing happened, but what the hell.

Clare said little as he piloted the BMW out of the foothills and back toward Phoenix. He made no move to force the conversation. They had talked a lot this evening, sometimes dancing around each other's subtle probes, sometimes agreeing, sometimes disagreeing, sometimes smiling at the same ironic observations.

This was an opportunity to see if they could be quiet together.

By the time he drove into the nearly deserted parking lot of the Desert Dawn Motel, the question had been answered. The silence in the front seat had not separated them, he decided. Instead, it seemed to him that the sense of closeness had become more binding. There was always the possibility that, hungry as he was for her, he was misreading the feminine signals he was picking up but he didn't think so.

He eased the car into a slot near the entrance, got out and walked with Clare to the lobby.

The same night clerk was on duty. He looked up from his magazine and gave Jake the same knowing smirk he had given him the night before. Jake contemplated the pleasant prospect of ripping the guy's throat open with his bare teeth.

"I'm going to see the lady to her room," he said instead.

Civilization at work. What a concept. No blood, no mess, no fun.

"Sure. Whatever." The night clerk went back to his reading.

Jake took Clare's arm and escorted her up the stairs. Then he guided her down the dimly lit hall, irritated again, as he had been the night before, by the knowledge that he was going to have to leave her here in this place with its dingy carpet and badly painted walls.

Clare got her door open and stepped across the threshold. She turned to look at Jake.

"Good night," she said. "Dinner was terrific."

"Glad you enjoyed it," he said. He braced one hand on the doorjamb. "Now promise me you'll check out of this place tomorrow morning."

"I'll only be here tonight and tomorrow night," she said. "No point moving."

"You're stubborn, hardheaded and you don't take good advice well," he said. "I like that in a woman."

She opened her mouth to respond.

"But there's such a thing as too much of a good thing," he added before she could say a word. "I want you to check out of here tomorrow."

She gave him a long, considering look. "I realize that you're accustomed to giving orders but there's something you're forgetting here."

"What's that?"

"I don't work for you."

"Probably just as well," he said. "Because I've got a feeling that I would have to fire you."

"For being stubborn and hardheaded?"

"No," he said. "So that I could do this."

He gripped the doorjamb, leaned into the opening and kissed her. He was very careful not to touch her with his hands. This way she had the option of stepping back out of range.

She didn't step back. Her mouth was soft and welcoming under his. She knew what he was and she wasn't afraid of him. In fact, she seemed to like what she saw.

Desire arced through him, hot and exultant.

He went through the opening, never taking his mouth off Clare's, and kicked the door closed with one foot.

Now he did put his hands on her, pulling her close so he could deepen the kiss. He heard her make a muffled, urgent little sound and felt her fingers curl around his shoulders. She gripped him hard, bracing herself, pulling him to her.

Her response to him revved up all his senses. This close to her he could sense her power. He knew she was probably picking up his as well. The effect was an exhilarating rush unlike anything he had ever experienced. The part of him that was never allowed out of control was suddenly running free in the night.

He urged her backward, driven by some vague notion of getting to the bed. But in the first chaotic moments of the kiss he had become disoriented. Clare stopped abruptly, her back against the wall, not a mattress. Desperate for her, he caught her wrists and pinned them on either side of her head

She nipped at his throat in retaliation, letting him feel the edge of her teeth. Then she punished him further by drawing the inside of her leg up along the outside of his calf. He could feel the spike heel of her shoe through the fabric of his trousers. The sensual warning was the most erotic challenge he had ever encountered. It was a wonder he didn't climax right then, he thought.

He fought back by capturing both her wrists in one hand and anchoring them over her head. The action freed his other hand. He used it to unfasten the clip that bound her hair. The silky tresses tumbled down over his fingers. He seized a fistful of the stuff and used it to hold her head still so he could kiss her again, openmouthed this time, wanting to taste her, needing to inhale her essence.

She twisted restlessly against him. He used his hips to nail her hard against the wall, letting her feel the size and shape of his erection. She reacted with a low, breathless moan. The spike heel of her shoe dug into his leg.

He slid his hand down the sweet curves of her breast and waist, all the way to her hip. There he paused and squeezed, savoring the resilient swell of feminine flesh and bone.

Clare was breathing faster now. Quick, shallow, hot little gasps that told him he was definitely not the only one on fire in this room.

When he raised his head he saw that she was watching him with dazed, unfocused eyes. He realized that she was surprised by her reaction.

"What?" he said, smiling a little. "You didn't see this freight train bearing down on us all evening?"

"It's not that." She shook her head as though to clear it. "It's just that I didn't realize how I . . . Never mind."

"Now, me, I knew it would be like this," he said against her mouth. "Knew it the first time I saw you."

"Did you?"

"Oh, yeah."

Inserting his fingers between the wall and Clare's sleek back he found the zipper of the sexy little dress and peeled it down. The front of the garment fell away, revealing a lacy black strapless bra.

He had to release his captive's hands in order to unfasten the bra. She responded by using her newfound freedom to yank at the buttons of his shirt with trembling fingers.

By the time the bra had disappeared, Clare had her hands flat against his bare chest. When he bent his mouth to taste one tight nipple she swayed against him. The leg that had been climbing his suddenly returned to the floor as she tried to steady herself.

"I don't know why we're doing this up against a wall when there's a bed handy," he muttered.

He scooped her into his arms and carried her out of the narrow confines of the entryway. He dropped her lightly onto the bed and put his hand on the buckle of his belt. Clare looked up at him with sultry welcome, lips parted in anticipation.

A series of sharp raps on the door reverberated through the room. Jake spun around. The sexual tension that had hardened every muscle in his body was instantly transmuted into another kind of tension via the dark, dangerous alchemy that linked sex and violence. In a heartbeat he had gone from wanting to claim his woman to wanting to protect her.

Talk about overreacting, he thought.

"If that's the guy from the room next door, I've got a few words of advice for him," he said.

"Wait," Clare whispered. "I'll handle this." She raised her voice. "Who is it?"

"Management." The familiar voice of the night clerk boomed loudly through the door. "Sorry to disturb you, Miss Lancaster, but we had a report that a second party was seen entering your room. And, uh, well, there's a rule. It says that only the person who is legally registered in the room can occupy it. So, unless you, uh, want to pay an additional fee and register that guy who's in there with you, I'm going to have to ask your guest to leave."

"Well," Clare murmured. "This is certainly one of life's more embarrassing little moments." She raised her voice again. "There's been a misunderstanding. Just a second."

She got to her feet, staggered, and would have toppled over if Jake hadn't caught her. She looked down and noticed her missing shoe. "I knew I shouldn't have bought these sandals."

"For what it's worth," Jake said, zipping up the dress, "I like them."

"Easy for you to say. You don't have to wear them."

She removed the remaining shoe and walked, barefoot, across the room. She paused, one hand on the door, and waited impatiently for Jake to finish buttoning his shirt.

He shoved the shirttails back inside the waistband of his trousers and spread his hands in a voilà gesture.

She jerked the door open and glared at the night clerk. "My business associate was concerned about the security in this room. He wanted to check it out before he left."

It was a good line, Jake thought, amused. And she had delivered it with just the right amount of irritated arrogance. She might have got away with it, too, if it hadn't been for the fact that, from her shoeless feet to her rumpled dress and tousled hair, she radiated the unmistakable aura of a woman who had just been thoroughly kissed.

"Right." The night clerk looked her up and down and then gave Jake another smirk. "Security check."

Jake looked at him. "I'm sure you're aware that the security lock on the sliding glass door is broken."

The clerk frowned. "Nobody reported any broken lock."

"I'm reporting it now," Jake said.

Clare folded her arms and raised her eyes to the ceiling.

The clerk moved hesitantly into the room, taking in the sight of the rumpled bedspread and the high-heeled sandals on the threadbare carpet. He fiddled with the sliding glass door a couple of times. There was a click as the lock slid into place.

The clerk regarded Jake with a triumphant expression. "The lock works just fine."

"Yeah?" Jake shook his head. "I'll be damned. Must have been a case of operator error." He turned to Clare. "Something tells me it's time for me to go."

She smiled wryly. "I think so, yes."

"I'll call you in the morning."

Laughter gleamed in her eyes. "They always say that."

"I don't always say it. But when I do, I mean it."

He touched the side of her cheek, bent his head slightly and kissed her. It wasn't a proper good night kiss. It was a message to the night clerk. *The lady is mine.*

When he raised his head he saw the sparkle of amused irritation in Clare's eyes. She understood the message that was being sent, too.

He went out into the hall and waited for the clerk to join him. Clare closed the door firmly behind them.

Jake started down the stairs. The clerk hurried to catch up.

"I'm just doing my job," the clerk said apologetically. "No unregistered guests in the rooms. That's the rule."

"And an excellent rule it is."

The door to room 208 opened again. This time the bald-headed man peered out. His gaze went first to Clare's door. But when he saw Jake he hurriedly ducked back inside his room.

"I think I can guess where the complaints came from," Jake said to the clerk.

"The wife in two-oh-eight is a little on the uptight side."

Jake went down the stairs, thinking about the two things that had been bothering him all evening. The first was Clare's effort to ensure that everyone in Stone Canyon with the exception of himself and Elizabeth believed that she was staying out at the airport. The second was the serious scare she had received in the mall parking garage that afternoon.

Taken independently, neither fact was enough to generate a great deal of concern, he thought. There were reasonable explanations for each. After witnessing Myra's obvious tension and Valerie's out-of-control rage at the cocktail party the night before, he could understand why Clare didn't want to advertise the address of her motel. Valerie, at least, was quite capable of showing up unannounced and causing a scene.

As for the incident in the garage, that could be explained away easily enough by an inattentive driver or a young punk bent on frightening a woman alone.

But the combination of the two made him uneasy. When he added in the fact that the last time Clare was in town she had discovered a dead body, he got downright edgy.

He checked his watch when he reached the lobby. It was nearly one o'clock in the morning. Time for an executive decision.

"You can check me in," he said to the clerk. "I want room two-twelve if it's available."

"Huh?"

"The room on the other side of Miss Lancaster's room. Is it available?"

"Well, yeah, I guess so, but —"

"I'll take it."

"Gee, I don't know. This is kind of an unusual situation."

"You got any problems registering a paying guest?"

"Well, when you put it like that —"

She had changed into her nightgown and was pulling back the covers on the bed when she heard him come back down the hall. She knew it was Jake. There was an unmistakable resonance to his long, prowling stride that reverberated through the cheap floorboards.

Startled, she hurried to the door and opened it a couple inches. She was in time to see Jake slide a key into the lock of the adjoining room. He had a small leather duffel bag in one hand.

"What do you think you're doing?" she demanded in a loud whisper.

"Spending the night in a third-rate motel." He got the door to his room open and looked at her. "Not my first choice but I hear the place is clean."

"Jake, you can't be serious."

"Trust me, I'm serious. See you in the morning." He started to enter the room.

Her senses verified the statement. Okay, so he was serious.

She leaned a little farther out into the hall, struggling to conceal her nightgown-clad body with the door.

"Wait," she said urgently. "What is this all about?"

He propped one shoulder against the wall, folded his arms across his chest and regarded her with a puzzled frown.

"I don't like the idea of you staying here," he said. "You refuse to move. Therefore I've got no choice but to stay here, too."

"That's ridiculous."

"Well, there is one other option."

"What's that, for heaven's sake?"

"I could spend the night in your room instead of this one but something tells me the mood has been shattered."

She blushed. He was right. Now that the dazzling energy of passion had faded to more manageable levels, she had come back to her senses. She needed to think about what was going on here. Wild flings with men she had known for only a couple of days were not her style. She had never been into one-night stands. When you were the product of one, you thought twice — make that three or four times — before you took that kind of risk. In addition, she was definitely not accustomed to being out of control the way she had been a few minutes before.

Yes, she certainly needed time to contemplate events.

"Very perceptive of you," she said. She frowned at the duffel bag. "Do you always keep an overnight kit packed in your car?"

"I was a Boy Scout. I take that 'Be prepared' stuff seriously."

She was abruptly incensed. "You do this kind of thing a lot?"

"Are you kidding?" He managed to look highly offended. "I haven't stayed in a low-rent joint like this since I got out of college."

"That's not what I meant, and you know it."

"Get some sleep, Clare. I'll treat you to breakfast in the morning."

"One more question."

He waited.

She cleared her throat and lowered her voice. "So, is it true that hunters can see like cats and owls in the dark or is that just part of the legend?"

His smile was slow and wicked. "Stick around, lady. Maybe one of these days I'll tell you the truth."

He went inside his room and closed the door.

She shut her own door, snapped the lock

into place and sagged back against the wooden panels. She spent a few minutes trying to figure out why Jake was so determined to keep an eye on her tonight. Surely he wasn't that worried about her choice of lodging. The Desert Dawn wasn't exactly a five-star resort but it was not a seedy flophouse, either, in spite of what appeared to be the general consensus of opinion.

He had picked up on her uneasiness, she thought. The hunter in him had no doubt detected her underlying fear. He hadn't pushed her for an explanation she was not ready to give. Instead he had decided to remain close in case she needed protection.

No man had ever done anything that romantic for her in her entire life. No man had ever tried to make her feel safe.

She went back to bed and lay there quietly for a time, listening to the faint sounds of movement that emanated through the thin wall that separated her room from Jake's.

She had a lot of questions about Jake Salter and very few answers. But one thing was certain. She would sleep a lot more soundly tonight than she had last night knowing he was right next door.

CHAPTER FOURTEEN

"You're joking." Elizabeth removed the chilled herbal eye mask and turned her head to look at Clare. "Jake Salter cooked dinner for you?"

"Uh-huh." Clare had already removed her eye mask. The weight of the thing together with the enforced darkness had made her feel claustrophobic. "What's more, I gotta tell you, the man can cook. Says it relaxes him."

"Who knew?" Elizabeth shook her head in amazement and replaced the eye mask. "Jake's an original, that's for sure."

"He certainly is different from any man I've ever met," Clare conceded. "And not just because he can cook. I dated a chef once. It wasn't the same thing at all."

She and Elizabeth were ensconced side by side on twin recliners in the spa's serene Contemplation Room. The space served as a waiting area for clients between treatments.

The other four recliners were vacant at the moment, the occupants having been led away by quiet, low-voiced attendants.

The ceiling was a rotunda lit with recessed lights and painted with a nighttime sky. Tiny "stars" twinkled overhead. New Agey music emanated from hidden speakers. The scent of herbal tea wafted through the air.

They had been given plush robes and flip-flops to wear while they went through the various spa therapy sessions. Thus far they had each experienced the steam room and the whole body massage. Next on the agenda for Clare was a trip to the Tropical Experience Chamber. She was looking forward to that, she thought. When you were in the desert anything that involved water sounded good.

"So what happened after dinner?" Elizabeth asked.

"He took me back to my motel."

"Does he think it's a dump, like I do?"

"I don't recall that he used the word 'dump,' but he did not approve," Clare said. "There was also, I regret to say, a slight misunderstanding with some of the other guests."

Elizabeth yanked the mask off again. "What sort of misunderstanding?"

"When Jake walked me to my room my

172

neighbors next door concluded that I was a call girl entertaining a client."

Elizabeth's eyes widened. Then she started to giggle. "I don't believe it. You? A call girl? You haven't had a real date in six months."

"Tell me about it."

"Until last night, that is," Elizabeth finished on a thoughtful note. "So? What's the bottom line here? Did Jake make a pass?"

"As a matter of fact —"

"Oh, my God. He *did* make a pass. Wow. That's even more amazing than your neighbors thinking you're a call girl."

"Why?"

"I told you, he seems so ordinary. Boring, even. A nice guy, I'm sure, but sort of monkish or something."

"I don't think he'd make a good monk," Clare said judiciously.

Elizabeth chuckled. "Obviously you have swept Mr. Salter off his feet."

"Something tells me Jake doesn't get swept anywhere he doesn't want to go."

"Okay, I can't stand it any longer," Elizabeth said. "I have to know. Did you and Jake spend the night together?"

"No. I slept alone."

"Your idea or his?"

"The manager's, actually. As I told you, there were complaints from the neighbors.

173

Jake was asked to leave my room."

Elizabeth slapped a palm over her mouth to stifle her laughter. "I don't believe it. You? And Jake? Ohmygod."

"Believe it."

"Amazing." Elizabeth's smile faded. "By the way, on a less amusing subject, I talked to Mom last night. Seems Dad told her about his plans to establish a foundation and put you in charge of it right after he talked to you."

"How did she take the news?"

"Not well, I'm afraid."

"She's probably afraid a large endowment will impact the size of the inheritance you and Matt receive. She's right."

"I don't think that's the only thing that's bothering her," Elizabeth replied.

Clare sighed. "She's also worried that I'll take the job Archer is offering me and that it will have the effect of bringing me more frequently into the family circle. She's probably suffering horrifying visions of me showing up at Thanksgiving and Christmas."

"Unfortunately she can't separate your existence from what happened in the past."

"What woman could?" Clare asked simply.

"It's not right. If she wants to hold on to her resentment against Dad for what happened over three decades ago, that's her

174

business. But she shouldn't blame you. It wasn't your fault Dad and your mother had an affair."

"It didn't even qualify as an affair," Clare said. "It was, as I understand it, a one-night stand after which both parties involved realized that it was a terrible mistake."

"I feel sorry for you, Clare. You know I do. I can't even imagine what it must have been like for you all those years, never knowing your father and your sister and brother. But, frankly, I'm damned grateful that you exist. Sometimes when I wake up in the middle of the night after a nightmare about Brad I start to think about what would have happened if you hadn't been out there and if you hadn't contacted me when you did."

Clare reached across the space that separated them and touched her arm. "But I was there and we did meet."

"Thank heavens," Elizabeth whispered. "If I could just get Mom to listen. But she keeps saying that it's best if we all forget about what happened and move on with our lives. I've never seen her so adamant. It's like she's in total denial."

"Let it go, Liz. If it's meant to be, it will be."

"I suppose your saving my life gets filed

under the no-good-deed-goes-unpunished rule."

Clare smiled. "I didn't save your life. You made the decision to trust me. In doing so, you saved your own life and very likely Archer's and Matt's as well, if our theory about Brad's motives is right."

"Our theory is correct," Elizabeth said. "I know it is, although we'll never be able to prove it now."

"Like I said, time to let it go."

Elizabeth was quiet for a moment.

"What are you doing for dinner tonight?" she asked.

Clare thought about the conversation at breakfast.

"I invited Jake out to dinner," she said. "He accepted."

"You invited him? This is getting exciting."

"Well, actually, he asked me out again but I declined."

"For heaven's sake, why?"

"Something tells me that with a man like him, it's probably a good idea to keep the score even. I don't want him to feel that he's running things in this relationship. Assuming you can call one date a relationship."

"No offense to your feminine instincts, Clare, but I honestly don't think letting him feed you dinner twice in a row would make him conclude that he's got the upper hand."

"I think it's sort of a game we're playing," Clare said. "Hard to explain."

"Sounds interesting. Where are you going to take him?"

"I haven't decided but after splurging on that dress and pair of shoes yesterday, I can guarantce you that it won't be one of the high-end resort restaurants. Got any suggestions?"

"Well, there's a little Mexican place that Dad raves about. They make their own tortillas, and according to Dad, who knows these things, they serve the best green corn tamales in the Valley. He and Owen go there a lot after a round of golf. It's right here in Stone Canyon."

"Sounds like just what I'm looking for."

"I'll give you the address. They don't take reservations so you may have a wait in the evenings."

Hushed footsteps sounded on the tile floor behind the recliners. Two spa attendants garbed in the establishment's pale green and brown uniforms and soft-soled athletic shoes appeared.

"Ms. Glazebrook, it's time for your facial," one of them said.

Elizabeth rose from the recliner. "See you in an hour, Clare. Enjoy the Tropical Experience Chamber."

The second attendant smiled at Clare. "If you'll follow me, Ms. Lancaster?"

Clare accompanied the woman down a tranquilly lit hall. "What's this Tropical Experience thing, exactly?" she asked. "The brochure said something about waterfalls."

"It's one of our most popular therapies," the attendant assured her. "I think you'll enjoy it."

She opened a door and ushered Clare into a small slice of a lush, tropical paradise. Palms, ferns and exotic blooming plants framed a large spa tub disguised as a rocky grotto. A waterfall shower cascaded into the tub creating a low, rushing, churning sound. The ceiling was decorated with a mock canopy of dark green leaves. The low, ambient lighting gave the room the aura of a jungle at dawn.

"I like it already," Clare announced. She untied the sash of her robe. "This is going to be fun."

"Take your time and relax," the attendant said. "This is a forty-minute experience. I'll come and get you when it's finished."

She let herself out into the hall and closed the door.

Clare hung the robe on a convenient hook and went up the spa steps. She stepped gingerly into the fake grotto pool. The jetted water was warm and fragrant.

She lowered herself onto an underwater seat, stretched her arms out on either side and prepared to savor the Good Life.

It occurred to her that the imitation grotto was large enough to hold two people. She allowed herself to slip into a pleasant fantasy that involved sharing the delightful tropical setting with someone interesting, Jake Salter for instance.

Probably not a good idea to be fantasizing about Jake, she thought. But fantasies were notoriously hard to control. That's why they called them fantasies, she reminded herself. No problem. As long as she kept Jake in the fantasy realm she was safe. Right?

Something told her that nothing connected to Jake Salter was safe; not for her, at any rate. Last night she had played with fire. Tonight she was planning to do it again. After a lifetime of caution around men the uncharacteristic streak of recklessness made her smile.

The water splashed and bubbled around her. She rested her head against a towel-covered pillow attached to the back of the spa tub and watched the waterfall. The cascading water was soothing, almost hypnotic.

She had no idea how much time had

passed when she heard the door open behind her.

"Is my forty minutes up already?" she asked.

There was no reply. Clare heard the sole of a hard leather shoe slap against the tile floor.

A leather shoe.

That was wrong. Everyone around here wore slippers or athletic shoes.

The same panicky awareness that had hit her the day before in the parking garage flashed through her again. It was as if someone had traced the length of her spine with a sliver of ice from an ancient glacier. Intense cold chilled her to the bone.

Acting on her fight-or-flight impulse, she shoved herself away from the side of the tub into the middle of the grotto pool. She whipped around in the water, turning to face the door.

She had a split second to register the bizarre sight of a figure garbed in a spa robe and towel turban standing at the far end of the tub. The intruder's features were obscured by a green-tinged mudlike facial mask.

The robed figure had a heavy-looking object clutched in both hands and was propelling it downward with ferocious energy.

A dumbbell, Clare realized an instant before it crashed against the pillow precisely where her head had been resting a second before.

Shocked, she instinctively threw herself farther back out of range.

The movement took her under the waterfall. A heavy rush of water pounded down on her, obscuring her vision.

She reeled away from under the cascading water, groping blindly for the steps and something, anything, she could use as a weapon. Her hand closed over a towel. *Useless.*

She opened her mouth to scream.

The intruder whirled and ran from the room, pausing just long enough to slam the door shut.

Clare scrambled up the spa tub steps, grabbed the robe off the hook and raced toward the door.

The hall outside the spa room was empty.

CHAPTER FIFTEEN

The assistant manager's name was Karen Trent. She was a very buff, very toned, very attractive blonde in her early thirties. She was also very concerned and very unhappy.

"Are you absolutely certain about what happened, Miss Lancaster?" she asked for the third time.

Clare, dressed once more in the black pants and brown T-shirt she had worn to the spa, faced her from the other side of the desk. Elizabeth, also dressed in her street clothes, and tight-lipped with anger, sat beside her.

"You saw that eight-pound dumbbell in the pool for yourself," Clare said. "How do you think it got there?"

"I'm not saying that someone didn't accidentally drop it into the spa tub," Karen said soothingly. "But I'm sure that it wasn't intentional."

Clare's senses stirred. Karen was lying but

that was hardly a surprise under the circumstances. The assistant manager obviously suspected that something unpleasant had happened in the Tropical Experience Chamber, but she was going to remain in denial if at all possible. A lot of folks in her position would have done the same. No one wanted this kind of trouble, especially in an upscale spa. Bad for business.

"You weren't there," Clare said. "I was. I know what I saw."

"I'm not disputing the events, only your interpretation of them," Karen said quickly. "I think it is much more plausible that one of the clients opened the door of the Tropical Experience room by mistake, got disconcerted when she realized that the grotto was already occupied and dropped the dumbbell."

The energy of the lie was tinged with desperation. Clare wondered if Karen was worried that her job might be at stake.

"The intruder tried to crush my skull with that dumbbell," Clare said evenly. "Trust me, it was no accident."

Elizabeth glowered at Karen. "Why do you think someone in the middle of a mudpack facial would go down the hall to the gym and borrow an eight-pound dumbbell in the first place?"

"Our clients are allowed free use of all the facilities, including the fitness center," Karen said. "You know that, Ms. Glazebrook. Sometimes people get bored waiting for a mudpack therapy to conclude. They wander into the Contemplation Room or the Tranquillity Room or the fitness center."

"You're not going to call the police, are you?" Clare said.

"I really don't see any reason to do so." Karen widened her hands. "Of course, you and Ms. Glazebrook are free to do as you wish. If you do choose to file a report, however, please be aware that you have no evidence to back up your version of events except the dumbbell. As I just said, its presence in the pool can be explained in other ways."

This was a waste of time, Clare decided. Now that she'd had some time to calm down she was starting to think more clearly again. It dawned on her that most of Stone Canyon still wondered if she had killed Brad McAllister six months ago. Karen Trent was probably lying because she was afraid she had a murderer sitting in her office.

There was another factor working against them, too, Clare thought. She exchanged a glance with Elizabeth and saw grim comprehension in her sister's eyes. They both knew that the rumors of Elizabeth's nervous breakdown had never gone away entirely.

Neither of them would be viewed as a star witness. The Glazebrook name would ensure that they were treated politely by the cops, but that was as far as the investigation would go.

Clare got to her feet. "Let's go," she said to Elizabeth.

Elizabeth rose, stiff with anger, and followed her.

In the spa lobby they put on their sunglasses and walked out into the intense early afternoon sun. Heat radiated in waves from the parking lot pavement, creating a visible shimmering effect. Brilliant light sparked off the fenders of the parked vehicles.

The interior of the Mercedes was an oven in spite of the silver sun screen that Elizabeth had placed behind the windshield to deflect the heat.

Elizabeth folded the reflective screen and dropped it behind the front seat. She slipped behind the wheel, switched on the engine and cranked up the air-conditioning. Clare got in beside her. The buckle of the seat belt was too hot to touch.

"You know who it was, don't you?" Elizabeth asked.

"I think so, yes," Clare said quietly. "So do you."

"That's why you didn't push Karen Trent into calling the police."

"That and also because she had a point. I have zilch in the way of proof." Clare gingerly fastened her seat belt. "Let's face it, we both know that I don't need any more trouble with the local authorities."

"What are we going to do?" Elizabeth turned urgently in the seat. "She just tried to *murder* you. We can't ignore that."

"It would probably be smart if I left town as soon as possible," Clare said. "It was my presence here that set her off."

"Valerie Shipley is just like her son." Elizabeth's voice was dull with dread. "She's crazy."

"I agree. But we couldn't prove that Brad was a wack job and I don't think we'll be able to prove that his mother is, either."

CHAPTER SIXTEEN

A light gold Jaguar was parked in the drive of the Shipley home. Clare halted the rented compact behind it and turned off the engine.

She looked at the double front doors at the entrance to the large, sprawling house. Raw determination warred with a morose sense of futility. What she planned to do probably wasn't going to work but it was the only option left. She could not think of any other way to get Valerie off her back.

She got out of the car and slung her purse over her shoulder. She gripped the strap so tightly she had a hunch she was leaving nail marks in the leather.

She hadn't told Elizabeth of her scheme because she knew that, at the very least, her sister would have insisted on accompanying her. But if the strategy failed Valerie might decide to turn her rage on Elizabeth. That would only make the situation worse. After all, Elizabeth had to live in this town.

She stopped on the tiled entranceway, stomach clenched as though anticipating a blow, and rang the doorbell.

No footsteps sounded in the entry hall on the other side of the door.

She leaned on the bell a second time.

Still no answer.

She stepped back, not knowing whether to be relieved or disappointed. Unfortunately, postponing the confrontation with Valerie Shipley was not going to improve matters. It only delayed the inevitable.

She left the entranceway, walked to where the gold Jaguar was parked and looked through the windows. She had no idea what she expected to see.

A crumpled white terrycloth turban lay on the floor on the passenger side. It looked as if someone had discarded it hurriedly, perhaps while fleeing the scene of an attempted murder.

Clare's stomach fluttered unpleasantly. It shouldn't come as a surprise, she thought. She had known, deep down, that the intruder in the Tropical Experience Chamber was Valerie. Nevertheless, the little piece of confirming evidence was disturbing.

Morbid curiosity compelled her to walk across the driveway to the three-car garage.

One of the garage doors was open, revealing an empty space that was no doubt meant for the Jaguar.

She stepped into the shadowy gloom, took off her sunglasses and surveyed the interior.

The second space inside the garage was also empty. But parked in the third space at the far end was a large, silver-gray SUV. It was identical to the one that had nearly run her down in the mall garage.

A shivery sensation swept through her. She had to remind herself to breathe.

She left the garage, wondering what to do next. Two of the Shipleys' three vehicles were here. Owen was probably gone, but the odds were that Valerie was inside the house, not answering the door.

What would an alcoholic most likely do after a failed attempt at murder?

Go home and have a stiff drink or two or six, Clare decided. Actually, it seemed like a reasonable thing for anyone to do under such circumstances.

She stopped and looked toward the far end of the breezeway that separated the house from the garage. She could see a wrought-iron gate set in the high stone wall that enclosed the pool terrace and garden behind the house.

Just beyond the terrace and gardens she could see the emerald green expanse of one of the fairways of the Stone Canyon Golf Course. There was only one cart in sight. It was some distance away on another fairway. Arizona golfers were a hardy lot but the relentless afternoon sun had proved too much for most of them today.

The wrought-iron gate was no doubt intended for the use of the gardeners and pool service people, Clare thought. It was very likely alarmed.

But maybe not at this time of day, especially if someone is home.

She contemplated her options. Forcing her way into the house was not only a good way to get arrested, it could also get her shot, especially here in Arizona, where owning a gun was a common lifestyle choice.

She walked to the gate, stopped and looked through the decorative curlicues and spikes. From where she stood she could see the gracefully curved pool.

There was someone in the bright, flashing water.

Valerie Shipley was not swimming. In fact, she was not moving at all. She was not wearing a bathing suit, either. She was fully clothed, in a pair of white pants and a sleeveless top.

She was floating facedown.

The gate was unlocked. Clare opened it

reluctantly. She did not want to check the body. She would rather have done anything else. But you were supposed to make certain in situations like this and there was no one else around to do what had to be done.

She dropped her purse and phone beside the pool and waded into the water. She knew as soon as she touched the body that Valerie was dead but she nevertheless checked carefully for a pulse. There was none.

That was enough, she told herself. She did not owe this woman anything more.

She climbed back up the pool steps. Dripping wet, she opened the door of the small cabana. There was a stack of clean towels on a rack. She helped herself to one. When her hands were dry, she left the cabana and made the 911 call.

"There's an aid car on the way," the operator assured her. There was a distinct pause. "Did you say your name is Clare Lancaster, ma'am?"

"Yes."

Clare Lancaster, Stone Canyon's all-purpose suspect.

She ended the call, finished drying herself off as well as she could and then went inside the house to unlock the door for the medics.

There was a cell phone on the white stone

coffee table next to a half-empty pitcher of martinis.

It would be a few minutes before the aid car arrived, Clare thought. She grabbed a couple paper napkins off the liquor cabinet and used them to pick up the phone.

It probably wasn't legal to take a quick look at the victim's phone log but she promised herself she would be very careful not to taint any evidence.

After a moment she realized she needed a pen and paper to jot down the numbers. She went back outside to get the items from her purse.

She was disappointed to discover that there were no calls, either incoming or outgoing, logged for that day. So much for being a psychic detective, she thought.

She could hear sirens in the distance. She still had a couple minutes. Unable to think of anything else to do, she jotted down numbers that Valerie had stored in the cell's phone book.

CHAPTER SEVENTEEN

"Don't leave the motel," Jake ordered, speaking into his cell phone. "It will take me about half an hour to get there. Stay right where you are."

"I'm sorry," Clare said, sounding unutterably weary. "But I'm going to have to cancel our arrangement for this evening. I don't think I'd make very good company for dinner."

Jake was on his feet, heading toward the door of his office.

"Forget it," he said. "A dinner date strikes me as the least of your concerns at the moment."

There was a short pause on the other end.

"Things aren't that bad," Clare said, rallying somewhat. "They didn't arrest me or anything. Actually, there are two schools of thought at the moment. One holds that Valerie got drunk, fell into the pool and drowned. The other theory is that she committed suicide. They're going to do an autopsy to test for drugs."

"I'm on my way."

"It's okay, Jake, really. Elizabeth is here with me."

"In that case, both of you stay put."

He ended the call and paused in front of the administrative assistant's desk.

Brenda Wilson regarded him with her customary severely serene expression. She was sixty years old, athletic-looking and unmarried. As far as Jake had been able to determine, she was dedicated to her job. Early on in their relationship she had informed him quite proudly that she had worked for the company for over thirty years. She had started out as Owen Shipley's secretary.

"Something has come up, " Jake told her. "I'll be out of the office for the rest of the afternoon. Hold all my calls."

"Yes, Mr. Salter," Brenda said crisply. "I assume this has something to do with the death of Mrs. Shipley?"

"You never fail to amaze me, Brenda. I just got the news five minutes ago. When did you hear it?"

"Four minutes ago, while you were on the phone. Mr. Glazebrook's assistant called to tell me the tragic news."

"Is Glazebrook still in his office?"

"No, he left shortly before noon. Said he wanted to go home and work on some special project."

"See you on Monday, Brenda."

"Have a good weekend, sir."

"Something tells me it's going to be a very long and complicated weekend."

"Things are always complicated when Clare Lancaster is involved," Brenda said.

The prim, suppressed anger in Brenda's tone stopped him cold. He turned back to face her.

"Is there anything you think I should know, Brenda?" he asked quietly.

She picked up a stack of printouts and tapped the papers briskly against the desktop to square them. "Rumor has it that it was Clare Lancaster who found Mrs. Shipley's body in the pool."

"I heard that." He waited.

Brenda cleared her throat. "By a strange coincidence it was Miss Lancaster who found the body of Mrs. Shipley's son, Brad, six months ago."

"Heard that, too. I get the impression that you don't believe in coincidence, Brenda."

"No, sir, I don't." She put the tightly squared stack of papers down and folded her competent hands on top of the pile. "Neither does anyone else around here. Not when the coincidence involves Clare Lancaster."

He went deliberately back across the room and stopped in front of her desk.

"I won't tell you what to think, Brenda," he said. "But I want to make it very, very clear that it would be a good idea if you kept your opinions of Miss Lancaster and the subject of coincidence to yourself."

Brenda went rigid. "Yes, sir."

He left, heading for the parking lot. He wondered what Brenda would have had to say if she knew that her tidy little condo was one of the many residences he had searched during his short stay in Stone Canyon. Unfortunately, he hadn't turned up evidence of anything other than a life devoted to work and office gossip.

Jake's phone rang just as he got out of the BMW and started toward the lobby of the Desert Dawn Motel. He recognized the number.

"Hello, Archer," he said.

"Where the hell are you? I just talked to Brenda. She said you left for the day and that it had something to do with Clare."

"As usual, Brenda is on top of the situation." Jake paused at the door. He did not want to have this conversation in front of the desk clerk. "I'm at Clare's motel."

"You're already at the airport?" Archer sounded startled. "You made damn good time, especially in Friday rush hour traffic."

"Got lucky," Jake said. "Traffic wasn't as bad as usual."

"You heard what happened?" Archer demanded.

"Yes. Where are you?"

"I'm on my way to the Shipley house. This is not a good situation, Jake. Not after what happened six months ago. I've already had calls from the local reporters."

"Don't give them anything," Jake said.

"You think I'm stupid? Of course I'm not taking the damned calls. What's worrying me is that I haven't been able to get in touch with Clare. She's not answering her cell phone."

"I'll let her know you want to talk to her," Jake said.

"What's the name of her motel? I'll try her there."

"You're breaking up, Archer. I can't hear you. I'll get back to you later."

"Hold on, damn it —"

Jake ended the call and walked into the lobby. The desk clerk looked up.

"Another night, huh?" he asked.

"No," Jake said. "Miss Lancaster won't be staying tonight, either. Get her bill ready.

She'll be checking out shortly."

"Yes, sir."

Jake loped up the stairs to the second floor. Elizabeth opened the door to 210.

"Jake." Relief lit her eyes. "Thank goodness you're here. Talk about a bad day at Black Rock."

The sliding glass door at the far end of the room was open, letting in the last of the late afternoon heat. The window-box air conditioner hummed mightily but it was a losing battle. The room was close and stifling.

He could see Clare out on the tiny balcony, gripping the railing with both hands. She appeared to be riveted by whatever was going on in the pool area below.

"How is she?" he asked quietly.

"Exhausted," Elizabeth said softly.

Clare straightened abruptly and turned her head to glare at Elizabeth and Jake through the dark shield of her sunglasses.

"For Pete's sake," she said briskly. "There's no need to act like this is an intensive care unit. You don't have to discuss my condition in hushed tones. I'm fine."

"Tough as nails, isn't she?" he observed to Elizabeth.

"They breed them hardy up there in San Francisco."

Clare made a rude noise.

198

"Don't let the attitude fool you." Elizabeth closed the door. "She puts on a great act but the truth is, she's been through a lot today."

"Finding a dead body can have that effect on a person," he agreed.

Elizabeth gave him a long, considering look. He got the feeling that she had come to some momentous decision.

"Especially when the dead body in question is that of the woman who tried to brain you with an eight-pound dumbbell a couple of hours earlier," Elizabeth said.

"I think," Jake said, "that the three of us need to talk."

CHAPTER EIGHTEEN

"I won't lie to you, Archer. I can't. We've been friends for too long." Owen leaned forward in the white leather chair and rested his elbows on his spread knees. He gazed through the wall of windows, contemplating the sparks of sunlight on the swimming pool. "It's a terrible thing to say but part of me felt a sense of relief when they told me what had happened. My first thought was, at least there won't be any more scenes."

"She was in a bad way." Archer carried the glass of whiskey he had just poured across the white carpet and put it into Owen's hand.

Owen looked down at the drink as if surprised to see it there. "She was my wife. I failed her. I should have got her into rehab."

"Don't beat yourself up over this." Archer sat down across from him. "You did your best. Myra said Valerie refused to even consider rehab."

Owen swallowed some of the whiskey and cradled the glass in both hands. "She got so upset whenever I tried to talk about it. I suggested she see a therapist, someone from the Society who would understand the sensitive side of her nature and help her process her grief."

Archer wasn't sure what to say so he sat quietly, just trying to be there for the man who had been his partner and friend for so many years.

Owen drank his whiskey. After a while he put down the glass.

"It was suicide," he said. "Not an accident."

Archer looked at him. "You're sure?"

"Yes. She talked about it the night she pushed Clare into the pool. She said she could not stand the sight of her son's killer. Said knowing that Clare was right here in Stone Canyon, acting as if nothing had happened, was too much to bear."

"Clare did not murder Brad."

Owen sighed. "You and I know that, Archer. But Valerie was obsessed, and I think starting to become delusional. To tell you the truth, I was about to warn you that Clare might be in danger from her."

Archer frowned. "You think she was becoming dangerous?"

"I believe so. Yes."

A tiny chime sounded. They both looked at Owen's high-tech watch.

Owen got to his feet. "It's time for my shot. I'll be right back."

He walked across the great room and went down the hall toward the kitchen.

Archer rose and went to stand at the wall of windows overlooking the pool. The strategist side of his nature quickly calculated the odds against Clare walking in on not one but two dead bodies within six months.

He didn't like the math. But the thing about accidental drowning deaths was that it was very hard to prove murder. The water washed away most of the evidence.

CHAPTER NINETEEN

They went downstairs to the Desert Dawn's minuscule pool and commandeered the single rickety plastic table and three of the four moldy plastic chairs. It was five-thirty. The late afternoon sun was setting on the far side of the hotel, leaving the pool in the shade. It wasn't what anyone would call cool yet but there was a light breeze and it seemed more comfortable to Jake than the close confines of the cheap motel room.

He shoved some money into the vending machine next to the stairwell and extracted three bottles of chilled water. He carried the plastic bottles back to the table and put them down.

Clare unscrewed the cap on one of the bottles and swallowed some water. She hadn't said a word since they had left her room.

"All right, let's have it," he said to both women. "I want the whole story."

Clare sat back in her chair and raised her

brows at Elizabeth. "You started this. You tell him."

Elizabeth put both hands on the table, making a triangle with her fingers around the base of her bottle of water. She faced Jake, earnest and determined.

"We all know that Valerie had a drinking problem," she said. "And there were rumors that she had found a doctor who was pretty loose with the prescription meds."

Jake nodded and drank some water. He had discovered long ago that people tended to chat more freely if you left them plenty of conversational space to fill. And in this instance Elizabeth seemed to want to talk.

Unlike Clare, he thought, studying her stony expression out of the corner of his eye. He got the feeling that if he'd had to depend on her to tell him the story, he would have had to pry the information out of her bit by bit.

"At Mom and Dad's party the other night you saw for yourself that Valerie was obsessed with the idea that Clare murdered Brad," Elizabeth continued.

"Yes," Jake said.

Elizabeth took a deep breath. "I know you're going to find this hard to believe, but this afternoon at the spa, Valerie tried to kill Clare."

It was as if he had just walked off the rim of a canyon in the middle of the night. There was nothing but a whole lot of darkness under his feet.

Slowly he lowered the plastic bottle and looked at Clare. She was gazing out at the pool, stoic, impassive. Waiting for him to tell her that she was nuts, he thought. Waiting for him to inform her that no one tried to kill her that afternoon, that things like that didn't happen in high-end spas.

"Explain," he said quietly.

Clare rested one arm on the table and drummed her fingers. "She tried to brain me."

He waited.

"Clare was in one of the treatment rooms," Elizabeth said quickly. "Alone. Sitting in a pool. Someone dressed in a white robe and a turban with a mudpack plastered over her face entered the room, rushed up behind Clare and tried to hit her with the dumbbell."

"Shit," Jake said. He was still falling through darkness. He tried to think. "You're sure it was Valerie Shipley?"

Clare shrugged. "As sure as I can be under the circumstances. I couldn't see her features because of the goop on her face but she was about Valerie's size. Thin. Frail-looking."

"Don't forget the turban," Elizabeth said quickly.

"What turban?" Jake asked.

"The person who tried to clobber me with the dumbbell wore a towel turban around her head," Clare said. "When I went out to the Shipley house this afternoon I found a turban just like it in the front seat of Valerie's Jaguar. She must have tossed it there when she was driving away from the spa."

"Take me through it, step by step," Jake said.

She looked at him. He saw barely veiled surprise and uncertainty in her eyes. She hadn't expected him to believe her, he thought.

"It was just like Elizabeth said." She tightened her grip on the bottle of water. "I was alone in the grotto tub. I heard the door open behind me. I thought the attendant had come to tell me my time was up. But I heard the person's shoe on the tiles."

"Her shoe?" Jake repeated.

"It was a street shoe. You know, one with leather soles. Everyone in the spa wore soft-soled shoes or slippers. But this person was wearing regular shoes. My first thought was that someone had walked in on me by mistake and there I was, stark naked in the hot tub. And then I got a panicky feeling, like

206

something terrible was about to happen."

"Your intuition kicked in," Elizabeth said wisely.

"That and the fact that the street shoe just sounded so wrong," Clare agreed.

"Go on," Jake said.

"I leaped for the middle of the pool. Valerie was already swinging the dumbbell. She had it clutched in both hands. It crashed into the pillow and fell into the pool."

"Clare came that close to having her skull crushed," Elizabeth said tightly. "She would have been dead or horribly injured by now if she hadn't moved when she did."

"What did you do next?" Jake asked Clare, careful to keep his voice neutral.

"Leaped out of the tub, of course," Clare said. "But Valerie was already off and running before I could grab my robe. By the time I got to the door, she had disappeared."

"You reported this, I assume," Jake said.

Clare and Elizabeth exchanged glances.

"We did tell the assistant manager," Clare said carefully.

"He called the cops?" Jake pressed.

"She," Elizabeth corrected. "Her name is Karen Trent. And no, she did not call the police. She didn't believe us when we told her what had happened. Claimed we misinterpreted events."

"The dumbbell," Jake said, thinking.

"Was still in the spa pool." Clare nodded. "But Ms. Trent seemed to think that it had been accidentally dropped by whoever mistakenly opened the door of the treatment room."

"Did you two call the police?" Jake asked.

Clare said nothing.

Elizabeth pressed her lips together.

Jake exhaled slowly. "You didn't call the cops."

"I have some issues with the Stone Canyon Police Department," Clare said.

"Because of what happened to Brad," Elizabeth explained hurriedly. "And no one would have taken *me* seriously without some hard evidence because everyone believes I had a nervous breakdown a while back."

Clare lowered her bottle and looked at Elizabeth. "There's also the little fact that you didn't actually see anything. You were in another therapy room at the time. It would have been my word against Valerie's."

"True," Elizabeth said. She turned back to Jake. "The Stone Canyon cops would have gone through the motions because of Dad but they wouldn't have turned up anything. The bottom line is that what evidence there was got washed off the dumbbell when it went into the water."

Maybe not all the evidence, Jake thought. He slouched back in his chair, stretched out his feet and drank some water.

"The SUV that tried to run you down in the mall yesterday," he said after a while. "Think that was Valerie?"

"There was an SUV parked in the Shipleys' garage this afternoon that looked identical," Clare said.

"Let me clarify," Jake said softly. "You went out to the Shipley house this afternoon all by yourself to confront this obsessed, crazy woman."

Clare blinked and then flushed a dull, angry pink. She did not take criticism well, he noted.

"I thought I might be able to talk to her," she said coldly. "Get her to see reason."

"Clare didn't tell me what she was planning to do," Elizabeth put in quickly, "or I would have gone with her."

Clare slumped deeper into her chair. "Okay, in hindsight going to see Valerie alone was probably not the smartest thing I've ever done."

He let that go. Snarling at her now probably wasn't going to accomplish much. Besides, the main reason he wanted to read her the riot act was because he couldn't think of any other way to work off some of the tension chewing up his insides. Nothing he said was going to change what had happened that afternoon, he reminded himself. It was time to focus on a plan of action.

"Where, exactly, do you stand with the Stone Canyon police on this thing?" he asked.

"I'm not an official suspect, if that's what you mean," she said. "But I was asked not to leave the Phoenix area for a while."

"Just until the medical examiner makes an official determination of accidental drowning or suicide," Elizabeth explained. "That shouldn't take long. After all, Valerie Shipley's death is a very high-profile case for the Stone Canyon police. I'm sure the authorities will rush the autopsy."

"Meanwhile, it looks like I'm going to have to do a little hand laundry in my bathroom sink tonight," Clare said wearily. "I'm out of clean clothes."

Elizabeth frowned. "I can take some of your things back to the house and have the housekeeper do them for you."

"That's okay. Thanks, anyway. I'm sure the management of the Desert Dawn Motel won't mind me hanging a few hand-washables out to dry on the balcony."

Jake glanced up at her room. "The sight of your lingerie hanging from the railing would probably add a certain colorful charm to this establishment. But I think there is a better solution."

"I know. Go shopping again." She made a face. "It may come to that if the Stone Canyon police won't let me leave town soon. But I'd like to avoid running up any additional expenses, if possible. This trip has already cost me a lot more than I intended to spend."

"Send the bills to Dad," Elizabeth said. "He's the one who asked you to come down here."

"I know, but I have this policy," Clare said softly.

" 'Never take money from Archer Glazebrook,' " Elizabeth quoted, irritated. "Yes, I am well aware of your dumb policy. But if you won't let Dad help you out, you'll have to take the money from me."

Clare sighed. "I'll keep the offer in mind. With luck it won't come to that. I'm still hoping to be on my way back to San Francisco in a couple of days."

Jake set his water bottle aside, sat forward and folded his arms on the table. "One thing's for sure, you're not spending the next few nights here at the Desert Dawn."

Clare gave him a quelling look.

Elizabeth brightened. "I agree with you,

Jake. This place is the pits."

"It's clean," Clare insisted.

"So is my place," Jake said.

Both women looked at him, lips parted in surprise.

"I've got plenty of room," he added. "And here's the clincher. I've got a washer and dryer."

Something that might have been relief lit Elizabeth's eyes. "It's not a bad idea, Clare."

Clare pulled herself together, straightening abruptly in her chair. "I really don't think —"

"It's settled," Jake said.

"This is ridiculous," Clare said heatedly.

"What's ridiculous is both of us camping out here at the Desert Dawn Motel when I've got a perfectly good house with a private pool and a decent kitchen," he said.

Clare bristled. "Nobody said you had to stay here, too."

"No, but that's what I'm going to do if you stay locked down in stubborn mode over this," he said mildly. "Let's try for some common sense here, shall we? You've had a hell of a day. You're exhausted. Elizabeth and I agree that you should not be alone tonight. I'm offering you a reasonable alternative to this third-rate motel."

Elizabeth rounded on Clare. "I think you

should accept his offer. It would certainly give me some peace of mind."

"Well," Clare said slowly. She subsided. "All right."

Jake relaxed. He'd won. She was too worn out to argue anymore.

That was enough for now. He'd get the answers he was after later, when he had Clare where he wanted her, on his territory.

"Go pack," he said. "I'll take you home to my place. Then I've got an errand to run."

Something about his tone must have alerted Clare. She frowned.

"What kind of errand?"

"I'm going to get in a short workout at the Stone Canyon spa before dinner."

CHAPTER TWENTY

The gym at the Stone Canyon spa was crowded with a trendy-looking after-work crowd. Every treadmill, stationary bicycle and rowing machine was occupied by someone wearing the latest in snappy workout attire.

Dressed in a pair of khaki shorts, faded T-shirt and running shoes, a towel draped around his neck, Jake wandered across the room to where an array of gleaming dumbbells was stacked.

He braced himself and selected the eight-pound weights.

When his hand closed around the one on the left, dark psychic energy splashed across his senses. Even though he had been prepared for it, the effect was a lot like getting hit with acid. It took every ounce of control he had not to let the dumbbell drop to the floor.

He tightened his grip on the weight and

opened his senses fully.

Fury, desperation, a terrible, ripping need to avenge, to kill. Hot satisfaction. So close.

Silent, shrieking anguish. Failure. Despair. Rage.

He took a deep, steadying breath and carefully replaced the dumbbells. The disturbing waves of energy ceased affecting his senses the instant he released the weight.

The ice-cold anger that took its place would last awhile.

CHAPTER TWENTY-ONE

Clare unzipped the small overnight suitcase and studied her extremely limited wardrobe. The rules of engagement between Jake and her had changed, she decided. The slinky dress she had worn the night before was out of the question this evening. She was a houseguest now, not a date.

The hard fact was that she had no clothing options. The pool-ruined black suit was out. She'd lost another pair of pants and a T-shirt when she waded into the pool to check Valerie's pulse. That left her with the pants and T-shirt she had on now.

Forget changing for dinner.

She crossed the bedroom to the sliding glass door. Through the floor-to-ceiling glass she could see the kitchen and the other wing of the house across the pool courtyard.

Jake had the kitchen sliders wide open. He was working at the center island. He must have sensed her watching him because he raised his hand in a casual wave.

Probably real hard to sneak up on a hunter.

This was to have been her night to do the entertaining, she thought. She had known from the outset that it would be a bad idea to let Jake get the upper hand. But here she was in his house, getting ready to drink his wine and eat the food that he prepared.

Jake was once again in charge.

She decided she was in no condition to analyze all the possible ramifications of that situation. It had been a very long day. She needed a shower and then she needed food and sleep.

Tomorrow morning she would worry about how to deal with Jake Salter.

When she walked into the kitchen a short time later, feeling slightly more human and even a bit more energetic, Jake handed her a large glass of wine and a small bowl of roasted almonds.

"Drink," he said. "Eat. You need the vitamins."

"You're right." She sat down at the table and reached for a fistful of nuts. "So? What did you learn at the spa?"

"Found the dumbbell Valerie used to try to brain you."

"Really?" Fascinated, she stared at him. "You could actually detect her psychic imprint on it?"

"I could sure as hell feel someone's energy." Jake stopped working long enough to munch some almonds. "Given what you told me and the turban in the car, it must have been Valerie's."

"What does that kind of energy feel like?"

He hesitated, looking thoughtful. "Raw. Elemental. Dark. It's like touching the heart of a tornado."

"Do you only pick up the kind of energy that is left in the wake of an act of violence? Or can you pick up other kinds of intense emotions as well?"

He looked at her. "The thing about being a hunter is that you only connect to the dark stuff."

"I see." She cleared her throat. "Sounds unpleasant."

"Probably no worse than getting hit with one of those ultraviolet lies you told me about. By the way, Archer called while you were in the shower. Second time I've heard from him in the past couple of hours. Says he's been trying to get ahold of you."

"I know. I saw the calls on my phone log."

"Going to respond?" Jake asked.

"Yes." Reluctantly she took her phone out

of her pocket and punched in Archer's private number. "He won't stop calling unless I do."

Archer answered on the first ring. "Where the hell are you?"

"With Jake."

"Doing what?"

"Jake is fixing dinner for me."

There was a short pause on the other end.

"Jake is cooking dinner? You're not at a restaurant?"

"Yes to the first question," Clare said. "No to the second. We're at his place."

Silence hummed again for a few seconds.

"Are you all right?" Archer asked after a while.

"Yes. Elizabeth baby-sat me for a while until Jake showed up."

"What's the name of your motel? No one seems to know. Even Brenda was confused."

"No point worrying about it now," she said lightly. "I checked out an hour ago. Jake offered me his spare bedroom. I accepted."

"What the frigging hell does he think he's doing? If you need a place to stay, you can damn well come over here."

She smiled in spite of her weary mood. "Bad idea, Archer. We both know that."

"Put Jake on the phone."

She held the phone out to Jake. "He wants

to talk to you."

Jake wiped his hands on a towel and took the device from her.

"Bad timing, Archer. I'm a little busy."

There was a short pause.

"Sure," Jake said. "The problem is, she doesn't want to go to your place. She's been pretty clear about that. You want to try to convince her?"

There was another listening moment.

"Yeah, I did notice the stubborn streak," Jake said. "Seems to run in the family. I'll talk to you tomorrow, Archer. Meanwhile you know where to find Clare. Don't worry, I'll take good care of her."

He ended the call and tossed the phone back to Clare.

It rang again before Clare could ask what Archer had said. She glanced at the number and sighed.

"Hi, Mom."

"Where are you, dear? Still in Stone Canyon?" Gwen Lancaster's voice was tinged with a hint of hopefulness. "Everything going well?"

"Still here," Clare said, tasting her wine. "Things have become complicated."

She gave her mother a quick summary of events, leaving out the close call in the parking garage and the dumbbell incident. When she used the words "dead body" and "police" in the same sentence, however, there was a horrified wail from the other end of the line.

"Not again."

Clare had to hold the phone several inches from her ear. Jake looked up from slicing a tomato. She knew he had heard Gwen's pained cry of dismay.

"Now, Mom, you don't have to make it sound like I trip over dead bodies all the time. There have only been two."

"Two in six months. Do you know what the odds are of that kind of thing happening if you're not a cop or in some sort of emergency work? And the two bodies we're discussing happen to be related to each other. Do you realize what that does to the probability factor?"

"Take it easy, Mom, you're going into full accounting mode here. You know I didn't get your talent for numbers."

"Do the police consider you a suspect?" Gwen asked sharply.

"No, I'm not a suspect." Clare kept her voice calm and soothing.

"Where is Archer in all this? Has he hired a lawyer for you?"

"I don't need a lawyer." Clare hesitated. "Not yet at any rate. Everyone seems to think Valerie Shipley's death will be ruled accidental. A bad mix of alcohol, tranquilizers and a convenient pool. Please don't worry. As soon as things are cleared up, I'll be on the first plane back to San Francisco."

"But what about the reason you went to Arizona in the first place? Did Archer tell you why he wanted to see you?"

There was no point putting off the inevitable, Clare thought.

"He says he intends to establish a private grant-making foundation. He wants to make me the director."

Gwen went very quiet on the other end of the line.

"I was right," she said eventually. "He wants to atone in some way for the past."

"I think he feels that he has a responsibility toward me," Clare said. "It's bothering him that I haven't been able to find a new job. He's trying to create one for me."

"Sounds like it." Gwen fell silent.

"Mom? Are you still there?"

"Yes," Gwen said. "I'm still here. But I'm very worried. I don't like this situation."

"Neither do I," Clare admitted. "But I think it will all go away in a couple of days after they do the autopsy and everyone concludes that Valerie Shipley's death was not murder."

"Are you still at the motel?"

"No, Mom, I'm not."

"You're with Elizabeth?" Gwen asked. "I thought she was staying with Archer and Myra until her condo closes. I know you don't like to go to the Glazebrook house if you can avoid it."

"I'm not there, either." Clare cleared her throat. "I'm staying with someone who is consulting for Archer. His name is Jake Salter."

"You're staying with a complete *stranger?*"

"He's not a stranger, Mom."

"But you've only known him a couple of days," Gwen said, sounding slightly stunned. "Is he married?"

"No," Clare said, watching Jake, "he's not married."

"You're there alone with him?"

"It's complicated, Mom."

"How did you meet him?"

"At the Glazebrook cocktail party. I guess you could say that Archer introduced us."

"No," Jake said, "I introduced myself."

"I heard that," Gwen said. "Is that him?"

"Yes," Clare said. "He's cooking dinner."

"Do you think it's wise to be staying at his house?"

"To be honest, at the moment I'm too tired to care."

223

"Clare —"

"It's been a very long day, Mom. I'm going to have a glass of wine, eat dinner and fall into bed."

Jake was dousing the vegetables with olive oil. She saw his mouth curve faintly in a very male smile. It dawned on her that the last part of her sentence left a lot to the imagination.

"Alone," she added hastily.

"Clare, I'm not sure about this," Gwen said.

"I love you, Mom, but I'm going to hang up now. I'm beat. Bye."

She ended the call and set the phone on the table.

"I'm thirty-two years old," she said. "I can't believe I'm still having conversations with my mother about where I will sleep. Do men have conversations like that with their mothers?"

"Can't speak for all of the other males on the planet." Jake crunched a chunk of blood-red bell pepper between his teeth. "But I sure as hell don't."

"Lucky you."

He sprinkled salt over the vegetables. "Doesn't mean there isn't some pressure, though."

She almost laughed. "I find it very hard to

believe that anyone, even your own mother, could apply serious pressure to you, Jake Salter."

"Never underestimate a mother when it comes to that kind of stuff."

"What pressure does your mother apply?"

"She'd like to see me get married again. She's after me to register at arcanematch.com."

"Are you going to do it?"

"I've been thinking about it," Jake said. "It's not like I've got anything to lose, right?"

Her heart sank. He might just as well have come straight out and told her that he didn't see any future for the two of them, she thought.

"Guess not," she said.

"Ever register yourself?" he asked.

"Tried it once." She drank some wine and lowered the glass.

"I'm getting a bad feeling here," Jake said. "I take it the matchmakers at Arcane House didn't come up with a match?"

She wrinkled her nose. "Let's just say that being told that you are unmatchable with any other member of the Society is hard to take, even for an optimistic, upbeat, positive thinker like myself."

"Are you still registered?"

"Good grief, no. It was too depressing

getting that stupid little 'Welcome to arcanematch.com, Clare Lancaster. Sorry, no match yet. Check back later' message."

"Think you'll give it another try some-day?"

"What's the point?" she asked.

"You might get lucky," he said.

"I doubt it. And I'm really not in the mood for any more rejection at the moment."

CHAPTER TWENTY-TWO

Clare came awake very suddenly from a dream in which Valerie Shipley was hunting her through an endless series of spa chambers. Each room contained a bottomless pool. In the dreamworld she knew she had to keep running, hoping to find a way out, but Valerie was closing the distance between them.

Valerie's gone. Let it go.

The image of Valerie's dead body floating in the turquoise blue pool refused to fade.

Think of something else.

She lay still for a moment, orienting herself to the unfamiliar bedroom, trying to pinpoint whatever it was that had awakened her. Eventually she turned on her side and looked at the clock.

It was just after midnight.

She had a vague memory of tumbling into bed almost immediately after dinner. Sleep had come, hard and fast, her body shutting down so that it could recover from the long, difficult day. But now the effects of the wine and exhaustion had worn off. She felt unnaturally alert and restless.

Shoving aside the covers, she got to her feet and padded barefoot to the sliding glass doors.

She pulled the curtains aside. The underwater lights were off. Half the pool lay in heavy shadows cast by the walls of the house. The other half was illuminated by the brilliant desert moon. When she saw the dark figure in the opaque, silvered water she stopped breathing for a couple heartbeats. Not again. She really could not deal with any more bodies.

Belatedly she realized that the person in the pool was not floating; he was swimming toward the far end, where the shadows were deepest, with smooth, powerful, controlled strokes.

Jake.

Impulsively she went into the bathroom, pulled on the robe she had borrowed from the Glazebrook house and went back to the glass doors.

She unlocked the slider, opened it and stepped out into the night.

The air was a pleasant temperature now. The stones that paved the pool terrace still radiated the warmth that had been absorbed during the day. She walked to the edge of the water.

Jake had seen her and changed direction. He swam to the side and looked up at her. Moonlight gleamed on his wet hair and sleek, powerful shoulders.

"You okay?" he asked.

"Yes. Slept like a log until a few minutes ago."

"Bad dreams?"

She hesitated. "Only to be expected under the circumstances."

"A swim might relax you so you can get back to sleep."

"I didn't bring a swimsuit with me."

"You don't need one. The lights are off. You can't see anything under the surface at night."

Automatically she glanced down into the water below his chest. He was right. She could not even see the dark outline of his body.

"Well," she said, thinking about it.

"Haven't you ever gone skinny-dipping?"

"Actually, no, I haven't."

"Try it. You'll like it."

The note of sensual amusement in his words stirred something deep inside her. She realized that she wanted very much to be in the water with Jake.

"All right," she said. "But you'll have to turn around while I get in."

"I wouldn't have taken you for the shy type. Pretend you're on one of those European beaches where everyone is nude."

"I'm not sure I'm capable of that degree of imagination, but I'll give it a shot."

She walked around the edge of the pool into the dense shadows at the far end. Feeling more than a little reckless and uncharacteristically, excitingly *brazen,* she untied the robe and tossed it onto a lounger.

She kept an eye on Jake, who was treading water at the opposite end. He was in the moonlit section, so she could see that he had his back to her.

Quickly she started down the steps.

Jake turned around just as the water reached her knees. She wasn't sure how much he could actually see in the shadows, but if even some of the rumors were true, his night vision was much better than average.

"No peeking," she yelped. She crossed her arms over her breasts and immediately sank neck-deep into the warm water. "You promised."

"No, I didn't." He made his way slowly toward her, cruising with the grace of a sea serpent. "I would have remembered a stupid promise like that. You *ordered* me not to look. Different matter entirely."

"You really can see in the dark, can't you?"

"I'm a hunter. Goes with the territory. Don't worry, you looked beautiful getting into the water. Think Botticelli's *Birth of Venus.*"

She smiled wryly. "Except I'm not a redhead."

"I noticed. Fine by me." He swam closer. "I like the dark, sultry, mysterious, exotic type better anyway."

Was that really how he saw her? she wondered. She had never considered herself any of those things. Okay, dark-haired, yes. But sultry, mysterious and exotic?

"You were right," she said, sweeping her hands lazily back and forth beneath the surface. "This does feel good."

"Especially after dark." He stopped a short distance away and stood chest deep in the water.

"Do you always swim at night?" she asked.

"My favorite time."

"I can't remember ever swimming in the moonlight," she said. She was unable to take her eyes off his looming silhouette. "It's a very unusual experience."

"So is this," he said.

His hands closed around her bare shoulders. He drew her up out of the water and against his chest. When his mouth came down on hers there was an inevitability about the kiss that thrilled her senses.

She had known this was going to happen when she got into the pool, she thought. And she was pretty sure he had known it, too.

Nevertheless, the fierce urgency that slammed through her took her breath. She *wanted* Jake. She *needed* him tonight. She yearned to abandon herself to the sheer physical sensation of being held close and tight and hard by this man.

The vibrant force of her own desire caught her off guard. She could feel Jake's hunger, as well. The combination was electrifying.

No one had ever affected her senses like this. Or maybe she had never allowed anyone to have this effect on her. Blame the trust issues, she thought. But her natural defenses had come down with a vengeance tonight. She was not afraid to make a leap in the dark.

She heard herself give a soft, hoarse cry. The small sound was muffled by Jake's mouth. He groaned, flattened one hand on the base of her spine and forced her hips against his own.

She wasn't the only one who was not wearing a swimsuit, she discovered.

He was heavily aroused. It gave her a glorious satisfaction to know that she was the cause. His erection pressed against her, rigid, demanding. She reached below the surface of the water and circled him with her fingers.

"Talk about larger than life," she whispered. She squeezed gently.

He inhaled sharply and raised his mouth an inch from hers. "It's been a while," he warned. "Don't think I can take much foreplay tonight."

"Tell me when to stop." She stroked him more firmly.

He gave a low, sexy growl of a laugh. "Don't hold your breath."

He bent his head and kissed the hollow of her shoulder. His fingertips slid between the cleft of her buttocks and then moved around the curve of her hips. He found the tight, urgent place between her legs and probed slowly. A delicious ache flowered inside her. She leaned into him.

"Jake."

"Are you going to have second thoughts in the morning?" he asked softly. "Because if so, I'd really appreciate it if you'd tell me now."

"No second thoughts," she said. She kissed his chest. "Not about tonight."

He scooped her up in his arms and carried her through the water to the steps. The night air felt cool after the warmth of the pool. She shivered a little.

He stood her on her feet and bundled her into her robe. When he left her to cross through the moonlight to pick up a towel she saw him briefly silhouetted in full profile. There was something profoundly compelling about the sight of his aroused body.

He wrapped the towel around his waist and came back for her. When he lifted her up into his arms again she thought about telling him that she was quite capable of walking to the bedroom. She kept her mouth shut. It was a lot more fun to be carried off into the night. For once it didn't matter that a man was making all the decisions. For the first time in her life she wanted to surrender to the experience.

He carried her through the open slider of his own bedroom. In the moonlight she could see that the bed was badly rumpled. The light blanket had been kicked partway off onto the carpet. The sheet was twisted and the pillow was dented in several places. Jake's sleep had been restless, she realized. That was probably what had driven him outdoors to swim.

She wondered what kind of thoughts kept

a man like Jake Salter awake at night.

He opened a drawer in the nightstand and took out a small packet. He had the condom on with a couple of quick, efficient moves. Then he was on the bed, gathering her in his arms.

The robe fell away. Jake loomed over her, caging her between his arms. He kissed her again, on her mouth, her throat, her breasts. He moved down the length of her body, raised her knees and found the tight, hard button between her legs with his tongue.

Alarm shot through her.

"Wait." She levered herself up on both elbows. "That's not my thing. I've never let anyone —" She broke off, floundering, feeling suddenly frantic.

He raised his head briefly. "Why not?"

She could not believe he was asking questions. "This is hardly the time for an extended discussion of the subject."

"Can't think of a better time, can you?"

"All right," she snapped, exasperated. "It's too personal. Too *intimate.* There. Satisfied?"

"No. Ever tried it?"

"No."

"Then you're not speaking from experience. You don't know what you're missing."

He lowered his mouth to her again.

She clawed at the bedding with both

hands, instinctively trying to retreat from the sheer intensity of the sensation. She found herself trapped when she came up hard against the head of the bed. Jake gripped her buttocks, sinking his fingers into her in order to hold her still.

"You taste so good I could eat you alive." He kissed the inside of her thigh. "Trust me, here."

And suddenly there was nothing she wanted to do more in the entire world.

"Jake."

She heard a low, sexy laugh.

"There's an old saying that suits this situation," Jake said, tightening his grip on her. "Something along the lines of 'Lie back and enjoy it.'"

"Why, you macho, arrogant son of a —"

Outraged, she fisted her hands in his hair, intending to push him away. Somehow she accidentally pulled him closer.

"Open up all of your senses," he whispered. "Run hot for me."

That was one risk she did not want to take tonight, she thought. She could not bear to discover that he was not as enthralled as she was by the passion that had flared between them.

He eased his thumbs into her, pressing upward, finding the perfect spot just inside. At the same time, his tongue stroked the sensitive bud.

She was suddenly clenched so tightly she had nothing left for the battle. She did the only thing she could do under the circumstances. She surrendered.

The climax rolled through her, sweeping away the last of her control. All her senses flashed into full awareness. Power danced in the shadows around her; hers and Jake's. She realized dimly that he was running wide open, too.

Her heels dug into the mattress. She heard a high, exultant shriek. She was screaming. She *never* screamed in bed. Then again, she had never had an orgasm with a man, either.

Jake moved swiftly up her body and sank deep inside her with a long, heavy thrust.

But she was impossibly sensitive now and he was much bigger than any of the handful of men she had gone to bed with in the past. The result was an overwhelming storm of sensation.

A second series of small shock waves reverberated through her. Instinctively she wrapped her legs around his hips.

"Yes," Jake muttered against her mouth. "Just like that. Tight and hot."

The muscles of his back went rigid beneath her palms. His skin was damp, not from the pool water; from perspiration. He drove himself into her again and again, hard and fast.

Seconds later his release slammed through him. She felt every wave.

When it was finally over he collapsed on top of her, pinning her to the bed with the weight of his utterly relaxed body.

"Knew it was going to be like that," he said into the pillow beside her.

He was telling the truth.

CHAPTER TWENTY-THREE

Jake finally gave up trying to ignore the pushing and prodding. He roused reluctantly, opened his eyes and levered himself up onto his elbows. The sight of Clare sprawled beneath him, her hair a tangled cloud, her face still flushed, filled him with a bone-deep satisfaction.

"What?" he asked, lazily kissing her nose. "I'm trying to get some sleep here."

"I noticed. But I want to get up."

"So? Get up."

"I can't. You're on top of me."

He looked down at her breasts. "Huh. You're right."

"Off."

"Okay, okay."

He flopped onto his back, folded one arm behind his head and admired the sweet, full globes of her rear as she disappeared into the bathroom.

"You know, you have a really terrific butt,"

he called after her.

There was a short, startled silence from inside the bath.

"Gosh, thanks," Clare said eventually. "Yours isn't bad, either."

He grinned, too relaxed to move. "I can't believe you've never gone skinny-dipping until tonight."

Clare reappeared, enveloped in his robe. Probably because hers was still damp, he decided. He smiled at the sight. She looked like she belonged to him, he thought.

She watched him steadily for a moment, thoughtful and sultry.

"I can't believe I let you do what you did to me," she said finally. "And swimming naked was the least of it."

He rolled off the bed and started toward her. "Let's get something straight here, lady. You didn't *let* me do anything. I had to fight you every inch of the way, remember? We even had an extended debate at one point."

"Yes, we did, didn't we?" She tipped her head slightly to one side. "I think I lost."

He stopped directly in front of her and planted both hands against the wall on either side of her head. "You were just overcome by my irrefutable logic."

"That's right. I remember now. Your brilliant arguments consisted of 'trust me' and 'lie back and enjoy it.' How could I have failed to be swayed by that kind of snappy logic?"

He smiled slowly. "So, was it good for you?"

She studied him for a moment with an unreadable expression. "If I tell you that this is the first time in my life that I have never had to fake an orgasm, will you become insufferably egotistical?"

"No, honest." He took one hand off the wall long enough to cross his heart. "I will be proud, of course, but very, very humble."

"Gee. Why does that statement lack the ring of truth?"

"Probably because I am lying through my teeth. You know, it's downright scary to think that if I hadn't come along, you might have spent the rest of your life never knowing the joys of sex with me."

"Think maybe I should get down on my knees and thank you at some point in the near future?" she asked with perfect innocence.

"Oh, wow," he breathed reverently. "The image that comes to mind is enough to make me feel a trifle faint."

She punched him lightly in the ribs. "You keep forgetting you're talking to someone who always knows when you're fibbing."

He laughed. "Want to know what really scares the hell out of me?"

"What?"

"The thought of never having met you."

"Is this your way of saying that it was good for you, too?"

"The best," he said simply.

He was telling the truth again. She was flabbergasted. She reminded herself that at that particular moment, awash in postcoital afterglow, he might actually believe what he had just said, in which case it was the truth. But only for tonight.

People always assumed that the truth was never as complicated as a lie. They were wrong.

He straightened and walked into the bathroom. "Now that we've got that settled, let's get back to your suggestion."

"What suggestion?" she asked from the doorway.

He turned on the faucet. "I'm not sure of all the details, but I believe it involved getting down on your knees to thank me personally for the best orgasm of your life."

"It's kind of late. I wouldn't dream of keeping you up past your bedtime."

"Not a problem. I'm already up."

She looked down at his heavily aroused body.

"Yes," she said. "I can see that. Well, Mom always told me that good manners are important."

"Nice to know that there are still some standards left."

CHAPTER TWENTY-FOUR

She felt him leave the bed shortly before dawn. There was the smallest of rustling sounds. A moment later she heard the soft slide of a zipper. The door slid open.

He had gone outside onto the patio. She wondered if he had left something out there last night: his watch or shoes, perhaps. When he did not return immediately, curiosity got the better of her. She sat up to see what he was doing.

The curtains were open. From the bed she had a clear view of the pool and the wrought-iron fence beyond. Jake had opened the gate. He stood at the edge of the patio, looking out at the rolling desert landscape. The calm, alert stillness of his stance told her that he was watching something very intently.

She rose from the bed and pulled on his robe. Tying the sash, she crossed the room and stepped outside onto the patio.

The exhilaration of the predawn atmosphere struck her full force. The sweet scents, the perfect temperature with the promise of the heat to come, the exotic light, all combined to give her an odd, thrilling rush of awareness.

Halfway across the patio she saw the first coyote. It was a few yards from where Jake stood, watching her with an unwavering gaze. After a few seconds she saw the second and then the third. The trio regarded her for a long moment, and then, evidently concluding she was not a problem, they went back to prowling the underbrush.

She came to a halt beside Jake. He put an arm around her shoulder and pulled her against his side.

"What's going on out here?" she whispered.

"Those three are hunting breakfast."

She winced. "I hope they don't find it while I'm standing here watching. Something tells me they don't eat a lot of soy burgers."

"At this hour they're probably after rabbits."

"What about you? Staking out your territory? Marking your boundaries?"

"In a way."

"It better not involve peeing on the fence.

245

I don't mind a little back-to-nature stuff, but I'd have to draw the line at that."

"Go ahead, take all the fun out of it."

She laughed and turned into the curve of his arm. He kissed her there in the light of the desert dawn, sending energy splashing across all her senses.

When he raised his head at last she could see the exciting heat in his eyes.

"I didn't buy you dinner last night," she said. "So I'll make breakfast instead."

"Works for me."

He walked into the kitchen some time later, showered and shaved and aware of a hungry anticipation that had nothing to do with food. Clare was at the center island, cracking eggs into a bowl. He could see that she had just come from the shower herself. Her hair was held back in a ponytail. She had on a pair of black pants and a rust-colored T-shirt. Both looked good on her. Both looked familiar.

He stopped in the doorway, giving himself a chance to enjoy the sight of her in his kitchen.

She looked up from the eggs, smiling a little shyly. "Hungry?"

"Oh, yeah."

"I meant for breakfast."

"That, too."

He went around the counter, picked up the teapot and poured Dragon Well green into a heavy white ceramic mug. He lounged back against the counter and watched Clare work on breakfast. She seemed to have made herself very much at home, he noticed. He liked that.

Too bad he was going to have to ruin the warm, romantic atmosphere.

"I'd like to take you up on that offer to make use of your washing machine and dryer after breakfast, if you don't mind," she said.

"No problem."

A non-stick frying pan was heating on the stove. Clare put a teaspoonful of Dijon mustard into the egg mixture and added some chopped fresh dill and a large dollop of ricotta.

"Something I need to ask you," he said.

She picked up a wire whisk and went to work on the egg mixture. "Hmm?"

"Who do you think killed Brad McAllister?"

She stopped whisking very abruptly. "I told you. I have no idea."

"But you're not buying the interrupted burglary theory, are you?"

"No. I didn't buy it six months ago and I

247

really can't buy it now. Not after what happened to Valerie Shipley."

"Got a theory of your own?"

She concentrated very hard on putting a dab of butter into the hot pan. Then she added the eggs. He could tell she was choosing her words carefully, deciding what and how much to tell him.

"The truth, Clare," he said.

She exhaled slowly. "I don't know who killed Brad but I'll tell you one thing."

"What?"

"Until yesterday, I was very grateful to that person."

"Because the killer came up with a permanent fix for Elizabeth's problem?"

"That, too," she admitted. "But there was another reason."

"What?"

Clare looked up from stirring the scrambled eggs. "I think he or she probably saved my life."

A chill went through him. "What are you saying?"

"I'm sure that Brad intended to kill me that night. Someone else got to him first."

CHAPTER TWENTY-FIVE

She knew she should be having some serious concerns about confiding in a man who was still, in far too many ways, a stranger. She had not talked to anyone, not even Elizabeth, about her darkest fears relating to the night of Brad's death.

She had an uneasy feeling that the intense intimacy of last night's blistering sexual encounter had broken through the last of her carefully constructed barricades. She had kept her secret too long, she thought. Only now did she fully realize how desperately she had wanted to discuss her nightmarish theory with someone.

If anyone could address her anxieties with cold reason, it would be Jake.

"I wake up sometimes in the middle of the night, wondering," she said. "But I never told anyone."

"Why would Brad McAllister want to kill you?"

"Because I was the one who pulled Elizabeth out from his clutches. The divorce was not yet final when he died. I think he figured that if he got rid of me, he could regain control of Elizabeth."

"From all accounts, Brad McAllister was an all-around terrific guy."

The eggs were done. Clare scooped them onto two plates and added toast.

"Brad was a manipulative sociopath," she said. "Make that a manipulative *para*-sociopath. And he was so good-looking and so charming and so damned smart that he got away with it. Elizabeth is sure he was having an affair while they were married but she could never prove it."

"He was a member of the Society. Archer checked that out."

"Yes. But I'm positive that Brad lied, not only about the level of his parasenses but the type, as well. I think he was a lot stronger than he let anyone know. Maybe he found some way to fake the Society testing process."

"What kind of talent do you think he had?" Jake asked.

"My guess is, he was a hypnotist or something along those lines. It would certainly explain how he managed to fool everyone, including Archer."

He sat down at the kitchen table. "But not you."

She shrugged. "I am what I am. He wasn't able to fool Elizabeth indefinitely, either. Not even the best hypnotist can keep someone in a trance twenty-four–seven for months on end."

"So how did he manage to keep her under control as long as he did?"

"Drugs." She sat down at the kitchen table. "He convinced a shrink that she was going crazy. I wouldn't be surprised if it turned out that Brad used his hypnotic talents on the doctor to encourage him to prescribe the meds. Then again, maybe he didn't have to work that hard. Like I said, the bastard was incredibly charismatic."

Jake ate some of the eggs while he contemplated that. "Why would McAllister want to make Elizabeth look like a nutcase? What was his agenda?"

"Our theory is that he did it to get control of her inheritance. Liz will eventually receive half of Glazebrook, Inc."

"But not until Archer dies. He looks to be in really good health."

She poured the tea and sat back. He was listening, she thought. He might not be convinced yet but at least he was paying attention.

"All right," she said, "here's the rest of the conspiracy theory that Elizabeth and I concocted. Neither one of us thinks that Archer would have been long for this world if Brad had lived."

"You think he intended to murder Archer?"

"Yes. Eventually. An accident of some sort, no doubt."

"McAllister would still have had Archer's son to deal with," Jake pointed out. "Matt is slated to take control of the company if anything happens to Archer."

"I don't think Matt would have survived long, either. If we're right, in the end control of the company would have wound up in Elizabeth's and Myra's hands. And it wouldn't have been hard to convince Myra to turn everything over to Brad. She thought he was great. Heck, everyone thought Brad was wonderful."

"I can see why you didn't go to the cops with this theory of yours," Jake said neutrally.

She sighed. "I know. It's pretty bizarre, isn't it? The cops would have laughed. And as for other members of the Society, well, they're already strongly inclined to believe that people like me are mentally unstable. I didn't want to add anything to that image.

I've got my future as a psychic investigator to consider."

He nodded, saying nothing, and finished his breakfast.

"Great eggs," he said finally, putting down the fork.

"Thanks. It's the ricotta."

"I'll remember that." He picked up his tea. "All right, for the sake of argument, let's come at this another way. Everyone says that Brad was a wealthy man in his own right. Why go to all the trouble and risk of driving his wife mad and killing a couple of people in order to get his hands on Glazebrook, Inc.?"

Clare sipped some tea. This was admittedly one of the weak points in the theory.

"Some people never have enough," she offered.

"True. Still, you have to admit the scenario you described is pretty extreme."

"Yes."

"How did you and Elizabeth first make contact?"

"I told you, I never intended to show up at the front door of the Glazebrook home and ruin their perfect family thing. But I kept track of all of them, especially Elizabeth, from a distance. I couldn't help myself. She was the sister I never had. Literally."

"Go on."

"Her wedding to Brad McAllister was photographed for one of the glossy Phoenix-area house-and-garden magazines. The spread was beautiful. Elizabeth was so lovely. Gorgeous gown, of course. Everyone looked so happy and pleased. But when I looked at the picture of Brad toasting the bride I got a cold chill."

He raised his brows. "You can detect someone lying in a picture?"

"It's dicey, at best. But there was something about the way he was looking at her that scared me. The wedding had occurred a few months before the photos appeared in the magazine, of course. By the time I saw them and contacted Elizabeth via e-mail she was already well into her supposed nervous breakdown. But she managed to get back to me with a single word."

"What was the word?"

" 'Help.' "

"That was all?"

"Yes. I e-mailed her back immediately and said that I would be in Phoenix on the three-forty P.M. flight from San Francisco that day. She said she would meet me at a bookstore in a mall. Turned out that was one of Brad's afternoons for visiting his girlfriend. He didn't know what had happened until he got home. By that time Elizabeth and I were on a plane headed back to San Francisco."

"How did you end up in Stone Canyon on the night Brad was murdered?" Jake asked.

"By then Elizabeth had recovered from the drugs and was herself again. She stayed with Archer and Myra and made it a point never to be alone with Brad while they went through the divorce proceedings. I kept an eye on things from San Francisco. It all seemed to be going well."

"Brad didn't fight the divorce?"

"He made a few attempts to convince everyone that he loved Elizabeth and didn't want the divorce but he must have realized that there was no chance of salvaging the marriage." She paused. "At least not as long as I was in the picture. He had to know that if the situation changed in any way, I'd come back to Arizona in a flash."

"Did you ever meet McAllister in person?"

"Yes. Once. I went with Elizabeth on the one occasion when she and Brad met with the lawyers together. She wanted me there in case Brad tried anything. But everyone was very nice and polite and civilized. I swear, there was something about McAllister that was colder than ice, though."

"Was that the first time you met Archer?"

"No, he flew up to San Francisco as soon as he found out I had spirited Elizabeth away."

"Did he try to talk you out of encouraging Elizabeth's divorce?"

She tipped her head to one side, thinking. "No, he didn't, as a matter of fact. Elizabeth was very firm about the decision. And Archer and I were both stepping very cautiously around each other at that point."

"Go on with your story."

"A couple of weeks after that, Elizabeth invited me down for a long weekend. I was due to arrive Friday evening. But that afternoon Elizabeth got an e-mail telling her that something had come up on my end and I wouldn't be able to get to Stone Canyon until the following morning. She attended a reception for the Stone Canyon Arts Academy with her parents, instead."

"The e-mail changing your arrival time was not from you, I take it?"

"No," Clare said. "I arrived on schedule Friday evening, picked up a car, drove to the house and found Brad's body."

"What about the e-mail message you supposedly sent?"

"It looked perfectly legitimate. The return address was mine."

He contemplated her across the table.

"You think Brad sent that fake e-mail, don't you?"

"It isn't that difficult to use a phony e-mail address. Spammers do it all the time."

"You think he wanted to lure you to the house that night in order to murder you because you were ruining his scheme." Jake's voice was disturbingly cool and very, very neutral.

She gripped the tea mug tightly. Maybe he wasn't going to believe her after all. Well, she could hardly blame him.

"Yes," she said.

"But someone else got to him first?"

"Yes."

"Sort of a large coincidence, isn't it?" Jake asked.

"Not if you go with the possibility that Brad's murder was deliberately timed to take place while I was here in town," she said.

"You think someone wanted to throw suspicion on you?"

"Maybe. Or maybe the killer staged things that way in case the police didn't buy the interrupted burglary scenario. Maybe I was just the fall gal."

"If you're right, it means that both Brad McAllister and his killer knew your flight schedule that Friday," he said.

"I'm sure it was no secret around Elizabeth's office that I was coming into town to see her."

"It also implies that someone knew Brad was planning to kill you."

"Someone he trusted," she agreed. "A partner in crime, maybe, who betrayed him that night."

"You've really been working on this theory, haven't you?" he asked.

"I've had six months to think about it but I had nothing to go on until now."

"You're referring to Valerie's death?"

She nodded. "I don't care what the autopsy says, I'm going to have a hard time believing it was an accident or a suicide."

"Murder by drowning is notoriously difficult to prove. Just ask any insurance company."

"I know," she said.

"Okay, how about a motive? Got one of those?"

"Not for Valerie's death," she admitted.

"All right, moving right along, I'll grant you that it's theoretically possible that Brad and his partner-killer knew your schedule six months ago. But how could anyone know that you were planning to go out to Valerie's house this afternoon?"

Restless, she stood and went to the window to look out at the pool. "I think that my finding the body this time probably was a genuine coincidence. The killer didn't have to worry about pointing suspicion else-where. Everyone knew Valerie was drinking heavily and using meds."

"In other words, your finding the body was just plain bad luck."

"Yes."

"All right, I can go along with that reasoning. Still, if Valerie was killed, it's damn interesting that the murderer chose to do it while you were here in town."

"I know. I've been thinking about that a lot. Why kill her now?"

"Why kill her at all?"

She turned suddenly to face him. "Jake, you were right the other night when you said that someone should have gone looking for answers six months ago. It's a little late, but I'm going to do it now."

His eyes narrowed faintly. "I was afraid you were going to say that."

"The problem is, I'm not sure how to go about it. I don't have the cash to hire a private investigator, and even if I did, I doubt he'd get far in Stone Canyon."

"That's a given," Jake said. "I can't see the fine folks out at the Stone Canyon Country Club talking to a PI, especially if they think it might involve them in a murder investigation."

"There's a lot of money in this town and that means there's a lot of dirty laundry. No one is going to want it aired."

He looked thoughtful. "Maybe you should talk to Archer before you do anything rash."

She shook her head. "He made it clear six months ago that he wants this whole thing to go away. I can't blame him."

"You're serious about looking for answers, aren't you?" he asked.

"Yes."

"In that case, I'll help you."

"Why?"

"Because you're with me now and I can't talk you out of this project. Doesn't leave me much choice."

"You don't have to do this."

"Yeah," he said. "I do."

"I don't know what to say." Tears welled up in her eyes. "Thank you."

"Don't thank me yet. Got a feeling we're going to be opening up a jar of scorpions here. We'll probably both regret it."

Clare waited. But Jake did not say anything else. Instead, he reached for the morning paper lying on the table. He opened it to read the headlines.

Clare cleared her throat. "Uh, got any idea where we should start?"

"Sure." He turned to the business section. "First we find out who Brad was sleeping with last year when he was killed."

CHAPTER TWENTY-SIX

The doorbell chimed just as Clare removed her panties and T-shirt from the dryer. Jake's footsteps sounded in the hall. She went to the door of the laundry room and listened.

"Where's Clare?" Archer's growl rumbled down the hall.

"She's doing her laundry," Jake said. "Come on into the kitchen. I'll make some coffee."

Clare gave the men a minute or two and then followed them into the kitchen. Archer was at the kitchen table. Jake was spooning coffee into a machine.

"Good morning, Archer," Clare said.

Archer scowled at the sight of her in the robe.

"You okay?" he demanded aggressively.

"I'm fine," she said. "Did you want to speak to Jake or are you here to discuss your plans for the foundation?"

"I'm here to talk to you. What the hell are

you doing running around in a robe at this hour?"

"I'm doing my laundry." She waved the T-shirt. "I didn't pack for an extended stay here in Stone Canyon. Ran out of fresh clothes yesterday. If you'll excuse me, I'll go get dressed." Turning on her heel, she headed for the door. "Maybe you'll be in a better mood when I come back."

"Don't count on it," Jake said in low tones as she walked past him.

She frowned. "What's that supposed to mean?"

Jake acted as if he hadn't heard her.

She spun back around to confront Archer. "Am I missing something here?"

Archer glowered. "We'll talk when you're decent."

She glanced pointedly down at the white robe that enveloped her from neck to toes. "I am decent."

"You should probably get dressed, Clare," Jake said.

She did not like the undercurrents that were flowing between Jake and Archer, but it was clear that neither man was going to explain. Probably a guy thing, she thought.

Stifling a sigh of exasperation, she went down the hall to her bedroom.

It took her only a few minutes to put on

the clean panties and bra, a T-shirt and one of two pairs of black trousers. Amazing how simple it was to get dressed when one's wardrobe was so limited, she thought. Now that she had decided to stay on in Stone Canyon for a while, she really would have to go shopping.

Extending her stay in Stone Canyon brought up other issues, she reminded herself. She was not ready to discuss her conspiracy theories with anyone other than Elizabeth and Jake. She was going to need a good excuse for hanging around, one that would satisfy Archer and everyone else who might wonder why she was still in town.

Luckily, Archer had handed her a ready-made reason for spending a little more time in Stone Canyon.

She went back into the kitchen. The bristly atmosphere had not changed. What was going on here?

"Anything new on Valerie Shipley's death?" she asked, for want of a better ice breaker.

Archer's expression darkened further. "Owen says they expect the autopsy results Tuesday. But he's convinced it was an accident or suicide."

"Seeing me the other night upset her," Clare said quietly.

Glazebrook image."

"That's not why he's pissed."

"What other reason could there be?"

"He's annoyed because you're here."

"Here?"

"With me."

"What?" She got her mouth closed. "Why should he care if I'm staying with you?"

"You're his daughter," Jake said with exaggerated patience. "Fathers always have a problem with the men their daughters are sleeping with when said daughters are not married to the men in question."

"You're joking."

Jake shook his head. "Don't blame him. Some kind of primitive instinct. Deep in his gut he's afraid that I'm taking advantage of you. Hell, I'd feel the same way if I had a daughter."

"I'm thirty-two years old," she yelped.

"And you were still trying to explain things to your mother yesterday, as I recall."

"Yes, but she's my *mother.*"

"So? Archer is your father."

"For heaven's sake, he didn't even know I existed until a few months ago."

"Doesn't make it any easier to deal with."

Jake's cool certainty gave her pause. "You seem to have this all figured out," she said.

"I knew it was going to be a problem."

Guilt assailed her. "Maybe I shouldn't stay here. I don't want to put you on the spot. You're working for Archer, after all."

"You're staying." He sat down at the kitchen table and took out a notebook. "There's no point arguing about it. Archer will do whatever he thinks he has to do. I'll deal with it when the time comes."

She eyed the notebook. "What's that for? Are you going to make notes about my conspiracy theories?"

He looked at the notebook. "I was thinking more in terms of a grocery shopping list. Now that I've got a guest in the house, I'm going to need more food."

CHAPTER TWENTY-SEVEN

"You want to know who Brad was sleeping with?" Elizabeth leaned back in the clean-lined red leather office chair, clearly startled by the question. "Why?"

They had agreed to meet at Elizabeth's office even though it was a Saturday afternoon and Glazebrook Interiors was technically closed for the weekend. There were a couple reasons for that decision. Clare knew that Elizabeth would not be comfortable discussing her relationship with Brad in front of Jake, which nixed Jake's house as a meeting place. The second reason was that Clare had no desire to go back to the Glazebrook estate.

Elizabeth's elegant business was located in a modern, upscale shopping arcade filled with high-end gift shops, exclusive furniture galleries and a variety of boutiques that featured one-of-a-kind accessories for the home.

"Because I've decided that I need to know more about what really happened when Brad was killed," Clare said.

Alarm flashed across Elizabeth's face. "I thought we agreed that it would be best if we both kept quiet about our conspiracy theories. No one wants to hear them, Clare. Not Mom and Dad, not the cops, no one."

"Yes," Clare said. "But things have changed. Trying to pretend that Brad really was killed by a burglar has been driving me nuts for months. Now, given what happened to Valerie Shipley, I can't stand it any longer. I need to know what really happened the night Brad died."

"I'm starting to think Mom is right. It's probably best not to stir up that hornet's nest."

"We'll be discreet," Clare said.

There was a short pause.

"We?" Elizabeth said cautiously.

Clare stacked her heels on the little red leather hassock in front of the black leather and chrome chair in which she was sitting.

"Jake and I will be discreet," she clarified.

Elizabeth's eyes widened. "Jake thinks this is a good idea?"

"No. He thinks the idea sucks. But he realizes that he can't talk me out of it so he's doing the only other thing he feels he can do under the circumstances. He's helping me."

"Why?"

"He claims he's doing it for his own sake. He was telling the truth, as far as it went."

Elizabeth drummed her fingers against the polished surface of the desk. "He's afraid that you're going to stir up trouble. This way, at least, he's got some control. The question, of course, is why does he feel it's his job to be in charge of you?"

Clare almost laughed. "Nature of the beast, I think."

Elizabeth blinked. "I beg your pardon?"

"Let's just say that Jake's the kind of guy who always likes to be in charge. But in this case he's my *partner,* whether he knows it or not. He is definitely not in control."

"Where is he, anyway?"

"Grocery shopping."

"Hmm. Odd thing for your average take-charge kind of guy to be doing, isn't it?"

"Jake's not average. In any way."

Elizabeth sighed. "Clare, if you and Jake start asking questions, everyone is going to get upset all over again."

"I'll be careful."

"Given the circumstances, that's going to be a little tricky, isn't it?"

"Hey, I've been in the charitable foundation business for the past few years. You

think I don't know how to be d
my work involved finesse and d
   Elizabeth raised her brows. "
other half involve?"
   "Detecting frauds and scam a
   "I know you're good when
picking out the cons, but we're t
a murder."
   "Maybe two murders, if I'm
Valerie Shipley."
   "That just makes it twice as
Elizabeth said. "The Stone Ca
haven't been able to turn up
Brad's death. What makes you tl
learn anything new after all this
   "I have to try, Liz. I can't stan
ing any longer. I want the truth.
   Elizabeth sat forward abrupt
aware of what you're planning tc
   "Jake's going to break it to
when they play golf tomorrow m
   "There's no gentle way to d
going to be furious. I've told yc
not want anyone in the family tc
tion the subject of Brad's death."
   "I know," Clare said.
   "Why are you so determined
what was going on six months a
ished. Brad is dead, and speaking
I'm certainly not shedding any tc

under the circumstances. He's helping me."

"Why?"

"He claims he's doing it for his own sake. He was telling the truth, as far as it went."

Elizabeth drummed her fingers against the polished surface of the desk. "He's afraid that you're going to stir up trouble. This way, at least, he's got some control. The question, of course, is why does he feel it's his job to be in charge of you?"

Clare almost laughed. "Nature of the beast, I think."

Elizabeth blinked. "I beg your pardon?"

"Let's just say that Jake's the kind of guy who always likes to be in charge. But in this case he's my *partner*, whether he knows it or not. He is definitely not in control."

"Where is he, anyway?"

"Grocery shopping."

"Hmm. Odd thing for your average take-charge kind of guy to be doing, isn't it?"

"Jake's not average. In any way."

Elizabeth sighed. "Clare, if you and Jake start asking questions, everyone is going to get upset all over again."

"I'll be careful."

"Given the circumstances, that's going to be a little tricky, isn't it?"

"Hey, I've been in the charitable founda-tion business for the past few years. You think I don't know how to be discreet? Half my work involved finesse and diplomacy."

Elizabeth raised her brows. "What did the other half involve?"

"Detecting frauds and scam artists."

"I know you're good when it comes to picking out the cons, but we're talking about a murder."

"Maybe two murders, if I'm right about Valerie Shipley."

"That just makes it twice as dangerous," Elizabeth said. "The Stone Canyon police haven't been able to turn up any leads in Brad's death. What makes you think you can learn anything new after all this time?"

"I have to try, Liz. I can't stand not knowing any longer. I want the truth."

Elizabeth sat forward abruptly. "Is Dad aware of what you're planning to do?"

"Jake's going to break it to him gently when they play golf tomorrow morning."

"There's no gentle way to do it. Dad's going to be furious. I've told you, he does not want anyone in the family to even mention the subject of Brad's death."

"I know," Clare said.

"Why are you so determined to find out what was going on six months ago? It's finished. Brad is dead, and speaking personally, I'm certainly not shedding any tears."

"Neither am I. But I told you, I've got a feeling that Valerie's death is linked to it."

"So what? Let the authorities deal with it."

"They're going to conclude she drowned accidentally. You know they are."

"I hate to sound cold-hearted about all this, but do either of us really care?" Elizabeth asked. "The woman tried to kill you. Twice. If we're right, she was the one who sabotaged your engagement and your career. Frankly, I'm relieved that she's gone, too."

"Don't you see? If we're right, it means that Brad wasn't the random victim of a home invasion robbery and neither was Valerie."

"Don't tell me you feel an obligation to avenge Brad and Valerie."

"No," Clare said. "What I don't like is that the killer took advantage of the fact that I happened to be in town to kill twice. Whoever he or she is, the murderer had to know that if there were any suspicions about either death, they would point toward me. I think I was the fallback plan in the event that questions were asked."

Elizabeth winced. "But it turned out okay in both cases. You're not a suspect."

"Thanks to the Glazebrook name, probably. Trust me, there's nothing I'd like more than finding out that I'm wrong and that there is no conspiracy. I'll sleep a lot better at night if that is the case."

"I have a feeling this is a really, really bad idea."

Clare smiled ruefully. "Wouldn't be my first."

Elizabeth turned thoughtful. "What about you and Jake?"

"I beg your pardon?"

"Don't give me that whatever-are-you-talking-about look. Something is going on between the two of you, isn't it? I can tell."

"You're guessing."

"No," Elizabeth said firmly. "I am not guessing."

Clare nodded. "Well, you are a level-five sensitive. That means you get lots of points for intuition."

"You're sleeping with him, aren't you?"

"Let's just say I have discovered a new hobby."

"What kind of hobby?"

"Skinny-dipping. Now will you answer my question?"

"About Brad's girlfriend?" Elizabeth swiveled back and forth a couple times in her chair. "I don't know who she was. I certainly don't have a name to give you. To tell you the truth, I was so doped up most of the time and so afraid I was having a real nervous breakdown that I didn't really care who she was. I just knew that he was seeing someone."

"Do you remember how you first found out?"

Elizabeth massaged her temples with her thumbs. "Brad and I stopped having sex about a month and a half into the marriage. I told you, before the wedding and for a while afterward, he was the perfect lover. He used his sexual skills the way he did his looks and charm."

"To manipulate people."

Elizabeth nodded. "Yes. But he also liked sex. A lot. That part of our life came to a halt, although Brad acted as if we had a normal relationship. He claimed that I forgot our lovemaking the next morning; that I was somehow blocking it psychologically."

"The fugue state thing."

"Yes. That was when he insisted that I start seeing Dr. Mowbray." Elizabeth shuddered. "It was awful. Brad used to wake me up in the morning with coffee in bed and tell me how passionate I'd been during the night. Then he would act hurt and concerned when I couldn't remember the sex."

"But you knew he was getting laid," Clare said.

"Oh, yes. As I said, sex was very important

to Brad. He wouldn't have gone without it for long. Not willingly, at any rate. But I didn't find any strong evidence until after he died. By then, of course, I didn't care."

"What was the evidence? You never mentioned it."

"You know the old saying 'Follow the money'?"

Clare nodded. "Sure."

"After Brad was killed I had to go through a lot of his papers and files. Even though he had moved out and I had started proceedings, we were still technically married at the time of his death."

"I remember that you had a lot of work to do to settle his estate."

"I turned everything I could over to the lawyer. Valerie got the bulk of Brad's money. Lord knows I didn't want it. Anyway, for months afterward, bills and credit card statements kept turning up in the mail."

"I think I'm getting the picture here." Clare was suddenly aware of her pulse. "Hard to carry on an affair without spending money."

"Turns out Brad had a credit card that I knew nothing about until the bills started arriving after his death. There was one recurring charge on the statements that caught my eye."

"What was it?"

"Once, sometimes twice a week for almost the entire time we were married he evidently spent an afternoon at a spa in Phoenix. My intuition tells me that is probably where he went to screw his lover."

CHAPTER TWENTY-EIGHT

"What the hell is going on between you and Clare?" Archer asked.

Jake dropped the club back into the bag and got behind the wheel of the golf cart.

He had been expecting the question since they teed off at the first hole. The only real surprise was that Archer had waited until the third hole to ask it. Glazebrook could be astonishingly nuanced and roundabout in his business dealings, but when it came to interpersonal relationships he was usually about as subtle as a brick.

It was Sunday morning, going on six o'-clock. The temperature was still pleasant but the sun was climbing rapidly. So was the brilliance of the light. He and Archer had already put on their dark glasses.

Since his arrival in Stone Canyon Jake had begun to look forward to his rounds of golf with Archer. It wasn't only because it gave them a secure place to talk, the golf itself was an interesting challenge. They had agreed from the beginning that, when it was just the two of them, they would play with all their senses wide open. When they were both running hot, the matches became an intriguing contest between his hunter talents and Archer's unique strategic abilities.

The outcomes were unpredictable. There were upsides to both talents, Jake reflected. There was no question that his hunter talents gave him an edge when it came to coordination and timing. But Archer's preternatural ability to plot strategy paid off just as often. Take today, for instance. They were both on the green in two. Now it all came down to the putting. And putting was half strategy and half timing and coordination. It could go either way.

"You don't really expect a detailed answer to that question, do you?" Jake asked, steering the cart along the narrow path to a point close to the green.

"Damn right I do. You haven't shown any interest in women since you got here. I was starting to wonder if maybe you weren't the type who likes 'em."

"Would that have been an issue for you?"

"Let's get something straight. I don't give a frigging damn who you sleep with so long as it doesn't create a problem for me or someone in my family."

"You're worried that a relationship between Clare and me might create a problem?"

"Yeah," Archer said. "That's exactly what's worrying me. This thing between the two of you blew up like a storm out of nowhere. A few days ago she hadn't even met you. Now she's living with you."

"That's how it happens sometimes."

"You think I don't know that? Clare is the direct result of my own personal experience with a sudden storm. I don't want her put into the same kind of position her mother found herself in all those years ago. Is that real clear, Salter?"

"Your concerns are noted."

"Don't give me that bullshit, damn you. This is my daughter we're talking about."

"Archer, I appreciate your point of view. But my personal life is just that. Personal. I don't discuss it in depth with anyone."

"The hell you don't. You're gonna damn well discuss it with me as long as your personal life involves Clare."

Jake braked the cart to a halt. He sat quietly for a moment, studying the situation on the green.

"I'm going to tell you something, Archer. You're not going to like it but maybe you'll

280

understand why I've got Clare living in my house."

"I'm listening."

"Clare is convinced that Brad McAllister was not the victim of a burglar he happened to interrupt in the course of a robbery. She thinks he was killed by someone who planned the murder very carefully in a way that would throw suspicion on her."

Archer stiffened. "That's crazy."

"What's more, she thinks that Valerie was murdered by the same person who killed McAllister. Someone who knew that if the authorities did have any questions about the death, they would be inclined to look at Clare, who just happened to be back in town."

"Shit."

"The reason she decided to hang around Stone Canyon for a few more days isn't because she wants to consider your job offer. She's staying because she plans to dig into the facts surrounding McAllister's death. She needs to prove to herself, one way or another, if her conspiracy theory is valid."

Archer looked as if he had taken a body blow. "Clare said that? She wants to find the killer?"

"Yes. I told her I'd help her."

"*That's* why you've got her staying with you?"

"Right." *And also because I want her in my bed,* Jake thought. But he decided not to add that part.

"Sweet hell," Archer whispered, sounding as if he had just been blindsided. "Talk about a major screwup."

"She's made up her mind. I can't stop her, Archer. Neither can you. But at least this way I can keep an eye on her."

"I never even thought about that possibility," Archer said. His voice was so low he might have been talking to himself. "Never dawned on me that it was someone else. Thought I had it all figured out."

"What are you talking about?" Understanding crackled through Jake. "Damn. I should have known. *That's* why you steered the Jones & Jones analysts away from the McAllister situation. And they bought your take on the murder because they knew what a hell of a strategist you are. If you didn't see a connection between McAllister and the other problem, everyone assumed there probably wasn't one."

"Yeah, well, even a superior strategist can make mistakes when there's personal stuff involved. It was just that I had it figured, you see. Everything fell into place. When that happens —" Archer broke off, shrugging. "You know how it is."

"When everything fits you stop looking for other answers."

"Damn right. When Elizabeth came back from her stay in San Francisco and filed for divorce, she was a changed woman. She was normal again. You don't recover from a nervous breakdown that fast. I realized then that McAllister had done something terrible to her."

"Clare thinks he may have been a powerful hypnotist. In addition he had a doctor feeding Elizabeth drugs."

Archer nodded somberly. "Didn't think about the possibility that McAllister was a hypnotist but that would explain a lot."

"Including why no one saw through him."

"Except Clare," Archer said.

"Except Clare."

Jake turned slightly in the seat to look at Archer. "I see where this is going. You came to the conclusion that Elizabeth wasn't going to be safe as long as Brad McAllister was alive."

"Bastard was too damn clever. And he had targeted my family for some crazy reason. Once the scales fell from my eyes, I figured I had to get rid of him."

"But when he turned up dead you assumed Clare got to him first, didn't you?" Jake asked.

"I knew she was feeling very protective of Elizabeth. Knew she didn't trust McAllister at all."

Jake whistled softly. "All these months you used your influence to squelch the Stone Canyon police investigation and you stonewalled Jones & Jones, as well."

Archer studied the green. "Didn't see any option, to tell you the truth."

"You thought Clare really did kill McAllister. You've been trying to protect her."

"I reckon I leaped to the conclusion that she killed McAllister because I was already locked into the same strategy, myself. Once I realized what he was capable of, I figured it was the only way to be sure that he didn't cause any more trouble for my family. But I was thinking of something more along the lines of a convenient accident."

Jake smiled appreciatively. "Yeah, I'd expect that kind of plan from you. Never did like the notion of you gunning him down."

Archer's brows rose. "You figured I might have been the killer?"

"Crossed my mind a few times."

Archer exhaled heavily. "Looks like I may have caused you some unnecessary problems, Jake. Didn't mean to mess up your project."

"You had your reasons. But it does leave us in an interesting situation."

"What do you mean by 'interesting'?" Archer asked, wary now.

"My gut tells me that the McAllister murder is related to my case here in Stone Canyon."

"How the hell do you figure that?"

"It's been bothering me from the beginning because it's the only thing that stands out as an anomaly in this situation. But J&J was so damned sure there was no connection I've been looking at other possibilities, instead." Jake shook his head, disgusted. "Waste of time."

Archer frowned. "No luck with any of those late-night searches you've been doing, huh?"

"None. But from the moment Clare arrived the other night, my senses have been running a little hot. I'm half jacked up all the time. Know what I mean?"

"Sure." Archer snorted. "In my day, we had other words for it, though."

"Believe it or not, this isn't just about the fact that I'm attracted to your daughter, Glazebrook. What I don't like is her connection to McAllister's murder."

"I don't like it, either. What's that got to do with this?"

"It all comes down to one thing. Given the low crime rate in this burg, what are the odds that she would find the bastard's body if she wasn't the one who murdered him?"

"Not good," Archer admitted. "That's why I tried to point you in another direction. But I don't see any way there could be a link between whatever the new cabal has going down here in Stone Canyon and my family."

"I don't have all the answers yet, but McAllister was involved in this mess somehow. I can feel it."

Archer was quiet for a couple beats, looking thoughtful.

"Instinct?" he asked finally.

Among the members of the Society, instinct carried a lot of weight.

"Hunter's instinct," Jake said.

CHAPTER TWENTY-NINE

Clare was in the kitchen when she heard the sound of a car in the drive. Hoping that it was Jake returning from the early Sunday morning golf game, she went down the hall to the front door and peered through the peephole.

Myra got out from behind the wheel of a sleek Mercedes and walked determinedly toward the front door.

Clare wondered if she could get away with pretending she was not at home. But even as that plan popped into her mind she saw Myra glance at the rented compact sitting in the drive.

Resigned, Clare opened the door just as Myra put her finger on the bell.

"Good morning," Clare said, summoning a polite smile. "If you're here to see Jake, he's not home. He's out on the golf course with Archer."

"I'm aware of that," Myra said evenly. "I

came to talk to you."

"I'm not sure that's a good idea," Clare said. "You and I don't get along very well, remember?"

"I need to discuss something with you," Myra said through set teeth.

Clare gave up. "Okay."

Myra moved past her into the hall and looked around with absent curiosity.

"First time you've been here?" Clare asked, closing the door.

"Yes, as a matter of fact, it is. Jake and Archer have met here on a few occasions to discuss business but I've never been in this house. I got the impression that Jake is a very private person."

"He is. Let's go into the front room. We can talk there."

Clare led the way down the hall and motioned Myra to one of the dark leather chairs.

Myra sat stiffly. She kept her purse on her lap. *Probably worried I might steal it,* Clare thought.

She sat down across from Myra. "Is this about Archer's plan to establish a charitable foundation?"

"Was it your idea?" Myra demanded in a tight, accusing voice.

"No. It came as a complete surprise to me.

I had a feeling you wouldn't be pleased."

"He wants you to run it."

"I know," Clare said.

"Are you going to take the job?"

"I've told him that I don't want it. But I am considering offering my services as a security consultant." Clare gave Myra a megawatt smile, hoping a little humor might diffuse the tension. "For a hefty fee, of course. I figure the Glazebrooks can afford me."

"I see." Myra did not look amused.

So much for humor.

"You're going to have a problem with that, aren't you?" Clare asked.

"As far as I'm concerned, you have caused nothing but trouble since the day you showed up here in Stone Canyon."

"It's not like things were going so awfully well before I arrived on the scene," Clare said quietly. "At least not for Elizabeth."

Myra flushed a dull red. "Elizabeth was severely depressed for a while. It affected her marriage, and you took advantage of that to move into our lives."

"You're wrong, Myra. Brad was poisoning Elizabeth. The man was a total sociopath. He married her to get control of Glazebrook, Inc."

"We were acquainted with Brad for several months before he married Elizabeth. We would have *known* if Brad was evil."

"No one, with the possible exception of Valerie, knew what he was capable of, and given that she was his mother, I wouldn't be at all surprised if she refused to see the truth."

Myra's fingers clenched around her purse. "For your information, not only did Archer have the Glazebrook, Inc., security department run a background check on Brad before the marriage, he also had a search done in the genealogy records at Arcane House. There was no indication whatsoever that Brad McAllister was anything but what he seemed to be."

"Then someone missed a few things."

"You think you're so clever, don't you? You've got Elizabeth convinced that you're her best friend. Archer plans to make you the director of his new foundation. Now you've started an affair with Jake Salter, one of the few men Archer trusts."

"Myra, please —"

"I don't know what you're after," Myra whispered. "It isn't just money, is it? You know Archer will make sure you get that. He feels a responsibility for you. So why are you here? Damn it, what do you want from my family?"

Tears spilled down Myra's face. She

groped in her purse, found a tissue and blotted her eyes.

A rush of guilt splashed through Clare. She got to her feet. "I'll be right back."

She went into the kitchen, opened the refrigerator and took out a bottle of Jake's favorite spring water. She opened it, poured the contents into a glass full of ice and carried the glass back out into the living room.

"I'm sorry," Clare said. "I didn't mean to upset you."

Myra stopped sniffling into the tissue. She took the water without a word, swallowed some and lowered the glass.

"I swore I wouldn't cry," she whispered.

"It's okay," Clare said. She sat back down. "We're women. It's allowed. I realize that every time you look at me the past slaps you in the face."

"I am aware that I have no right to blame you for what your mother and Archer did all those years ago," Myra said.

Startled, Clare gave her a tentative smile. "Thank you for that much. I did promise myself that I would never intrude on your life. If I hadn't been so sure that Elizabeth needed help before now, I wouldn't be here."

"I will never understand why she felt she couldn't trust her own family, her own *mother.* I suppose her fear of confiding in us was a symptom of her anxiety and depression."

"Mostly it was because none of you believed her when she tried to tell you that Brad was a very scary guy."

"That is not true, damn you. I talked to her doctor personally. Dr. Mowbray confirmed that Elizabeth was suffering from severe depression complicated by an unusual neurosis brought on by her sensitive nature."

"Dr. Mowbray is a sensitive?"

"Yes. He trained at Arcane House. He explained everything to me. He also told me that Brad was doing his best to help her. But Elizabeth was actually delusional. I was terrified she was going to kill herself."

More tears leaked from Myra's eyes.

There was no point arguing anymore, Clare thought. Elizabeth was right. Myra was in denial. She did not want to believe that she had urged her daughter into a truly horrendous marriage. Talk about the ultimate bad guilt trip for a mother.

"Mrs. Glazebrook, if it's any consolation, I am well aware that when I show up here in Stone Canyon, I don't usually bring joy and sunshine into your life," Clare said. "But I swear it isn't my intention to hurt anyone."

"Then why don't you leave?" Myra asked baldly.

"I intend to," Clare promised.

"When?"

"Soon."

Myra's mouth pursed in frustration. She looked around the well-furnished great room. "Why have you gotten involved with Jake?"

"It just happened."

"That sort of thing doesn't *just happen.* Men may choose to believe that when it suits them but women know the truth."

Clare pondered briefly. Myra had a point. "Okay, I'll give you that."

Myra crushed the tissue in one hand. "Are you trying to seduce Jake the same way you seduced Brad?"

Anger flashed through Clare. "One more time for the record. I never, ever slept with Brad McAllister. He was a dangerous, vicious liar and probably a very strong parahypnotist into the bargain."

Myra's eyes widened in outrage. "He was not a hypnotist. I told you, Archer had a thorough background check done. Brad McAllister was a level-four strategist. If he had been false in any way, Archer would have seen through him immediately. Archer is an *eight,* for heaven's sake."

"And I'm a level-ten lie detector. Trust me, I know a liar when I meet one."

Myra rose suddenly. "There is an old saying in the Society. No one can tell a lie as well as a human lie detector."

Clare stood. "I am not here to hurt your family."

"You want revenge, don't you? For all the things you missed because you didn't grow up as Archer Glazebrook's daughter."

"That's not true."

Myra ignored that. "What else are you after, Clare? Why have you set your sights on Jake Salter? Do you think you can use him somehow to further your own agenda?"

Clare tightened her hands into fists at her sides. "That's enough, Myra."

"I'm giving you fair warning, Clare. I will do whatever I must to save my family."

Myra turned and walked very quickly across the great room, heading for the front hall.

Clare hurried after her. "Listen to me. Please."

Myra wrenched open the front door. She stopped and looked back at Clare, radiating the fierceness of a lioness protecting her cubs.

"I want to make one thing very clear," Myra said. "I promise you that I will not stand by and allow you to wreak any more vengeance on this family."

She went out, slamming the door behind her.

CHAPTER THIRTY

Jake pulled into the drive, got out of the BMW and started toward the front door.

The door opened just as he reached for his key. Clare stood there. She had a glass of iced green tea in one hand. The black pants she had on looked familiar but he was certain he hadn't seen the blouse before.

He stopped a couple paces short of the door and let himself take in the sight of her standing in the opening, waiting for him. It hit him that he had been anticipating this moment ever since he left the clubhouse.

"I heard your car in the drive," she said. She held up the iced tea. "Thought you might need this after dealing with Archer all morning."

"You must be psychic." He moved into the hall and took the tea from her hand.

She closed the door and turned to look at him. "How did it go? Did he give you the third degree?"

"Sure. I was expecting it." He kissed her on the mouth and then swallowed some of the cold tea.

"Well?" she prompted. "What did you say?"

"I confirmed his worst fears. Told him you were with me."

Her dark brows snapped together. "That's all?"

"No. After that I really ruined his day."

"You beat him at golf?"

He nodded once. "That, too."

A wary expression tightened her eyes. "What else did you do?"

"I told him that you want to find out what happened to Brad McAllister and that you plan to stick around Stone Canyon until you get some answers."

"I'm not sure that was a good idea."

"Well, he wasn't real thrilled, I can tell you that. But he had his reasons. Do you know that he thought you were the one who murdered McAllister?"

"What?"

"He's been doing his best to squelch any and all inquiries into the matter for the past six months."

"Good grief." She looked stunned. "He was trying to protect me?"

"He's your father. He might be late to the

party but that doesn't change his sense of obligation. Besides, he decided that Brad had it coming."

"But now he must realize that I had nothing to do with Brad's murder. I certainly wouldn't be looking into the situation if I was the killer."

"That little fact did alter his view of things," Jake agreed. "The upshot is that he is now taking a more philosophical attitude toward our current living arrangements, however."

She groaned. "In other words, he's decided that if I'm going to open up a can of worms, it would be best if you kept an eye on me."

He took another long pull on the tea and lowered the glass. "That pretty much sums up his take on things."

"Damn. People keep saying stuff like that."

"Like what?"

" 'Well, at least Jake will be able to keep an eye on you.' I got the same line from Elizabeth." She went past him along the wide hall, heading for the kitchen. "It's very irritating. The only one who doesn't see things that way is Myra."

He followed her into the kitchen and sat down at the table to drink his tea. "You saw Myra today?"

"About an hour ago." Clare opened the refrigerator, took out the jug of iced tea and poured herself a glass. "Let me tell you, if you think my conspiracy theories are over the top, just wait until you hear hers. She thinks that I have worked my wicked wiles on you and have you in my power."

He smiled. "That sounds interesting."

She sat down across from him. "Turns out she's convinced that I'm determined to have my revenge on the Glazebrook family, first by destroying Elizabeth's marriage and now by seducing you into assisting me with some diabolical scheme."

He thought about that. "She give any indication of what she believes the nature of this diabolical scheme might be?"

"No. She's still working on that part of her theory." Clare sat back, drank some tea and lowered the glass. "But she knows that whatever it is, it will be bad for the Glazebrooks."

"Don't worry about Myra. She'll come around in her own time."

"Maybe. Maybe not. But on another front, I did accomplish one thing today. I made an appointment for myself this afternoon at the spa in Phoenix where Elizabeth thinks Brad went to meet his girlfriend."

An icy chill gripped Jake's insides. The cold had nothing to do with the iced tea.

"You did *what?*" he said.

CHAPTER THIRTY-ONE

Jake hadn't actually raised his voice but Clare winced anyway.

"I thought it would be a discreet way to check the place out," she said, baffled by his reaction.

"You're not some kind of undercover cop, Clare. You can't just go marching in and start asking blunt questions about a sensational murder."

She was starting to get irritated. It annoyed her that he did not immediately appreciate the cleverness of her scheme.

"Give me some credit here," she said. "Until recently I've made a pretty good living detecting frauds and scam artists. I am not a complete amateur at this kind of thing."

"You may be good with scammers but you're a total amateur at investigating a murder. I do not want you going to that spa alone."

"Don't worry, I'll be careful," she said, striving to make her voice soothing. "What could possibly happen?"

"Let me think. Right, I remember now. The last time you went to a spa you nearly got brained with an eight-pound dumbbell."

She shuddered. "Okay, point taken. But the person wielding the dumbbell is gone, so dumbbells shouldn't be a problem. Besides, no one at the Phoenix spa knows me. I've never been there before in my life."

"You can't be sure you won't be recognized."

"I booked my appointment under a phony name," she said, proud of that bit of initiative. "I'm going to pay in cash. No one will see a credit card."

"I still don't like it," he said.

"I appreciate your concern."

"It's not concern you're hearing," he said. "It's panic."

"I'm sure that expensive business consultants do not panic. Look, I just wanted to let you know where I'm going to be this afternoon in case I'm late getting back here. My appointment is at four o'clock. I booked a fifty-minute massage, so what with changing clothes and paying the bill, I should be out a little after five. But it's a long drive so I might not return until close to six."

"Book an appointment for me, too," Jake said flatly. "I'm coming with you."

"That's not necessary."

"Book an appointment for me, too," Jake repeated. "Or I'll do it myself."

"Okay, okay," she said. "What kind of treatment do you want? Massage? Steam?"

"I don't give a damn as long as you don't sign me up for anything that involves wax."

Jake was still in a grim mood when he drove the BMW into the parking lot of the Secret Springs Day Spa.

"You know," Clare said, "if you're going to get like this every time I make a decision you don't approve of, we may have a problem with this partnership."

"Relationship." He unsnapped his seat belt, got out and closed the door a little too deliberately.

She scrambled out and looked at him over the roof of the car.

"What is that supposed to mean?" she demanded.

"You called what we have a partnership." Sunlight sparked dangerously off the black lenses of his sunglasses. "It's a relationship."

"Oh." She wasn't sure how to take that. "Well, you know what I mean."

"No," he said deliberately, "I don't always

know what you mean, especially when you use a word like 'partnership.' In my world partnership has serious business connotations. Try another term." He paused a beat. "Unless, of course, you want to sign a written contract with me."

She blinked, feeling more than a little flummoxed. Then, out of nowhere, laughter bubbled up inside her.

"Something tells me I'd be a fool to sign a contract with you, Jake. You're a business consultant. I'm sure that when it comes to wheeling and dealing you're way out of my league."

His jaw tightened. His face was now a stony mask. So much for trying to coax him out of a bad mood with a little humor, she thought. She hadn't had much luck with Myra, either. Obviously she wasn't going down well as a stand-up comedian today.

Then to her astonishment, the corner of Jake's mouth edged upward in a humorless smile.

"You can bet I'd enforce every damn clause," he said.

He delivered the warning in soft, ice-and-lava tones that gave her the exciting little-hair-stirring-on-the-nape-of-her-neck sensation. She could not come up with an adequate response, so she decided to keep

303

her mouth shut.

Jake opened one of the heavy glass doors, held it for her and then followed her into the air-conditioned, artistically lit reception area.

She took off her sunglasses and surveyed the polished stone floors, the long, gleaming granite desk and the two generically beautiful receptionists. One male, one female.

The male receptionist smiled at her, showing perfect white teeth. "May I help you?"

"We're the Smiths," Clare said smoothly, moving toward the granite desk. "We have an appointment."

"Smith?" Jake muttered in a voice that did not reach beyond Clare's ear. "That's the best you could come up with?"

She ignored him and came to a halt in front of the desk. Something about the extraordinarily warm, welcoming smile the female receptionist was bestowing upon Jake irritated her. The name on the little bronze and black tag pinned to the woman's obviously enhanced chest was Tiffany.

"I have you right here, Mrs. Smith," the male receptionist said. His name tag read Harris. "You're booked for the Ritual of Renewal treatment, and Mr. Smith will be enjoying the Ritual of Relaxation Massage." Harris paused briefly, checking his computer screen. "It says here that you requested a female therapist, Mrs. Smith."

"That's right," she said.

Tiffany brightened her smile for Jake. "Do you have a preference, Mr. Smith?"

"Well —" Jake began.

"Mr. Smith wants a masseur," Clare said quickly. She frowned at Tiffany. "I made that request when I booked the appointment today. I was told that a male therapist would be available."

Out of the corner of her eye she saw Jake smile benignly. He was enjoying this, she realized.

He looked at Tiffany. "Whatever Mrs. Smith says."

Tiffany did a little eye-rolling, signaling her sympathy for his plight as a henpecked husband. Clare gave serious consideration to climbing over the granite counter and throttling her.

"I'll have someone show you both to the dressing rooms," Harris said. "You will begin your rituals by changing into robes and slippers."

He pressed a button behind the counter. A few seconds later an attendant appeared.

"Please follow me, Mr. and Mrs. Smith," the attendant said.

CHAPTER THIRTY-TWO

The therapist's name was Anya. She was built like a Viking goddess. Her English was accented with traces of a language that had its roots in a country that had once taken directions from Moscow. She was very powerful.

"Easy," Clare gasped, sucking in her breath as the woman leaned into her work. "Not so hard, please."

"Perhaps madam is not accustomed to exfoliating treatments." Anya stroked heavily down Clare's right leg. "It is necessary to use force if one wishes to obtain the greatest benefit."

"I think you may be removing an entire layer of my skin."

"That is the whole point, madam."

"It feels like you're scrubbing me with sandpaper."

"When I am finished, you will feel like a new woman," Anya promised. "Your skin will glow."

"In the dark?"

"Hah, hah. Madam has a sense of humor."

Anya went to work on Clare's other leg, lathering on the salt rub mixture before massaging it heavily into the skin. Clare gritted her teeth and tried to focus on the reason she was subjecting herself to the torture.

"Have you, *uh,* been at this spa long, Anya?"

"Five years, madam." Anya's voice rang with pride. She scraped the salt concoction off the back of Clare's calf. "I was among the first therapists hired."

"Really? Impressive. I have always heard that there is a high turnover in your profession."

"That is true but I am happy here. This spa has an excellent reputation."

"I know all about the spa's reputation. In fact, I've been looking forward to this experience for months, ever since I made plans to come to Phoenix."

"Madam is not from around here?"

"No. I'm visiting from San Francisco."

"You have picked the wrong time of the year. It is very hot now."

"I noticed."

She felt Anya take hold of her right foot. She cringed.

"You should come back in the winter or

early spring," Anya said, kneading the sole of Clare's bare foot with her knuckles. "The climate is much better then. Perfect, in fact."

Clare inhaled sharply, wondering if Anya had broken something in her foot. When the pain eased she tried to get back on track.

"But during the high season it would probably be very difficult to get into this spa, let alone book the services of an expert such as yourself," she said. It wasn't easy staying chatty through the pain.

"This is true," Anya said, pulling hard on a toe. "Madam's feet require much treatment. I recommend that you purchase some of our excellent foot rejuvenation cream before you leave today."

"Thanks." Clare gripped the edges of the bed, hanging on for dear life as Anya went to work on the other foot. "I got the name of this spa from a man I met at a business conference several months ago. He said he came here frequently. Once a week, in fact."

"We do have many regular clients here in the Phoenix area. I told you, this is a very well-respected spa."

"Maybe you know the man I'm talking about. His name was McAllister."

Anya's hands stilled on Clare's foot. "Mr. McAllister? That does not sound familiar."

"I've got a picture." Clare had left her spa

robe within reach. She dug the photo of Brad out of one of the pockets. "This is him."

Anya peered at the photograph. "Ah, that is Mr. Stowe."

Disapproval rang in the words.

"Was he a client of yours?" Clare asked.

"No. He always requested another masseuse." Anya went back to work on Clare's foot. "I did not care for that man. He was a terrible womanizer."

"Did he hit on you?"

"Absolutely not." Indignation flared in Anya's face. "I do not allow my male clients to hit me."

"I mean, did he take liberties with your person? Did he insult you with sexual advances?"

"Ah yes, I understand now," Anya said. "As I told you, I never had him for a client so there was never an opportunity for him to 'hit on' me. But I promise you that if he had tried such a thing I would have gone straight to my manager. I am a professional. I do not tolerate professional insults."

Clare did not doubt that for a moment. "If he was the type to insult professional therapists, it's a wonder he was allowed to come here on a regular basis. Or was the management always careful to make certain that he had a male therapist?"

"I told you, Mr. Stowe always requested one particular therapist. He took his treatments from her and no one else. And if you ask me, what went on during those sessions was not at all professional."

"So, what are you?" Rodney studied the photo that Jake had handed to him. "Some kind of private investigator?"

Rodney was a pro, Jake concluded. The masseur was in his late thirties. His thinning hair was shaved very close to his skull and the arms that extended beneath the sleeves of his crew-necked T-shirt rippled with the kind of muscles that come from endless bodybuilding. When Jake made it clear that there was some serious tip money in the offing, he had proved ready, willing and eager to talk.

"Not exactly," Jake said. He got up from the massage table and pulled on the spa robe. "I'm an heir tracer."

"What's that?"

"Law firms representing large estates hire me to track down lost heirs. If this guy is the one I'm looking for he's got some money coming from a recently deceased relative he probably never met and may not even know existed."

Rodney snorted. "If you ask me, the last thing Stowe needs is more money. You should have seen the guy's clothes. Those jackets had to come from Italy. Shirts and shoes, too, probably. He drove a Porsche."

"That's how it goes. The rich get richer, usually because of inheritances. You said the man's name is Stowe?"

"Yeah." Rodney gave him an odd look. "Why?"

"There seems to be some confusion," Jake said. "The name on the paperwork I was given is McAllister."

"Well, all I can tell you is that the guy in that photo is Stowe. No mistaking that jacket. I lusted after that jacket."

"Maybe he changed his name for some reason," Jake said easily. "People do that sometimes. Is Stowe a regular here?"

"Used to be. But he stopped coming around about six months back." Rodney chuckled. "No coincidence there."

"Why do you say that?"

"Stowe always requested Kimberley Todd. The two of them went at it like bunnies back there in the Ocean Garden Room. Everyone on the staff knew what was going on. After she left, he never returned."

"People in your line get hit on a lot?"

"Hazard of the trade." Rodney assumed a

philosophical air. "But it's not so bad here at Secret Springs. It was a lot worse at the spa where I worked in Vegas. You wouldn't believe some of the things the clients did there."

"Vegas is Vegas. Some people think anything goes."

"Tell me about it." Rodney looked knowing. "Here in Arizona, people tend to be better behaved. Most of the time, that is."

"You say Stowe stopped coming here about six months back?"

Rodney nodded. "Didn't see him again after Kimberley quit. My guess is he followed her to wherever she went after she left this place."

"Todd moved to another spa?"

"We all assumed that's why she quit. It's the usual reason. Massage therapists move around a lot. Here in the Valley there's always a new high-end spa opening up, often in conjunction with a new resort. First thing a new operation does is lure away the top therapists from other spas."

"Better money?"

"The more upscale the spa, the bigger the tips. In this business, that's what it's all about."

Rodney watched the Smiths drive out of the parking lot. After a few minutes he went back into the empty therapy room, took out his personal phone and called the number he had been given.

"Is the offer still good?" he said.

"Someone asked about Kimberley Todd?"

"Not more than twenty minutes ago. Two people. A man and a woman."

"Did you get a description?"

The curt question was laced with tension.

"Sure," Rodney said. "And a license plate."

"The money will be waiting for you in an envelope that will be left at the front desk in the morning."

"Five hundred?"

"As promised."

Rodney gave the descriptions and the license plate and ended the call.

In this business, it was all about the tips.

CHAPTER THIRTY-THREE

Clare picked up the notepad and pen and settled deeper into the pool lounger. The blast furnace the locals fondly referred to as the sun had finally been extinguished for the day. The seductive desert night had descended. She could get used to being able to wear sandals and a T-shirt after dark, she thought.

"All right, let's see what we've got." She tapped the notepad with the tip of the pen. "For starters, we have a name for the woman Brad was seeing on a regular basis while he was married to Elizabeth. Kimberley Todd."

"Who just happens to have quit her job at the Secret Springs Day Spa right around the time Brad got killed," Jake said.

"Convenient."

She watched him put a tray down on the patio table. Arranged on the tray were a bottle of chilled Chardonnay, two glasses and several small dishes containing a variety of interesting tidbits. The selection included three kinds of olives, crackers, some artichoke and Parmesan dip that Jake had made the day before, a hunk of rich, crumbly English cheddar, radishes, raw snow peas and some crusty sourdough bread.

The one thing that all the items had in common was that none of them had required cooking. Neither she nor Jake had felt like going to the trouble of preparing a meal after returning from the spa, so they raided the refrigerator and the pantry together.

"I dunno." Jake poured wine into the glasses. "Some might see Kimberley leaving her job as a reasonable response under the circumstances."

"Brokenhearted lover plunges into despair upon learning of the death of her boyfriend, quits job and goes back to wherever she came from? Maybe. But my instincts tell me there's more to the story."

"So do mine." Jake handed her one of the glasses of wine.

"We really need to find Kimberley Todd," Clare said.

"It shouldn't be too hard."

"Unless she's trying to hide because she is a potential witness or maybe even a suspect in an unsolved murder."

"That could complicate things," Jake

agreed. "But I know someone who is very good at tracking people online. I'll give him a call tonight."

"Someone back at your home office?"

"Sort of."

When he did not offer anything further, she decided to move on to another subject.

"Elizabeth and I are going to talk to Dr. Mowbray tomorrow," she said. "He was the one who treated her during her so-called depression episode."

"Did you make an appointment?"

"No. I thought we might have better luck if we surprise him. I don't want to give him time to prepare. If he saw Elizabeth's name on his schedule, he might be worried that she's contemplating some legal action for the lousy diagnosis he gave her and call his lawyer."

Jake leaned back in the lounger. "I like the way you think."

"Thanks." She was oddly pleased by the compliment.

He drank some wine and munched a cracker saddled with a slice of cheddar. "Got to say that you really do have a flair for this kind of work."

"I told you, I've had some experience with scam artists. And when you come right down to it, that's what Brad McAllister was."

"Looks that way. But the thing that's bothering me is why he was willing to go to so much trouble to get control of Glazebrook, Inc. It was a huge gamble at best, not a sure thing. And it involved a hell of a lot of risk, what with trying to make Elizabeth think she was crazy and then planning a couple of what would have been very high-profile murders."

"Brad wasn't a typical scam artist, that's for sure," she said slowly. "They usually hang around just long enough to collect the money and then they vanish." She put down the notepad and pen. "Maybe he just liked the idea of being a major player in the business world. If he had gained control of Glazebrook, Inc., he would have commanded a lot of power and respect here in Arizona."

"Or maybe he had another agenda," Jake said quietly. "One we haven't figured out."

She waited for him in a swath of moonlight. He turned off the bathroom light and walked toward her, a towel around his hips.

When he reached the bed he stopped, indulging himself in the sheer elemental satisfaction the sight of her gave him. Her hair was a dark wave on the white pillow. In the shadows her eyes were even deeper and

317

more mysterious than they appeared in day-light.

She smiled, welcoming him.

He did not try to examine too closely the unfamiliar hunger and urgency that drove him. He accepted the sensations, the same way that he accepted the predictability of the sunrise.

He got rid of the towel, pulled back the covers and looked down at her. The night-gown reached just to the top of her thighs. He could see dark, inviting shadows between her legs.

He lowered himself slowly on top of her, opening up his senses to fully savor the moment. The world around him took on another dimension. He became aware of colors that had no names and sounds that were otherwise muffled. Sensation intensified. The heat of Clare's body compelled him. Her scent was a powerful, arousing drug. But it was the knowledge that she wanted him as much as he wanted her that had the most exhilarating effect.

Energy pulsed in the atmosphere around them.

"You're running hot, aren't you?" he asked, sinking down along the length of her body.

"Yes."

"Then you'll know I'm telling you the truth when I say I want you so badly I think I would go crazy if I couldn't have you tonight."

"*Jake.*"

Her arms went around him. He felt her nails sinking into his back. He liked the fact that she was leaving her marks on him. He intended to leave his own on her tonight. The need to bind her to him, to imprint himself on her in such a way that she never forgot him was vital. He wanted her and she wanted him. That was all that mattered.

He slid one hand down her side and up under the hem of the nightgown. He kissed her, long and deep, and cupped her firmly. It only took a few strokes of his fingers to bring forth the telltale dampness that let him know she was aroused.

His body ached with the need to sheath himself inside her tight, wet heat but he forced himself to wait until she was twisting beneath him, until her soft pleas became sharp commands.

"Now." She clutched him. "Do. It. Now."

Glorying in the small triumph, he rolled onto his back, dragging her with him. When she was astride his body he used both hands to tug off the nightgown. He dropped the garment on the rug beside the bed and gripped her waist.

The feel of her inner thighs pressing warmly against the sides of his body was enough to push him to his limits. It took everything he had to stay in control.

He was about to guide her onto his erection when she surprised him by changing position. Leaning forward, she kissed him lightly on the mouth. Then she moved her lips to his chest.

He was enthralled by the sight of her dark hair spilling across his bare skin. Her mouth was wet and hot. He shuddered.

"I think I know where you're going with this," he managed. "But now isn't a good time."

She raised her head and looked at him through a veil of silken hair.

"Why not?" she asked.

It was, he realized, the same question he had asked her when she tried to resist. He wanted to laugh but the sound came out as a husky groan.

"Because I'm already on the edge," he admitted. "I'll be lucky to last long enough to get inside you."

"Doesn't sound like a good reason to me. Got any other excuses?"

"I thought that was a pretty good one," he said.

"Nope. Speaking as one control freak to another, may I suggest that you just lie back and enjoy it?"

"You're going to make me pay for that crack, aren't you?"

"Oh, yeah." She lowered her head and went back to what she had been doing.

A moment later her mouth closed over him. He sucked in a lungful of air and discovered that the oxygen level in the room had declined markedly in the past few minutes. It was all he could do to breathe, let alone drag her away from his erection.

He reached down and gripped her head with both hands, intending to pull her free and reposition her where he wanted her.

But her tongue was coiling around him and she was stroking the tight, sensitive skin at the base of his erection with her fingertip.

He hovered on the precipice, knowing he could not last much longer. He was torn between the fierce need to take her and the unfamiliar, equally urgent desire to let himself be taken.

The hot urge to brand her as his own won out. He tightened his grip on her head, hauling her up the length of his body. She struggled but he could tell that the erotic combat was only making both of them more excited.

It was one of those situations where sheer muscle power dictated the outcome. He knew from the expression on Clare's face that she understood that as well as he did. But it only made her more determined.

He heaved upward and forced her down onto her back, pinning her to the bed.

"You ever hear of the concept of taking defeat gracefully?" he asked.

"Heard about it." Her teeth gleamed in a wicked, seductive laugh. "But I don't buy it. What about you?"

"Can't say that I'm a fan of it, either."

"I'll bet you like variety, though, don't you?" she asked smoothly.

"Variety, huh? Now that sounds interesting."

She smiled again. "That's what I'm offering here. A little change of pace."

"Well, why didn't you say so?"

He rolled onto his back. She came down on top of him.

It didn't take long. They were both too close.

"Jake."

He felt her constrict around him and knew that she had made the leap. He wanted to luxuriate in the sensation of her climax but the pulses of her release pulled him over the edge with her.

Together they fell, weightless, into the night.

CHAPTER THIRTY-FOUR

"So Brad was screwing his massage therapist?" Elizabeth asked.

"By all accounts, yes," Clare said.

They were sitting in Elizabeth's Mercedes, which was parked in the lot in front of a sleek steel-and-glass office building. The nine-story commercial tower that housed the practice of Dr. Ronald Mowbray glinted like armor in the hot sun.

"And she just up and disappeared around the time Brad was killed," Elizabeth said. She tapped a forefinger on the steering wheel. "Well, well, well. Isn't that interesting?"

"There may be nothing terribly sinister about it," Clare cautioned. "At this point we simply don't know much about Kimberley Todd."

"You're wrong," Elizabeth said. Her fingers closed tightly around the steering wheel, whitening her knuckles. "We do know one thing about her for sure."

"What's that?"

"Whatever else she is, she must be a very, very good massage therapist."

"Only the best for Brad?"

"Only the best." Elizabeth opened the door on the driver's side and got out of the car.

Clare popped her own door and emerged into the full glare of the sun. She examined the landscaped commercial park through the protective shield of her sunglasses. It was mid-morning, not yet eleven o'clock. The pavement was already radiating steady, palpable waves of heat. The sparkling fountains and impossibly green lawns that graced the office tower looked like an artificial oasis.

She glanced at Elizabeth across the roof of the Mercedes. "Nice real estate."

Elizabeth's smile was brittle. "Nothing but the best shrink in town for Brad McAllister's poor, mentally ill wife."

"Are you sure you're okay with this?"

"To tell you the truth, I've been dreading it since you suggested it," Elizabeth said. "When I woke up this morning, coming here was the last thing on earth I wanted to do. But now that I'm actually here, I'm looking forward to telling Dr. Mowbray what I think of his third-rate medical skills."

Clare walked with her toward the heavily tinted glass doors of the lobby. "Probably can't blame him entirely for being taken in by Brad. Everyone else was, too."

"I've read that sociopaths can even fool lie detectors."

"Heard that, too."

Elizabeth smiled. "But he didn't fool you."

"No."

Clare braced for the blast of icy, machine-chilled air that she knew awaited her and followed Elizabeth inside the building.

The lobby had the sleek, polished feel typical of modern office buildings. Walls of black glass that reduced the intense sunlight to a comfortable level and gleaming slate floors generated the impression that only dignified, important business was carried on here.

Elizabeth did not pause at the directory. She marched straight toward the bank of elevators and punched the button.

"Dr. Mowbray's office is on the fourth floor," she said. "Not something I'm likely to forget."

Clare followed her into the elevator. She glanced down at the white-knuckled grip Elizabeth had on the strap of her purse. She didn't say anything, just reached out a hand and touched her sister's arm.

Elizabeth gave her a tremulous smile. "I'm okay. Really."

"I know," Clare said.

The doors opened on the fourth floor. They went along a carpeted corridor, passing two small accounting firms and a law office.

"I don't see any other doctors' offices or clinics on this floor," Clare said. "Don't medical professionals tend to hang out together?"

"Depends on the type of medicine they practice," Elizabeth explained. "It isn't uncommon for psychologists and psychiatrists to establish their businesses in office buildings like this one. It allows patients more privacy when they arrive for appointments."

"Makes sense. A person walking into that lobby downstairs could just as well be on her way to visit a lawyer or an accountant or a stockbroker. No need to advertise that she's seeing a shrink."

"Not that Brad went to any great effort to conceal the fact that I was being treated by a psychiatrist," Elizabeth added bitterly.

She led the way around a corner and stopped in front of number 410. Squaring her shoulders, she reached for the doorknob.

Clare glanced at the sign on the door. It read "J. C. Connors, Attorney-at-Law."

"Hang on," she said. "Wrong door."

Elizabeth's hand froze on the knob. She, too, stared at the sign.

"This is the right door," she whispered. "I'm positive."

She opened the door. Clare followed her into a modestly appointed reception room. The middle-aged woman behind the desk had been filing her nails. She looked up quickly.

"May I help you?"

"We're looking for Dr. Mowbray's office," Clare said.

"This isn't it," the receptionist said. "Did you check the directory downstairs?"

Elizabeth took a step closer to the desk. There was a brittle tension about her that worried Clare.

"I'm sure this is the right office," Elizabeth said. "I remember coming here. I know this was the place."

The receptionist was starting to look uneasy. She reached for the phone. "I'll call the manager's office. I'm sure he can tell you where Dr. Mowbray is."

"This is his office," Elizabeth insisted.

"I'm sorry." The receptionist gave Clare a pleading glance.

"How long have you been here?" Clare asked, moving to stand beside Elizabeth.

The receptionist hesitated. Then the glimmering of relief appeared in her eyes. "Miss Connors opened her office about three months ago. She hired me at that time. Perhaps Dr. Mowbray was the former tenant."

"That explains it," Clare said. She smiled. "My sister came to this office over six months ago. Obviously Dr. Mowbray has moved his practice."

"Obviously," the receptionist said. She gave Elizabeth a wary look. "That explains the mix-up."

Elizabeth relaxed visibly. "Yes, it does. Sorry to have bothered you. Do you have any idea where Dr. Mowbray went?"

"No, I don't."

"Thank you," Clare said. She took Elizabeth's arm and steered her toward the door. "We'll talk to the building manager."

"His office is on the first floor," the receptionist volunteered, clearly eager to see her visitors gone.

"Thank you," Clare said.

Outside in the hall, Elizabeth took a deep breath. "Sorry about that. I almost lost it in there. When the receptionist said she'd never heard of Dr. Mowbray, those dreadful months with Brad flashed before my eyes."

"I had a hunch that was what was going on."

"All I could think about for a few seconds was how Brad convinced everyone that I was having fugue states in which I blanked out and couldn't recall anything I'd said or done."

"Well, now you know that you didn't forget a thing," Clare said. "You remembered the exact location of Mowbray's office. Let's go find the building manager."

"He just disappeared," Raul Estrada said.

The building manager was in his mid-thirties, professionally dressed in a crisp white shirt and dark trousers. His desk was covered with neatly stacked piles of papers, notebooks and logs. There was also a computer on the desk. Next to it was a photograph. The picture showed Raul, smiling proudly, together with a pretty, dark-haired, dark-eyed woman and two laughing children.

Clare suppressed the little pang she always got whenever she saw a happy family portrait. Probably not a perfect family, she thought. No family was perfect. But something about the Estrada family picture gave her the feeling that whatever bad stuff might come, the Estradas would handle it as a family.

"No forwarding address?" Clare asked.

Raul shook his head. "Left owing a lot of

rent. We tried to track him down but no luck."

"Do you happen to know the date he vanished?" Elizabeth asked urgently.

Raul eyed her thoughtfully for a moment. "This is important, isn't it?"

"It's critical," Elizabeth said. "I used to be one of Dr. Mowbray's patients."

"More like his only patient," Raul said.

Clare tensed. Beside her Elizabeth did the same.

"Are you sure about that?" Clare said carefully.

Raul nodded. "After he vanished I talked to some of the other tenants on that floor. They all said that Mowbray kept to himself. He spent very little time in his office. Folks up there on four could only recall seeing one couple who showed up on a regular basis. They assumed the woman was the patient and the guy with her was her husband."

"He had no other patients at all?" Elizabeth asked faintly.

"I can't swear to it," Raul said. "But I think it's safe to say Mowbray didn't have a large practice. I can tell you this much. Until you two showed up today, no one has come around looking for him."

"Any mail or package deliveries?" Clare asked.

"No," Raul said. "It's like the guy never existed."

Elizabeth sagged back into her chair, stunned. "He was a complete phony."

Clare looked at Raul. "It would help us a lot if you could tell us the date he vanished."

Raul watched Elizabeth for a long moment.

He swung around in his chair and pulled a logbook off a shelf. Swiveling back, he opened the log on the desk and flipped through several pages before stopping to examine one page more closely.

"Here we go. January seventeenth," Raul said. "That was a Saturday. The weekend security guard made a note that Mowbray showed up very early that morning, collected some files and left again. Haven't seen him since."

"What about his office furniture?" Clare asked.

"The furniture was all rented." Raul closed the log. "He left it behind. The rental company wasn't too happy with him, either. He left owing them a couple thousand bucks. I checked with their accounting department a few months ago to see if they'd had any luck finding him. But they came to a dead end, too."

Clare couldn't think of anything else to

ask. She rose from the chair. Elizabeth did the same.

"Thank you very much," Clare said to Raul. "You've been very helpful."

"Let me know if you find Mowbray." Raul got to his feet and came around the side of the desk. "He still owes us for breaking the lease."

"We will contact you if we learn anything," Elizabeth assured him.

Clare looked at the family picture on his desk. "Cute kids."

Raul grinned. "Thanks. My son's birthday is coming up next week. We're all going to San Diego to play on the beach for a weekend. It will give us a break from the heat. I've got a new camera I'm looking forward to trying out."

Clare thought about the pictures that would be taken over the course of the weekend on the beach. There would no doubt be lots and lots of images of two happy kids frolicking in the surf with Mom and Dad.

No such thing as a perfect family, she reminded herself. But what the Estradas had looked pretty good.

"Have fun," she said.

The interior of the Mercedes had turned into a sauna again by the time Clare and

333

Elizabeth returned to the vehicle. Elizabeth went through the ritual of lowering the windows, taking down the sunscreen, switching on the engine and firing up the air conditioner. She pulled two bottles of water out of the small ice chest behind the seat and handed one to Clare. She opened her own bottle and studied the office tower with a strange expression.

"Okay, this is getting really weird," she said.

"I'm not so sure about that." Clare reached for the seat belt buckle. The metal edge was so hot it singed her hand. "Ouch." She wrapped her fingers around the bottle of water to cool them. "If you ask me, things are starting to fall into place. What do you want to bet that Dr. Mowbray wasn't a real shrink at all, just some scam artist Brad knew and hired to pose as a psychiatrist?"

Elizabeth smiled ruefully. "You sound positively thrilled at the notion."

"Yes. Because it explains so much." Clare finally got the buckle fastened.

Elizabeth exhaled slowly. "Like why Mowbray was so quick to declare me a wack job." She paused. "How was he able to get the drugs?"

"Come on, Liz. A fourteen-year-old kid can buy just about any kind of drugs he wants on a street corner if he knows what he's doing. How hard could it be for a couple of professional scam artists to get ahold of a few bottles of psychoactive meds?"

"True." Elizabeth fastened her own seat belt, put the Mercedes in gear and reversed out of the parking space. "Wonder where Dr. Mowbray is now?"

"I don't know, but I'd sure like to find him."

"Me, too," Elizabeth said with great depth of feeling. "I have a few things to say to that bastard."

CHAPTER THIRTY-FIVE

Jones & Jones had screwed up, Jake thought. He could feel it in his gut. It wasn't the analysts' fault, not entirely. They'd had a lot of help. The intelligence had been bad from the beginning, and Archer Glazebrook's efforts to protect Clare had sent everyone looking in the wrong direction.

But the biggest problem of all was that no one knew what the enemy's real agenda was in Stone Canyon. Until he had that information he was chasing phantoms in the dark.

He brought the BMW to a halt and sat looking at the old, abandoned ranch house. It was six o'clock in the evening. The sun was sinking fast in the sky, turning the mountains a dozen shades of purple.

He got out and walked toward the skeleton of the old house. The soles of his low boots left little impression on the hard, dry ground.

He had come across the tumbledown

house shortly after arriving in Stone Canyon. The ramshackle structure was perched on a hillside overlooking the town and the Valley beyond. Jake liked the view. He also liked the sensations he got here. The wildness of the desert was a stimulating balm to his senses, allowing him to think more clearly.

He heard a soft rustling noise to his left. A covey of quail bolted out from the cover of some nearby brush and raced madly toward the safety of the shadows beneath the porch.

He opened his senses, taking in the unseen energy of the desert. In this environment life was reduced to its most basic elements. Small creatures darted, skittered and slithered, intent on the next meal or on not becoming a meal, or on mating. Nothing else mattered. Survival and reproduction were the only goals.

He walked through the bones of the old house and out onto the remains of the front porch. When the quail heard his footsteps overhead, they scurried out from under the sagging boards and dashed for some other cover.

He halted, studying the landscape. This afternoon he came out here because he needed to think without distractions. It was time to revise the strategy of the hunt.

The problem was Clare. His instincts were to get her out of the picture entirely; to keep her safe. But that was not going to be possible. He knew her well enough already to realize that nothing he could say would deflect her from her own agenda. And the truth was, he needed her help. If it hadn't been for her he would still be going down the wrong path.

It was time to tell her the truth. Fallon wouldn't like it, Jake thought. But it was understood that once he was out in the field, he had the discretion to make decisions of this nature. The reality of the situation was that, thanks to Clare, an entire new avenue of investigation had opened up.

It was definitely time to bring Clare into the loop.

Light glinted amid a mound of boulders on the hillside to his left. His hunter instincts, already fully aroused, reacted in less than a heartbeat.

The speed of his reflexes was all that saved him. Even with that, he was not able to move fast enough to avoid some damage.

The shot from the rifle seared his left shoulder instead of sinking deep into his chest. The impact spun him partway around and off his feet.

There was an audible whack as the bullet tore through flesh and continued on, plowing into the wall behind him.

The initial sensation of icy shock in his shoulder gave way to fire. When he looked down he saw that his shirtsleeve was already saturated with blood.

CHAPTER THIRTY-SIX

"Where is he? I know he's here somewhere. Let me see him. I demand that you tell me his condition."

Clare's voice reverberated through the thick glass doors that separated the emergency room reception area from the treatment rooms. Jake could hear her very clearly. He smiled.

"Sounds like my ride is here," he said to the young ER doctor and the uniformed representative of the Stone Canyon Police Department who accompanied him.

"That would be the lady out there in the waiting room?" Dr. Benton asked, watching Clare through the glass doors.

"That's her," Jake said.

"Don't give me that privacy stuff." Clare leaned toward the hapless woman behind the desk. "I'm the closest thing he's got to next of kin in this town."

"Your wife?" Officer Thompson inquired politely.

"No," Jake said.

"Must be a good friend, then," Thompson concluded.

"Oh, yeah," Jake said.

"Sounds like she's real concerned about you," Thompson offered.

"It does, doesn't it?" Jake said, pleased.

Benton hit the code to unlock the doors. Jake and his two companions ambled out into the lightly crowded reception room.

Clare had her back to him. She was still engaged in an intense conversation with the woman behind the desk.

"No, I'm not his wife," Clare said tightly. "I'm a friend, the one who got the call from you a few minutes ago telling me that he had been injured."

"I'm sorry, ma'am," the beleaguered receptionist said. "I can't authorize someone who is not a family member —" She broke off at the sight of Jake. Relief brightened her face. "Here is Mr. Salter now."

Clare whirled around. *"Jake."*

"Sorry I'm late for dinner, honey," Jake said. "Got held up at work."

She rushed toward him. He had the distinct impression that she was about to throw her arms around him. But to his great disappointment she stopped short, horrified at the large white bandage that enveloped the upper portion of his left arm.

It dawned on him that he probably looked more than a little rough around the edges. The ER team had cut off his shirt. He was leaving the hospital bare to the waist. No one had bothered to clean him up, either. There was a lot of dried blood on his pants and boots.

"How bad is it?" Clare whispered.

"I probably won't be playing golf for a while," Jake said, feeling quite cheerful. "You look lovely. Is that a new T-shirt?"

Clare frowned worriedly and turned to the doctor. "He sounds out of it."

"He may be," Benton said, frowning a little. "I gave him something for the pain. Some people react in odd ways to painkillers. Which reminds me." He pulled out a notepad. "Here's a prescription for an antibiotic and some more pain meds. He's going to feel that arm when the local wears off."

"Are you sure he's ready to go home?" Clare asked.

"Yep," Jake said, rocking a little on his heels. "I'm ready."

"He'll be fine," Benton said to Clare. "If I had any real concerns I'd admit him for twenty-four hours. But as long as he has someone to stay with him, I don't see any problem. Keep Mr. Salter quiet for a couple of days and watch for a fever or any other sign of infection. There will be some seepage from the wound, but if he starts to bleed heavily get him back here right away."

"How badly was he hurt?" Clare asked.

"It was just a flesh wound," Jake assured her. "You know, like in those old Westerns where the hero gets shot from behind. Except I was shot from the front. Sort of. More like on an angle, maybe. The guy was up on the hillside hiding in some boulders."

He wondered if he had become invisible. No one was paying any attention to him.

"There's some soft tissue trauma, naturally," Benton said to Clare, "but no damage to the bone. He did an excellent job of getting the bleeding under control right away."

"Thank goodness." Clare's shoulders relaxed slightly. "Stitches, I assume?"

"Sure," Benton said, "lots of 'em. He'll need to make an appointment to have them removed in a few days. Will you be the one changing the bandages in the meantime?"

Jake got a sudden visual of the gory state of his left arm.

"Hell, no," he said loudly. "I look like something that was sewn together by Dr. Frankenstein. I'll take care of my own arm."

Neither Clare nor Benton looked at him.

"Yes, I'll deal with the bandages," Clare said.

"In that case, here are the instructions for wound care," Benton said, handing her a sheet of paper and the prescriptions he had just written.

Clare scanned the list of instructions. "I assume I can get these things at any good drugstore?"

"Shouldn't be a problem," Benton said. "Or you can pick them up at the hospital pharmacy on your way out. You can fill the prescriptions there, too."

"I'll do that," Clare said. She folded the paper and tucked it into her shoulder bag. "Thank you, Doctor."

"Hey, it's what I do," Benton said, smiling broadly. "Got to tell you, Mr. Salter was definitely one of the more interesting cases I've seen in a while. We don't get a lot of gunshot wounds here in Stone Canyon. They show up all the time at the big hospitals in Phoenix and Tucson, of course. But this town is not exactly Crime Central." He glanced at Thompson. "Isn't that right?"

"We like to think we have a nice, safe little community here." Thompson studied Clare with a considering expression. "Haven't had a gunshot fatality in six months."

"Right, the McAllister murder," Benton

344

said genially. "I didn't start working here until a couple of months after it happened but people were still talking about it. McAllister's death was a big sensation at the time. They never caught the killer, did they?"

Jake was starting to get irritated by the way Thompson was looking at Clare.

"Case is still open," Thompson said.

Benton nodded thoughtfully. "Officially they chalked it up to an interrupted burglary, but as I recall there were a lot of rumors going around. Everyone seemed to think the truth was that McAllister was murdered by his lover, who just happened to be his wife's half sister. One of those messy love-triangle situations."

"Something like that," Thompson agreed.

"I guess it only goes to show that just because a family is rich and powerful doesn't mean it can't be just as screwed up and dysfunctional as any other family," Benton said. He punched in the code to unlock the security doors again. "Well, folks, you'll have to excuse me. Got a long night ahead. Lives to save and coffee to drink, you know. Hope I don't see you in here again anytime soon, Mr. Salter."

The doors closed solidly behind him.

Jake looked at Clare. Her mouth was very

tight at the corners.

Thompson had removed a notebook from his pocket. "I didn't catch your name, ma'am."

Well, damn, Jake thought. He could almost see Thompson's cop-brain grinding away. He tried to shake off the fuzzy, disoriented sensation that had enveloped him.

"Clare Lancaster," Clare said politely.

"Thought so," Thompson said. He made a note.

"Hey," Jake growled. "Stop that."

Neither Thompson nor Clare looked at him.

"Do you have any idea who shot Jake?" Clare asked aggressively.

"Not yet," Thompson said.

Clare narrowed her eyes. "Shouldn't you be out looking?"

"We're working on it. I just finished taking Mr. Salter's statement. Do you mind telling me where you were around six o'clock this evening, Miss Lancaster?"

"I was at Mr. Salter's house," Clare said. "Cooking dinner."

Jake put his good arm around her shoulders. "Nothing a man looks forward to more after a hard day's work getting shot than coming home to a nice home-cooked meal. What are we having, sweetheart?"

"Grilled salmon with pesto sauce," she said.

"Excellent," Jake said. He winked at Thompson. "Fish is good for you, I hear."

Thompson made a note, but Jake didn't think it had anything to do with the benefits of eating fish.

Thompson was looking very hard at Clare again. "Anyone else there at the house with you?"

"No," Clare said.

"Make any phone calls?" he asked.

"No," Clare said.

This was not going well, Jake thought. Probably ought to do something. But it was hard to think through the murky haze the painkiller had created in his brain.

Thompson wrote something else on his notepad. "Anyone call you, Miss Lancaster?"

"The only call I got was the one from this hospital telling me that Jake had been injured," Clare said evenly.

Jake tried revving up his senses to beat back the pleasant mushy-headed sensation. When the psi energy pulsed through him he managed to glimpse some clarity amid the clouds.

"Get a grip here, Thompson," he said. "I was shot with a scoped rifle, remember?

You've got the bullet I dug out of that stud. You know as well as I do that you're looking for some guy who likes to hunt."

Thompson nodded. "Yes, sir."

"Well then, that proves it," Jake said.

Thompson's brow furrowed. "Proves what, sir?"

"That Clare had nothing to do with my getting shot, of course." Jake gave her an affectionate little pat on the top of her head. "Doubt if my little Clare has ever hunted a day in her life. Right, sweetie?"

Clare stiffened. "Hunting is certainly not my thing."

"See there, Thompson?" Jake said, "What did I tell you?"

Thompson made the derisive snort all hunters make when someone informs them that not everyone considers shooting animals to be a fabulous way to spend an afternoon.

"Feel sorry for Bambi?" Thompson asked Clare.

"I know that there are some legitimate reasons to hunt," Clare said through her teeth. "Thinning the herds by removing diseased animals appears to be at the top of everyone's list of justifications. But why anyone would want to kill and eat a diseased animal is beyond me."

Thompson scowled. "That's not the only reason."

"Well, I suppose there is the sport factor," she agreed politely. "But in my opinion gunning down unarmed creatures with a high-powered weapon does not strike me as something that a civilized person would do for the sheer fun of it."

"She's not from around here," Jake explained confidentially to Thompson.

"Yeah, I got that impression," Thompson said.

"Comes from San Francisco." Jake patted Clare on the head again. "CFL territory."

"What," Clare asked in a dangerous tone, "does CFL stand for?"

"Certified Flaming Liberal," Jake explained. "Yes, sir," he said, turning back to Thompson. "I think it's safe to say that my little Clare is a genuine, card-carrying member of the bleeding heart antigun lobby."

"Speaking of bleeding," Clare said, giving him a steely smile. "We need to get you home and into bed. You heard what the doctor said. You're supposed to rest."

"Okay," Jake said. He looked around, trying to be helpful. "Which way is home?"

"This way." Clare took his good arm. She glanced at Thompson. "Can we leave now?

Jake looks like he might collapse at any moment."

"Nah," Jake said. "Steady as a rock. That's me."

The room tilted on its axis. Clare steadied him.

"The doc was right," Thompson said. "Whatever was in that pain shot is hitting him hard."

"Yes." Clare steered Jake toward the door. "You know where to reach us if you have any more questions."

"You need some help with him?" Thompson asked.

"No, thanks," Clare said. "I can manage."

Jake smiled benignly. "She's stronger than she looks."

He allowed himself to be maneuvered through another set of glass doors and out into a hallway. He was vaguely aware of Clare pushing him gently into a chair while she made some purchases at the hospital pharmacy.

A few minutes later she eased him carefully into the passenger seat of her rental car.

He closed his eyes and leaned his head against the back of the seat. He heard Clare's door open and close. Then he felt her fumbling with his seat belt.

"You know what Thompson was thinking,"

he said without opening his eyes.

"Not hard to guess." She fired up the engine. "Another mysterious crime here in the fair town of Stone Canyon, Arizona, and what do you know? Clare Lancaster just happens to be in the vicinity again."

"You do seem inclined toward a lot of bad luck whenever you're in this burg," Jake said.

"You're the one who got the rotten luck today. Dear God, Jake. Someone tried to *murder* you."

He forced himself to focus hard on the subject. "Could have been a hunter's stray shot."

"I don't believe that for a second and neither do you. It's connected to the fact that you're helping me find out what was going on in Brad McAllister's life at the time he was killed. It has to be."

He opened his eyes. "I'll admit that getting shot today did sort of strike me as something of a coincidence."

"Did you tell that cop that we're investigating the circumstances of Brad's death?"

"Hell, no."

"Why not?"

"It's kind of complicated," Jake said.

"I'm getting a bad feeling here. Define 'complicated.'"

Time to level with her, he thought.

"This is Jones & Jones business," he said.

"Damn," Clare whispered. "I knew you were lying right from the start."

Jake felt that he should probably try to respond to that accusation but he couldn't seem to think anymore.

So he went to sleep, instead.

CHAPTER THIRTY-SEVEN

She pulled into the drive, switched off the engine and looked over at Jake. He was still asleep. The only thing that had kept him from sprawling forward against the dashboard was the seat belt.

"Jake?" She leaned around him to shake his right shoulder very gently. "Wake up. We're home."

He raised his lashes a little and looked at her with unfocused eyes. "Home?"

"Yes." She unfastened his seat belt. "Do you think you can make it into the house?"

He inhaled deeply. "You smell good."

"Pay attention, Jake. You're going to have to help me here. I can't carry you inside."

"Too bad. Sounds like fun. Never been carried over a threshold before."

She got out and went around to his side of the car. When she opened the door he almost toppled out onto the driveway. She barely caught him in time.

"Hang on, let's try this." She inserted her arm between his back and the seat and maneuvered him out of the vehicle.

When she got him on his feet he gripped the edge of the car door to steady himself. He peered at the entrance.

"No sweat," he said. "Piece of cake."

"Good." She draped his good arm around her shoulder. "Here we go."

She was breathing hard by the time she got him into the front hall. When they finally reached his bedroom he was leaning on her so heavily she was afraid she might go down beneath his weight. If that happened she would have to leave him on the floor for the night, she thought.

But he managed to make it as far as the bed. His eyes closed as soon as his head hit the pillow.

She took off his shoes and placed them neatly on the floor beside the bed. After briefly considering his blood-spattered pants, she elected not to remove them. He was asleep now and she did not want to disturb him anymore. Even an agent of the legendary firm of Jones & Jones probably needed a little rest after taking a bullet.

She checked the bandage one last time. There was no sign of increased bleeding.

Satisfied, she turned out the lamp beside

the bed and went to the door.

"Clare?"

She paused and looked back at him. "Yes?"

"You'll be here in the morning?"

"I'll be here," she said.

"Good."

She stood there for a long time, watching him sleep. Her insides were still tied up in the ice-cold knot that had formed when she got the call from the emergency room.

She went into the kitchen and made a large pot of tea. When it was ready she filled a mug to the brim and went back down the hall to Jake's bedroom.

He was sound asleep. She put her palm on his forehead and then on the bare skin around the bandages. Satisfied that he was not in the grip of a raging fever, she sat down in the reading chair near the window, put her feet up on the hassock and took a sip of tea.

She did a meditation on the moonlit night and prepared to wait for the coyotes of dawn.

CHAPTER THIRTY-EIGHT

She was in the kitchen whipping up eggs when she heard the sound of a car in the drive. Given that it was not yet eight o'clock in the morning, the arrival of a visitor did not bode well, she thought.

The news of the shooting incident was in the morning edition of the *Stone Canyon Herald* lying on the table. By now most of the local residents had probably read it.

She set the bowl of beaten eggs in the refrigerator and went down the hall to open the door.

Elizabeth was on the front step. Unfortunately, she was not alone. Archer and Myra were with her.

"What the hell is going on here?" Archer demanded. "Paper says Jake was shot last night."

"Is he all right?" Elizabeth asked anxiously. "I called the hospital but they said he hadn't been admitted."

"He's here." Clare stood back, holding the door. "Still asleep. Please keep your voices down."

Myra was the first one into the hall. Her eyes were shadowed with accusation. "The paper says the police believe Jake may have been the victim of someone who was hunting out of season. Is that true?"

"Probably not," Clare said.

Myra frowned. "What is that supposed to mean?"

"Long story," Clare said.

"What about you?" Elizabeth said. "Are you all right? You look terrible."

"Thanks." Clare managed a wan smile. "One of the great things about having a sister. Total honesty."

Myra gave her a second cursory glance. "You do look a little pale. What's wrong?"

"Nothing major." Clare closed the door. "I didn't get much sleep last night, that's all. Why don't you come into the kitchen? I'll make some coffee."

She got Elizabeth, Myra and Archer seated at the kitchen table and went to the counter to make a pot of coffee.

"Let's have it," Archer said.

"I think someone tried to murder Jake yesterday." Clare concentrated on spooning coffee into the filter. "Probably the same

357

person who killed Valerie Shipley and Brad McAllister."

Archer blew out a long sigh. "I was afraid you were going to say something like that."

"That's not possible," Myra insisted, sounding desperate. "Brad was killed by a burglar. Valerie drowned accidentally. There isn't any connection."

Elizabeth said nothing. Clare turned on the coffeemaker.

"I think there is a link, Myra," Jake said from the doorway.

Clare gave him a quick, head-to-toe survey. He had run a comb through his hair and put on a fresh pair of trousers and a clean shirt. The shirt was unbuttoned, the left sleeve hanging empty. Jake had managed to drape the garment in such a way that it concealed the bandage on his arm.

The clean clothes did nothing to soften the impression he made. The hard lines of his face were rendered more starkly ominous than usual by the dark shadows of his morning beard.

Archer whistled softly. "Well, hell, Salter. You look like you just got back from the gunfight at the O.K. Corral."

"Feels that way, too," Jake said.

Elizabeth's eyes widened. "How badly does it hurt?"

He rubbed the stubble on his chin. "Let's just say that I'm aware that whatever the doc gave me last night has worn off."

"I'll get the pain pills," Clare said quickly.

"No, thanks." He shook his head. "I need to do some thinking. That stuff fuzzes up my senses."

Clare hesitated, saw the stubborn look in his eyes and decided to abandon the argument.

"Are you sure you should be out of bed, Jake?" Myra asked uneasily.

"I'm okay, Myra," he said. "I just need some tea and some food."

"You also need rest," Clare reminded him. She ran water into a kettle. "The doctor said you're supposed to take it easy for a couple of days."

"Yeah, sure," Jake said. He sat down at the table.

His careless agreement told her that he had no intention of loafing around in bed for the next forty-eight hours. She wanted to lecture him, but this did not seem to be the appropriate time so she gave him a severe frown instead. He smiled slightly, his eyes warming.

Archer scowled at Jake. "You think this is all connected to the other business, don't you?"

"Yes," Jake said flatly. "I do."

359

Clare glanced quickly at Myra and Elizabeth. They looked as blank as she felt. She wasn't the only one who didn't know what was going on around here.

"Okay, Mr. Hotshot Jones & Jones agent," she said. "I think it's time you told us just what this 'other business' is."

"Jones & Jones?" Elizabeth looked genuinely shocked.

Myra was appalled. "There can't be anything going on here in Stone Canyon that would attract the attention of Jones & Jones."

"Looks like there is," Jake said. "I was sent here to investigate it. Things got a little screwed up."

"My fault," Archer said. He rubbed the back of his neck in an oddly weary gesture. "I deliberately pointed you away from the McAllister murder."

"It wasn't just you," Jake said. He looked at Clare. "The intelligence J&J had pointed away from it, too."

Clare groaned. "Jones and Jones thought that I killed Brad?"

"Your name came up at the top of the list of possibilities that the probability analysts put together," Jake said.

She frowned. "What was number two on the list?"

"The interrupted burglary scenario."

"Great," Clare muttered. "Just great. No wonder I can't get a job at J&J."

"The bottom line was that Jones and Jones wasn't interested in McAllister's death as long as it appeared to be nothing more than a messy love triangle," Jake said.

Archer raised his brows. "But given recent events, you think it's more than that."

Jake nodded. "I think there is a very direct link to my own investigation."

No more Mr. Bland Consultant, Clare thought. The hunter had come to the surface, big time. The man from Jones & Jones was taking charge.

Myra rounded on Archer. "What is this all about?"

Archer blew out another long breath and slouched in his chair. He exchanged one last look with Jake and then shrugged.

"You're not going to like this," he said, looking directly at Myra. "I was hoping you would never have to know."

"Just tell me," Myra pleaded. "I can deal with anything once I know what it is. You know that. It's the uncertainty that I can't bear."

Archer smiled ruefully. "I know. But in this case, I've been wishing that it would all go away before I had to say something."

Elizabeth frowned. "What is going on here, Dad?"

Clare folded her arms beneath her breasts. She fixed both men with a hard look.

"Well, gentlemen?" she said coolly.

"I didn't hire Jake to consult on the Glaze-brook pension and benefits plan," Archer said. "Jones & Jones requested that I provide cover for him here in Stone Canyon so that he could pursue a classified investigation."

Myra studied Jake. "You're an exotic, aren't you? Jones & Jones is rumored to use a lot of them."

"Yes," Jake admitted.

Myra sighed. "You seemed like such a nice man."

CHAPTER THIRTY-NINE

"I'm not a full-time agent for Jones & Jones," Jake said. "The firm doesn't maintain a large, permanent staff of agents. Most of us are freelance. Like a lot of the other agents, I've got my own investigation business. But I'm on call for what the Council likes to refer to as 'extraordinary situations.' That usually translates into 'messy.'"

"What about Salter Business Consulting?" Clare asked. "Is that just a cover?"

He shrugged. "My MBA is for real but I use it primarily as a cover when I need it for corporate security investigations. That's the bulk of my business."

Myra gripped the edge of the table with both hands and glared hard at Archer. "Why didn't you tell me what was going on?"

"Jones & Jones asked me to keep Jake's real role here a secret," he said.

"Oh, screw that damned J&J," Myra shot back. She leaped to her feet. "I'm your wife.

You should have told me what was going on."

There was a short, startled pause. Jake and everyone else stared at Myra, astonished by the uncharacteristic outburst.

Elizabeth smiled slowly. "Gosh, Mom. Why don't you tell us how you really feel?"

Archer grinned sheepishly. "Your mother doesn't lose her temper very often, Lizzie, but when she does, it's always impressive."

Myra ignored the byplay. She rounded on Jake. "I can't believe that I introduced you to all my friends and acquaintances as a highly respected business consultant."

"I'm sorry, Myra," he said. "I needed to be accepted into your social circle."

"For heaven's sake, why?" Myra swept out her arms. "Just what sort of investigation was so important that you and Jones & Jones felt justified in using me for my social connections?"

"Now, honey, that's not how it was," Archer said, placating. "We didn't use you."

"Yes," Myra spat back. "You did."

Clare elevated her brows in a way that Jake knew did not bode well.

"Sure sounds to me like the two of you and Jones & Jones used her," she said.

Myra cast an uncertain glance at Clare.

"It certainly does," Elizabeth agreed. "No

doubt about it. You guys definitely used Mom."

Jake looked at Archer, instinctively seeking guidance from an older and, he hoped, wiser male who had the advantage of several more years of experience dealing with the opposite sex.

Archer did another heavy exhale and sank deeper into his seat. He gave Jake an apologetic look.

No help from that quarter, Jake thought. He was on his own. Clare, Myra and Elizabeth were all watching him with expressions that would have been appropriate to three female judges about to render sentence on a convicted purse snatcher. And they hadn't even heard the really bad stuff yet. He had saved that for last.

"I'm after a member of what appears to be a new Arcane Society cabal," he said.

Clare drew a sharp breath and sat down hard on the edge of a chair.

Elizabeth and Myra were equally stunned.

"But the cabal is just a legend," Myra managed faintly.

"Not exactly," Jake said.

Clare was already moving beyond startled to intrigued. He wasn't surprised. She was into conspiracy theories. For the members of the Arcane Society the cabals were the ultimate conspiracy theories.

Clare glanced at Elizabeth and Myra and then went back to Jake. "I don't think any of us doubt that there was a cabal at one time or that it was a very dangerous group. But that was back in the late 1800s, when Hippolyte Jones was the Master of the Arcane Society."

"That's right," Elizabeth said. "I remember the story from one of the Arcane House history classes. The leader of the First Cabal was hunted down by a member of the Jones family."

"Caleb Jones," Archer put in, evidently trying to be helpful.

Myra glowered at him. Archer shut up.

"Jones had the assistance of the woman who later became his wife," Clare added, excitement lighting her eyes. "The conspiracy was destroyed. According to the records, the remaining members of the First Cabal were all kicked out of the Society."

"The basic organization of the First Cabal looked a lot like what we would call a cult today," Jake said patiently. "It had ascending circles of secrecy and a leader at the top who was a strong sensitive obsessed with power. Most of the rank-and-file members were nothing more than eccentrics and weakminded individuals who could be manipulated. When the original conspiracy was disbanded, the majority of those affiliated with it tottered off and disappeared."

"Precisely," Myra declared. "The First Cabal is now nothing more than just another old Arcane Society legend. Like so many of those fanciful tales, it was associated with one of the Jones men. Personally, I think that fact alone makes this entire story highly suspect."

Jake looked at her. "There is a reason why it was eventually called the *First* Cabal, Myra."

Myra's lips thinned. "I am aware that over the years there have been rumors of attempts to form new cabals. But we all know that they came to nothing."

"Only because Jones & Jones was able to stop them in time," Archer said.

"Jones & Jones," Myra said with cold emphasis, "was established by Caleb Jones and his wife. It is no secret that all the various branches have been headed by the descendents of the Jones family ever since. That family turns out a lot of exotics."

Elizabeth winced. "Mom, please."

Myra had the grace to redden. "I'm sorry if I offended you by using the term 'exotic,' Jake, but we all know the facts here."

"Don't worry about it, Myra." He watched

Clare pour boiling water into the pot. He really needed that tea. "You're right. In any event, I've got bigger issues at the moment."

"Go on, Jake," Elizabeth said.

"Like it or not," he said, "every so often some member of the Society with a wacked-out psychic profile and usually a very high level of sensitivity to go with it gets inspired by the legend of the First Cabal and decides to fire up a new version. Jones & Jones has reason to believe that has happened again."

Myra continued to look stubborn for a moment. Then a resigned expression stole over her face.

"You're serious, aren't you?" she said.

Jake nodded. "I'm not the only one working on this thing. It's the West Coast branch's highest priority at the moment. There are a number of avenues and leads being pursued. But the only thing J&J has at this point is a murky outline of a group that appears to have recruited some Society members into its ranks."

"That's it?" Clare asked, looking disappointed. "Just a vague notion of a conspiracy?"

"That and a couple of missing lab researchers, a dead technician and a dead informant," he said. "If I'm right, we can also add Brad's and Valerie's deaths to the list."

Clare swallowed hard. "I see."

"This thing is dangerous, Clare."

"Yeah, I get that now," she said. "Can we assume that this new outfit is after what all the other cabals have been after? The founder's formula?"

"They may already have it," Jake said.

"Oh," Clare said. "Wow."

Myra groaned. "Not that old legend again."

"Afraid so," Jake said. "Let me give you a little background here. It's not well known among the members, but the Society runs its own drug research program. The main objective is to tweak already existing psychoactive pharmaceuticals so that they are more effective on people with paranormal senses. We all know that a lot of the modern antidepressants, tranquilizers and even some painkillers have unpredictable effects on those of us who are sensitives."

"That's true," Elizabeth agreed.

"The Society maintains its own private research facility but the work done there is performed under the auspices of a government agency that, of course, shall remain unnamed," Jake said.

Clare smiled. "The government just can't resist dabbling in paranormal research, can it?"

Jake spread his hands wide. "As we all know, it's got a long, lurid and mostly clandestine history of doing just that."

"Well, it only stands to reason," Archer pointed out, "given that statistically speaking, a small percentage of people who have found their way into government work over the years have probably had some degree of paranormal talent. Some of them would certainly have encouraged psychic research."

"The thing is," Jake said, "from the very beginning of the research program the Council has always given strict orders that absolutely no work was to be done on the founder's formula or any variation thereof."

"Let me guess," Clare said drily. "Sooner or later, a sensitive who thinks he's a modern-day alchemist comes along who can't resist going there."

"That's exactly what Fallon believes has happened this time," Jake said. "And it looks like the freak has recruited a couple of the Society's researchers to help him."

Clare poured three mugs of coffee and carried them to the table.

"What made Jones & Jones think there was a cabal connection here in Stone Canyon?" she asked.

"Shortly before he turned up dead, an informant got a message to an agent telling him that the new cabal had some kind of operation in play here," Jake said. "The informant did not know who was involved but he indicated that the individual was moving in expensive social circles."

"Why was my family dragged into this business?" Myra asked.

"I think I can guess how that happened," Clare said. She went back to the counter and took two more mugs out of the cupboard. "When Jones & Jones realized there was a family of socially well-connected members of the Society living here in town, it contacted Archer to see if he would cooperate. Right?"

Elizabeth, Myra and Clare looked at Archer.

"That's pretty much how it went down," Archer admitted. "I was assured that no one in my family would be involved in the investigation or put in harm's way. All I had to do was provide camouflage for Jake."

Jake leaned back against the counter. "After Archer gave his consent, I got a call from Jones & Jones."

"Why you in particular?" Clare asked.

"Given that one of my covers is a business consulting firm, I was the logical choice." He paused a beat. "That and the fact that I'm a hunter."

Elizabeth blinked. "Really? I've never met a hunter before."

Myra sighed. "And to think that I introduced you to everyone at the country club as a respectable consultant."

"How is your investigation connected to Brad?" Elizabeth asked quickly.

"It wasn't," Jake said. "At least not at the beginning. Jones & Jones did take a look at the murder because the victim was a member of the Society who was married to another member. But as I said, it concluded that McAllister was not linked to the conspiracy. They dismissed his death as a routine police matter."

"I have to admit that I encouraged that view," Archer added.

"Because you thought I killed Brad," Clare said. She felt a rush of warmth and wonder. "You were trying to protect me. You shut down an entire police investigation as well as a J&J inquiry just to keep me from becoming a serious murder suspect."

Archer spread his hands. "That's what fathers are for."

Jake noticed that Myra had gone rigid in her chair. An odd expression crossed her face.

"I was also convinced that it wasn't J&J business," Archer said to Clare. "If you were the one who killed McAllister it was because you were afraid he was an ongoing threat to Elizabeth, not because of some cabal conspiracy. By then I'd finally begun to realize that McAllister was not what he seemed and that he was dangerous. Figured he had it coming for what he did to Elizabeth."

Clare glowed. "Thanks, Dad."

She turned away, grabbed a napkin and dabbed at her eyes.

Archer grinned with delight.

Elizabeth stared at Archer, incredulous. "You never said anything about Brad being dangerous, Dad."

"I was just trying to make it all go away," Archer explained. "The cops were happy with the interrupted burglary scenario. But if it had come out that there was a strong motive for killing McAllister, things could have gotten real sticky for both you and Clare. I didn't want them looking at either of you too hard."

"Oh, Lord," Myra said faintly. She put a hand to her breast. "I was so sure —" She broke off abruptly.

They all looked at her.

"You were so sure of what, Mom?" Elizabeth prompted.

She turned to Archer. "I thought *you* were the one who shot Brad. Heaven knows he deserved it after what he did to our Elizabeth. I have to admit that I considered killing him myself."

Jake watched the shocked expressions take hold on every face except Archer's. His grin just got bigger.

"See, that's what I love about your mother," he said to Elizabeth. "She's a lady on the surface and a tiger underneath."

"So that's why you discouraged me from talking about my marriage to anyone outside the family," Elizabeth said. Wonder and admiration lit her face. "You were afraid that Dad was the killer. You were trying to protect him."

Myra sighed. "Like Archer, I was trying to downplay anything the police might view as a potential motive for murder. But there was another reason why I didn't want you to talk about what Brad did to you."

"Two words, I'll bet," Clare said. "Valerie Shipley."

"Yes," Myra said.

"What?" Elizabeth stared at her, open-mouthed. "You never said anything about Valerie to me, Mom."

"It was obvious that after Brad was killed she became dangerously obsessed." Myra looked at Clare. "I thought that you were safe as long as you stayed in San Francisco."

"Out of her sight, you mean," Clare said.

"Precisely," Myra said. "Valerie didn't show any signs of wanting to follow you and do you harm. Owen promised to let me know immediately if he thought she was about to do anything like that. But he assured me that she was in such a disorganized state from all the drinking and the pills that she could not possibly put together a coherent plan that involved getting on an airplane and staging a murder."

Clare winced. "Good to know."

"But Elizabeth was here in Stone Canyon," Myra continued. "She seemed so much more vulnerable."

Clare looked at Elizabeth. "Because she was right under Valerie's nose. I understand."

Myra shook her head. "I was afraid that if she talked too much about how bad things had been with Brad, Valerie would hear the gossip and start to wonder if Elizabeth was the one who killed him."

Elizabeth smiled slowly. "You were trying to protect all three of us, weren't you, Mom?"

"The only thing I could think of to do was to encourage Owen to put Valerie into rehab," Myra said. "He agreed that she needed to go. We were working on that when

Clare showed up the other night."

Archer grimaced. "Hell. That's why you and Owen seemed so close lately."

Myra frowned. "What on earth are you talking about?"

"Forget it," Archer said gruffly. "Just a slight misunderstanding on my part."

Myra shook her head, baffled now. "Did you really think that Owen and I were — ? Oh, for pity's sake, Archer."

Elizabeth grinned. "You were jealous, weren't you, Dad?"

Archer flushed. "Yeah, well, your mother is a beautiful woman. And there was a time when Owen and I were both chasing her like crazy." He looked at Myra. "Seeing the two of you together so often these past few weeks made me wonder if maybe you were thinking you'd made the wrong choice all those years ago."

Myra blushed. She tried to glare but Jake could see the glow of warmth in her eyes when she looked at Archer.

Jake took the mug of tea Clare was handing to him. "Thanks," he said.

He took a cautious sip. The brew was hot and bracing.

"Okay, folks," he said. "We now know that, between them, Mr. and Mrs. Glazebrook managed to single-handedly deflect a top-secret J&J investigation. I, for one, have no plans to mention this little glitch to anyone, as it would make me look like a complete idiot."

"That's not true," Archer said.

"Yes, it is," Jake said. "So, moving right along, let's see if we can reconstruct this puzzle. In light of recent events, I'm going to assume, until proven otherwise, that Brad McAllister was murdered because of his connection to the new cabal."

"What about Valerie's death?" Clare asked.

"That's still an open question as far as I'm concerned," he said. "I admit I don't like the coincidence of both Brad and his mother winding up dead. On the other hand, Valerie was clearly getting more and more obsessed, and everyone knows that she was using booze and pills. But the real piece of evidence that makes me doubt that she was connected to the cabal is that the two attempts she made on your life can only be described as clumsy."

"Hey," Clare interrupted. "You may have your definition of 'clumsy' but let me tell you, I've got my own."

Archer looked at her. "What Jake means is that neither attempt had the stamp of a sophisticated cabal operation."

Clare looked at Jake for confirmation.

"He's right," Jake said. "I know the incidents were frightening, but they were both the sort of actions you'd expect from a maddened crazy person acting on impulse, not a calculating killer."

"Okay, point taken." Clare looked at his arm. "But what about what happened to you last night? Going to write that off as an impulse?"

"I'm not sure yet," Jake said.

"What do you mean?" Clare demanded. "Someone shot you with a high-powered rifle, for heaven's sake. We're not talking parking garages and dumbbells here."

"The guy definitely knew what he was doing," Jake said. "He was a good shot and he was careful to use a deer hunting rifle, not a weapon that might have made the local cops think they had a professional killer running around the neighborhood. It wasn't exactly an act of impulse but I think it may have been a case of someone seizing an opportunity."

"There's a difference?" Elizabeth asked.

"Yes," Jake said. "A guy who has set a long-range plan in motion and thinks someone is about to put the strategy in jeopardy might look for an opening to take out the problem in the quickest, most efficient manner."

"Nothing more efficient than a rifle,"

Archer noted. "Trouble is, here in Arizona that leaves you with a whole lot of suspects."

"I know," Jake said. He felt a pleasant tingle across his senses. "But I'm going with a glass-half-full attitude here. Getting shot at last night is one of the few good breaks I've had since I arrived in Stone Canyon."

Clare shuddered. "If almost getting killed is your idea of catching a break, I'd hate to see what you call bad news."

"What happens next?" Elizabeth asked.

"A whole lot of stuff," Jake said. "First, I'll contact J&J and have the analysts take another look at the murder of Brad McAllister. I think it's a safe bet they missed something the first time around. Also, it probably goes without saying but I'm going to say it anyway. No one in this room is to breathe a word of what we talked about here to anyone who isn't in this room right now. Understood?"

There was a series of somber nods.

Jake heard the burble of his cell phone. He took it out of his pocket and glanced at the coded identity of the caller.

"Jones & Jones," he said to the others. "I asked Fallon to see if he could locate Kimberley Todd and Dr. Ronald Mowbray. Maybe we're going to get lucky again." He took the call. "What have you got for me, Fallon?"

"Not much on Kimberley Todd, yet," Fallon said. "All I can tell you at this point is that she isn't a registered member of the Society. But it wasn't too hard to track down Mowbray. He's a level-five sensitive who makes his living fleecing seniors in various retirement communities. Looks like he's been working in Tucson for the past year. Before that he was in Florida. He rarely stays more than a year in any one location. It takes that long to establish the scam, attract the victims and persuade them to turn over their life savings."

Jake took out a pen and reached for the notepad on the counter. "What name is he using in Tucson?"

"Nelson Ingle. Ingle Investments."

Fallon rattled off the address.

"Thanks," Jake said. "Keep looking for Kimberley Todd. She's important."

"I will, but at the moment she seems to have fallen off the face of the planet. Anything else?"

"No, but someone took a shot at me last night so I think we're finally making progress."

There was a short pause.

"You okay?" Fallon asked.

"A few stitches, that's all."

"Want me to send in backup?"

"If you do our guy will probably spot whoever you send. This is a small town. Tell you
what, let me talk to Ingle first. Maybe afterward I'll have a better idea of what I'm going
to need."

"All right. Stay in touch."

"I will." He realized that Clare was glaring
at the phone.

"Hang on," Fallon said. "One more thing.
What about the Lancaster woman? Any
problems there?"

"Not for me," Jake said. "But you may
have one eventually."

"What the hell does that mean?"

Jake smiled at Clare. "I think she's pretty
well decided that there's no point sending in
any more applications to J&J. She's going to
open her own psychic detective agency."

"She's going to do *what?*"

"Something about not wanting to work for
you after all."

"She mentioned me specifically?" Fallon
said cautiously.

"Let's just say that the word 'dumbass' and
your name all appear in the same sentence
with some frequency."

"She called me a dumbass?" Fallon was
clearly baffled. "She's never even met me."

"You've never met her, either," Jake said.
"But that didn't stop you from rejecting

every application she sent in. That's it for now, Fallon. I'll call you later and let you know how things are going."

"Hold on here, just one damn minute. About the Lancaster woman —"

"Gotta run."

"Don't hang up on me. Damn it, Jake —"

Jake ended the call and looked at the others. "They found Dr. Ronald Mowbray. He's in Tucson, running a scam under the name Ingle. I'm going to track him down this afternoon."

"I'm coming, too," Elizabeth announced.

Archer got to his feet. "I'll ride shotgun."

Myra frowned. "I will accompany you, also. I have a few things to say to him."

Jake surveyed the ring of determined faces. "I usually work alone."

"Guess what," Clare said. "This time you've got a team."

Resistance was futile, Jake thought. There wasn't much that could stand up to a united Glazebrook front. The only thing he could do was try to stay in charge.

"All right," he said. "But we do this my way."

Clare smiled slowly. "Actually, it might work better if we did it my way. I'm the expert when it comes to dealing with scam artists, remember?"

CHAPTER FORTY

The office of Ingle Investments was located in a strip mall on Tucson's east side. With its faux-adobe architecture, red-tile roof trim, shaded sidewalks and acres of parking, the row of stores and boutiques looked like every other strip mall Clare had seen in Arizona.

"Not exactly upscale office space for an investment firm," she said, surveying the stores through the windshield. She could see a couple of casual clothing boutiques, a bakery, an ice cream shop and some small eateries.

"But not cheap, either," Jake said. He studied the door of Ingle Investments. "Looks like he prefers to maintain a low profile."

The trip from Phoenix had taken a good two hours. Jake would no doubt have made better time but Clare had done the driving because of his injured arm. She had been intensely aware of the controlled anticipation simmering inside him every mile along the way. Something similar had sparked all her senses, too.

They were both dressed casually. She was in what had become her Arizona uniform: black trousers and a T-shirt. Jake wore a denim shirt that covered the bandage and a pair of khakis. Aside from the fact that he kept his left arm close to his side, there was nothing to indicate he had been injured.

"He's trying to project an approachable, reassuring image," Clare said. "His clientele consists of seniors who are living on fixed incomes and hoarding their savings for the kids. His prime target will be a little old lady who is widowed or divorced. She has her Social Security, maybe a small pension from her years teaching school, some income from the investments that she and her husband made over the years and the money she got when she sold the family home. That's what he'll go after."

"The money she made off the real estate?"

Clare nodded. "It will be sitting in a bank somewhere, probably in nice, safe certificates of deposit. She doesn't want to put it at risk because she's determined to leave an inheritance for her children. Nelson Ingle's prime objective will be to convince her that her money will be just as safe in one of his investment schemes. He'll guarantee to triple or quadruple the interest income."

Jake turned his head to look at her through the shield of his dark glasses. "You know guys like this."

She shrugged. "You read predators. I read liars. Whatever else he is, we know for a fact that Nelson Ingle is a liar."

Jake looked at the door again. "I lied to you."

"I know." She smiled faintly. "You were good at it, too. Takes a lot of talent to keep me guessing."

"So, do you hate my guts now that you know the truth?" he asked, still watching the door.

Startled, she turned slightly in the seat. Jake's profile could have been carved in granite.

"You're talking about the fact that you didn't mention that you happen to be working for Jones & Jones, aren't you?" she asked.

"Yes."

"Good grief. Why would I hate you? You have a job to do."

He turned his head to look at her with hard eyes. "You were never supposed to be part of the job."

"But I became part of it. Not your fault. It's all right, Jake. I understand."

"You really do have a slightly offbeat philosophy on the subject of lying, don't you?"

"Like I said, the ability to lie is a tool, as far as I'm concerned. What matters is context."

He started to smile.

"That does not mean, however, that I have changed my mind about Fallon Jones," she added crisply.

His teeth gleamed in a wolfish grin. "I don't give a damn how you feel about Fallon as long as you'll still sleep with me."

"I'm glad you have your priorities straight. Now, I think we should postpone the rest of this conversation until a more convenient time. This is where we get to corner one of the bad guys and scare him into spilling all his evil secrets, remember?"

"Yeah," Jake said. "This is the fun part."

"You know, you remind me of those coyotes that come around hunting in the morning."

"Is my tongue hanging out yet? I hate it when my tongue hangs out. Kind of embarrassing."

"I don't see any tongue."

"That's good." He unbuckled his seat belt, cracked open the door and got out. "Let's do this."

She braced for the blast of heat and opened her own door.

Jake joined her on the sidewalk. Together they went to the front door of Ingle Investments. Jake pushed open the door with his good arm.

A draft of arctic air enveloped Clare. She took off her dark glasses and did a quick assessment.

Ingle's office could only be described as nondescript. The carpeting was beige. A couple of standard-issue Arizona-sunset paintings hung on the walls. There were two chairs and a low table. A newspaper and some magazines were neatly stacked on the table. There was no receptionist.

The door to the inner office was closed. Clare could hear low voices on the other side.

An elderly woman with a helmet of tight gray curls sat in one of the two client chairs. She peered suspiciously at Clare and Jake through her reading glasses.

"Mr. Ingle's with a client," she announced loudly. "I'm next."

"Thank you for telling us," Clare said politely.

Reassured that the newcomers weren't showing any signs of trying to move to the head of the line, the woman relaxed.

"Hot enough for you?" she asked.

"It certainly is," Clare said.

"Gonna be a real scorcher tomorrow," the woman assured her. "Heard it on the news this morning. Lucky we're not over there in Phoenix. Always ten degrees hotter there than it is here."

"Heard that," Jake said.

The door to the inner office opened. A distinguished-looking man in his mid-forties held it for a white-haired lady who was pushing a walker. The man had to be Ingle, Clare decided. He was just as Elizabeth had described. Patrician and conservatively dressed in a white shirt and tie, he had the air of an old-fashioned family lawyer. The kind of guy most people would trust on sight, she thought.

But not her.

"Good-bye, Mrs. Donnelly," Ingle said in a rich, warm tone. "It was a pleasure to meet you. I hope I was able to answer your questions about the investment to your satisfaction."

"Yes, you did, Mr. Ingle." The woman beamed, clearly pleased with whatever had been said about the investment. "It sounds like just what I've been looking for."

"Please don't hesitate to give me a call if you have any more questions," Ingle said. "Otherwise, I'll see you on Friday. I'll have the papers drawn up and ready to sign."

"I just want to be sure that my money will be safe," Mrs. Donnelly said. "At my age one can't afford to risk the principal, you know."

"It will be rock-solid safe and insured, just like in a bank." Ingle smiled. "But you will have the advantage of making at least twenty-five percent return on your money."

The lie fell into the ultraviolet range.

Unpleasant little frissons of energy snapped across Clare's senses, sparking the familiar, nerve-jarring fight-or-flight response. Ingle enjoyed his work. The unwholesome lust that tainted the energy pulsing from him sent shivers through her.

Automatically she fought the jangling mental alarms that threatened to overwhelm her senses. *Fight, not flight.*

Outrage kicked in on cue, dampening the panic.

She glanced at Jake. Energy was coming off him in waves. Of course, it didn't take any special sensitivity to recognize Ingle's blatant deception. No legitimate investment adviser could guarantee a twenty-five percent return on a *safe, insured* investment, not in this market. That kind of profit could only be had at the price of taking a huge financial risk — just the sort of risk that a person living on a modest fixed income had no business taking.

In all fairness, Claire thought, as far as Ingle was concerned, the woman's money wasn't going to be put at risk. The senior's life savings were undoubtedly destined for Ingle's own private offshore bank account.

Clare looked at Mrs. Donnelly. "Never believe anyone who tells you he can get you that kind of return on a supposedly insured investment," she said. "Ingle is lying through his teeth."

There was an audible gasp from the woman seated in the reception room.

Mrs. Donnelly's jaw sagged. "What on earth?"

"Leave this to me, Mrs. Donnelly," Ingle said, righteously stern. He took an ominous step toward Clare. "I don't know who you are, but I do know that you have no right to be here. I'm going to call the police."

"Suit yourself," Clare said. "But first you're going to talk to me and my associate."

Ingle frowned at Jake. Jake smiled.

Ingle took what looked like an unconscious step back. He glanced at Clare. "Just who the hell do you think you are?"

She reached inside her purse, extracted her wallet and flipped it open to display her driver's license.

"Clare Lancaster, Arizona State Anti-Fraud Bureau," she said briskly. She snapped the wallet closed before Ingle could get a close look at it. "We're here to talk to you about a little matter of investment fraud, Ingle."

"*Fraud?*" Mrs. Donnelly repeated, alarmed.

"What's this?" The woman in the chair grabbed her cane and struggled to stand. "Did you say 'fraud'?"

Ingle's initial alarm gave way to anger. "There is no such thing as an Arizona State Anti-Fraud Bureau."

"Okay," she said easily. "Make it the Arizona State Anti–Fraudulent Licenses Bureau, Dr. Ronald Mowbray."

"See here," Mrs. Donnelly said. "Mr. Ingle's not a doctor."

"He certainly isn't," Clare agreed. "But he recently posed as one in Phoenix."

Shock and something that might have been fear flashed across Ingle's aristocratic features.

Now that was interesting, she thought. Ingle knew her license was a fake, but the mention of his stint as a phony shrink had unnerved him a lot more than the reference to his investment scams.

"Who are you people?" he demanded. His gaze flitted uneasily back and forth between Clare and Jake. "What do you want?"

"We should probably have this chat in private," Jake said. He looked at the two seniors. "Ladies, if you'll excuse us?"

"Now, hold on," Ingle said quickly. "There's no need for them to leave."

He really was afraid, Clare realized. So much so that he actually wanted the two women to stay. Maybe he thought their presence offered some protection.

Jake moved, gliding toward Ingle with the lethal grace of the hunter closing in on prey. Clare felt the familiar brush of unseen energy lifting the hair on the nape of her neck.

Ingle probably felt it, too. He was a sensitive, after all. He fell back another couple of steps. Jake pursued him into the inner office.

Clare followed quickly, closing the door on the astonished faces of the two women.

"You can't do this," Ingle said. Panic roughened his voice.

"Sit," Clare said.

"You're the scam artists, not me," Ingle shot back, desperate. "How dare you barge in here like this?"

"You heard the lady," Jake said. "Sit."

Ingle swallowed hard. He turned, went very quickly behind his desk and sat down abruptly.

Jake moved again, as fast or even faster than the first time. It seemed to Clare that in

392

the blink of an eye he had circled the desk and grabbed Ingle's right wrist.

"No guns," Jake said.

He opened the drawer that Ingle had been reaching for and removed a pistol. Then he made a quick check of the rest of the drawers and felt around under the desktop. When he was satisfied, he stood back, holding the gun loosely at his side.

"Put your hands on the desk," he said to Ingle. "Leave them there where I can see them."

Clare looked at Jake, raising her brows inquiringly.

He shook his head. "Pretty sure this wasn't the pistol that was used to kill McAllister or anyone else, for that matter. There aren't any traces on it. It's clean."

"What are you talking about?" Ingle yelped. "I didn't kill McAllister."

Clare turned back to him. "Somebody did."

"Not me." Ingle seemed to fold in on himself. He flattened his palms on the desk. "All right, I understand what's going on here. Let's get to the bottom line. What's this going to cost me?"

Clare sat down in one of two client chairs and crossed her legs. "You're going to get off cheap. All we want are answers."

"Bullshit." Ingle rallied a little. "I know a couple of blackmailers when I see them. You want money."

"No." She smiled coldly. "Just answers."

"About what?" he asked warily.

"Let's start with your role as Dr. Ronald Mowbray in Phoenix," Clare said.

Ingle looked at her for a moment and then turned to Jake. "First, tell me who I'm dealing with."

"I'm with Jones & Jones," Jake said.

Ingle was startled. "I haven't done anything to attract the attention of Jones & Jones."

"Yes," Jake said, "you have. Otherwise, I wouldn't be here, would I?"

Ingle regarded him carefully. "What are you? One of the throwbacks they say work for J&J?"

Clare was on her feet without conscious thought. She swept past Jake and came to a halt in front of the desk. Planting her palms on the gleaming surface not far from Ingle's hands, she leaned forward and lowered her voice.

"Mr. Salter is not a throwback," she said. "He is an *investigative consultant.* You will show him respect. Is that understood?"

"Hell, everyone knows about the exotics Jones & Jones uses," Ingle said.

394

"Let me put it this way," Clare interrupted. "If you do not show Mr. Salter the appropriate degree of professional respect, I will see to it that you are turned over to the Tucson police this afternoon along with all the evidence they will need to send you to jail for fraud. Your name and face will be on the evening news and in tomorrow morning's papers. Do we have an understanding, Ingle?"

Ingle's jaw flexed a couple of times. "Certainly, Miss Lancaster. Whatever you say. I am, of course, happy to cooperate with Jones & Jones."

The sarcasm was only barely concealed but she decided to let it go. Time was a factor, after all.

She took her hands off the desk, turned and walked back to her chair. Out of the corner of her eye she could see that Jake was amused. She flushed. As if he needed her to defend him, she thought.

For the second time she sat down and crossed her legs.

"Now then, about your career as Dr. Ronald Mowbray," she said to Ingle.

Ingle seemed to relax a little. He was obviously less concerned now that he knew Clare and Jake were connected to Jones & Jones. *What did he fear more than the Arcane Soci-*

ety's investigators? Clare wondered.

"Brad McAllister contacted me," Ingle said. "He told me that he wanted me to play the part of a shrink for a couple of months. Said it would only require two days a week and that it wouldn't interfere with my business here in Tucson."

"Were you two acquainted before he contacted you?" Clare asked.

"No," Ingle said. He smiled humorlessly. "We weren't exactly in the same league. McAllister was a major player. He must have made millions over the years. In case you didn't notice, my clients don't come from the higher tax brackets."

"How did McAllister know you'd be a good candidate for the scam in Phoenix?" Jake asked.

Ingle shrugged. "He said he'd heard about me. Admired my work. He made me an offer I couldn't refuse. When he told me he was running an operation involving the Glazebrook family, I had some second thoughts. Like I said, I'm not used to playing in those circles. But everything went off like clockwork, at least at first."

"Then what happened?" Clare asked.

Ingle smiled coldly. "Then you showed up, Miss Lancaster. You snatched Elizabeth away so fast, McAllister was left flailing.

Took him a while to understand what had hit him. Congratulations. I doubt if many people were capable of taking him by surprise."

Clare stilled. "He talked to you about me?"

"Yes," Ingle said. "He told me that you were a problem that he had not anticipated but eventually he indicated that he had a plan to deal with you. Frankly, I more or less expected you to suffer an unfortunate but highly convenient accident. When McAllister turned up dead instead I figured you'd just moved a little faster than he had, that's all."

"You thought I killed McAllister?" she asked.

He elevated one brow. "You were the one who found the body. I knew you had a motive. You wanted to save Elizabeth from McAllister's clutches. True, it wasn't the motive that the rumors attributed to you, but it seemed like a reasonable one to me."

"You knew that I wasn't having an affair with Brad McAllister," she said.

"Didn't seem very likely under the circumstances."

Jake watched him with a feral stare. "You were aware that Miss Lancaster was in mortal danger from McAllister but you made no move to warn her?"

"I assure you it was just guesswork on my

part," Ingle said, politely innocent. He grimaced. "Not like I knew what the guy was really thinking. I doubt if anyone knew what was going on in McAllister's head. The longer I worked with him, the more I realized he was some kind of wack job."

Clare leaned forward slightly. "Why do you say that?"

"Hard to explain." Ingle reflected briefly. "At first he came across as another pro. Talked a lot about how we were in the same business. He said I was too good to be working at such a low level. Made me feel like I was his equal. I knew it wasn't true but for some reason he actually convinced me that I could become what he was, a serious player."

"In other words," Jake said, "he conned you, just like he conned everyone else."

Ingle's mouth twisted. "There's an old saying to the effect that the easiest person to sell to is another salesman."

"Or, in this case," Clare said coolly, "the easiest person to scam is another scam artist."

"I, of course, prefer the term 'salesman,'" Ingle said.

"I suspect that McAllister was a hypnotist of some kind," Clare continued. "A powerful one. What do you think?"

"That possibility crossed my mind after I

saw how he had dazzled everyone in Stone Canyon, including Archer Glazebrook," Ingle admitted. "I once asked him about his particular talent."

"What did he tell you?" Jake asked.

"He claimed he was a sensitive but not a strong one. A four on the Jones Scale. Good with numbers and strategy."

"Everything he *told* you was probably a lie," Clare said. "But what about the things you observed?"

Ingle's brows crinkled. "I beg your pardon?"

"You've been a successful scam artist for several years," she said. "You obviously have some talent for the business."

His expression hardened. "What are you implying?"

"Only that you must be a very good observer of human nature." She injected a note of admiration into her tone. A pro on the opposite side of the fence letting another pro know that she respected his skills. "Don't tell me what he told you about himself. Tell me what you *saw.* If you were sizing him up as a prospect for your little investment plan, how would you approach him?"

"Are you kidding?" Ingle uttered a short, harsh laugh. "I wouldn't have touched him."

"Why not?"

Ingle gave that a moment of serious reflection. Then he exhaled softly. "Miss Lancaster, my skill lies in being able to discern what a prospect wants most and then convincing that prospect that I can deliver it. But I never did figure out what Brad McAllister wanted. And that's why I would not have targeted him for any of my investment opportunities. The reason I have survived this long is because I have been very careful when it comes to selecting my, uh, clients."

Clare was aware that Jake was watching Ingle with the rapt attention of a predator getting ready to go for the throat.

"I would have thought it was obvious what McAllister wanted," Clare said. "He was after his wife's inheritance, half of Glazebrook, Inc."

"I don't doubt that was his immediate goal," Ingle agreed. "What I could never figure out was why he wanted it."

"Money?" Jake asked neutrally.

"McAllister had money, a lot of it," Ingle said. "If he wanted more, he could have set up another one of his astonishingly successful investment schemes. Trust me when I tell you that in our line he was considered a true artist. He also had a reputation for working alone. Why take on a risky project like going

400

after Glazebrook, Inc.? I mean, think about it. Doping the daughter of a prominent family and trying to convince everyone that she was crazy? Talk about extreme."

"Yet he got you to assist him," Clare pointed out.

Ingle winced. "When I look back on it, I still can't believe I allowed him to drag me into that project. He really must have been a hypnotist. A damned strong one, as you say."

"There are only a few objectives that would make a guy like McAllister go to all that trouble," Jake said. "Money, power and love are the top three."

Ingle nearly choked. "You can forget love as a motivator. Believe me, McAllister didn't have anything resembling sentimental feelings for anyone."

"Not even his mother, Valerie Shipley?" Clare asked.

Ingle blinked and turned thoughtful again. "Valerie Shipley was probably the only person on earth McAllister actually trusted. But I wouldn't go so far as to say that he loved her. She doted on him, however. I'll admit I'm not a real psychiatrist, but even I could see that she was obsessed with him in a manner that could only be described as unhealthy. She would have done anything for him and McAllister knew it. He used that weakness to manipulate her."

"We know McAllister had a lover," Clare said. "A massage therapist who worked at the Secret Springs Day Spa in Phoenix."

"Doesn't surprise me that he was screwing someone," Ingle said. He started to move one hand in a dismissive gesture, caught Jake watching and hurriedly flattened his palm on the desktop again. "But I can guarantee you that he wasn't in love with her."

"All right, that brings us back to money and power as motivators," Clare said.

Ingle met her eyes. "I'm not saying McAllister did not want those things. He certainly did. But I got the impression that he didn't want Glazebrook, Inc., just because it was a lucrative enterprise. It was more than that. I think he *needed* the company."

"Why?" Clare asked.

Ingle shook his head. "Damned if I know. All I can tell you is that there was a lot going on beneath the surface with Brad McAllister. Speaking personally, I was not inclined to look too deeply."

"When did you start to get nervous?" Clare asked.

"When you came along and it became obvious that things were falling apart. It made me extremely uneasy when I realized that McAllister wasn't going to do what most

people in our profession do under those circumstances."

Clare understood. "He didn't shut down
the operation and disappear."

"Exactly," Ingle said. "When his wife left
him and filed for divorce, I thought for sure
McAllister would pull the plug. It's what I
would have done. Instead —"

"Instead, what?" Clare prompted.

Ingle made a small, fluttering motion with
one elegantly manicured nail. "Well, I won't
say he panicked. He was too much of a pro
for that. But he definitely became extremely
agitated. He seemed absolutely obsessed
with salvaging what was clearly an unsal-
vageable operation. I know this is going to
sound weird, but it was almost as if —"

Jake's eyes tightened a little. "As if?"

Ingle spread his hands. "As if failure was
not an option. But that should not have been
the case, not for an expert. One must always
be prepared to abandon a project if it turns
sour. It is the first law of survival in the profession."

"Do you think he might have been working
for someone else?" Clare asked. "Someone
who would not tolerate failure?"

Ingle frowned. "Hard to imagine McAllister taking orders, to be honest. I'll tell you
one thing, though."

"What's that?" Clare asked.

"If he was working for someone it would have been because that person could give him something that he wanted very, very badly. Something he could not get on his own. And if you're not the one who killed him, Miss Lancaster — ?"

"Wasn't me," Clare said.

"Then the only other likely possibility is the one you hinted at. Perhaps McAllister was killed because he had failed."

Jake looked at him. "Does that mean you don't buy the interrupted burglary scenario, either?"

"No," Ingle said, "I don't. You may have noticed that I closed down the office of Dr. Ronald Mowbray the morning after the news of his murder hit the papers. The only reason I went back at all was to make certain I had not left anything behind that could be used to track me down." He grimaced. "Clearly I missed something. Mind telling me how you found me?"

"The J&J analysts located you," Jake said.

Ingle sighed. "Of course."

Clare contemplated things for another moment and then got to her feet. "All right, I think that does it."

Ingle watched her uneasily. "We have a deal, right? You said you wouldn't go to the cops if I told you what I know."

"Relax." She slung her purse over her shoulder and nodded at Jake, indicating that it was time to leave. "We're not going to report you to the local police."

"What about Jones & Jones?" Ingle asked, darting an uneasy glance at Jake.

Jake smiled his wide, cold, predator's smile. "It isn't Jones & Jones you have to worry about now, Inglc. You've got a more pressing problem."

"What the hell is that supposed to mean?" Ingle demanded.

Clare opened the door, allowing him a clear view of the three people waiting in his reception room.

"Meet the family," she said, gesturing toward Archer, Myra and Elizabeth with a small flourish. "Sure the Glazebrooks are a little dysfunctional, but hey, what family isn't?"

Archer stalked into the office. Myra and Elizabeth were right behind him.

"So you're the son of a bitch who tried to make us think our daughter was going crazy," Archer said softly.

"Hello, Dr. Mowbray," Elizabeth said with an unholy smile. "I'm sure you'll be pleased to know that I've made a miraculous recovery."

Myra gave Ingle a look that would have frozen whole oceans. "Rest assured, after today you won't be doing any more business here in Arizona."

"No, wait." Ingle leaped to his feet, horrified. "You don't understand. I cooperated with Jones & Jones."

"Here's the bad news," Archer said. "We're not with Jones & Jones. This is personal."

CHAPTER FORTY-ONE

"I hope Archer doesn't do anything too violent to Ingle," Clare said. She cast a worried glance back toward the closed door of Ingle Investments before she reversed out of the parking space. "I know he'd like nothing better than to beat that bastard to a pulp. I don't blame him. But the last thing we need now is a lot of attention from the police and the press."

"Don't worry," Jake said. "Archer is a strategist, remember?"

"So?"

"So he isn't going to take his revenge physically. At least not to the extent that it might land Ingle in the ER. It wouldn't do much good to turn him over to the cops, either."

Clare made a face. "Scam artists always seem to skate. It's a white-collar crime, after all. Worst-case scenario is that you get out on bail and leave the country. Even if you do wind up in court a lot of your victims won't testify because they feel humiliated. That's especially true of seniors."

"Because they're afraid to let their adult children know they've been conned?"

"Yes. They're terrified that the kids will conclude they're losing it." She glanced at him. "What *is* Archer going to do?"

Jake savored a little rush of satisfaction. "He's going to destroy Ingle in the way it will hurt the most."

"Professionally?"

"Right," Jake said. "First he'll force him to turn over the codes to his offshore accounts and a list of people who got bilked here in Tucson and in past schemes, so that as much as possible of the money that was stolen can be repaid."

"That's probably a heck of a lot more than the police could accomplish," Clare said.

"When that's done, Archer will put a scare into Ingle."

"How?"

"By informing him that Jones & Jones will be adding his name to its Watch List. If Ingle goes back to his old ways, the analysts will notice fairly quickly. They'll see to it that local law enforcement is notified. That will keep Ingle on the move, if nothing else. It's a form of harassment, but it is fairly effective. J&J uses it to deter guys like him who try to put their talents to use fleecing folks and committing other kinds of low-level crimes."

"Didn't know Jones & Jones had a Watch List."

"Probably because you didn't ever go to work for them."

"Blame Dumbass Fallon Jones for that." Clare paused for a stoplight and gave him a quick, searching look. "Are you okay?"

"Yeah, sure." He did a quick staccato with his fingers on the seat, realized what he was doing and made himself stop. "Still running hot, that's all."

She surprised him with a small laugh. "Call of the wild, huh?"

He wasn't sure how to take that. "You think it's funny?"

"No, of course not. Sorry." The light changed. She accelerated smoothly through the intersection. "But I don't think it's such a big deal, either."

He studied the street scene. He couldn't *help* but examine it. His senses were still on full alert, which meant that he was automatically registering the details of his immediate environment, looking for a threat, seeking prey. The phrase "call of the wild" was uncomfortably close to the mark.

Throwback.

Then he thought about how Clare had leaped to his defense when Ingle called him that. Some of the prowling tension inside him started to ease.

"What's it like for you?" he asked quietly.

She did not ask him what he meant.

"When I first came into my parasenses and awoke to a world full of lies I had wave after wave of uncontrollable panic attacks," she said.

"That was before you learned to filter the lies?"

"Yes. The Arcane House experts have very little experience in dealing with my type of sensitivity because it's so rare. But eventually a parapsychologist realized that my particular senses are hardwired to the good old fight-or-flight response."

"Sure," he said, thinking it through. "Lies, in general, even the harmless type, always represent a potential threat, after all. You were reacting appropriately."

"My therapist helped me create a psychic filter. It wasn't easy. But the only alternative was to become a total hermit so that I could avoid all lies."

"Sure glad you didn't go that route."

She smiled. "Me, too."

"You were good back there with Ingle," he said. "You worked him brilliantly."

"Not the first time I've dealt with scam artists."

"That was obvious. Fallon sure screwed up by not hiring you."

"That is certainly my opinion."

Jake settled back a little, shutting down his senses with an act of will. He needed to think and he didn't always do his best thinking when he was running hot. One of the downsides to being a hunter.

"You know," he said, "that part about McAllister getting agitated when the Glazebrook operation went south but refusing to call it off was interesting."

"Yes, it was. Very interesting. Ingle was right. Most scammers in that situation would have disappeared. There must have been a very compelling reason to make a professional con stick with a bad project after it became clear that it would probably fail."

"I keep coming back to the possibility that failure was not an option. Historically, the Arcane Society cabals have been very Darwinian organizations. If you want to ascend to the higher levels, you have to prove yourself every step of the way by accomplishing certain tasks that are assigned by the guys at the top."

"If Brad McAllister was working for this

new cabal it means that the organization must have sent him to acquire control of Glazebrook," Clare said. "He may have been executed when it became clear that he had failed. In which case, the killer is probably long gone."

"Maybe," Jake agreed. "But I'm not going to close any more doors; I made that mistake back at the beginning of the investigation. Once was enough."

"I keep wondering where Kimberley Todd fits into this thing," Clare mused.

"You and me both. The fact that the analysts at J&J haven't been able to find her yet may mean that she's dead and buried somewhere out in the desert. Part of a cleanup operation after the project failed."

Clare shuddered. "Think they got rid of her because she knew too much?"

"It's a possibility."

"Maybe that's why Valerie Shipley was killed, too. You heard what Ingle said. She was the one person Brad trusted. The cabal might have been worried that he confided the plan to her." Clare tensed. "Good grief, I just thought of something."

"What?"

"I wonder if Owen Shipley is in any danger. After all, he was married to Valerie. The cabal may decide he knows too much, too."

Jake contemplated that briefly. "Elizabeth was married to Brad, but so far there's been no attempt on her life. My guess is the cabal crowd would rather avoid gunning down every prominent resident of Stone Canyon who ever got near McAllister. It would attract way too much attention."

"Someone tried to gun you down yesterday," she reminded him.

"I know. But I'm not a pillar of the community. I'm just a passing consultant. Here today, gone tomorrow."

She slanted him a disapproving glance. "I wish you didn't sound so cheerful when you talk about someone trying to murder you in cold blood."

"Sorry. Like I said, it tells me that I'm getting close."

"Wonder why the cabal wanted Glazebrook, Inc., so badly."

"In case you haven't noticed, it happens to be an extremely profitable company," Jake said. "Every organization needs money."

"Yes, but why Glazebrook? There must be hundreds if not thousands of very successful businesses that generate plenty of cash."

"But not all are closely held, family-owned enterprises that can be quietly taken over without arousing the attention of a board of directors, shareholders and government watchdogs."

"I see what you mean," she said. "Nevertheless, it can't be a complete coincidence that the cabal chose a very successful company that just happens to be owned by a member of the Society."

"No big mystery there," Jake said. "The leader or leaders of the cabal would naturally be inclined to go after companies they can research thoroughly. The genealogy records at Arcane House are open to all members of the Society."

"Members do tend to marry other members," Clare said. "They often form partnerships and close friendships with people connected to the Society. You're right, the cabal would have been able to provide an enormous amount of background material to McAllister before he made his attempt to grab Glazebrook."

"All right," Jake said. "So much for looking at the deaths of McAllister and his mother from a cabal conspiracy point of view. Let's try another approach."

"Such as?"

"I wonder if we're working too hard to connect them both to the cabal."

Clare frowned. "I thought we agreed they had to be connected."

"It's a possibility, not a fact. Until you

414

know for sure, you have to be able to step back and come at the problem from different directions."

"Is that something they teach you at Jones & Jones?"

"No," Jake said. "I learned it the hard way over the years."

"Okay, let's try your approach. Who else would have had a motive to murder Valerie?"

He looked at her. "If you were not a devout conspiracy theorist and if I wasn't a hotshot undercover investigator for Jones & Jones who was sent out to track down a cabal freak, we'd be looking at an entirely different scenario to explain Valerie Shipley's death."

"Think she really did commit suicide?"

"That is still a possibility," he said. "But if that isn't the answer then we've been over-looking the most obvious suspect, the one person who is always at the top of everyone's list when a wife is murdered."

"Oh Lord, of course." Clare's hands clenched around the steering wheel. "The husband."

CHAPTER FORTY-TWO

Moonlight glinted on the tile roof of the large house. Jake studied the Shipley residence from the cover of a shallow arroyo. The bright moon meant that he would have to take extra care approaching the residence, but once inside it would be an advantage. Together with his jacked-up senses he would not even need the flashlight he had tucked into a pocket.

Clare had spent the evening trying to talk him out of his plan to search the Shipley house but he knew that, underneath the anxiety, she understood as clearly as he did that this was one of the few alternatives they had left.

Tonight was the obvious night to do the job because Owen had been invited out to dinner by Alison Henton, one of the many sympathetic, deeply concerned divorcées in Stone Canyon who were lining up to comfort and console him. Jake had seen enough of Alison in action at the country club during the past two weeks to know that Owen would be lucky to escape before midnight.

He made his way along the dry wash to the point that was closest to the house. There he halted again, pushing his senses to the limit. There was, as always, a lot of activity going on in the desert at that hour, but as far as he could tell nothing human moved in the vicinity of the house.

His preternatural instincts objected to the short dash through the open to the sheltering shadows at the side of the house. He suppressed the atavistic dislike of being exposed in the moonlight long enough to get to his destination.

His night vision was excellent. He could walk through the deepest shadows at the side of the house without fear of bumping into objects or tripping over a hose.

Contrary to the rumors about his kind, it wasn't quite the equivalent of being able to see in the dark and it wasn't like using night vision goggles, either. His eyes were human, after all, not those of a cat or an owl. They could only do so much with minimal illumination. But his psychic abilities afforded him a different way of perceiving objects and other living things when there was little light available.

He stopped at the side door. He had a clear idea of the layout of the interior of the residence because he had grilled Myra and Archer earlier that evening. Both had been frequent visitors to the Shipley home over the years.

Best of all, the Glazebrooks had a key to the house and the code to silence the alarm. He could have gotten in without those assets, thanks to the small J&J tool kit he carried, but having them made things easier. Owen had given both the key and the code to the Glazebrooks years ago in the event of an emergency while he was out of town.

He pulled on the plastic medical gloves he had brought with him and took the key out of his pocket. He opened the door and moved quickly into the hall. The alarm pad was right where Archer had said it would be.

He closed the door and punched in the code, disarming the system.

Slowly, he walked through the house, registering impressions on both the normal and paranormal planes.

He was searching for the special emanations of psi energy that clung to scenes where violence had taken place. But that was not all he hoped to find. He was here to do some old-fashioned detective work. In his experience that was usually what it came down to in the end.

People were people, regardless of whether or not they possessed a degree of psychic ability. The same emotions and motivations governed their actions. Once you knew an individual's agenda and had an idea of how far he or she would go to achieve it, you had all you really needed to know to close a case.

His goal tonight was to nail down Owen Shipley's agenda.

He replayed the conversation with Clare in his head.

"But why would Owen kill her?" she asked.

"I can think of a couple of reasons, starting with the obvious fact that she had become an embarrassing problem. The woman was a full-blown alcoholic and she was getting worse."

"If Owen wanted to get rid of her, he could have simply divorced her."

"Now, why would he do that when she had just inherited the bulk of McAllister's estate?"

"Oh. Good point." She paused. "On the other hand, Owen doesn't need Valerie's money. He's rich in his own right."

"As we have observed on previous occasions, that doesn't mean he might not want to get richer."

"I don't know," Clare said, dubious now. "Murder is a high-risk enterprise."

"Sure. So is sex with strangers, but people

do it for money all the time."

"One more small problem," Clare said. "Owen has an alibi. He was playing golf the afternoon that Valerie died, remember?"

"He was playing alone, in the middle of the afternoon on one of the hottest days of the year. He probably had the course to himself."

"And the Shipley house is located on the twelfth fairway."

"All he had to do was drive the cart into the arroyo behind the house, go inside long enough to drown Valerie and then return to the fairway to finish his game."

"Pretty cold."

"Yes," Jake said. "Ice cold."

Moonlight slanted through the windows of the pale great room. It didn't seem likely that Owen would conceal his secrets in such an open area where visitors came and went freely. But he decided to give the place a quick going-over before moving into the bedroom wing.

He studied the wet bar and the liquor cabinet. Chances were good that Valerie had made heavy use of those particular items of furniture.

He checked the drawers beneath the small sink first. They were filled with the paraphernalia associated with the preparation of cocktails: bottle openers, corkscrews, napkins and spoons.

He closed the bottom drawer and reached for the handle of the small refrigerator.

The faint but explosive traces of violent psychic energy crackled through him, leaving an invisible energy burn. His already heightened senses flared even higher, sharpening to a feverish intensity. The spoor of violence was not fresh, but it was not very old, either. He concentrated, trying to feel what the killer had experienced at the moment when he opened the refrigerator.

Thirsty. Heart pounding. Hot, dark excitement pumping through his blood . . .

Suddenly, he *knew* what had happened. Shipley had come in off the blistering hot golf course and found Valerie deep into a pitcher of martinis. Maybe she had taken one of her pills to calm down after the failed attempt on Clare at the spa. Shipley told her he stopped to get a bottle of water. The afternoon sun was unrelenting out on the course.

He had also been sweating, not just from the heat of the day but from the anticipation of what he was about to do. So he opened the small refrigerator and took out a bottle of water.

He no doubt overpowered Valerie easily

421

enough. He was a strong, athletic man. Valerie had been scrawny and frail from the months of heavy drinking.

He would have had to take a few minutes to go inside the house and change his clothes. Carefully he'd chosen a second pair of golf slacks and a shirt in the same colors as the pants and shirt he had been wearing when he started the round. Then he went back out onto the course.

He probably planned to finish the game and have a few drinks at the club with friends before inviting an acquaintance home for cocktails. That way he would have a witness with him when he "discovered" the body.

It must have come as a shock to be told that Valerie had been found much sooner than he had intended.

Clare had been right, Jake thought. Valerie was murdered. It also seemed logical that Shipley was the killer, but unfortunately there was no way to prove that yet.

The psychic spoor left by someone who had committed an act of violence was as distinctive as a fingerprint. But unlike a fingerprint, it was given off only when the individual was physically aroused by, and in the grip of, intense, violent emotions. The energy of such emotions was so strong that it resonated on the paranormal plane and clung to surfaces for a long time.

Jones & Jones would take his findings seriously, but psychic traces were not much good in a courtroom. *"Well, Your Honor, I was walking through the dead woman's house and I sensed the psi energy of her killer. Yeah, sure, I could identify him if he leaves any more of the same kind of energy behind. But he's got to be in a killing mood, if you see what I mean. What's that, Your Honor? Yes, as a matter of fact, I do think that I'm a psychic detective. Why do you ask?"*

There was a reason why members of the Society who wanted to lead normal lives did not go around claiming a connection to a group of people who all believed they had psychic powers. That kind of thing came under the heading of *family secrets.*

Now that he knew he was looking in the right place, it was time to find some more traditional evidence to turn over to the local police.

There was a large wine vault adjacent to the kitchen. He took the black leather case out of his pocket and used one of the items inside to unlock the door. It took a few minutes to go through the rows of elegantly stored bottles. He also looked inside the white wine chiller.

He found nothing except a lot of very expensive wine.

He let himself out of the vault and went down a wide hall that led to the other wing of the big house. Archer had told him that Shipley's study was the first door on the left. That seemed like a reasonable place to continue the search.

He paused when he caught sight of a small object sitting on an end table. A cell phone.

He crossed the living room and picked up the device. More of the vicious energy scalded his senses. Shipley had picked up the phone while still in a killing rage. Maybe Valerie, realizing she was in danger, had tried to dial 911. Or maybe Shipley had wanted to erase any record of her incoming and outgoing calls.

He put the phone down on the end table.

The study door was open. From the entrance Jake could see a heavy wooden desk, a couple file cabinets and a bookcase. A computer sat on the desk.

He powered up the computer and slapped the small storage device he had brought along into the USB port. While the files listed on the screen were being copied, he went through the desk drawers. Nothing jumped out and screamed incriminating evidence.

When the copying was complete he removed the storage device, dropped it into a pocket and powered down the computer.

He went back out into the hall and started toward the master bedroom suite.

The faint change in air pressure in the hall ruffled his senses. Someone had entered the house. Whoever he was, he was moving in a stealthy manner.

Another intruder. That was interesting. Who else had a reason to come here tonight?

Hungry, predatory excitement splashed through him. He glided into the deep shadows of a bedroom doorway and waited. The other intruder might or might not be a sensitive but either way, he would be jacked, too. Adrenaline was adrenaline, whether or not you were running hot. People got killed fairly easily, often accidentally, when the stuff was flowing.

If the guy was any good, it wouldn't be long before the newcomer realized he was not alone in the house.

Let the hunt begin.

He realized his mistake an instant later when the psychic firestorm electrified his senses. The ferocious energy forced him to his knees. Instinctively he gripped his head in both hands, as though he could somehow dampen the blast.

Another scalding flash of energy struck him. This one was followed by a massive wave of night that swamped him in a sea of endless darkness.

CHAPTER FORTY-THREE

Anxiety sparked through Clare, sharp and jagged as a burst of lightning. The panic attack rolled out of nowhere, trampling her defenses before she even had time to erect them.

She was sitting on the sofa, one leg curled under her, poring over the list of numbers she had copied off Valerie Shipley's cell phone when the disturbing energy frazzled all her senses.

The clanging of every single one of her private alarm bells brought her to her feet, heart pounding, pulse racing. Her palms went cold. Adrenaline rushed through her bloodstream. Everything inside her was at full throttle. She was ready to flee to safety or fight for her life.

No, not her life. Someone else's. She had never experienced a panic attack quite like this one.

Jake. Yes, she was sure of it now. This involved Jake. He was in terrible danger. But it was impossible for her to know that, she reminded herself. There was no such thing as telepathy or mind reading. The researchers in the Society had investigated the numerous anecdotal stories for decades but had never been able to reproduce the experience in the lab.

Breathe. Calm down. You're worried about Jake out there at the Shipley house. That's what triggered this episode.

She started to pace, making herself focus on her breathing while she painstakingly erected the psychic defense mechanisms she had worked so hard to create.

The sensation of intense awareness winked out as swiftly as it had hit. It was as if someone had turned off a switch.

After a couple minutes she felt steadier, more in control.

She glanced at her watch. It was nearly midnight. Jake had been gone for more than two hours. How long did it take to search a whole house?

He ought to be home by now. She pulled her cell phone out of her pocket and looked at it longingly. But she dared not call him. Surely he had turned his phone off when he entered the Shipley home but what if he had neglected to do so? She didn't want to risk placing a call that would create a problem for him on his end.

There was always the possibility that a neighbor had noticed something at the Shipley residence and went to investigate. Or called the police.

Please, don't let it be the police, she thought. The last thing they needed now was for Jake to get hauled in on breaking-and-entering charges.

But something was very wrong. She knew it with a dread certainty that did not diminish even as the initial adrenaline charge of the panic attack faded.

It's your imagination, she thought. *Let it go. Get a grip.*

But she couldn't get past the absolute certainty that Jake was in trouble.

No matter what the Arcane House experts claimed, everyone with half an ounce of sensitivity — members of the Society or not — knew that once in a while two people who had an intimate bond sometimes experienced brief flashes of psychic intimacy. When she and Jake made love they shared some kind of psychic connection. Why would it be strange if she could somehow sense that he was in danger?

Maybe she was coming at this from the wrong angle. It was possible that the panic attack had been triggered by what she had been doing a few minutes ago.

The notebook had fallen to the floor. She scooped it up and looked at the numbers she had written down. When she had found the cell phone on the coffee table in the Shipleys' house, she was disappointed because there were no incoming or outgoing calls logged on the day of Valerie's death. In addition, none of the few numbers that Valerie had entered into the device's phone book seemed unusual.

But tonight when she had gone over the phone book list a second time, one jumped out at her. Valerie had evidently called it with some frequency because she had put it on speed dial.

Take it easy, she thought. It was possible that a lot of women in town had the Stone Canyon Day Spa on speed dial.

Nevertheless, there was one other person in the world who had evidently loved Brad McAllister. And Kimberley Todd was a professional massage therapist who had vanished from her job. Everyone at the Secret Springs Day Spa assumed she had found another position.

What if that was precisely what had happened? What if her new position was right here in Stone Canyon?

What were the odds?

Probably about a million to one, Clare thought. She tossed the notebook on the coffee table and checked her watch again. What was keeping Jake? She was going to go nuts waiting for him.

Lights speared the night outside the window. A car was coming up the road. Relief flooded through her. Jake was home at last.

She rushed down the hall and opened the door just as the vehicle pulled into the driveway.

The car halted but Jake didn't turn off the engine. The headlights blazed straight into her eyes. Instinctively she put up an arm to cut the glare.

The door on the driver's side opened. A figure got out. The blinding brilliance of the high-beam lights made it impossible to see anything more than a vague silhouette. Alarm flashed through her.

"Jake? Is everything okay? I was getting worried."

"I'm afraid Jake has been badly hurt," Owen Shipley said. "I found him unconscious in my house when I got home tonight. He's in the emergency room. I'll take you to him."

The ultraviolet lie ignited her already sensitized senses. The monster of all panic attacks arced through her.

In the wake of the wave of terror that pounded through her she fought to control her reaction. She could not succumb to the panic. She had to stay in control so she could help Jake.

The searing blast of psychic energy came out of nowhere, frying her fully open senses. She felt herself falling through space, and then darkness descended.

CHAPTER FORTY-FOUR

The faint hissing sound finally became so irritating that Clare opened her eyes. She found herself gazing up into an eerie twilight sky. She could feel hard tiles beneath her back. Artistically arrayed benches designed to resemble rocky outcroppings rose up the walls.

"Oh, damn," she said.

"I think I said something similar when I came around a few minutes ago," Jake said. "Maybe a little stronger."

"Jake?" She sat up suddenly. That proved to be a mistake. The interior of the Stone Canyon Day Spa steam chamber whirled precariously around her.

"Take it easy." Jake crouched beside her, steadying her with a hand on her shoulder. "The dizziness will pass in a minute. At least it did for me. How do you feel?"

"Weird." Memory tore through her. She remembered Owen getting out of his car, lying to her about Jake.

"I was so afraid he had killed you," she whispered. Her throat tightened. Panic flickered.

"Breathe," Jake said.

She did, albeit cautiously because she expected the action to fire up a splitting headache. To her enormous relief, there was no new wave of pain. The blast of psychic energy that had seared her senses had been intense while it lasted but evidently it did not leave a residual effect.

"What did Owen do to us?" she asked.

"I'm not sure. Some kind of trick that temporarily shorted out our senses, I think."

"I've never heard of anyone being able to do that."

"There are some references to something similar in the old archives concerning the founder's formula."

She frowned. "I've studied the history of the Society. I don't recall any stuff about mind blasts."

"The details are in the private archives of the Jones family."

"Those files are not open to the regular membership of the Society," she said. "Only the Master and the Council have access. And the members of the Jones family, I suppose. How did you get to see them?"

"It's sort of complicated."

"A J&J thing, huh? Never mind." Glumly she surveyed the steam room. "We've got other priorities here."

"Yes, we do."

"I don't suppose you have your cell phone?"

"When I woke up it was gone. Shipley must have taken it off me. You don't have one on you, either. I checked before you opened your eyes."

"Not good."

"No." Jake straightened and began to prowl the chamber. "Gotta tell you, this hunting-cabal-freaks stuff is for the young hotshots. I'm too old for this kind of excitement."

She couldn't help it. In spite of everything, a little laugh bubbled out of her. "You're lying through your teeth, Jake Salter. You live for hunting bad guys. You *need* to hunt them."

"Maybe the old saying is right." There was no inflection at all in his words. "It's in the blood."

"Yep." She struggled unsteadily to her feet. "Just like lie detecting is in mine."

He looked at her, not speaking.

She spread her hands. "Hey, we are what we are, Jake, a couple of exotics. We aren't the first in the Society and we won't be the last. I say ditch the angst. You know, we might make a good team."

"You offering me a partnership?"

"Why not? If the two of us work together, we could not only handle a wider variety of cases, we could sell our consulting services to Jones & Jones as a package deal. Think about it. How many lie-detector and hunter investigative firms are out there? Probably none. What we have to offer will be impossible to duplicate."

There was a short, startled silence. Then Jake took two long strides across the chamber, wrapped a hand around the nape of her neck and kissed her hard and deep.

When he raised his head she was a little breathless again, but not from panic.

"Damn," Jake said. "I really like the way you think."

She smiled modestly. "Guess a flair for business runs in the family."

"Guess so." He released her and went back to studying the ceiling.

"Where's Owen?" Clare asked.

"Still here in the building," Jake said. "I can feel him. He's throwing off a lot of weird energy."

"Weird how?"

"I can sense when someone else is running hot. Shipley is definitely at full throttle. But his energy waves feel distorted somehow. Abnormal. Twisted. I don't know how to explain it."

"What's he doing?"

"Waiting, probably."

"Waiting for what?"

"Well —" Jake didn't finish the sentence.

The temperature was starting to rise. Clouds of steam were forming. Clare looked around uneasily.

"Does it feel like it's getting warmer in here?" she asked.

"Someone fired up the steam system after dumping us in here. Full blast."

"That can't be good." She rubbed her arms uneasily and looked around. "Somehow I can't see Owen worrying about our personal comfort."

"No."

She could feel her skin growing moist. Jake's shirt was already plastered to his back.

"I wonder how hot this room gets," she said.

"I've been thinking about that myself."

"There must be some sort of safety valve to control the temperature," she said.

"Probably."

"What aren't you telling me, Jake?"

He vaulted up to the highest stone bench and stretched his arm straight up. She saw that his fingers just barely reached the surround that concealed the recessed lighting fixtures.

"The problem with any kind of mechanical temperature control," he said, "is that there is almost always a way to remove it or override it."

"Why would anyone want to —" She broke off, horror shafting through her. "Oh, Lord. Don't bother to answer that."

"Okay," he said, "I won't."

She tried to take her mind off the implications of what he had just said. "What are you looking for?"

"An access panel. Given all the high-tech plumbing and the HVAC stuff in this chamber, there has to be one."

"HVAC?"

"Heat, ventilating and air-conditioning."

"Oh, right." She shivered again in spite of the heat. "You don't really think Owen plans to steam us to death as if we were a couple of oversized artichokes, do you?"

"If you put yourself in his position, that scenario does offer some distinct advantages," he said.

"Describe your idea of advantages."

"When our bodies are discovered in the morning, it will probably look like we died of heatstroke."

"For crying out loud," Clare yelped. "People don't croak from sitting too long in a steam room."

"Sure they do." He glanced at the wall near the door. "Why do you think they put up those little signs warning you not to spend more than a few minutes inside one?"

She swallowed hard. "But if they find our bodies in here tomorrow morning, the first thing everyone is going to ask is what were we doing in the steam room after hours. The second question is going to be, why didn't we just open the door and walk out when it got too hot?"

"Answer to Question Number One will probably be that we booked a couples special in this chamber last night in order to enjoy hot sex. *Very* hot sex. Nobody noticed that we hadn't come out by closing time. Maybe we were having such a great time we didn't want to be discovered."

"What about the answer to Question Number Two?"

"We got accidentally locked in here when the staff closed up for the night."

"Terrific. What about the steam? Why didn't it shut off?"

"Mechanical malfunction."

"Archer isn't going to believe that for a minute," she said.

"Jones & Jones won't buy it, either. But by then it will be too late for us."

"But Owen must know our deaths will only serve to bring the full resources of Archer Glazebrook and the firm of J&J down on his head."

"You're forgetting one very important thing," Jake said.

"What?"

"No one but you and I know that Shipley is the cabal freak."

She felt a little flare of psi power. She was no hunter but she was definitely becoming sensitive to Jake's energy, she thought. It had the same unique, intimate, compelling impact on her senses as his scent and the sound of his voice.

Jake gripped the lighting surround with both hands and hoisted himself up into the shallow recessed area. She saw his face tighten into a stark, grim mask. A dark crimson stain appeared on his left shirtsleeve.

"Jake, your arm."

"Some of the stitches ripped. I'm okay."

The recessed lighting shelf was not very wide. Jake had to remain on his side to wedge himself into it.

He probed the painted ceiling directly over his head. She had a hard time seeing exactly what he was doing with his hands because the clouds of steam had grown so thick. But a moment later she heard him give a small sound of satisfaction.

"Got it," he said.

A section of the ceiling swung downward on hinges. He scrambled up out of sight through the shadowy opening. A rising current of steam followed him, billowing upward into the darkness.

He reappeared, leaning partway over the edge of the panel. His belt dangled from a loop he had made around the wrist of his right arm.

"Grab the end with both hands, wrap it around one of your wrists and hang on tight," he ordered.

She climbed up onto the highest bench as he had done, reached up and grabbed the end of the belt.

He hauled her up swiftly. The leather strap burned into her wrist but somehow the pain didn't seem like a big deal at the moment. She set her teeth and tightened her grip.

When she reached the level of the lighting fixtures, she managed to find purchase with one foot on the surround. That took some of the pressure off her wrist. From that vantage point Jake helped her slither awkwardly into the recessed opening.

She became aware of the hum and whine

of the building's air-conditioning system re-verberating through the darkness.

"You're good," she whispered. "You're really good."

"I had some strong motivation."

He leaned out of the opening again, caught hold of the panel and pulled it closed. An intense darkness enveloped her. A tingle of panic, the non-psychic kind, flickered through her.

"With luck Shipley won't check to see if we're fork-tender for a while," Jake whispered.

She shuddered. "You can skip the visuals. But I think you're right. By now he must know that you're a hunter and that you're bound to be really pissed off. It would be dangerous to open the door until we're, uh, done."

"That should buy us a little time."

"Wonder why he didn't tie us up," Clare said.

"He wouldn't want the authorities to find any restraint marks on the bodies."

She winced. "Got it. Doesn't fit with the death-by-accidental-steaming scenario."

"Right. Follow me."

"Glad to, but I don't think that's going to work," she said. "I can't see anything except the crack of light around the access panel."

"I can." His fingers closed around her wrist. "Stick close. There are air-conditioning ducts and pipes running everywhere up here. And whatever you do, try not to make any noise. Take off your shoes. We don't want any squeaking in the ceiling if we can avoid it."

"Hang on. What, exactly, are you going to do if you find Owen?"

"Ripping out his throat comes to mind as an option." Jake sounded inordinately cheerful.

"Get a grip here," she whispered. "What about his psychic freeze trick?"

"I'll take him down before he even knows I'm in the vicinity."

His confidence worried her. She suspected that it was rooted, in part, in the fact that he was running hot.

"No offense," she said, "but I think we should have a Plan B."

"Got one?"

"I've been thinking," she said. "When Owen did his mind blast thing to you were your senses wide open?"

"Yeah. Why?"

"Mine were on edge but I wasn't running hot, at least not at the moment when he got out of the car. I was expecting you. Then Owen spoke to me, told me a lie. That was when my senses kicked in. And that was when I felt the full blast of whatever it was he used to knock me out."

"You think his trick only works on our psi senses?"

"Maybe. There's no way to know for sure without doing some tests. But it seems logical that since his power is generated on the paranormal plane, it would be most effective against that side of our natures, doesn't it?"

"All right," Jake said. "I'll keep that in mind. But I still prefer Plan A, the one where I rip his throat out before he even knows I'm around."

"You don't like taking directions, do you?"

"No, but on occasion I've been known to be reasonable."

"That's very reassuring." She slipped out of her loafers and held them in her left hand. "Okay, I'm ready."

She followed him through the inky darkness, aware of the objects in their path only when he altered course to avoid them. When they detoured around a large, vibrating heat pump she saw another rectangular crack of light indicating another access panel. The room below was illuminated.

Jake's fingers tightened around her wrist.

The hunter had scented his prey.

They crept closer. She could hear the low, muffled sound of voices now. Owen and a woman were speaking. The female voice sounded vaguely familiar.

Jake put his mouth very close to her ear. "Got a hunch we just located Kimberley Todd."

"I *know* that voice," Clare whispered. "I've heard it somewhere. Good grief, it's Karen Trent."

"Who?"

"The assistant manager here at the spa. The one who didn't believe me when I told her that someone tried to brain me with the dumbbell."

"Like I said, I think we just found Kimberley Todd." Satisfaction reverberated through Jake's low voice.

"Damn. She was here at the spa all the time."

"All right," Jake said. "Here's what we're going to do. First, I want you out of this place. I'll open one of the other panels and lower you into an empty room. Get clear of the building, find a phone and call the cops. Understood?"

"I don't think I should leave you here alone with those two."

"I can handle this," he said. "But I can do

it even better if I know you're safe."

This was the kind of thing he was born to do, she reminded herself. It was time to let Jake hunt.

CHAPTER FORTY-FIVE

He opened an access panel above a darkened massage therapy room. Taking hold of both of Clare's wrists, he lowered her until she could stand on the white-sheeted table. He was aware of the pain in his left arm but with his senses wide open he could push the sensation to the edge of his awareness, at least for a while.

Clare found her footing on the table and looked up at him. He knew she could not see him in the dense shadows of the ceiling crawl space.

"Be careful," she said softly. "Please."

"I will," he promised. "Go on, get out of here."

He waited until she had opened the door and slipped out into the hall. There was enough moonlight filtering through the skylights out there to illuminate her way to the lobby.

When she was gone, he made his way back

across the ceiling to the illuminated access panel. The voices of the two people in the room below were loud and clear, thanks to his jacked-up hearing.

He realized at once that something had changed in the atmosphere. Shipley was throwing off even more of the disturbing, abnormal psychic energy.

"You *bastard*," Kimberley shrieked. "What do you think you're doing? You can't kill me."

"Of course I can," Owen said calmly. "In fact, it is absolutely necessary. I need to throw some red meat to Glazebrook and the local cops."

"You're crazy. You need me. We have a plan, damn you."

"I have a plan," Owen said. "Sadly, it is somewhat different from the one we discussed. You are going to commit suicide."

"No one will believe that."

"Of course they will. As the months went past you became despondent after you murdered McAllister. The gun you used to kill him will be found in your desk drawer. I put it there myself a few minutes ago."

"You can't do this," Kimberley said, frantic now.

"Valerie's death will remain a probable accident as a result of drugs and alcohol. You will leave a suicide note on your computer explaining the other deaths, however. You murdered Brad McAllister because he dumped you in favor of Clare. When she came back to Stone Canyon, you couldn't stand it. You lured her here to the spa with the intention of murdering her tonight. Unfortunately for him, Jake Salter showed up with Clare, no doubt anticipating a couples' massage. You had no choice but to get rid of him, too. You locked them both in the steam chamber."

"We're partners in this," Kimberley pleaded.

"As I said, there has been a slight change of plan."

"You need me."

"Not any longer," Owen said. "In a few days Archer Glazebrook will suffer a heart attack following the shock of Clare's death. His son, Matt, will die in a car crash on the way home to his father's funeral. And in their grief, Myra and Elizabeth will turn to me, an old friend of the family. I will take control of the company and lift that burden from their shoulders."

Jake sensed movement in the room below. Kimberley was edging toward the door. She was probably going to make a desperate bid to flee into the hall. That would be good. He could use the distraction.

"You can't shoot me from across the room," Kimberley said. "No one will believe I committed suicide if you do."

"I am fully prepared to make adjustments to my plan," Owen said, unruffled. "If you make me kill you this way, I will simply take your body into the steam room and stage what will appear to be a battle over the gun. You lost."

Jake let the access panel swing open. He put one hand on the edge of the dropped ceiling and plummeted, feet first, straight down.

Owen's head jerked up at the sound of the panel falling open. Startled shock and then rage flashed across his face. Instinctively he brought the gun around, trying to aim for an impossibly awkward shot.

Jake landed inches from his prey. He brought his hand down in a short, chopping action, striking Owen's arm. The gun clattered to the floor.

Owen skittered backward, clawing at the desk for support.

"Son of a bitch," Owen snarled, his face a demented mask. "You want to know how bad it can get? I'll show you."

Pain slashed across Jake's senses, enough to make him stagger, but not enough to cause the lights to go out again. It wasn't easy keeping his senses dampened when everything in him wanted to make the kill.

"Clare's right," he said. "Your little psychic trick doesn't work nearly as well when I'm running cold."

Owen's eyes widened with real fear for the first time.

"No," he breathed. "Wait —"

"Still hurts, though," Jake said. "And that really pisses me off."

Owen threw up his hands to protect himself. Jake delivered two solid blows to Owen's midsection. Owen clutched at his belly and sank to his knees, gasping for air.

Jake turned quickly, seeking other prey. Kimberley Todd was gone. So was the gun.

That would not have happened if he'd been working at full capacity, he thought.

He used his belt to secure Owen's wrists behind his back.

"We both know you aren't going to kill me," Owen said. "And there's no evidence Jones & Jones can give to the local cops. Kimberley murdered McAllister, not me."

"But you murdered Valerie, didn't you?"

"You can't prove that."

"Maybe not. But it shouldn't be too hard to prove that you conspired with Kimberley to murder Clare Lancaster and me tonight."

"Wait. Listen to me. You don't know what's going on here. I'm using a new version of the founder's formula. It works, damn it. I can get some for you, too."

"No thanks."

"Hear me out. We're talking power here. Incredible power. I can make you a member of the new cabal. Once you've taken the drug you'll see what I mean. Nothing can stop you when you're running hot on the formula."

"People have said that before. They've all come to a bad end."

Jake drew the small leather tool kit out of his pocket and removed the prefilled syringe.

Owen's eyes followed Jake's hands. "What's that?"

Jake jabbed the needle into Shipley's arm.

"It's a J&J thing," he said.

Owen slumped forward, unconscious.

Jake headed out into the dark hall, all senses wide open.

Time to continue the hunt.

CHAPTER FORTY-SIX

Getting out of the building proved harder than Clare had anticipated. The heavy glass doors in the lobby were locked. There was a keypad on the wall but she had no clue about the code.

She swung around, searching for an emergency exit. There was a sign pointing the way over a door behind the long stone desk.

Running footsteps sounded in the hall that led to the changing rooms. A woman, she thought. Kimberley. Something had gone wrong.

She hurried around the desk and ducked behind the chest-high counter.

The footsteps grew louder. She could hear panicky breathing. Not her own.

A split second later Kimberley pounded out of the hall. She headed straight for the emergency exit door behind the long desk.

Intent only on escape, she never looked around.

Clare straightened, grabbed the heavy glass bowl full of brochures off the desk and swung it with all her might at Kimberley's head.

At the last instant Kimberley sensed movement and started to turn. The motion converted what would have been a solid crack to the skull into a glancing blow. But the impact was enough to make Kimberley stumble sideways and lose her balance. She sprawled on the floor. The object in her hand landed with a harsh clang on the tile.

Clare looked down. There was just enough light to make out the gun. She crouched and grabbed the weapon in both hands.

"Don't move," she said. "Trust me, after what I've been through lately, I am not feeling particularly squeamish. It won't bother me at all to pull this trigger."

Kimberley looked up at her, enraged. "Bitch."

"You got that right."

Jake materialized from the shadows of the hall. He took in the situation in an instant.

"You okay?" he said to Clare.

"Yes. You?"

"Turns out you were right about Shipley's psychic blast thing. Running cold dulled the effects enough to keep me on my feet."

Kimberley looked at each of them in turn.

"What are you talking about? Psychic blast? You're crazier than Shipley."

Clare ignored her, concentrating on Jake. "What did you do with Owen?"

"He's unconscious at the moment," Jake said.

"But when he comes around, he'll be dangerous to anyone who is a sensitive, even if he's tied up."

"Not for quite a while," Jake said. "I gave him a shot of a heavy-duty tranquilizer. His senses will be in neutral for at least forty-eight hours. Long enough for Jones & Jones to figure out how to handle the situation."

"What about Kimberley here?"

Kimberley jerked in alarm. "How do you know my name?"

"We're good," Clare explained.

"Who *are* you people?" Kimberley demanded.

"He's from J&J," Clare said. "I'm freelance."

"What's J&J?" Kimberley asked.

"A private investigation firm," Clare said.

Kimberley wrinkled her nose. "Shit."

"We'll hand her over to the local cops along with Shipley," Jake said to Clare. "They'll finally be able to close the case on McAllister's death."

"No one can prove that I killed Brad,"

Kimberley said urgently.

"The gun that Shipley planted in your desk drawer should be enough to tie you to that crime," Jake said. "And then there's the little matter of your attempt to kill Clare and me tonight. Lots of evidence for that."

"It was Shipley's idea," Kimberley snapped. "He was trying to set me up to take the fall. Hell, he blackmailed me into this whole thing."

"Because he knew that you murdered Brad?" Clare asked smoothly. "Was that what he used to force you to help him?"

Kimberley stiffened. She said nothing.

"I'm sure the cops will enjoy hearing your version of events and comparing it to Shipley's," Jake said. "Nothing like a partnership gone bad when it comes to this kind of stuff. Both parties can't wait to spill their guts if it means ratting out the other person."

Clare looked at Jake. "What are you going to tell the police?"

Jake shrugged. "That I'm a private investigator with the old and distinguished firm of Jones & Jones. I was hired by Archer Glazebrook to look into the death of his son-in-law."

Clare smiled. "You sure do that truth-veiled-in-a-lie thing well."

"We all have our talents."

Clare looked at Kimberley. "Out of sheer curiosity, mind telling me how you got involved with Brad McAllister in the first place?"

Without warning, Kimberley started to sob. Everything about her seemed to crumple.

"We met at the spa where I was working," she whimpered. "Became lovers. He brought me out here to Arizona with him. Said he had a major business operation going down in Stone Canyon. Said it was probably going to take several months, maybe a year or more to pull it off, but when it was finished we could be married."

"When did you realize that he had lied to you?" Clare asked.

Kimberley sniffed back tears. "I began to get suspicious when Brad insisted that no one could know about our relationship, not even his mother or his business partner. He kept me stashed away clear across the Valley as if he was ashamed of me."

Jake looked thoughtful. "Valerie and Shipley didn't know about you?"

"Not at first," Kimberley said. Her voice had gone flat. "But eventually Shipley found out about us. He was furious with Brad. I overheard them arguing. Shipley accused Brad of putting the whole plan in jeopardy by bringing me along."

"Did Brad or Shipley ever tell you about their scheme?" Jake asked.

Kimberley shrugged. "Something to do with a takeover of Glazebrook." She gave Clare a fulminating look. "When you showed up and convinced Elizabeth to file for divorce, Brad went a little crazy. I'd never seen him like that. He kept talking about how he was going to get rid of you. He was so sure that if you were out of the picture he could salvage the deal."

"You figured out how and when he intended to kill me, didn't you?" Clare asked.

"I didn't have to figure out anything." Kimberley's hand clenched into a fist. "Brad *told* me how he planned to do it. He was so damned obsessed with getting rid of you that he *wanted* to talk about the scheme. That's when I finally began to realize that whatever he had going on here in Stone Canyon was a lot more important to him than I would ever be."

"What happened next?" Clare asked.

"I asked him about our future," Kimberley whispered in a choked voice. "The bastard laughed. He actually had the gall to *laugh.* Said I was very good in bed but that if he ever wanted to get married again he would look a lot higher than a massage therapist."

"So you shot him," Clare said.

"On the night he planned to kill you," Kimberley agreed. "I knew that when you found the body everyone would think you were the murderer. That's the way it works, isn't it?"

"Shipley guessed right away that you were the killer, though, didn't he?" Jake asked.

Kimberley used her sleeve to dry her eyes. "He promised me he wouldn't tell anyone, not even Valerie, if I agreed to help him. He said he would make me his business partner. He got me a new identity and then recommended me to the management here at the spa. I was hired immediately."

"Of course," Clare said. "No one in Stone Canyon would say no to Owen Shipley. What did Owen tell you he wanted you to do for him?"

"He said he wanted me to make friends with Valerie. I was supposed to keep her focused on her obsession with you until the time came to get rid of her. But tonight I finally realized he was just keeping me handy so that I could take the fall when he finally needed someone to give to the cops."

"You called Valerie the day I was here at the spa, didn't you?" Clare said. "You told her I was scheduled for a couple of treatments. Did you invite her to come on over and take a whack at me with that dumb-bell?"

Kimberley made a disgusted sound. "That was all her idea. I called her, yes, but only because I had told her I would let her know if you showed up here. I wasn't aware of what she had done until you came into my office complaining that someone had tried to kill you. I realized right away it must have been Valerie who attacked you. After you left that day I called Shipley and let him know that Valerie was out of control. He was at the country club. He said he'd take care of the problem."

"He went out, played a round of golf and murdered her," Jake said.

Clare studied Kimberley. "Why didn't Owen ever tell Valerie that you were the one who killed Brad?"

It was Jake who answered. "He couldn't. With Brad gone, Shipley needed help to further his plans. Valerie was useless to him. She was too obsessed with her grief. Kimberley was all he had to work with. He had to protect her until he needed her."

"I loved Brad," Kimberley said. "I thought the bastard loved me. He lied right from the start."

"Yes," Clare said. "He did."

CHAPTER FORTY-SEVEN

Five-fifteen A.M., *Scargill Cove . . .*

Fallon sat at his desk, gazing into the glowing screen of the computer. He had been working steadily on Owen Shipley's journal since Jake awakened him three hours before and informed him that he was sending an encrypted file via e-mail attachment. It had been easy to break the password code. Shipley had not been what anyone would call a techno whiz.

Unfortunately there wasn't nearly as much material as Fallon had hoped to find. Shipley had been only a low-level member of the cabal. But there were some hints and clues at last. The kaleidoscope in Fallon's head was starting to produce more than tantalizing glimpses. He could see pictures forming. Disturbing pictures.

He got to his feet and walked to the window. The first light of dawn was waking the cove. Physically he was exhausted but he knew he wouldn't be able to sleep for a long time.

CHAPTER FORTY-EIGHT

Eight-ten A.M., Portland, Oregon . . .

It was raining when John Stilwell Nash left his private club. The monthly breakfast meeting and the guest speaker who had followed had been incredibly boring as usual. He disliked wasting his time on such trivial matters. But it was important to maintain his image in the Portland business community.

A number of city and state VIPs belonged to the club. It was the only reason he had joined. It gave him a sense of predatory satisfaction to rub shoulders with the movers and shakers of the region. He felt like a shark swimming among a school of oblivious prey fish whenever he dined at the club. He savored the secret knowledge that he already owned some of the politicians and business executives in the room. Eventually, he would have governors, senators and presidents in his grasp.

The rain was steady, relentless. He did not like the city. He didn't like anything about the Northwest. But his instincts had told him that this would be a good place in which to establish the organization. No one would think to look for the man who intended to take over the Arcane Society here in Portland.

His phone chimed as he waited for his car to be brought around. He checked the number and took the call.

"Yes?" he said.

"The Stone Canyon operation has been terminated. Shipley was picked up by the authorities late last night."

A searing flash of rage snapped through Nash; the raw anger of the hunter when the prey manages to wriggle free and escape. He worked frantically to control the intense sensation. He had been half expecting the news for some time now, he reminded himself. He had known things were going badly in Arizona. Nevertheless, he wanted Glazebrook. The company would have made an ideal acquisition, perfectly suited to the cabal's purposes.

He took a couple deep breaths and waited until he was sure he had himself in hand.

"Any loose ends?" he asked, pleased that his voice was calm and cold. It was vital not to show strong emotion in front of the members of his staff. A display of temper was a display of weakness. Self-control was everything.

"No. Shipley is still unconscious. They must have given him something. A heavy tranq, maybe."

Deprived of the drug, Shipley would soon sink into a bottomless well of insanity, John thought. Jones & Jones would no doubt pick up a few glimmerings of the Plan, but that could not be helped. He would deal with those problems if and when they occurred.

"What about the Todd woman?" he asked.

"She doesn't know enough to do any damage."

Neither did Shipley, John assured himself.

"Shipley would have had a small supply of the drug left," he said. "The local authorities don't have any reason to be interested in it but I'd rather it didn't fall into the hands of J&J."

"Any idea where Shipley kept the drug?"

"No. But given its value to him, it is probably in a secure location. Try the wine cellar. The white wine chiller."

"The house is a crime scene. They'll probably have the tape up for a day or so. It would be impossible to get anyone inside long enough to conduct a thorough search until tonight, after the authorities leave."

The rage threatened to flare again. John clenched the phone very tightly. "As far as I am concerned, you are partly responsible for the unfortunate outcome in Stone Canyon. If you have any expectation of rising higher in the organization, you will follow orders. Understood?"

"Yes, Mr. Nash. I'm in Phoenix now. With the morning traffic, it will take me at least forty-five minutes to get to Stone Canyon."

"Just get the damn drug."

The parking attendant arrived with the car. John ended the call and got into the vehicle. He sat for a moment, hands gripping the wheel. He could still feel the heat generated by his frustration and anger vibrating through him, churning his senses. It was not a good sign. The rushes of sudden, almost uncontrollable rages were coming more often. He was beginning to suspect they were a side effect of his own, private version of the drug.

The stuff was definitely faster-acting and it was certainly expanding the range of his psychic powers. In addition to his natural hunter talents, he was developing hypnotic and strategic abilities. But there appeared to be a downside.

He needed to get back into the lab immediately.

CHAPTER FORTY-NINE

Eight-fifteen A.M., *Stone Canyon* . . .

They gathered on the veranda at the Glaze-brook house. It was just a little after eight but the overhead fans and misters were already cranking at full speed, making the heat tolerable. There was a large pitcher of iced tea and five glasses on the table.

Myra poured the tea. When she handed a glass to Clare, she actually smiled.

"Thank you," Clare said very politely. She wasn't sure if she would ever feel entirely comfortable in the very heart of Glazebrook Territory, but she had to admit that much of the tension seemed to have dissipated.

Jake walked out of the house to join the small group. He was talking on his cell phone. He ended the call when he reached the table.

"That was Fallon," he said, taking a seat.

"Well?" Clare asked. "What did Dumbass

467

have to say this time?"

Jake smiled. "He said to give you his best."

"Yeah, I'll bet he did."

"I believe he also said something about taking another look at your last application. He thinks you may have potential as a J&J agent, after all."

"Hah." Satisfaction swept through her. Revenge was sweet. "If Dumbass thinks he's going to get me cheap, he can think again."

Jake settled into the chair. "Be that as it may, he cracked that copy of the encrypted file that I took off Owen's computer. It was Shipley's personal diary of his involvement with the cabal."

"Oh, wow," Clare said. Excitement bubbled up inside. "Good stuff, huh?"

"There is a fair amount of information that will be useful in other, related J&J investigations," Jake said, "but not nearly as much detailed data on the new cabal as Fallon wanted."

Clare rolled her eyes. "Jones is a difficult person to please."

"No argument there," Jake said. "But in this case, I can understand his frustration. Looks like this new cabal is very good at keeping its secrets. Unfortunately Shipley was not high enough in the organization to know much."

"Bad news for Jones & Jones," Archer observed.

"True," Jake agreed. "But Fallon says Shipley's diary did provide a lot of details about the project here in Stone Canyon. That is proving extremely helpful because from that information he's getting a fix on how the new organization works and its probable agenda."

"Owen was the cabal guy all along?" Elizabeth asked. "The one you were sent here to find?"

"Right," Jake said. "According to his notes, the cabal recruited him a year and a half ago. His first major assignment was to take control of Glazebrook, Inc. They figured that if anyone could do that, he could because he enjoyed Archer's trust."

Archer grimaced. "He sure did. For damn near thirty-five years. Still hard to believe he was the bad guy in all this."

"Shipley came up with what can only be called a breathtaking strategy," Jake continued. "Among other things, he was promised by his superiors that success would enable him to ascend to the next level of power."

"What the hell did the cabal want with my company?" Archer growled.

"One word," Jake said. "Money. Lots of it. Glazebrook, Inc., is nothing if not a cash cow. As I told Clare, your company also had other distinct advantages. It's a privately held firm. There would have been no stockholders or outside board of directors to answer to when the money started to get funneled into the cabal's own secret projects."

Clare wrinkled her nose. "Define 'secret projects.'"

Jake looked at her. "Shipley didn't know what they were. But Fallon believes that the new cabal is in an acquisitions mode and is probably trying to take control of a number of privately held companies. He thinks it is assembling a strong financial base that will generate a reliable cash flow for the next several years."

Elizabeth frowned. "The cabal is just out to make money? They didn't need to form a secret club and kill people to do that. All that's required is a business license."

"It's not quite that simple if you're trying to put together a corporate empire that will generate an ongoing revenue stream that can be used to fund secret parapharmaceutical research," Jake said.

They all stared at him. Every mouth was open.

Archer whistled softly. "Damn. These guys aren't just out to re-create the founder's formula. They're planning to take it into full-scale production."

Myra frowned. "It's not just the Arcane Society that would look askance at an illicit drug lab doing unregulated pharmaceutical research. The Feds would be down on the new cabal in a nanosecond if they found out about it."

"Any way you look at it, the cabal has a lot of good reasons to keep their empire building secret," Jake said.

Archer exhaled heavily. "I thought Owen was my friend. Hell, after all we went through together."

"His resentment of you began years ago," Jake said quietly. "Fallon found that in the diary, too."

"What the hell did I ever do to Owen except help him make a ton of money?" Archer demanded.

Clare waited a moment for one of the others to state the obvious. When no one did, she shrugged.

"You got the girl," she said. "Mom told me the whole story about how Owen tried to persuade Myra to marry him. But Myra chose you, instead."

There was a short, startled pause. Everyone looked at Myra again.

"I was never in love with Owen and he never loved me," she said briskly. "Not really. He was only in love with the notion of marrying the senator's daughter. He wanted the connections and the lifestyle that he thought I could bring him. I knew that from the start."

"Then why the hell did you date him?" Archer demanded, outraged.

Myra raised her brows. "To make you sit up and take notice, of course. It was very hard to get your attention in those days, Archer Glazebrook. You were too busy building your precious company."

For an instant, Clare thought Archer was going to roar. Then he surprised them all with a thoroughly wicked grin.

"I've said it once and I'll say it again." Archer leaned back in his chair and hooked his thumbs in the waistband of his jeans. He looked smugly satisfied. He also looked like a man very much in love with his wife. "Never play cards with this woman."

Clare could have sworn that Myra blushed.

Jake cleared his throat. "Getting back to Shipley, his resentment of you may have started when he didn't get the girl, as Clare said, but it was fed by the knowledge that you were the real genius behind Glazebrook. At the same time, he wanted very badly what the company's success gave him."

"Money, connections and a degree of power," Clare said.

Archer shook his head. "He got all three but apparently they didn't satisfy him."

"No," Jake said. "His envy festered over the years. In short, by the time the cabal identified him as a potential recruit, he was more than ready to leap at the opportunity not only to take revenge, but to become a more powerful talent than you. The cabal gave him a variant of the formula genetically engineered just for him along with the promise of advancement within the organization to clinch the deal. All he had to do was deliver Glazebrook, Inc., on a platter."

Clare drank some tea and lowered the glass. "What about the others? How did Shipley find Brad McAllister and Valerie, the mom from hell?"

"Shipley decided that the slickest way to get his hands on Glazebrook was to promote a marriage with Elizabeth that would ensure that her husband got her share of the company when Archer conveniently died. Shipley, of course, is in his early sixties," Jake said. "He knew there was no chance he could ever make himself look like good husband material to Elizabeth."

"Heavens, no," Myra said. "He's much too old for her."

"You can say that again." Elizabeth made a face. "I think of him, or rather *thought* of him, as an *uncle.*"

"Shipley worked out his strategy and then contacted his superiors in the cabal," Jake continued. "It all hinged on bringing someone who looked like the ideal husband into the Glazebrook circle. The guy had to be able to successfully court Elizabeth and get the approval of her family. The cabal helped Shipley locate a world-class scam artist, one Brad McAllister."

"Who was not only good-looking, charming and smart, he was also a strong hypnotist," Clare said. "I'll bet that was his biggest asset as far as Shipley was concerned. If charm didn't work, Brad could always use his talent to dazzle everyone."

"What did Owen offer Brad to make him risk getting involved in the conspiracy?" Myra asked.

"According to the diary, it wasn't what Shipley offered that convinced McAllister to sign on for the project," Jake said. "It was what the cabal offered."

"Got it," Elizabeth said. "The cabal made the same offer to Owen that it made to Brad. Power and high status in the organization."

"And his very own genetically tailored supply of the enhancement drug," Jake said.

"The diary indicates that Brad McAllister was a level-eight hypnotist before he started taking the drugs. Whatever the cabal gave him boosted him straight off the charts."

Elizabeth sighed. "So that was how he was able to manipulate everyone so well."

"Everyone except Clare," Archer said proudly.

Myra smiled. "Yes, everyone except Clare. Thank God."

Clare felt an odd little rush of warmth. She had to grab a napkin and blot the moisture from her eyes. When she looked up, blinking, she saw that Jake was watching her with an amused expression.

"It was Brad's idea to have Shipley marry Valerie," Jake said. "It was the perfect way to slide Brad into your social circle here in Stone Canyon. What better credentials could a suitor have than being the son of your best friend's wife, Archer?"

Archer scowled. "I had McAllister checked out seven ways from Sunday. There was nothing in the member database to indicate that he was anything but what he claimed to be. Hell, McAllister not only came out clean, arcanematch.com said he was just right for Elizabeth."

Jake lounged deeper into his chair. "Here's one of the really nasty bits as far as Fallon is concerned. He thinks the cabal has managed to hack into the Society's genealogical records and arcanematch.com and that it is able to make alterations to the records."

Archer exhaled slowly. "That's going to be a problem for J&J."

"A big one," Jake agreed.

"One thing I don't understand," Archer said. "Why didn't Owen pull the plug on his scheme after Brad was murdered? What did he hope to accomplish?"

"He didn't have any choice but to come up with a new angle," Jake said. "Traditionally the cabals do not tolerate failure. The revised plan required several additional murders, namely Valerie's, Kimberley's, mine and Clare's, but by then he was desperate enough, or maybe crazy enough, to take the risk."

"I can tell you that the drug the cabal gave Owen worked," Archer said grimly. "He didn't always have that psychic freeze trick up his sleeve. No way he could have concealed it from me all these years. Hell, he was only a mid-range sensitive with a talent for strategy."

"Fallon agrees with you," Jake said. "It's obvious that the new cabal already has a functioning lab up and running somewhere."

Archer looked thoughtful. "Owen always was a pretty good shot with a hunting rifle. I assume he was the one who tried to take you out that day at the old ranch house?"

"Right," Jake said. "He followed me when I left the Glazebrook offices that day. It was a desperate, preemptive attempt to get rid of me. When that failed he went back to the drawing board and came up with the steamed veggie plan instead."

"Bizarre," Myra said.

"Yeah," Jake said. "So bizarre I wouldn't be surprised if the enhancement drug had begun to affect the rational side of his mind."

Archer's brows bunched. "How the hell did he know you were going to search his house that night after you returned from Tucson?"

"He didn't," Jake said. "But he was watching my place, waiting for an opportunity to collect Clare and me to cart us off to the spa. He saw me drive away just as he was getting ready to move in on us. He followed me."

"Straight back to his house," Elizabeth said. "Where he took you out with his psychic mind blast."

"I'd appreciate it if you wouldn't circulate that story too widely," Jake said. "I don't think it would be good for business."

Elizabeth chuckled. "Don't worry. Who, aside from a few folks at Jones & Jones, would believe us if we told them that Owen Shipley was a psychically enhanced sociopath involved with a mysterious cabal intent on building secret labs to create new versions of an ancient alchemical formula?"

Myra shuddered. "Don't even think about telling anyone in Stone Canyon. We would be asked to cancel our membership at the country club, and I would very likely have to step down from any number of boards. I assure you, no one around here would want a person who took psychic cabals and alchemical formulas seriously to be president of the board of directors of the Arts Academy."

Archer sat forward abruptly, startling all of them.

"Hell," he said, "those injections Owen was taking. I'll bet that was the para-enhancer."

"What injections?" Jake asked.

"A couple of times when I was with him Owen had to stop and give himself a shot," Archer explained. "The last time was on the day Valerie died. He told me it was medication for some kind of neurological problem. Said he didn't want anyone to know about it because he had his image to maintain."

Jake drummed his fingers on the table.

"Wonder if there's any of the stuff left at the Shipley house. Fallon would give a lot to get his hands on it to run some tests."

"The refrigerator," Myra said slowly.

"What are you talking about, Mom?" Elizabeth asked.

"I went to see Valerie one afternoon about a week ago," Myra said. "Owen asked me to do it. He was trying to cement the image of Valerie being in need of rehab, I suppose."

"What happened?" Clare asked.

"Valerie was drunk, as usual," Myra said. "She offered me a cocktail. I said no. She said there was a fresh pitcher of iced tea in the refrigerator in the kitchen and told me to help myself. So I did."

Archer gave her an inquiring look. "What are you getting at, honey?"

"There was a glass vial stored in the very back on the top shelf. It looked like a regular medicine bottle but I remember thinking it was odd that there was no label on it. You know how carefully pharmacies label meds."

Jake was on his feet, anticipation flowing off him in waves. "The drug must require refrigeration. Not many places in a household can provide that. Damn. I've got to get over there before the cops think to search the kitchen."

CHAPTER FIFTY

No one looked pleased to see him when he arrived at the Shipley house, but he was waved inside.

"Guess we owe you that much," the detective in charge said. "And you're a pro. You know enough to stay out of the way and not contaminate anything. Not that we're turning up anything useful here."

Jake wandered into the kitchen. There was no one in the room. He opened the refrigerator. The unlabeled bottle of clear fluid was still sitting on the top shelf.

He tucked the bottle inside a pocket and made his way leisurely to the front door. A man stood just outside, trying to talk his way into the crime scene.

"The name is Taylor," the stranger said. He sounded edgy. "I'm with the *Phoenix Star.*"

"Sorry, Mr. Taylor, no press allowed inside," the young officer said firmly.

"Look, my editor is going to be really

pissed if I don't get this story," Taylor said. "Give me a break here."

Jake felt his hunter senses stir. Taylor practically vibrated with tension. Definitely not your typical hard-bitten, seen-it-all-and-written-about-it crime reporter. *Running hot.*

"Excuse me," Jake said, moving past Taylor and the cop.

Taylor swung around abruptly, eyes darkening with sudden suspicion. "Who are you?"

"Knew the family," Jake said casually. Clare was right. He did do the truth-veiled-in-a-lie thing rather well.

He walked back to the car and got inside. Taylor threw him one last uneasy look and then resumed his urgent appeal to the cop.

Jake reached into the glove compartment, removed the small digital camera he kept there and took a shot of the reporter.

Might be nothing at all, he thought. But he would e-mail it to Fallon when he got home. Couldn't hurt.

When he loaded the photo onto his computer a short time later he realized that he had taken a pretty good picture. Taylor's features were very clear. Fallon ought to be able to identify him fairly easily.

He studied the picture for a long moment

and concluded that he had been right back at the Shipley house. The hunter in him had sensed more than tension in Taylor. What he had detected was fear.

He picked up his phone and dialed the familiar number.

"What have you got?" Fallon asked.

"I think the cabal sent someone out to collect what was left of the drug Shipley was taking. Guy called himself Taylor. Said he was a reporter. I've got a photo for you."

"What about the drug?" Fallon asked urgently.

"Got that, too."

"You just earned that inflated consulting fee that you're charging J&J."

CHAPTER FIFTY-ONE

Two days later . . .

"Owen Shipley was committed to a psychiatric hospital for observation?" Clare lowered the morning edition of the *Stone Canyon Herald* and looked at Jake, who had just ended a call.

"He was sent to one outside Phoenix yesterday." Jake put the phone down on the counter and went back to flipping the blue corn pancakes on the griddle. "Fallon says the local authorities think he just snapped. Apparently he's delusional and incoherent and getting worse by the hour. No one expects him to be declared competent to stand trial."

"What does Dumbass think really happened?"

"Fallon says the initial tests on that drug I took out of the Shipley refrigerator indicate that it is powerful but very short-acting. He

483

suspects there are devastating effects if it is withdrawn abruptly. He thinks Shipley started to slip into insanity as soon as his supply of the stuff was cut off. Either that's an unpleasant downside of the drug or else the cabal lab techs engineered the stuff that way in order to limit the amount of damage that could be done by any of their members who wound up in custody."

She shuddered. "Talk about cold-blooded."

"But effective. By controlling the drug, they control their people." Jake lifted the pancakes off the griddle and divided them between two plates. "This way they don't have to worry about any cabal member giving too much information to law enforcement or to J&J."

"The organization really knows how to cover its tracks, doesn't it?"

"Looks that way. J&J is going to be very busy for the foreseeable future."

Clare thought about that while she used a fork to cut a bite of the pancakes. "They'll probably need some occasional, expert, *very expensive* consulting from a hunter and a human lie detector."

Jake smiled slowly. "I believe I mentioned on at least one prior occasion that I like the way you think."

CHAPTER FIFTY-TWO

She felt him leave the bed just before dawn. A small flicker of her senses told Clare that Jake was using some of his hunter talent in order to avoid awakening her. She smiled to herself. He could be as stealthy as he wanted. She would always know when he was near her and when he was not.

She gave him a few minutes to collect his jeans and leave the room. He went down the hall toward the kitchen. He was probably going to make the morning tea. That sounded like a good idea.

She gave him some time to get the kettle going. Then she eased the covers aside and rose from the bed. The white robe was hanging on a hook in the bathroom. She pulled it on, tied the sash and took a few minutes to run a brush through her hair.

When she reached the kitchen she saw a pot of freshly brewed tea on the counter. She poured a mug for herself, savoring the delicate aroma of the clean, elegant green.

Jake's computer was open and glowing malevolently on the kitchen table. She wondered what he had been researching at this hour of the day.

The sliding glass door stood open, allowing the exhilarating predawn air and the fantastic light into the room. There was nothing like morning in the desert, she thought. It gave her a rush. Or maybe she was still riding last night's afterglow from their lovemaking.

She could see Jake on the other side of the pool security gate, standing at the edge of the patio. He was watching the three coyotes, a mug in one hand.

She started across the kitchen with the notion of joining him outside to savor the very special time of day.

When she went past the table she caught a glimpse of an all-too-familiar logo on the bright computer screen. A jolting chill swept through her. She stopped abruptly.

Welcome back to Arcanematch.com, Jake Salter Jones. Congratulations, we have a match for you! Please click on the link below to see a profile of the woman who is perfect for you.

She staggered a little under the impact of what could only be described as a double whammy. First she had to deal with the shock of what was apparently Jake's real last name. There were plenty of Joneses in the world but when it came to members of the Arcane Society, the name always gave one pause. Given Jake's strong hunter senses, it was probably not a coincidence. Odds were pretty high that Jake was a direct descendent of Sylvester Jones, the founder of the Society.

No wonder he had concealed his real name while he was working undercover in Stone Canyon, she thought. But why had he let her find out the truth in this stark fashion?

Because he didn't know how to tell her that he had just been matched by www.arcanematch.com, she thought. After last night's passionate lovemaking, he hadn't been able to face her with the news.

She was going to lose him to some unknown woman the matchmakers had dredged up out of their damn computer files. It wasn't right. It wasn't fair. She and Jake were made for each other. Ideal. Perfect. Surely he could see that.

She wasn't supposed to be able to pick up the psychic vibes of an electronic lie but she was certain that the arcanematch.com computers lied.

The panic attack screamed through her, igniting all her senses. Fight or flight.

Her first instinct was to run. *Get away from this place. Save yourself. You can't continue with this affair now that you know they've found someone else for him. If you stay here your heart is going to be broken for all time. Pack. Now. Where are the car keys? Run. Hide.*

Belatedly, the psychic reflexes she had built up over the years slammed into place, damming the torrent of mindless panic. *Fight. You can do this. Get a grip. You have to try. You're not going to run. Not yet, at any rate. This is worth fighting for.*

She dragged her attention away from the cruel words on the computer screen. Jake was still out there at the edge of his territory. His back was to her.

If you run, there's no hope. You want him? Fight for him.

The heat of battle rushed through her veins. She went through the open slider, circled the pool and stalked out to the edge of the patio.

"Those stupid matchmakers at arcanematch.com are wrong," she announced.

She didn't realize how loud her voice was

until she saw the three coyotes whip around to face her, ears rigidly erect. Jake turned, too, albeit in a more relaxed manner. Four sets of watchful, intelligent eyes gazed at her. Probably trying to calculate whether or not she qualified as prey.

"No," she said to the coyotes. "In case you're too slow to figure it out, I'm not breakfast."

Jake smiled slowly. "But you taste great."

The wicked humor infuriated her. She marched closer to him, stopping just two steps away.

"Don't you dare talk to me like that." Automatically she started to put her hands on her hips, but she realized that was impossible because she was still gripping the mug. "Not after what I just saw on that computer of yours."

The amusement faded from his expression. "What, exactly, did you see?"

"The arcanematch.com people say they found a match for you."

"Yeah?"

"They lie."

Paranormal energy was invisible to the human eye, but she could have sworn that the air around him was suddenly shimmering with the stuff. She could feel the potent waves pulsing invisibly in the atmosphere.

"You sure about that?" he asked.

"Oh, yeah." She moved another step closer. "I am absolutely positive they're wrong."

"Why?"

"Because you belong to me, that's why." She swept out her free hand. "We're perfect for each other. I love you. Why do you need arcanematch.com? What's that woman they claim they found for you got that I don't have?"

The dangerous energy that had swirled around him shifted with disconcerting abruptness into sensual hunger.

"Interesting question," he said.

"The answer is nothing. Zero. Zip. Nada. She's got absolutely nothing that I don't have. Don't bother to set up a date with her because there will be three of us there and I don't think she's going to feel real comfortable chatting with me, do you?"

"Don't know," he said. "It would certainly make for an unusual first date."

"Skip the snappy repartee. I am dead serious, Jake Salter *Jones.*"

His mouth tweaked up at the corners. Heat burned in his eyes. "About me?"

"About you. And me. We're a match. Can't you see that?"

"Yes."

"What's more, there's no frickin' way those arcanematch.com people could have found anyone who will love you more than I do."

"Okay, if you say so."

She stopped cold. "You're laughing at me."

"No. Honest. I'm not laughing at you."

"Liar." Scalding tears of outrage welled in her eyes. She jabbed him in the chest with a forefinger. "Why are you laughing at me?"

"Let's go inside." He took her arm. "I'll show you."

He walked her back into the kitchen and halted at the table where the dreadful news from arcanematch.com still glowed with macabre good cheer.

Jake clicked on the link that was set up to take him to a profile of his perfect mate. She watched, stomach clenched, dread in her heart, as a screen full of data and a photograph popped up. The photo was shockingly familiar.

Meet: Clare Lancaster.
Parasensitivity level: Ten*
Description: Extreme sensitivity to the inconsistent psychic energy generated by those engaged in willful prevarication and/or deception.

Clare stopped reading. "That's *me*."

"Thought I noticed a resemblance." Jake studied the photo on the screen with an air of satisfaction. "Great picture. I like your hair that way. The ice princess look is cool. It's got a real touch-me-if-you-dare thing going on. I think I can feel my pulse kicking up."

"Where did they get that photo?" she yelped. "That was taken for the annual report of the Draper Trust last year. I never sent it to arcanematch.com."

"Wasn't hard to find. I just looked up a copy of the annual report online."

"*You* sent it to arcanematch.com?"

"Sure." He poured himself a second cup of tea. "I got Fallon Jones to ask one of his computer techs to dig out the old registration you filed with arcanematch.com a couple of years ago. Figured Fallon owed me that much."

She was dazed. "But I pulled my registration file."

"Nothing ever disappears completely once it's online. It's always out there, somewhere."

"And the computer matched us?"

"That's what it says."

"Good grief." She sat down slowly, unable to take her eyes off the screen. "I don't understand. Did you do it so you could find out whether or not we really are meant for each other?"

"No," Jake said. "I already knew that. I did it so *you* could be sure. Given your trust issues and all, I figured you needed some objective confirmation."

Truth rang in every word, so dazzling and crystal-sharp that it stole her breath. She did not know whether she was going to laugh or cry. She covered her face with both hands and did both.

"Hey," Jake said, suddenly anxious. He touched her shoulder. "Are you okay? I didn't mean to make you cry. Damn. That's the last thing I wanted to do."

She raised her head. The tears were spilling down her cheeks but she smiled anyway. "When I saw that they'd matched you I was ready to hunt down those dip squat arcanematch.com matchmakers, wrap my hands around their scrawny little necks and start squeezing."

"I did get that impression," Jake said. He looked both relieved and pleased.

"Now, of course, I realize that I should wrap my hands around *your* neck, which is not scrawny. Nevertheless —"

"If you insist. But if you're in the mood to squeeze something maybe you would like to consider wrapping your hands around another portion of my anatomy?"

"You are absolutely impossible."

"Maybe. But I love you, Clare."

Once again the pure, silvery energy of truth shimmered in the atmosphere.

She leaped to her feet. "I love you so much."

His arms closed around her, warm, tight, strong. This was where she belonged, she thought. This was her true mate.

"About your last name," she said. "Can I assume that is not a coincidence? Are you one of those Joneses?"

"Afraid so."

"And Dumbass Fallon Jones?"

"A cousin. I've got a lot of 'em."

"Family, hmm?" She smiled slowly. "In that case we will definitely quadruple our consulting fees whenever we take on contract work for J&J."

Jake laughed. "I'll leave the negotiations up to you."

He started to kiss her. She put her fingers on his mouth.

"One more thing," she said.

"Yeah?"

She took her fingers away from his lips. "What would you have done if the arcanematch.com crowd hadn't matched us?"

"No problem. I would have called Fallon and told him I needed one of his techs to hack into the arcanematch.com database to make a few adjustments to our profiles."

"You would have crafted a whopping great lie just to convince me to marry you?"

"In a heartbeat."

She smiled. Love rushed through her, hot and sweet and true.

"Right answer, Jones."